The Best Seat ... se

Michael hesita... ...rborne 'Mech, still sh... ...s relentlessly throwing ... ...at was happening, or whe... ...um. But the laser hits kept coming ...

FLASH—his *P...* ...rifted to the left, spinning out of control, still rising on its remaining plasma-vent lifters.

FLASH—one hundred tons of armor, weapons, and control systems hurtled back against the ferroglass shield and detonator grid protecting the screaming, bloodthirsty fans in the stands. A cascade of bright, white-hot sparks lit up an entire quadrant of the arena as the underpowered grid tried to push back the huge 'Mech.

There was no chance.

FLASH—Michael could only hold on for dear life as the *Pillager* smashed through the detonator grid and ferroglass shield to plunge into the Coliseum's filled stadium seating.

Then the fans started screaming for real. . . .

BATTLETECH®

ILLUSIONS OF VICTORY

Loren L. Coleman

A ROC BOOK

ROC
Published by New American Library, a division of
Penguin Putnam Inc., 375 Hudson Street,
New York, New York 10014, U.S.A.
Penguin Books Ltd, 27 Wrights Lane,
London W8 5TZ, England
Penguin Books Australia Ltd, Ringwood,
Victoria, Australia
Penguin Books Canada Ltd, 10 Alcorn Avenue,
Toronto, Ontario, Canada M4V 3B2
Penguin Books (N.Z.) Ltd, 182–190 Wairau Road,
Auckland 10, New Zealand

Penguin Books Ltd, Registered Offices:
Harmondsworth, Middlesex, England

First published by Roc, an imprint of New American Library,
a division of Penguin Putnam Inc.

First Printing, May 2000
10 9 8 7 6 5 4 3 2 1

Copyright © FASA Corporation, 2000
All rights reserved

Series Editor: Donna Ippolito
Mechanical Drawings: Duane Loose and the FASA art department
Cover art by Peter Peebles

 REGISTERED TRADEMARK—MARCA REGISTRADA

To Bryan Nystul and Randall Bills,
for your enthusiasm and support.

I would like to bring the following people under the camera's eye, each of whom in many ways contributed to this novel. Appearance so rarely stands up to the reality that the author is never alone.

Jim LeMonds, Dean Wesley Smith, Kristine Kathryn Rusch, and Mike Stackpole, for their various turns at the roles of teachers, business associates, and friends.

Bryan Nystul and Randall Bills, who keep the BattleTech universe moving and jumped on the "Return to Solaris" bandwagon early. Donna Ippolito and Annalise Raziq, for putting up with one more tight deadline and working with me to make this the best book possible. Jordan Weisman and Ross Babcock, still the powers behind the throne.

My parents, LaRon and Dawn Coleman, who continue to take an active interest in my life. Even, surprisingly enough, to the benefit of their son.

"The Group." By which I mean Russell Loveday, Keith Mick, Allen and Amy Mattila, Vince Foley, Matt Dillahunty, Tim Tousely, Tim Huffer, and the returned Mr. Raymond Sainz.

The BattleForce IRC community, especially Chas, Ed, and Camille. Group W, who just couldn't be slipped into the pages this time.

My agent, Don Maass, who never seems too busy for "just one more question."

My wife, Heather Joy. My energetic sons, Talon LaRon and Conner Rhys Monroe. My lovely new daughter, Alexia Joy.

Oh, and the cats—Chaos, Rumor, and Ranger—who always seem to know when I start a new book, and stare.

Detail of the Inner Sphere
Circa 3062-63

Coreward

Spinward

Anti-spinward

Rimward

SKYE PROVINCE

DRACONIS COMBINE

Freedom
Izar
Marlik
Ryde
Kimball II
Konstance
Kornephoros
Kessel
Ellarin
Kaus Borealis
Kaus Australis
Kaus Media
Ascella
Carnwath
Glengarry
La Blon
Alrakis
Dromini VI
Kochab
Unukalhai
Skye
Alphecca
Skondia
Sabik
Altria
Moore
Lambrecht
Alkalurops
Zebebelgenubi
Syrma
Nusakan
Ko
Lyons
Imbros III
Dyev
Pike IV
Athenry
Alcor
Gatatea
Toril
Asta
Diosd
Styx
Summer
Mizar
Menkent
Zollikofen
Muphrid
Biham
Altair
Cor Caroli
Alioth
Chara
Milton
Lipton
Thorin
Rigil Kentarus
Alchiba
Denebola
New Earth
Zavijava
Terra
Sirius
Keid
Caph
Wyatt
Zosma
Oliver
Graham IV
Aiuta
Australis
Procyon
New Home
Bryant
Marcus

SKYE PROVINCE
DRACONIS COMBINE BORDER
LEGEND

8 PARSECS

40 PARSECS OR 130.4 LIGHT YEARS

SCALE: 1/8 INCH = 1 PARSEC = 3.26 LIGHT YEARS = 19,164,277,860,000 STATUTE MILES

MAXIMUM JUMP: APPROXIMATELY 30 LIGHT YEARS
FOR NAVIGATIONAL PURPOSES USE 9 PARSECS = 29.34 LY

© 3063 COMSTAR CARTOGRAPHIC CORPS

Prelude
(Three Years Before)

Solaris Spaceport, International Zone
Solaris City, Solaris VII
Freedom Theater, Lyran Alliance
21 September 3059

The line of steerage passengers shuffled out of the DropShip and slowly down the covered gantry, winding its way into the West Terminal of Solaris City Spaceport. Behind the passengers, the large *Monarch* Class vessel sat steaming on the tarmac as residual heat from reentry into atmosphere fought a short-lived battle against the gray drizzle falling from an overcast sky. The heat made the air rank with the scents of scorched ferrocrete and human sweat. People cursed as a sharp wind blew rain in under the lip of the gantry overhang. The gust was biting and cruel, bringing no true relief. Muttering under their breaths, the passengers pressed forward, anxious to gain the protection of the terminal, ignoring the dark glances from those in front of them while casting similar glances at those behind.

This was how Michael Searcy arrived on Solaris VII, the Game World. Young and eager. And *dispossessed*.

He threaded his way through the tight knot of people who blocked the gantry exit meeting up with relatives or asking the harried Monopole Line official posted there for directions available on any of the several nearby signs. At one point he stopped to let an elderly couple past, preventing an impatient mother towing three wrangling children from bustling into the pair. Then he, in turn, was pushed aside by security, who formed an instant corridor through the tangled mass of passengers to make way for a pair of agents escorting a man restrained by fetters and manacles. Michael spearheaded the rush to fill the void left by the departing security, breaking through the congestion at the arrival gate and into the terminal proper.

To be immediately confronted by a *Gunslinger*.

The replica of the assault 'Mech stood three meters tall, only a fourth the size of the actual eighty-five-ton BattleMech but still towering over the crowd. Several passengers had stopped to stare in awe, while Michael examined it for how faithful it memorialized BattleMech designs from all across the Inner Sphere as well as what was known of Clan 'Mechs.

The *Gunslinger* was a classic example of the war machines that ruled thirty-first-century battlefields. Built along humanoid lines, its broad-chested torso sat on thick, tree-stump legs, and its arms ended in the wide-bore barrels of gauss rifles. The 'Mech also boasted a pair of medium-class lasers on shoulder-mounted turrets for when combat got up close and personal.

A man and wife stood nearby, gazing up at the *Gunslinger*'s head, where a bright red light glowed behind the cockpit viewscreen. It lent the 'Mech a menacing air, though Michael knew that 'Mech cockpits were mostly dark, cramped spaces lit only by the muted glow of instrument panels, a few monitor screens, and various caution and warning lights that a 'Warrior never wanted to see. Theatrics, he decided about the red lighting. Just like the replica's metallic blue paint and the illuminated sign dangling from the ceiling. Flashing, the sign commanded: LET THE GAMES BEGIN.

"I wonder which BattleMech this is?" The wife was peering into the barrel of the left-arm gauss rifle. She shuddered. "It certainly looks deadly enough."

The husband looked up toward the cockpit. "*Crusader,* maybe? You remember, like the one from that

Allard-Liao and Cox team match against a Skye Tiger team a few years back . . ." He trailed off speculatively.

Michael wanted to laugh. If you shaved off twenty tons and reconfigured the offensive capability for missiles rather than direct-fire weaponry, then *maybe* by a wild stretch of imagination it might be a *Crusader*—a 'Mech antiquated on the modern battlefields.

"It's a *Gunslinger*," he said quietly. "Designation Gun-One E-R-D. Eighty-five-ton assault class BattleMech. Twin gauss rifles in the arms and quad lasers riding over the shoulders."

The couple looked him over with sudden interest, eyeing his dress military uniform, which gave away his heritage. The white jacket, blue trousers piped with gold and red, and the dark blue sash were all unmistakably Federated Suns—the *Davion* half of the fractured Davion-Steiner alliance. He'd eschewed the cape, feeling it would be out of place among steerage, but too proud to give up his uniform yet.

And why not? His official discharge wouldn't be final for a few months yet. And while it would be on record as OTH—other than honorable—Michael would never accept what had happened. His 'Mech *had* shut down from overheating on New Canton, despite his former commander's charges of suspected pusillanimity—a fancy way of calling him a coward. He couldn't think of it without getting a lump in his throat. The hurt was still raw.

"Leftenant Michael Searcy," he said, thinking now was as good a time as any to start getting to know the people of his new home. He planned to make a fresh start here on Solaris VII.

The man's wife turned away with an audible sniff. "A Davionist," she said under her breath, just as surely giving away her own loyalties. That would make the couple citizens of the Lyran Alliance, former sister-state of the Federated Suns. The two great nations had once been joined as the mighty Federated Commonwealth, but had recently split apart, with each star empire championing its own member of the ruling Steiner-Davion line. Archon Katherine—Katrina to her people—for the Alliance and Prince Victor with the Commonwealth *née* Federated Suns. Bad blood there.

"AFFC, eh?" The husband ignored his wife's politics. "You see any action against the Clans?" A natural question, with Prince Victor and the FedCom military currently spearheading a retaliatory strike against the Clanners. A real headliner, and the likely reason he gave Michael any grace at all.

"No, sir, I'm sorry to say. Just the action on New Canton, trying to hold off the Liao-Marik offensive in '57. I was"—he tried to keep his voice strong—"*discharged* before the main assault against Clan Smoke Jaguar began." What he didn't say was that he'd been court-martialed and stripped of his 'Mech—dispossessed—a fate worse than death for a MechWarrior.

But the man apparently did not want to hear about '57 and was even less interested in any MechWarrior's humble attitude. Not here on Solaris VII. He grunted something noncommittal and let his wife pull him away from the *Gunslinger* to rejoin the crowd.

Michael turned back toward the 'Mech, his face hot with embarrassment. Lesson number one, he decided. People here wanted flash and glamour. They *wanted* theatrics. He ran his fingers back through his short-cropped hair. Come to think of it, the same thing was also true in the regular military where you were expected to be part of a team. If you knew how to think for yourself, you'd better show a strong performance to justify your actions. While Michael hadn't. Abandoned by his commander in the path of Confederation forces, he'd been caught alone in a 'Mech that had shut down from overheating. He'd had no choice but to punch out, but his commanding officer gave a different version of the facts. The court found Michael guilty as charged, refusing to give him a second chance. That was what had brought him to Solaris VII, the hope of proving himself worthy. He glanced up again at the flashing sign.

LET THE GAMES BEGIN.

And they did, just the other side of the *Gunslinger* replica. A row of bank machines was interspersed with betting terminals in a long line stretching away from each terminal. Betting stubs littered the tiled floor, dashed hopes cast away as people readied a new series of wagers. The custodians merely swept the stubs aside like so much dust, forming small drifts along the walls that young children took delight in kicking through.

Michael watched as the couple he'd talked with joined a line at one computer to place their first bets. No care for the odds or even a glance at the latest betting sheets. They were here to gamble and live the dark adventure that was the promise and the lure of the Game World. On Solaris the wars of the Inner Sphere were recreated for the pleasure of the viewing audience as BattleMechs were pitted against each other in the arenas. Michael shook his head, still unable to fully grasp the idea of a place where MechWarriors fought—and sometimes died—for *sport*. Nowhere else in the Inner Sphere could this system work.

But then Solaris City was a microcosm of the rest of the Inner Sphere, each of its sectors corresponding to one of the ruling Great Houses. The spaceport was in the International Zone, a small sector in the southwestern corner of the city. It handled DropShip travel and the higher-level government functions. Most other duties changed hands at the sector borders. The city was divided by the Solaris River, which ran almost exactly across the center. South of the river were the International Zone, followed by the Black Hills, Cathay, and then Silesia, which bled a few neighborhoods to the northeast bank of the river. On the north bank of the river were the sectors of Montenegro and Kobe.

It was ironic that the leaders of the Inner Sphere had finally managed to resurrect the Star League in the face of the Clan invasion, but here on Solaris VII the old rivalries and many new ones ran too deep to be so easily put aside. Rivalries that were flaunted and exploited every night as the various House-affiliated stables battled each other in the arenas, each one clawing for dominion over the rest.

Several monitors suspended over the bank of automated tellers and betting terminals showed clips from the latest bouts and promoted the evening's upcoming matches. Commentators talked over one another while the distant sounds of combat added to the din. Michael moved closer to one showing the latest box scores, fishing deep into a uniform pocket for his own betting receipts. The DropShip that brought him here had been fitted with impressive theaters for viewing the fights, and no one had been immune to the draw. Michael had hoped his four years in the AFFC might give him a betting edge. Instead he ended up crumpling one ticket after another, missing the spreads by a few seconds in one fight, by a ton of armor in another. Finding a straight-up bet on the games wasn't easy; the simple win-lose wagers were reserved for long-odds upsets. That was how the entertainment commission kept a handle on the gambling, balancing out everything until only the savviest aficionados could hope to find the best wagers.

Michael knew this, but it hadn't kept him from trying. Nothing would ever keep him from *trying*. He found one winning bet among his tickets. It was the one where he'd taken the odds that Theodore Gross, the number one-ranked warrior on Solaris VII and this year's Champion, would successfully defend his title, but that the match would run better than ten minutes. An eternity in one of Gross's matches, but the bet had paid off and Michael recovered half of his initial stake.

On the next monitor over, one of the screens with louder accompanying sound was showing holovid footage of just that fight, with a Game World vidcaster sagely offering his commentary.

"Theodore Gross has never been put on the defensive so quickly, but that lucky shot found a flaw in his armor and managed to crack the shielding surrounding his fusion engine. The *Katana* was bleeding waste heat. In the Jungle, that can be a death sentence for a 'Mech."

An outline of the huge, pyramidal Cathay arena was displayed on the screen. Michael knew that the interior was filled with a lush tropical forest and maintained at temperatures that often pushed a BattleMech to the edge of overheating. An engine hit would be bad in there. He also recognized the vidcaster as Julian Nero, one of the more popular commentators on Solaris VII. Nero usually reported the fights at the Steiner Coliseum and was developing a reputation for accurate predictions. His "sure bets" often set off immediate and rapid fluctuations among the odds-makers.

"Fortunately for the defending Champion, Stephen Neils got too eager. Once the young warrior came within range of the *Katana*'s jump jets, allowing Gross to slip in behind him, it was all over." Nero winked at the camera. "Sorry, Stephen. I warned you."

Then back to business. "And now the Champion is set to defend his title for the fourth time at the Steiner arena in two months. What can he expect from veteran Ervine Rebelke? We have this statement."

Nero's chiseled features were replaced with the rough visage of a battle-scarred veteran. Michael wondered what battle had caused the ugly gash running from Rebelke's upper brow to his left ear. A real-life battle or an arena match? And was there really much difference between the two?

Rebelke apparently didn't think so as he sneered for the camera. "Theodore's good, but he's already past his prime. I'll bring the Drac down. In the Coliseum I'll *own* him."

So much smoke, Michael thought. Nero seemed to agree, shaking his head once as the camera cut back to him. "I certainly wish Mr. Rebelke luck. It promises to be a fast and brutal fight. That's for sure. The kind Theodore Gross enjoys, with his training in the Ishiyama Arena. A good evening's entertainment, for those of you with tickets for the live show.

"This from Julian Nero. Your man in the know."

The names and places were a buzz in the back of Michael's mind. Gross and Rebelke. Ishiyama and the Coliseum. Would he fight these men? In those arenas? That was why he was here, to restore his pride and to prove his worth to anyone with eyes to see. He knew he had it in him. All he needed was a chance.

Which meant first getting a dueling license, a sponsor, and a BattleMech. Even then he would have to fight his way up through the secondary arenas, before gaining equal footing with the likes of Gross and Rebelke in the Class Six Open Arenas of Solaris City. That could take years, while careers in the 'Mech games were too often measured in months. Months! Unless he could find a way to make himself a hot ticket.

Coming to the Game World was no idle whim; Michael had researched it as thoroughly as possible. The ones who lasted in the games, in the ratings, were those who made themselves memorable—loved or loathed, that didn't matter. So long as people *remembered*.

Theatrics, yes. But on Solaris VII appearances were important, and Michael had better get used to it. Quickly.

Engine, Engine
Number Nine

SOLARIS CITY

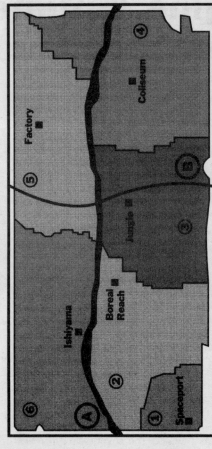

1. International Zone (Lyran Alliance)
2. Black Hills (Federated Suns)
3. Cathay (Capellan Confederation)

4. Silesia (Lyran Alliance)
5. Montenegro (Free Worlds League)
6. Kobe (Draconis Combine)

A. Solaris River   B. Solaris Highway
■ Arenas

DBC Studios, Silesia
Solaris City, Solaris VII
Freedom Theater, Lyran Alliance
10 August 3062

On the holovid wall screen in Donegal Broadcasting's studio number five, two 'Mechs stalked a nightmare battlefield. Walls rose and fell at random intervals, creating an ever-changing maze. Gouts of flame burst from the floor, bathing the contestants in flickering, hellish daylight before the twilight dimness reclaimed the arena.

The BattleMechs looked less like machines and more like avatars of war as they closed, pummeling each other with an incredible array of weaponry. Lasers stabbed out from both 'Mechs, the backwash of gem-colored light playing over the armored machines in a garish display. The *Orion* staggered, two new scars slashed into its broad chest. The edges of those scars glowed bright orange at first, though faded quickly back to an ember-red. Recovering its balance, the seventy-five-ton BattleMech pressed the attack. Three of its four launched missiles corkscrewed out on gray contrails to hammer at the advancing *Penetrator,* sending a shower of armor fragments to the ground. Then a tongue of flame licked out from a side-mounted barrel, accompanied by the metallic scream of the *Orion*'s eighty-millimeter autocannon. Tracers staggered into the ammunition feed flared in a brief stream of greenish sparks, marking the hail of depleted-uranium slugs that tore across the *Penetrator*'s right arm.

A new color effect, Michael Searcy noted, his expert eyes missing nothing. He was seated to the left of Todd Richards, host of the "MechTalk" show. He knew that his was the secondary seat, but here in the Lyran sector of Solaris City, wasn't he the enemy? Sitting to Richards' right was the afternoon's principal guest, Jarman "The Ripper" Bauer.

Bauer leaned forward from the edge of his chair, riveted to the wall screen and twitching with every exchange of weapons fire as if reliving his exciting battle against the *Orion*. He wore the green leather jacket with gold piping of Overlord Stables, while Michael was garbed in black and copper Blackstar livery. Physically, the two MechWarriors were as different as the colors under which they fought. Bauer's thicker build, dark hair, and beard contrasted Michael's trim form and clean-cut, blond good looks. The bruiser versus the artist. The bear versus the fox.

Steiner versus Davion.

Not that such differences would matter tomorrow, Day One of the Grand Tournament. In tomorrow's contest, the best warrior would prevail, no matter how he looked or sounded. Michael had no worries on that score; he had no doubt who was the better man. But until then appearances mattered very much. The betrayal on New Canton and his subsequent court-martial had taught Michael a lesson only reinforced by his three years on the Game World. "Appearance is so easily accepted as reality" was one of Drew Hasek-Davion's favorite sayings. Nowhere was that more true than on Solaris VII.

Todd Richards had half-turned from the live studio audience, showing off his strong profile to the cameras as he watched the battle unfold on the wall screen. He winced and nodded and made appreciative noises in all the right places, catering to Bauer. He, too, leaned in as if anticipating the crushing blow that would come at any time. The live audience also sat enthralled, though most—if not all—of them had certainly caught the highlights the night before. Michael wondered how many in the audience had lost money on Bauer's upset.

More than likely every last one of them had bet. The people couldn't help themselves. In the six centuries that 'Mechs had dominated the battlefields of the Inner Sphere, humanity had never lost its fascination with the lethal machines. Or with the warriors who piloted them. And for more than three hundred years, the games on Solaris VII had mirrored the reality of continuous warfare, only in a safe environment that soon gave rise to the most successful sporting event ever.

Solaris City was even modeled after the rest of the Inner Sphere, its five main sectors corresponding to each of the Great Houses. Michael had known all that when he arrived three years before, but he hadn't truly appreciated the depths of the bitterness that divided one sector from another. He had made the Black Hills his home, the sector affiliated so strongly with House Davion and the Federated Suns that it had never officially acknowledged the thirty-year alliance with House Steiner.

Then there was Kobe, reflecting the samurai culture of the Draconis Combine, and chaotic Montenegro, representing the fractious Free Worlds League. Shattered Cathay also seemed to mirror House Liao's troubled Confederation. There were even a few Clanners fighting in the arenas! But if Michael understood right, these 'Warriors were ostracized by their own kind for stooping to make a game of combat. Maybe they were like him and had come to the Game World seeking to redeem their honor.

Today Michael was in Silesia, land of the enemy. Where the Lyrans and the people of the Federated Suns had once united to create the great alliance of the Federated Commonwealth, its people were now united only in their bitterness in speaking out for or against Katrina Steiner-Davion usurping her brother's throne. The unofficial feud divided people on every world, and Solaris VII was no exception, except that the lines were more clearly drawn. Here FedSun loyalists had always clung to the Black Hills. Now, with tensions running so high in the outside world, entertainment again imitated reality as fighters rededicated themselves to the old loyalties. Fights between Federated Sun warriors and Lyrans were high-profile tickets and among the most savage battles fought.

Like the one Michael sat watching now. It was a duel between an *Orion* and a *Penetrator,* two Lyran warriors scrambling for one of the last slots in the Grand Tournament that would decide this year's Champion.

Michael leaned back in his chair, arms folded over his chest as he pretended for the viewing audience that the fight left him unimpressed. It wasn't too difficult. There were reasons this battle looked exceptionally fierce, and Michael could identify almost every one. The low-angle shots that made the 'Mechs look even bigger than their actual three-story height. The dim setting, for better display of a laser-light fight. And the pyrotechnics, of course, which were great crowd-pleasers but distracted only the greenest MechWarrior. You didn't come up through the Solaris games without learning something about production.

Or tactics, and from the start Michael had known that the *Orion* was in trouble. Right away it had gotten pinned into a corner of the arena. Lacking jump jets, it couldn't hope to escape Bauer's advancing *Penetrator.* Bauer had worked in to point-blank range, and now the *Penetrator*'s six medium pulse lasers spat out a flurry of ruby darts. The staggered bursts of energy flashed away the last of the *Orion*'s armor and cut deeply into its midline. It was this armor-shredding power that made the *Penetrator* such a devastating in-fighter and a favorite among the fans. The *Orion* shuddered violently as the rabid energies slagged its gyroscopic stabilizer into ruin. Seventy-five tons of upright metal suddenly lost their fight with gravity and toppled clumsily. The ground shook with the impact, and then the lights came up to show the *Penetrator* standing over the fallen *Orion.*

The image froze there—the *Penetrator* raising its arms in victory. The sounds of combat faded out to the canned ovation cut into the footage, now matched by cued applause from the audience.

"Well, a very intense finish to that bout," Todd Richards said, segueing back into the live interview. "And I'm certain the fans in Steiner Stadium appreciated it as much as . . ." Richards trailed off as the sound of belated, slow clapping interrupted him.

Michael continued to applaud as both Richards and the show's star guest turned to stare. In an instant, Todd Richards rolled with the interruption, almost as if it had been planned. Which, in a way it had. Everyone in the studio knew how the interview was supposed to end.

"You don't agree, Mr. Searcy?"

Michael shrugged, but stopped clapping. He slipped his hands into his jacket pockets as he slouched back. Matched up against Bauer on the first day of the Grand Tournament, he knew his role on the show was to provide a foil for Bauer and to ramp up the tension and the betting. Well, they asked for it.

"Oh, it was amusing, but hardly a real battle," Michael said, while Jarman Bauer glowered. Turning toward the camera, Michael caught the eye of his bodyguard waiting off to one side, behind camera number three. The big man tensed, then nodded while Michael said, "Nice light show. Poor tactics."

Raising one hand to forestall an outburst from Bauer, Richards took the bait. "Poor tactics by William Paulson, you mean. After all, Mr. Bauer won the fight and will meet you next in the Grand Tournament." Richards, too, had turned toward the camera now, trying to regain control of the conversation. "Day One tomorrow, sports fans. One hundred and twenty-eight of Solaris VII's finest beginning the week that will test their endurance and skill in the various Open Class arenas."

Michael stared icily at Richards, who had, fortunately, left him an opening. "Skill is exactly my point. Paulson is a better fighter than Bauer any day of the week, even after his daily bottle of Glengarry Reserve." There, let that bit of information trickle out into the tabloids.

He stabbed a finger toward the screen, where the victorious *Penetrator* was still displayed. "That wasn't a battle. It was a slugging match. Bauer's idea of tactical surprise is to hold back his medium lasers—which any Solaran third-grader knows he's got—until he can make a showy finish to his opponent. The fact that Paulson walked into it makes me wonder if the Steiner-affiliated stables didn't get together and flip coins for the victory." He leaned in conspiratorially. "Tell me, Jarman, was the fix in?"

"Damn Davionist!" Bauer jumped to his feet, nearly upsetting his chair. "Who the hell do you think you are, Searcy?" He looked ready to grab Michael by the throat. Only a wide, low table strategically placed between the two MechWarriors kept them apart. Even the minor prop was no accident, but had been carefully placed to buy time for more invective.

Never one to let a challenge slip by—not *Stormin'* Michael Searcy—Michael also leapt to his feet. He pulled his right hand, already balled into a tight fist, out of his pocket. With his left he grabbed the lip of the table and flipped it out of the way. The prop clattered across the studio floor.

Bauer blinked his surprise; he was supposed to have kicked the table to the side—later. Michael sailed into the other man's confusion. "I'm someone who didn't fail Jaime Wolf's class in strategy and tactics on Outreach," he shot back, definitely a low blow. Bauer's pained expression—and on camera no less!—suddenly made the cash outlay for that information a bargain. "But what can you expect from a Lyran?"

Bauer took a step forward, as if ready to swing, then faltered and looked to his host for some sign. Richards, getting more than he'd hoped for on the show, was staying out of the way until the two MechWarriors got to the point that was his cue.

"It'll take more than Lyran money to make you Champion," Michael taunted. What was it going to take to get Jarman to come at him?

Bauer had apparently decided to stick to the loose script arranged beforehand, hovering back as if the table still blocked the two of them from coming to blows. "You wait till I get you into Ishiyama," he said. "I'm going to bury you under Stone Mountain!"

Enough of this, Michael decided. Any more and it would begin to look comical. He stepped forward, pushing against Bauer's chest and shoving the larger man back a good few meters. "C'mon, Jarman. Right now! Let's go, *farmer*!"

On cue, or close enough, Todd Richards leapt forward to position himself between the two. From off-stage a pair of big men also raced out to restrain them— Michael's and Bauer's bodyguards. Still shouting curses and challenges, Michael and Bauer managed to work back close enough to place themselves in the same close-up shot with Todd Richards. Richards would segue into a break, and the show would cut to commercial. That was how the game was played.

Then Michael slipped his bodyguard's grip.

Right arm cocked back and ready, he lurched forward and pistoned his fist into Jarman Bauer's jaw. That one punch rocked the other MechWarrior back, knocking him unconscious to the floor.

A few seconds of stunned silence fell over the studio. That wasn't part of the script. Todd Richards stared dumbly at Bauer, for several long seconds forgetting to call for commercial. Then came the cut, and Michael's bodyguard was hurrying him off the floor and into the studio wings. From there, they went down a short hall cluttered with props and a few stagehands, and out a side door where an Avanti luxury hover sedan waited in the light afternoon rain.

The Avanti's driver was holding the rear passenger-side door open. Michael paused to wave to some Mech-bunnies being restrained by security. They were mostly teens and not adverse to staking out the studio doors in hopes of catching a glimpse of a favorite arena warrior. Maybe score an autograph or, in Michael's case, offer some lively curses for his future. One of the Lyran teens threw a half-full bottle of soda in his direction, shattering it against the sedan's forward fender.

Michael piled in, still wired from adrenaline, his body-guard close behind. He settled back into the plush leather seat as the Avanti rose up on a cushion of air and glided away from the curb, moving away from the small mob and into the streets of Silesia. His bodyguard took the rear-facing seat cross-corner to Michael and directly facing the portly man who'd been waiting for them in the hovercar.

The man was Drew Hasek-Davion, Michael's boss. Fortyish and overweight, he looked more like an old-time robber baron than the master of Blackstar Stables. He also affected a thin oily mustache that gave his face a ratlike appearance. Michael grinned at the man, expecting praise for his performance.

"What was that bit about 'farmer'?" he asked Michael, his tone sharp.

"Bauer is the German word for farmer," Michael said. "It will become a derogatory nickname for him within a day. What's more, it's also Solaran slang. A farmer is a warrior who drives a *tractor*."

Drew caught on quickly. "A BattleMech unworthy of the arenas. Or, the converse, a warrior who is unworthy of his BattleMech." He nodded. Yellow teeth showed as he made a brief stab at a smile of his own, a smile that died almost before it was born. "And the information about Paulson's drinking habit and Bauer's training failures?"

"All true, and paid for from my own pocket."

Drew frowned but nodded again. "Well played, then." He didn't sound so certain. He tapped the gold-plated lion's head of his walking stick against one thigh. "Still, you should leave the planning to me, Michael."

Michael shrugged, annoyed by Drew's condescension. "I'll bet you my percentage of the Day One purse that Bauer will lose the three percentage points his upset over Paulson netted him."

He watched as Drew's self-importance and the desire to rake in a good pot warred with the possibility of being raked himself. Meanwhile, the sedan gained Narvik Street to head west as the Silesia sector gave way to fragmented Cathay. In the end, Hasek-Davion shrugged off the challenge. "I only take wagers where I have a hand in the outcome."

"You like a stacked deck, you mean."

"Which is why I own you, dear boy." Drew settled back into the plush seat. "Try not to forget that." He paused to lend the veiled threat some additional weight. "Fortunately, you paid off again, dropping Mr. Bauer with a single blow. Now you merely have to end the feud tomorrow. And quickly, as you did today."

Michael decided not to take issue with Drew's belief that he owned the Federated Suns favorite. He had personally groomed and trained Michael in his fighter's persona, holding up the young man—and by proxy himself—as the great hope of Davion supporters on Solaris VII. Episodes such as tonight's interview helped cement that image. He also held Michael's contract, and that was close enough to ownership on Solaris VII if a 'Warrior wished to keep fighting. Which was what Michael wished more than anything. It was why he was here on the Game World.

Far more insulting, though, was the insinuation that Michael might lose to a pretender like Bauer, or to any Lyran for that matter. He wouldn't—couldn't—let that happen. It would threaten everything he'd worked toward these last three years. No, his first serious competition wouldn't come until Day Three, when he would likely fight Bromley Stables' Evelyn Czerny. She was the best Marik-affiliated fighter and ranked number two overall, five above Searcy himself. Now, she could be a problem. As for Bauer . . .

"Did your man find one of the new light gauss rifles?" Michael asked, and Drew nodded. "So we switch out the regular gauss rifle on my *Dragon Fire* for the lighter version and rip out the ECM package, then upgrade my autocannon to the twelve-centimeter bore of a Defiance Disintegrator. Bauer will close quickly. It's all he knows how to do, and I'll allow it. Then I'll rip that *Penetrator* to scrap." His smile was devoid of humor. Bauer had already lost, and tomorrow would merely be confirmation.

Did Drew smile in answer? "It seems I am not the only one in this car who appreciates a stacked deck."

Michael cocked his head to one side, as if considering. Then he tossed the roll of coins he'd been holding in his fist while sitting across from Bauer on the set. He'd kept them hidden in his hand until just before the argument came to blows. Nothing like a little extra advantage-insurance that one punch would drop his enemy. The bodyguard looked away, careful not to see anything.

Drew Hasek-Davion quirked one eyebrow, his only sign of surprise, then nodded. Once. High praise from the owner of Blackstar Stables, a man always quicker with criticism than compliments. Respect, now that felt good.

Massaging the bruised knuckle on his right hand, Michael turned to the window and smiled out at the rain-soaked city.

There were times he really enjoyed this world.

2

The Coliseum, Silesia
Solaris City, Solaris VII
Freedom Theater, Lyran Alliance
12 August 3062

The *Caesar*'s nickel-ferrous gauss slug smashed into the *Striker*'s left shoulder, crushing ferroceramic armor. Broken plates fell away amid a rain of shards and splinters, showering the BattleMech's protection over the sandy floor of the Coliseum. A fair percentage of the crowd roared with delight at the blow, probably because they'd bet against the 'Warrior piloting the *Striker* in this Day Two Grand Tournament match.

Hearing the cheer even from inside his insulated cockpit, Victor Vandergriff ground his teeth in fury as he rode out the brutal shove imparted by the gauss slug. His restraining harness held him securely to his seat, while the massive gyroscopic stabilizer set into the *Striker*'s lower torso fought gravity to keep the eighty-ton 'Mech upright. Neuroreceptors built into his bulky helmet fed his own sense of balance down into the stabilizer in a feedback loop that let the pilot worry less about walking around in a bipedal war machine and more about his opponent.

Right now Victor Vandergriff was *very* worried about his opponent, Davion dog though he was.

The arena's main partition was already rising again, about to conceal the contenders from each other. Victor wrenched hard on his control sticks, dragging the red targeting cross hairs across his cockpit viewscreen and settling them over Stephen Neils's *Caesar*. The reticle flashed between red and gold and then burned a steady golden hue as the computer acquired a hard lock. Mashing down on both thumb buttons as well as his right-hand trigger, Victor lashed out with the *Striker*'s three main weapons. The sapphire beam of his large laser cut into the *Caesar*'s left arm, sloughing away a half-ton of armor. The blue lightning of his particle projection cannon scored next, carving into the other 'Mech's left side, but his autocannon missed low, spending its depleted-uranium slugs against the rising barricade.

The temperature in the *Striker*'s cockpit shot up as the 'Mech's fusion reactor spiked to meet the power demand. Nothing to be too concerned about, not in this kind of fight. The heat levels would drop quickly enough. Meanwhile the coolant flushing through the small tubes of his bulky cooling vest helped keep down his core body temperature. Victor would have preferred one of the new full-body coolant suits, maybe even one with built-in neuroreceptors that did away with the antiquated neurohelmet, but that technology was still too expensive for Lynch Stables. Besides, the brief rise in temperature was only enough to raise a light sweat.

Although hurt by the *Striker*'s weapons, Neils wasn't about to surrender his advantage so easily. With the barricade almost up, his *Caesar* extended its right arm to angle one last shot at Victor. The hand-held PPC flared another cascade of manmade lightning across the field, burning into the *Striker*'s midline and carving a new molten-edged scar into the BattleMech's chest. One more hit and Neils would be through the armor there. Victor swore silently, though the stadium crowd went crazy with the hard-hitting exchange. Protected now by the barricade, he allowed himself a glance in their direction.

The Steiner arena was Silesia's pride. Built to resemble a giant Roman-era coliseum, its center was an open expanse where the BattleMechs fought. Surrounding the combat area were row upon row of seats from which the fans could watch the action live rather than by closed-circuit video. The sandy floor could be left wide open or confused with pop-up barricades like the kind chosen for tonight's tournament bout. Three stories above the ground and just over the heads of most 'Mechs, two levels of private boxes ringed the arena for those wealthy enough to afford such luxury. Above them the general seating was packed with forty thousand riotous fans, all of them infected with the tension of tonight's battle, the Grand Tournament's second Steiner-Davion match-up. Some pressed forward against the ferroglass shields, hammering on it with their fists as they shouted support or derision for one or both gladiatorial Mech-Warriors.

Victor Vandergriff despised them all.

The rich and the poor. Stable owners, nobles, merchants, laborers. The gamblers wagering money they did not have and the few "peekers" out there pretending to have large sums riding on the outcome of the battle. Even other MechWarriors were included in his wrath. Victor hated them because he was dependent upon them, and because he could remember a time when that wasn't so. A time when he'd fought for himself, one of the best 'Warriors on Solaris VII and destined for great things.

And then something went wrong, right about the time he'd lost the big fight against Allard-Liao and that Davion puppet Galen Cox. He'd lost before, but never with so devastating an effect on his career. The fans deserted him, many turning on him overnight and others drifting away slowly over the years as more defeats plagued him. A "zombie," that was what they called Victor now. One of the walking dead. Never mind that Theodore Gross, current Champion of Solaris defending his title for the fifth year, was three years older. Now Gross was on top of the world while Victor had fallen from favor.

Vandergriff had never climbed higher in the rankings than twelfth before starting his backward slide. The Skye Tigers stable had traded him as a bad investment despite his ranking, and Trevor Lynch had picked up the contract because he desperately needed a high-ranking fighter. Now Victor held on by his fingernails and a certain amount of desperation in his fighting style to the last spot in the vaunted Top Twenty. He might never make the Championship finals, but he could still claim to fight among the best the Game World had to offer. He had that, yes, but it didn't keep the knowledge that he'd fallen so far from eating away at him.

He'd stayed at the party too long. And now the party was all he had left.

The X-shaped partition that divided the arena into unequal quarters dropped again. Never so far that the competitors could cross it in the scant few seconds before it rose again. To try and reach point-blank range, Victor would have to run around the ends, while Neils would simply counter by walking the *Caesar* away. It was at the request of White Hand stables that Coliseum officials had reluctantly agreed to use the barricade to make up for the ten tons Victor's *Striker* had on Neils' BattleMech. No doubt they would have preferred to give Victor, the Lyran fighter, the edge, but in the Grand Tournament any match where an obvious inequality existed had to be handicapped.

With the barricade still falling toward the waist-high level it would maintain for a few desperate seconds, Victor and Neils were already positioning their 'Mechs for the best angles they could get. The *Caesar*'s right arm came up, mirrored by the *Striker*'s left. Neils was a touch faster on his PPC, which flayed away more armor from the *Striker*'s right arm. Melted ferroceramic composite runneled to the ground, splashing into the sand. In return, Vandergriff's forty-millimeter autocannon chewed into the side of the *Caesar*'s wedge-shaped head. Not enough to penetrate the armor but exacting some small measure of revenge as it rattled the warrior inside.

The barricade stopped while still at a height of five meters. His left-side armor hammered into memory, Victor throttled his *Striker* into a walk to the left while twisting his torso back to the right to fire. The move partially protected what was left of the savaged armor over his autocannon ammunition bin. He stopped just short of the end of the barricade. Just as he'd guessed, Neils countered by moving his *Caesar* to its left. There followed another exchange of weapons fire, Victor's laser and PPC answering Neils's gauss rifle, which tore away the *Striker*'s right arm at the shoulder joint. The loss threw the *Striker* severely off balance, past the gyro's ability to automatically compensate, and Victor had to fight his controls to keep the 'Mech on its feet.

The partition rose before he could recover, and a parting shot from Neils' energy cannon slashed another scar along his right side. The commline crackled to life immediately after, fighting off the interference from the PPC as Neils's voice whispered into his ear over the open channel they shared for trading insults.

"Haven't you got anything better to give, zombie?" Neils sneered.

The fans were on their feet screaming. A major fight had broken out in the stands between FedRat supporters and their Lyran rivals and was quickly spreading to other sections. Victor could well imagine the despair of the pro-Steiner fans, watching tonight's defender of Lyran honor being beaten down just as the despised Michael Searcy had smashed Jarman "The Farmer" Bauer the day before.

Sweat beaded on Victor's face, and he knew it was more from fear for his life than for the *Striker*'s heat levels. Furious at this sudden weakness, he almost targeted the upper stands. In the back of his mind he knew it would do no good. The arena's detonator grid protected the spectators, bleeding off energy weapons and deflecting any stray missiles or autocannon fire that might endanger the crowd. The grid, a rare piece of lostech, was the only thing that made direct-view seating possible.

Victor held his fire. He knew it wasn't the fans that had raised his ire. Not even the Davionists among them. It was Neils.

Stephen Neils, who was trying to kill him!

The request for a low barricade and the pattern of the *Caesar*'s attacks now seemed to fit into a devious scheme meant to shame and possibly kill Victor Vandergriff. While the barricade dropped or rose, he stood at a disadvantage, able to use his arm-mounted light autocannon against the superior power of Neils's PPC. When it was down, Neils abandoned his energy cannon to make carefully aimed attacks with the *Caesar*'s torso-mounted gauss rifle. One of the heavy gauss slugs would eventually punch through the head of the *Striker,* smashing the BattleMech's sensors, controls . . . and cockpit. No 'Mech design in existence could protect its pilot from that kind of destructive power.

Rage flooded over Victor as he wrenched the *Striker* around to the left and maneuvered it toward the end of the barricade's first arm. Rage, and contempt for the treachery of his Davionist opponent. He heard the dull roar of the fans—either cheering him on, warning their own champion, or shouting amid the brawl—but no longer cared. He raced forward, gambling for as much ground as possible as the partition began to drop again. He wouldn't make it. The second arm was too far, just out of reach. And when Neils saw him closing, he would slip around to the other side of the arena and again hammer at Victor with that deadly gauss rifle.

If Victor gave him the shot.

It was a strategy born of desperation, the kind that had become a Vandergriff trademark these last few years. Still at a full run, Victor rocked forward quickly to throw a tremor into his gyro as the neurofeedback loop read his sudden shift of balance. Then he reached forward, overbalancing the *Striker,* which toppled head-first toward the ground. The 'Mech hit hard, its armor crushed in the impact of eighty tons meeting unyielding floor, its momentum driving it forward in a parody of a baseball slide.

The move almost completed Stephen Neils's earlier work, mercilessly shaking Victor in the grip of his harness. The *Striker*'s head scraped against the arena floor, digging through the sand and treating its pilot to an even rougher ride. Victor's neurohelmet smacked hard into the back of his seat, and his mind swam at the edge of consciousness. The *Striker* piled up against the lowered barrier, its chest nearly stripped of armor.

Victor had five precious seconds to shake off the effects of the fall and another five to work the *Striker* back to its feet. Seconds were eternities in a 'Mech battle, especially in the Game World arenas. Winning and losing—sometimes even living and dying—often hinged on a crucial instant or two. He worked the *Striker*'s single arm under its own heavy body and used it to rock back to one knee and then to his feet just as the barricade completed its return to full upright.

Now Victor needed to know what Neils had done when his *Striker* had dived out of sight. MagRes imaging wouldn't have helped, not in the shadow of a barricade. Thermal *might* have showed enough waste heat bleeding into the air to tell Neils where Victor had ended up, but had Neils thought of that and made the switch in time? Victor could see fans in the main seating pushed up to the glass and gesturing, but some were pointing at him while others pointed the way they thought Neils should move. He didn't think Neils would find much help there.

It had become a guessing game. Neils must have thought Victor would move to the right, trying to shadow his *Caesar*. He'd countered by moving to the left. Neils had guessed wrong.

When Victor came around the side of the barricade, there was Neils in his *Caesar* standing just opposite him. Neils was quick to act, twisting his 'Mech around on its turret-style waist to bring the right-arm PPC to bear, but still too late. The energy whip drilled into the right side of the *Striker,* but found no critical components that could turn Victor's newly claimed advantage.

Victor fired back with his laser, the sapphire beam slicing into the *Caesar*'s back, biting deep through armor and the titanium substructure to carve away the bulky engine shielding of its 280XL engine. His PPC scored a long gash along the back of the *Caesar*'s left leg, but the autocannon made the hit that counted. Its depleted-uranium slugs hammered in behind the laser wound to smash the energy-storing capacitors of the gauss rifle. With a brilliant blue flare, the capacitors dumped their pent-up energy straight into the *Caesar*'s heart, gutting the right side. Engine shielding collapsed, threatening release of the raw power of a fusion reaction.

Neils was able to drop the dampening fields into place, shutting down the power plant and saving his life and his 'Mech. The fight, however, was lost. Thrown off-balance by the massive strike and now without the power needed for the gyro to stabilize the machine, the

Caesar toppled forward like a titan's discarded toy to smash face-down into the arena floor.

"You asked for it," Victor said to himself, not bothering to key open the transmitter.

The barricade dropped away, leaving Victor Vandergriff and his *Striker* commanding the Coliseum floor in plain view of every stadium patron. The arena officials piped in roars of Lyran approval even as the Davion-Steiner brawl continued to spread among the stands. And for all his earlier cynicism about the fickleness of fame, Victor Vandergriff soaked up the adulation.

It was, as he knew, all he had left.

═══ 3 ═══

The Coliseum, Silesia
Solaris City, Solaris VII
Freedom Theater, Lyran Alliance
12 August 3062

"**A** spectacular upset by Lynch Stables' Victor Vandergriff, one of Silesia's own. Everyone was hoping he had it in him, and tonight he certainly delivered."

Julian Nero stabbed at the mute button to keep his voice from going out over the closed-circuit channel. Then he elbowed the video controller sitting beside him. "Cut away from Vandergriff and give me a feed of the crowd, will you? No, not the Mechbunnies cheering. Give me that fight in the stadium's upper levels."

The match was over, and Julian knew that anyone paying attention to the closed-circuit video for his commentary wouldn't care much about Vandergriff's history or hopes for the future. The fact was that Vandergriff didn't have much of a future left on the Game World. If Julian was going to get any extra minutes picked up on the syndicated broadcasts, it would be in clips of the brawl quickly turning into a riot.

Julian also had his reputation to protect, having moved in the last few years from "*your* man in the know" to "*the* man in the know." It would be foolish to focus on Vandergriff, who was basically a loser. Nero remembered when Vandergriff still fought for the Skye Tigers back in '56. He'd teamed up with the great—and *late*—Glen Edenhoffer to battle Galen Cox and then-Champion Kai Allard-Liao. What a disappointment. And with five days to go in this year's Great Tournament, the odds were long that the aging MechWarrior would make it to the finals. He never had.

Better to segue into the brawl. The fighting in the arena stands was particularly vicious, with several brawlers already lying unconscious in the aisles. Nero knew that fights like this often spilled out into the streets of Silesia. He'd seen it before. He nodded a quick decision; *there* was his lead-in . . .

"I've seen this happen before," he said. "Anyone in the stadium who's not yet caught up in the fighting should find a place near a security station and ride it out. There's a full-blown riot starting up in the northeast section of the main seating. From what I can see, the Federated Suns supporters had the upper hand at the start of the brawl, but the Lyran fans are holding their own now."

How easy it was to slide from 'Mech battle commentary to covering the growing riot. He doubted the people glued to the closed-circuit holovid footage would even notice. They had paid for an evening of destruction and mayhem. Did the specifics matter so much?

"I count ten—make that twenty—bodies already unconscious," he went on. "No fireworks, none visible anyway, but that doesn't mean someone out there isn't concealing a hold-out laser."

Julian was barely warming to his subject when the image cut off unexpectedly, leaving him at a loss for words until the video controller fed him a new signal. It took a few precious seconds for him to roll with the new feed. When Julian finally saw what was going on, his mouth ran dry with excitement and some small measure of dread.

"As always, we stay right on top of the latest developments." Julian shot the video controller a hard glare for the lack of warning. "What you see here are the paramedics crowding around the head of Stephen Neils's fallen *Caesar*. It looks like they're having trouble extracting him. The egress hatch is open, but Neils could already be injured from that stunning fall he took. In your lower left-hand corner you can see a medic signaling for more help."

A dark shadow fell over the tech team, and Vandergriff's *Striker* leaned into the picture. The video controller panned back to get the big BattleMech into the scene. Was Vandergriff about to deliver a coup de grâce? Headhunter actions were frowned upon in the arenas, but they happened anyway. And this one was coming a bit late. Attacking Stephen Neils now could easily make Vandergriff liable for criminal charges. Harassment. Battery. Even assault with intent.

Not that they would stick, not while Vandergriff was still in the Grand Tournament. The powers that be on Solaris VII—namely the stable owners—would see to it that nothing interfered with the selection of a new Champion. Too much money rode on this week's events, and the percentages certain to find a way into the Solaran bank accounts of government officials, law enforcement chiefs, and even the world's media moguls would almost guarantee that no idealistic young reporter would make too much of a late-delivered blow.

Julian remembered his own early days and knew the score. The most Vandergriff risked was a fine for unsportsmanlike conduct, though if he'd thought ahead and covered the right bet, the 'Warrior could easily make up for it. Nero leaned in toward the screen, willing the answer from Vandergriff while he waited as anxiously as any spectator.

Vandergriff's *Striker* moved with a slow precision that looked odd in an eighty-ton 'Mech. It spoke of a comfortable synergy between man and machine that few MechWarriors ever achieved. Well, Julian had never claimed that Vandergriff wasn't a fine MechWarrior—in his day. Almost casually, the *Striker* hooked one of its arms under the shoulder of Neils's *Caesar,* then lifted and rolled the fallen 'Mech onto its side.

The words Julian Nero spoke on seeing the smashed-in cockpit had nothing to do with ratings, syndication, or playing to the viewing audience. The phrase slipped out without thought, an ages-old epithet.

"Blake's blood," he whispered as the image zoomed in to fill his screen with twisted and torn metal supports and the jagged edges that were all that was left of the ferroglass cockpit canopy. The enhanced video caught the tinge of color along one jagged shard.

Well, not Blake's.

All in all, a good evening's work.

Working her way clear of the Coliseum, Megan Church climbed over the metal bench someone had used as an improvised battering ram, then slipped through a shattered doorframe. The door was twisted nearly free from its hinges, and no loner barred either entry or exit. The angry shouting and pain-filled yells behind her were matched by similar noises ahead. Chaos had gripped the Steiner arena and spread into the surrounding streets of Silesia.

As she went, Megan nearly tripped over two unconscious security men crumpled against the outer wall. She checked and found them still alive, though missing their sidearms. A dark bruise blossomed on the side of one's ashen face. Megan spotted two guide-rope posts nearby, part of the makeshift fencing that was used to funnel a crowd into some semblance of a line for admission. They'd been used as clubs not too long ago, she decided, then abandoned in favor of the guards' better weapons.

The security men were in no immediate danger, so she decided to leave them. A quick shakedown netted her three betting slips and a *tonfun*-styled nightstick. That was better than her sap filled with lead shot or the wooden walking stick she'd lifted off an unconscious man inside. She threw the cane away and slipped the cosh into a pocket of her black leather jacket. Gripping the heavy plastic baton by its cross-grip, she continued on her way.

Ducking behind fluted columns and sidling along a wall, Megan worked to avoid the free-for-all taking place outside the eastern entrance under a light evening rain. The riot had spread outside faster than she'd have thought—the riot she'd *helped* to create. A shove here, some choice words there—it wasn't hard to spark a fight or keep it going in Silesia's Romanesque arena, where the violence of live BattleMech combat heightened tensions and set everyone on edge.

But even with many outside the arena listening to the live soundcasts, mere reports of the riot wouldn't have sparked so much violence. People shoved and hit, striking out at any threat real or imagined, kicking those already fallen. The same people who'd been lined up for the late-evening ticket, waiting to replace the cheering and jeering crowd that had witnessed Victor Vandergriff's amazing win.

Allies and enemies were easy enough to distinguish; people came to the games wearing T-shirts and jackets bearing the images of their favorite fighters or the colors of a favored 'Mech stable. Some wore patches of House alignment, openly declaring their allegiance to Archon-Princess Katrina Steiner-Davion or Chancellor Sun-Tzu Liao or Captain-General Thomas Marik. Not surprisingly, Megan noticed that the most violent brawlers were shouting anti-Seiner and anti-Davion curses at each other. The unrest created by Katrina's theft of her brother's throne continued to plague Silesia and the Black Hills, but it wasn't simply one side against the other. Megan knew there were Silesians who supported Prince Victor, just as some Black Hills residents touted Katrina. *Those* factions were just more silent. More careful.

So, any opposing nationality was fair game, and there were even factions within a single nation. Megan saw one man fly into the sidelines of the fight shouting. "The Blessed Blake and no quarter!" Flailing at anyone within reach, he plunged into the heaviest fighting, then was swallowed up in the brawl. Megan couldn't tell which side the man supported.

She doubted the man ever knew himself.

A different man stumbled into her, shoved out of the main fracas, and she quickly pinned him against one of the large columns using the long edge of the security baton. At one point six meters she wasn't exactly a tall woman, and the man had at least forty centimeters and thirty kilograms of advantage. But her compact frame was trained to wiry strength, and the baton gave her an additional edge. This guy wore a jacket displaying the old sword-and-sun emblem of the Federated Suns. Fair game.

He shrugged Megan's arm away and made a grab for her shoulder, but his fingers slid on the rain-slicked leather of her jacket. She spun the *tonfun* around, cracking him across the elbow with the baton's heavy plastic. He yelped in pain as his arm dropped to his side, numbed by the blow. Jabbing the baton into his soft gut, Megan left him retching on the sidewalk. A quick spin of the *tonfun* would have knocked him out, but she wanted him to recover quickly enough with a burn to rejoin the fight with a vengeance.

Vaulting a low concrete barrier, she gained one of the enormous parking lots near a line of cabs that continuously dropped off and picked up passengers, the drivers seemingly oblivious to the riot. If they thought anything of the fistfights illuminated by their headlights, it was likely to wonder if any brawlers left standing would need a cab. She brushed her hands free of some grit, dusting off any responsibility for tonight's violence. Relaxing her vigilance nearly cost her, and she dove aside with only centimeters to spare as an arriving cab braked too late and slammed into the concrete divider.

Instead of jumping out to check the damage to his cab or to Megan, the driver turned to argue loudly with his passenger. Something about Stephen Neils getting just what he deserved and so what if the FedRat died? Them's the breaks. That was news to Megan, that Neils had been killed at the end of the match. No wonder the crowd was out of control. It would make her work easier.

A loud popping noise punched a hole through the cab's front window and stretched a spiderweb of cracks across the glass. Now the two men inside were wrestling for control of a gun. Ignoring the argument, Megan picked up a chunk of broken cement and hurried toward the head of the line of cabs. She chucked the heavy fragment back into the crowd on the other side of the barriers, aiming for one of the heated fights where the names of Prince Victor and Archon Katrina were on everyone's lips.

Ducking into a cab, she ordered the operator to drive—just drive. It was time to go. Someone back there was about to become much more upset, she decided. Lyran or FedRat, it didn't make much difference to Megan this time. A stone was a non-lethal object for the most part. The injury would only fuel the rage in that particular fight and in the riot overall. And that was fine.

It was, after all, what she had been paid to do.

═══ 4 ═══

Ishiyama, Kobe
Solaris City, Solaris VII
Freedom Theater, Lyran Alliance
13 August 3062

Day Three of the Grand Tournament and already Michael Searcy was back in Kobe, fighting at Ishiyama arena. He'd defeated Jarman Bauer here on Day One, but Yoki Susuma was proving a much tougher opponent.

Sweat-salt had dried on his face, burning at the corners of his eyes, but his full-body coolant suit maintained his body's temperature well enough against the waste heat escaping the *Dragon Fire*'s fusion engine. However, even his high-technology life-support system couldn't keep his muscles from aching in the drawn-out battle. For the sixth time this evening Michael prowled the tight confines of The Knot, searching for his opponent. The Knot, a tangle of rock-faced chambers and tunnels of Gordian complexity, was the most difficult stretch of Ishiyama and the one no 'Warrior had ever truly mastered. He kept using its twists and turns to evade Susuma, hoping to infuriate the Combine MechWarrior—and the Combine audience as well.

Michael had been expecting to fight Evelyn Czerny tonight, but that was before she'd tangled with Susuma in the Davion arena the day before. Coming out of no-where, Susuma had staged a major upset by blasting the number-two-ranked Czerny out of her *Albatross* and completely out of the tourney. Susuma wasn't even ranked in the top two hundred, and it was already some-thing of a miracle that he'd won a spot in the Grand Tournament at all. Though maybe it shouldn't have been such a surprise. Kurita-affiliated MechWarriors had begun to dominate the games ever since the Draconis Combine legalized broadcasting of the Solaris matches within their realm. It was like they were riding some kind of warrior high.

That would have to end.

In an interview with the Federated Suns News Service, Michael had vowed to end Susuma's mayfly streak. It wasn't the usual anti-Drac rhetoric, but the promise of a pro against a flash-in-the-pan upstart in over his head. All in all, Michael thought, snakes weren't so bad.

With Susuma's upset and the difference in their rank-ings, the Combine fighter was given the choice of venue. Ishiyama was the deadliest arena on Solaris VII, with the greatest home-arena advantage for its usual fighters. It was the obvious choice for Susuma. And tonight he had acted in typical Combine fashion, going for an im-mediate and decisive win. The samurai traditions of House Kurita vaunted such efforts. Stormin' Michael Searcy had countered in the most obnoxious fashion possible.

He ran away.

Never for long, though, and not so far that anyone could accuse him of *cowardice*! That specter still haunted his thoughts. But Michael meant to have this win, to proceed along the Grand Tournament to the prize. He would be Champion, he was sure of it. Only then would he feel vindicated for his humiliation after New Canton. And victory meant fighting the battle his way, not Susu-ma's. Michael would retreat, then come back again to nip at his enemy's *Maelstrom* before fading away once more. First he shaved a half-ton of armor from the *Mael-strom*'s left flank. Then he delivered a pair of light gauss slugs, one hammered into each leg. Always watching for the advantage.

For the most part it was a straight-up match. Susuma held an edge in maneuverability while Michael owned it in firepower. In armor, however, they were even. Michael didn't intend to be drawn into a close-range slugging brawl where the *Maelstrom*'s better movement curve would be decisive. The Knot provided for his escape each time. He was no fool. He was the future Champion.

Susuma might think Michael was merely trying to dodge him, not realizing it was all part of a plan. There it was, the turn-off he'd been looking for. He took a hard left that took him into a tunnel barely large enough for his *Dragon Fire* to move through without scraping its sides against the artificial rock. If he'd judged correctly, it would slope down into the grand chasm, where he'd already skirmished a couple of times with the Combine gladiator.

The chamber did slope downward, and quickly, but not into the chasm he expected. Instead it took him to the edge of a giant underground lake, its black waters rippling under a roof of artificial stalactites. The lake was two hundred meters across at the widest point, and who knew how deep. Four chambers opened up onto its waters. The main chamber was lit with a bright phosphorescence along the walls and ceiling that resembled glowing algae or moss, except nothing in nature could have made such a glow. It was all part of the effort to make Ishiyama's terrain seem natural. Michael had never been in this part of the vast underground complex and didn't think now was the moment to start exploring it.

He backed up, preparing to turn around and try The Knot again, when his sensors screamed for his attention.

He wasn't the only one who'd taken a wrong turn out of the labyrinth of passages above. As if summoned to this dark place, Yoki Susuma's *Maelstrom* stepped down to the water's edge, just across a short, sixty-meter stretch of the lake. With both 'Mechs slightly out of line with each other, it became a race to see who could twist the fastest and bring weapons to bear. A race Susuma won, using the extra swing his arms gave him to snap off a shot with his right-arm laser. A ruby beam lanced out, flashing across the water to cut away at the fresh armor on the *Dragon Fire*'s right leg.

The damage threw a slight tremor into the 'Mech's stance, easily compensated for by the neuroreceptors build into his bodysuit's cowl. Michael held for a full salvo, waiting that extra second until he could bring his torso-mounted weapons into play. The large pulse laser he'd added after his fight with Bauer, replacing his close-range lasers, stabbed out a flurry of sapphire darts, flashing away armor off the *Maelstrom*'s chest. His light gauss rifle missed wide, sending the silvery blur of its propelled nickel-ferrous slug ricocheting back into the dark passages of Ishiyama. The Defiance Disintegrator autocannon made up the difference by pounding a stream of twelve-centimeter slugs into the other 'Mech's right side. The lethal barrage smashed away the last of the *Maelstrom*'s remaining armor, digging deep and then chipping away at the physical shielding of the reactor. He saw the blossom of waste heat show up on an auxiliary screen like a white heart opening up over the *Maelstrom*'s profile.

That would hurt it, Michael knew. The 'Mech depended on lighter weight but heat-inefficient weapons.

As the echoes of his autocannon fire faded away, Michael backed his 'Mech into the passage from which he'd come. Susuma fired one last shot, trying to catch Michael before his profile disappeared, but the laser missed short and only succeeded in melting a scar into the rocky wall instead. Just out of sight, Michael stopped the *Dragon Fire,* counted five long and painful heartbeats, then throttled up into a run that would take him straight back down to the lake's edge. Now he would see if his earlier patience in this fight had paid off.

And it had. Frustrated with chasing Michael and wanting to come to blows in a decisive match, Yoki Susuma had plunged into the water trying to catch the *Dragon Fire* before it made the safety of The Knot. When Michael burst back into the cavern, his cross hairs already leveled for an angle into the lake, Susuma was halfway across, wading through the deep water.

Trapped by his own impatience, the Kurita fighter could do nothing but try and slog forward while firing his weapons as fast as they would recharge. It was the stand-up fight he wanted, but on Michael's terms, one where the *Maelstrom*'s faster movement curve was negated. It was just the kind of finish that spoke of champions, that spoke of *the* Champion.

Multi-colored light flared in the cavern, a ruby lance trading with the sapphire darts of Michael's pulse laser. Armor ran molten orange on both sides of the engagement, dripping off the *Maelstrom* to be quenched by black waters. Steam rose up, wreathing the seventy-five-ton 'Mech in a haze quickly dissipated by the arcing cascade of lightning from Susuma's energy cannon. The azure whip dug into the *Dragon Fire*'s already-wounded right side, probing for the ammunition bin but not quite able to pierce the armor protection. Michael's heavy-bore autocannon tore into the *Maelstrom*'s right arm, cutting through the titanium humerus and dropping the PPC into the lake. His gauss slug found its target this time, punching right through the last of the center-line armor to smash the gyroscopic stabilizer into ruin.

The gyro tore itself into a rain of high-velocity metal spitting out from the wound, and the *Maelstrom* collapsed beneath the water's surface.

Yoki Susuma splashed to the surface a moment later, while Michael was still trying to decide which would play better to the media—standing there victorious over his opponent or wading in to help the other 'Mech to shore. Then he decided that wading in would only give Susuma a chance to swipe at him to try and knock the *Dragon Fire* to equal footing—or lack thereof. The MechWarrior's appearance solved the problem, though Michael winced briefly in sympathy, imagining the problems of drying out the other 'Mech's cockpit.

But that minor twinge of conscience vanished with the thought that he was victorious. Again. Day Four tomorrow and he would fight the winner of tonight's Karufel/Metz ticket. That match was sure to be hard-fought, the rival House Liao stables squaring off against each other in the Jungle. After that, Vandergriff or Mayetska. Then Theodore Gross? In his mind's eye Michael saw himself walking into the finals having dethroned the current Champion. In fact, so preoccupied was he that he didn't even notice Susuma swimming to shore, where he stood dripping, offering a formal bow in acknowledgement of his defeat.

Michael's mind was already on victories to come.

The private viewing box Blackstar Stables had reserved for the evening was large enough to double as a private lounge. Michael wasn't surprised when Drew Hasek-Davion met him at the door to claim his share of the victory.

"Well fought, Michael," Drew said as applause for the Davion favorite swept up from behind him.

A flush of pride warmed Michael's face as he glanced around the room. The next Ishiyama battle—a filler to kill time between Championship matches—was already underway on a giant holovid screen covering one entire wall. The sound was muted, and the fight played out against the buzz of idle conversation. Other Blackstar fighters were also present, ones Drew Hasek-Davion wanted to show off or spotlight on the coattails of Michael's success. The usual media hacks were also there and would surely try to weasel a private interview. The rest were minor nobles, local politicos, and other associates of Drew Hasek-Davion. Few people Michael routinely dealt with, or wanted to. But it didn't matter what he thought of these people; *he* knew he'd done a good job.

Drew peered further back into the corridor, impatiently tapping the golden lion's head of his walking stick against the palm of one hand. "Susuma?" he asked.

"Politely declined our invitation," Michael said. Riding high on his victory, no snub could dampen his spirits. How Yoki Susuma chose to deal with his mistake wasn't Michael's to decide. He knew from experience that couch-warriors would be second-guessing the Combine MechWarrior's actions for weeks to come. He privately wished the young gladiator luck.

"That is perhaps for the best," Drew said. "Garrett will be more likely to behave himself without a Combine 'Warrior around to provoke him."

Michael shrugged. How Drew's pet Clanner comported himself did not concern him. He saw Garrett lurking alone on the other side of the room, refusing a drink being offered to him by a server. It surprised Michael that the man had deigned to come into Kobe sector at all. Garrett was one of the Smoke Jaguar warrior renegades who'd chosen to make Solaris VII his home after the destruction of his Clan. Until just eighteen months ago he'd also been a prime contender in the arenas.

Garrett had developed a hatred that bordered on pathological for anything smacking of House Kurita. If he was at this party, it was at the command of Drew Hasek-Davion, possibly with the aim of engineering a new grudge match against any available Combine-stable fighter. That was fine with Michael. He didn't care what games Drew played at with Garrett, so long as they didn't interfere with his own rise to the top.

Then he spied another lone figure moving through the crowded room, a whipcord-thin man who Michael recognized at once. "I should greet some of these folks," Michael said, trying to disentangle himself from Hasek-Davion.

Drew's gaze had followed Michael's. "Consorting with the enemy again?" he asked. The tone was light enough, but Michael sensed the dark undercurrents of disapproval.

"Karl Edward is not the enemy," he said, defending his friend.

"He belongs to Starlight Stables. You to Blackstar. What *would* you call him?"

Michael conceded that the owner of Starlight Stables certainly went out of his way to interfere with Drew's plans for Blackstar, though it was nothing compared to the animosity that raged between Blackstar and the Skye Tigers. The difference was that Starlight, like Blackstar, was known for its ties to House Davion's Federated Suns, while the Skye Tigers backed the Lyran Alliance. And though rivalry between the various stables—even supposedly *friendly* stables—was unavoidable, Michael couldn't buy into it when it came to Karl. He was the only man Michael trusted on all of Solaris, a place where it was nearly impossible to find a true friend among so many only looking out for themselves.

"The loyal opposition?" Michael ventured, half in jest.

"Karl promised to monitor some fights for me tonight. I'd like to get his take on them."

Drew wasn't giving up so easily. "I have others acquiring vids of those fights." He guided his young star toward a knot of people gathered at the room's center as if holding it by force against all comers. Michael recognized a few Black Hills politicos as well as some corporate honchos. A few of the guests also wore the dress uniforms of the Armed Forces of the Federated Commonwealth. "They can get you any information you require."

"I prefer Karl's opinion," Michael said, keeping a wary eye on those uniformed figures. Even from here he could identify the shoulder patches as belonging to the Capellan March, an area with long-time ties to the Hasek and Hasek-Davion families. Michael saw too that these officers belonged to the same AFFC division from which he'd been cashiered. How far back had Hasek-Davion dug into his past?

He stopped in his tracks, forcing Drew to halt as well. Hasek-Davion had to know that trying to drag Michael where he didn't want to go wouldn't play well to their audience. Michael glared at him. "Are you wanting another pet MechWarrior or a Champion?"

Drew glared back, knowing that his protégé was using the fact that they were out in public to manipulate the situation. "You've learned well," he said. Then he pretended to notice Karl Edward for the first time and steered Michael in that direction.

"Very well, dear boy, I will indulge you." He put heavy emphasis on the word *boy,* reminding Michael who held the important cards, a hand that would be played only behind closed doors. "You think you know Karl Edward, but this is Solaris. Don't forget that he's still your *opposition,* even though you left him behind in the standings. He's jealous and would betray you if it was to his advantage."

Jealous? Perhaps a little. With only three years on the Game World, Michael was already ranked seventh overall. Stormin' Michael Searcy might not be Kai Allard-Liao, who had fought his way to the top in a single year back in '54, but he was damned good. Karl, on the other hand, had only recently earned the Class Six license that allowed him to fight in the Open Arenas of Solaris City. He was rising in the ranks, but slowly. That he didn't make the Grand Tournament roster simply gave him a goal to shoot for in '63. Maybe '64.

But betrayal? That was a subject about which Michael had learned more than he ever wanted to know. The Lyran officer who had cut short his military career had taught him well. If Karl Edward was that kind of man, Michael would have known it by now. Not that he left himself vulnerable to anyone, but at times it helped to know who you could trust at your back. Or at least, who would be the least damaging.

As he and Drew came up to Karl, Drew stepped over to speak with Garrett while Michael greeted his friend with an easy hand clasp. As a native of Solaris VII, Karl was technically a Lyran by birth. He'd fought his way up through the blood pits—the lower-echelon arenas outside Solaris City—then had met up with Michael on the Class-Three circuit shortly after Michael's arrival. He'd refused early sponsorship in a stable known for its long-time ties to House Steiner. That public—and dramatic—refusal had earned him very high marks in Michael's book at the time.

Michael and Karl had watched out for each other in the lower-class arenas, doing their best to resist the strong-arm tactics local tongs employed when trying to fix the fights. For a few months they'd even shared a ride—an old, beat-up *Centurion*. The 'Mech had been well past its prime in the technological renaissance the Inner Sphere was enjoying, but with a few good fights left in it.

Karl had switched to citizenship in the Federated Suns only two months before he and Michael were both picked up by Blackstar, though he'd been traded away quickly to Starlight. Since then Karl had become a vocal advocate of Prince Victor and, more important to both Michael *and* Drew Hasek-Davion, a critic of Katrina Steiner. Which was very possibly the real reason Drew tolerated the inter-stable friendship.

"Who do you want to hear about first?" Karl asked

without preamble. No congratulations. He was all business this evening.

It set Michael immediately on his guard. "I'm assuming Theodore Gross won at Boreal Reach, or else everyone would be talking about it," he said, accepting a nonalcoholic drink from a server. No liquor for him this week, but he needed something to replace the fluids sweated away earlier. "So then, how about Kelley Metz?"

Karl's eyes sparked with brief interest. "She won, but she was shaken up pretty bad. You'll get a bye if she can't fight tomorrow night."

Michael sipped his drink, a fruity mixture that would have gone very nicely with some alcohol. "Her win can't be sitting well with Zelazni Stables. It'll spark a new round of grudge matches as soon as the tourney is over." He mentally reviewed other matches set for Day Three, considering only the top players. "What about Craig Orme?" he asked, mentioning one of the Steiner-affiliated champions. "How is he looking?"

"Dead."

The answer came from over Michael's shoulder as Garrett intruded on their conversation. The former Clansman wore a Spartan gray uniform, its only decoration the Blackstar patch on his right sleeve and a Smoke Jaguar crest on his left breast. His mouth was a hard, cruel line drawn across a stern face. Michael might have put the intrusion down to the slight enmity he and Garrett shared, except for two things. That Garrett did not immediately leave the conversation and that Drew Hasek-Davion was standing nearby, close enough to eavesdrop if he so desired.

"Teresa Dale fired a PPC point-blank into the head of Orme's *Rakshasa*. It burned right through the cockpit," Garrett said.

"They ruled it an accident," Karl said at once, but he sounded dubious.

Of course there would be questions. Two fatalities in the Grand Tournament and both in matches between Federated Suns and Lyran Alliance MechWarriors. Still, 'Warriors sometimes died in the games. All the rules and restrictions, all the safety precautions, couldn't prevent it.

"An *accident,*" Garrett said, his tone mocking Karl's. "Try explaining that to the witnesses." The Clanner still couldn't abide calling the spectators an *audience.* To him, they were witnesses to a contest of skill. Paying witnesses perhaps, but Garrett did not fight for *them.* "They nearly tore Boreal Reach apart. Two MechWarriors exchanged live fire in the main BattleMech bay, damaging a power relay for the arena's holoprojectors."

Michael shook his head as he listened. More rioting in the streets of Solaris City. And this time Boreal Reach had been damaged! The high-tech arena in the Davion sector was impressive, using holographic media to generate a variety of terrain and conditions. It made the Steiner coliseum's detonator grid a poor second, in Michael's opinion.

"Who fired first?"

For some reason Karl flashed him a look of irritation, but Garrett was ready with an answer. "Sarah Anne Wilder," he said, "of *Starlight* Stables. She was disqualified from the Grand Tournament, though she claims it was self-defense." To Karl's credit, he didn't rise to the Clanner's bait, though it must have been galling to be needled on a point of honor by a Smoke Jaguar.

What would have happened next, no one would ever know. Drew Hasek-Davion was already shouldering his way into their little group. "Garrett," he said, as if surprised to see him. "I was wondering where you'd gotten off to. A word, please." The tone of the request brooked no refusal and instantly cut off any further discussion.

"You knew about Orme's death?" Michael demanded before Drew could turn and walk off with Garrett. Drew should have given him information of such import immediately, rather than arranging for Garrett to give him the news.

"Of course," Drew said smoothly. "That ought to shake things up a bit, don't you think? Some of the ticket-filler matches have already been rearranged to meet this new demand for Steiner-Davion brawls." Drew's blue eyes cut hard at Karl. "Speaking of which, good luck in the Coliseum on Thursday, Mr. Edward."

Then Drew and Garrett withdrew, though the Clanner looked sullen as he went.

"What's this about the Coliseum?" Michael asked, rounding on Karl. He would be fighting in the Coliseum in two days as well, providing he beat Metz tomorrow night.

"It's my grudge match with Tom Payne. We're being bumped up a week." Karl shrugged uncomfortably. "If you win—*when* you win tomorrow—I'll end up following your Day Five match."

And with their friendship a known fact, Karl would gain some publicity for his match by leeching off Michael's prominence. It was a smart move by Starlight Stables. Michael only wished that Drew hadn't tried to plant doubts in his mind about Karl's loyalty. He preferred to believe that Karl wouldn't actively seek to capitalize on their friendship, but why hadn't Karl mentioned it himself?

As if reading his mind, Karl said, "I was informed by messenger during your match with Susuma."

Nodding, Michael offered his friend a camera-shoot smile. "It's all right, Karl." But from the awkward silence that followed, both of them knew that it wasn't quite *all* right. But it would be, Michael decided. When he was Champion, everything else would pale by comparison. And Karl would be welcome to a piece of that. Drew Hasek-Davion, too. As a Blackstar fighter even Garrett would benefit. It would be something he'd always known he could achieve. Something truly noteworthy. Something historic.

And something no one could ever take away from him. Ever.

Across the room, Drew Hasek-Davion leaned on his walking stick and sipped at a watered-down bourbon. He nodded at all the right places as some Black Hills bureaucrat droned on about the cost of each hour of rioting. Drew wasn't about to explain how for each of those hours he made back at least triple the cost to the city. The man simply did not know how the games were actually played on Solaris VII. But, then, not many people did. Only the true masters of the world—the stable owners, the media, and the big entertainment concerns. Oh, and the criminal element, though they seemed mostly content to allow men like Drew to handle the day-to-day affairs while they plotted long-term rape on the flow of money the 'Mech games released. Drew had his fingers in more than a few of those deals as well.

So instead of debating the bureaucrat's delusional view of what Solaris City *should* be like, he observed Michael and Karl Edward's conversation over the smaller man's shoulder. His interest was much more than curiosity, though not quite pleasure. Very little in life gave Drew actual pleasure, though some things came close. Power was by far the leading candidate. The power he wielded on Solaris and back in the Federated Suns. Power over profitable ventures and over the lives of the people around him.

Power over Michael Searcy.

Through carefully nurtured paranoia, he had Michael second-guessing everything outside the arena, even his friendships, which was how Drew wanted it. Michael would soon believe he had nowhere to turn except to the master of Blackstar Stables. Drew had seen that the young firebrand was destined for greatness from the start. Under his coaching and care, Michael Searcy now stood within reach of what he'd wanted for so long. What they both wanted.

A pet MechWarrior? Not hardly. Drew had a stable full of those. No, he wanted a Champion. And more than that. He wanted to *own* a Champion, not just manage one. He would own Michael Searcy. And then all the prestige and influence of the Championship would also be *his* to use in furthering his plans, just as once that power had been allied against him. Drew had enemies to deal with, such as the Skye Tigers on the other side of Solaris City. He also had alliances to forge.

Michael Searcy would be Champion. He'd been groomed for it, just as one might breed and train a race-horse. Drew didn't even mind if the 'Warrior believed he was winning for his own reasons, his own purposes. Perhaps he was. He guessed that Michael thought Drew's plans nothing more than little games, power-plays meant to make it look like Drew was the ultimate source of Searcy's successes. Michael wouldn't see until it was too late that not only was appearance easily accepted as reality, but that all too often it *became* reality.

Drew Hasek-Davion smiled thin and hard, knowing that he represented a greater danger to Michael Searcy than any opponent the Davion favorite might face in combat. But in Hasek-Davion's arena, the young 'Warrior never stood a chance.

5

Today, the Paradise would become an arena as deadly as any in Solaris City, though not as a threat to life and limb. It would be the site of a more subtle duel, and one not for public consumption. Here, influence and alliances of convenience would rule the day, might even affect who would reign supreme over the Game World, if only for a few days or weeks or months.

Drew Hasek-Davion was already seated in the restaurant's private dining room, waiting as the fragile-looking *hana josei* silently escorted the other stable owners to their places at the low, round table. The women seemed to glide over the hardwood floor in their silk kimonos. Each wore her raven hair tied up in a simple bun, and the only color on their pale, white-powdered faces was deep red lipstick and high spots of rouge on their cheeks. They stood by patiently as the guests awkwardly arranged their bodies on low stools that let them rest in a half-kneeling position without putting strain on their legs.

When everyone was seated, the women bowed deeply

as they retreated from the room, tracing an unerring path backward to the door. One stopped, knelt, and pulled open the shoji panel, and then all glided through as silently as they'd come. Another then knelt on the other side to pull the panel shut.

Gathered around the low table, various members of the group commented on the restaurant's rich hardwoods and authentic Japanese antiques imported from Terra itself—the statuettes worked in bronze to exquisite detail, a Shinto shrine of light gray and blue marble, shoji panels that seemed sewn together from the wings of butterflies, and elegant charcoal sketches on ricepaper. Alongside the antiques were contemporary works of fragile beauty to contrast the timeless pieces.

Drew had arrived early enough that he'd already drunk his fill of the Emperor's Chamber. Joining him now were his fellow members of the Solaris Stable Owners Association, each with fighters still in the Grand Tournament. His peers. His enemies. He watched them with some amusement as the sweet and spicy scents of the food finally pulled their attention back to the table— laid out just before their arrival so that no rattling dishes or clumsy servers might ruin the atmosphere of the Paradise.

Only Thomas DeLon seemed as comfortable in these elegant surroundings as Drew. He sat directly opposite at the table and waited for Drew to open the meeting. DeLon could be trouble. As stable master for Theodore Gross, the defending Champion, his word carried some extra weight. DeLon and his 'Warriors did not indulge in the usual pre-fight rhetoric to jack up the challenges, grudges, and normal rivalries on which the Game World thrived. He didn't need to; his fights were always in high demand.

Drew shrugged that aside. The Combine was a different culture where showy displays were not as admired. Also, the games were still a new treat for its people, having become legally available only these last six years. DeLon could afford to hold back, for now. But that would change. Drew had the history of the Game World on his side. On Solaris nothing remained constant. Though Drew had nearly been ruined learning that lesson, eventually he'd used it to raise his personal fortune, and fortunes, to new heights. Now here he was, master of Blackstar, one of the strongest stables on Solaris VII. Vying for leadership against DeLon and a very few others for the power to direct the course of the Game World.

"My friends," he lied, "welcome to Paradise. I would like to thank Mr. DeLon for helping me arrange this afternoon's meeting."

Jerry Stroud was the owner of Skye Tiger Stables and possibly the second-most dangerous man after Drew on Solaris VII. "Why is this meeting being held in Kobe?" he asked, voice carefully guarded. While Stroud often affected an upper-class manner, Drew knew that it concealed a ruthless and predatory nature. "And why today?" he went on. "The SSOA mid-tournament lunch is usually held tomorrow, before the Day Five matches when the playing field has been narrowed to the final eight."

Drew wasn't about to admit that he'd chosen Kobe because it was inconvenient for the two Silesians present. "Coming from a man whose final contender is predicted to fall in the first sixty seconds against Theodore Gross tonight, I would think you'd appreciate an early meeting so that you might attend."

Stroud glowered, but didn't take the bait. Drew decided to prod him again. "In answer to your question, we meet today instead of tomorrow because Thomas DeLon has raised the issue of the recent"—he paused—"*troubles* between the Black Hills and Silesia. Damage to the Boreal Reach arena is a serious concern. The Kobe sector seemed to be more neutral ground. You have no objection to meeting me on equal footing, do you, Jerry?"

Seated between Drew and Stroud, Nicole Singh smiled and stifled a laugh. Perhaps she was recalling another meeting of a few months back, when Stroud had accused Drew of hiring some local mercenaries to sabotage the Clan OmniMech he'd just managed to purchase. The powerful machine might have won Skye Tiger a prime position and made possible some interesting matches against Singh's outcast Diamond Shark warrior and

Drew's Clan Smoke Jaguar renegade. There were still many who enjoyed seeing the former Clanners beat on each other. At the time Stroud had commented that Drew wanted the 'Mech destroyed because he was afraid to meet Stroud on equal footing.

Stroud flushed with anger. "If I ever find proof, you'd better watch out, Hasek."

Drew pulled himself up proudly. "Hasek-*Davion,*" he snapped, though that sword certainly cut both ways. He had appropriated the Davion name years before, though his only tie was remote, through marriage twice-removed rather than by blood. He'd once hoped it would win him a political boost among those who opposed the ruling Davion line, especially in the Capellan March where the Haseks governed and a Hasek-Davion had once held great power and prominence. So far that path to greater power had been a dead end. People seemed ill-disposed to turn on the current ruling Hasek line.

Though he kept his new name, Drew had then embraced the more hard-core anti-Davion sentiment, opposing the merger between the Federated Suns and the old Lyran state. Only to find himself once again on the losing side of a wager. And now, this year, here he was one of the strongest Davion supporters. At least, in front of the cameras. The viewing public had a very short memory.

"Don't waste your time, Jerry. There's no proof to find." That was because Drew had guaranteed that sabotage of the OmniMech could not be linked back to him. Both men knew the showdown was coming, though by unspoken consent they were waiting until a new Champion emerged from the Grand Tournament. At least, Drew *appeared* to be waiting.

"Shall we table business matters until after we've eaten?" Drew asked the group in general. Besides Nicole Singh, Stroud, and DeLon, also seated at the table were Tran Ky Bo, another Black Hills stable master, and beyond him Jurgen Gaalf, representing the interests of Montenegro. Only the Liao-affiliated stables were not represented, though by choice rather than exclusion. Jerry Stroud did not look ready to drop the argument, but retreated when no one else offered to back him up.

The beautifully prepared dishes had been set on ceramic plates arranged around a revolving wheel that comprised the table's center. The Paradise's specialty was tea-smoked riverwader, the Solaran equivalent of duck. The tender meat seemed to dissolve on the tongue, leaving behind a wonderful smoky taste. There were also plates of hot and spicy chicken served over a large bed of rice, shrimp tempura, and yakisoba, in quantities the stable owners could not possibly ever eat.

The moment they touched their food, a trio of the *hana josei* returned with green tea, sake, and a dark plum wine, which they poured for everyone. Not a drop was spilled or a cup rattled against saucer. So light was their presence that it was almost as if they did not exist at all, but were simply beautiful apparitions conjured to serve. They reappeared occasionally, sweeping through the room to see that glasses were filled and to whisk away dishes as necessary—one at a time rather than risk unnecessary noise with stacking. Even Drew, who had been waiting for the meal to finish, could not say for certain when the last dish disappeared and suddenly the stable owners were left alone with their drinks and a clear table over which to talk.

"Time for business," he said, opening the meeting. "I know Thomas is worried about what happened under Boreal Reach last evening, the live fire that damaged the Davion arena. Also the violence in the streets that has continued even to this morning. I think there may have been a few deaths." He knew very well that five residents of the Black Hills and twelve Silesians had been killed in the sporadic rioting. So far. "I believe we should address the issue."

Jurgen Gaalf nodded. "I agree. We've got to do something about it, but what?"

At first everyone was silent. After all, Drew had already spoken for DeLon, preempting what might have been an impassioned plea for calm and control—neither of which suited Drew's plans. He folded his pudgy hands on the edge of the table and softened his voice as he spoke. "Or, should we do nothing about it?"

Gaalf seemed shocked by the very idea, as did Tran Ky Bo. The others kept their poker faces in place. "Is it our business to put down riots?" Drew asked. "Why should the stable owners cut into their own profits because of Solaris City's lunatic fringe?"

"When our fighters are the nucleus of the trouble, it is our inherent responsibility to hold ourselves accountable," Gaalf stated emphatically.

Noble sentiments from a stable cloaking itself in virtuous white-knight behavior, but Jurgen Gaalf didn't fool Drew for a minute. The man didn't have to get involved in name-calling and political posturing because everyone else did the work for him. His people could play at being above such petty squabbles, and by saying so publicly—and quite often—actually contributed to the rivalries. If that idea were not so limiting in its options, Drew might have been jealous.

Tran Ky Bo was already nodding vigorously in support of Gaalf, though he would likely do so on any matter that opposed Drew Hasek-Davion. That one-sided feud was well known, and the owner of Starlight automatically set himself against anything he thought might favor Drew. That was all right with Drew; he saved his efforts for more dangerous game.

Such as Thomas DeLon, who was far more influential. "The fighters should not be making these matches personal," DeLon said. "There is plenty of profit potential without the theatrics. And without trying to turn our fighters and the fans against each other."

Someone else would have to answer DeLon, or else Drew would seem isolated, and then like sharks on a bleeding brother the others would all turn on him. And against Blackstar Stables. Fortunately, though, Blackstar wasn't the only outfit that counted on the personality cults of its 'Warriors and the strong rivalries that resulted in impressive ticket sales and lucrative broadcast rights. He would have preferred to see Jerry Stroud step in—had counted on it—but Nicole Singh jumped in next.

"That's very easy for you to say, Mr. DeLon." Young enough to be DeLon's granddaughter, Nicole felt obliged to address him with utmost respect. "After all, Kobe is again the wealthiest sector in Solaris City ever since the Combine opened its doors to the games. And I believe you own three fighters in the top twenty. Your fortunes are safe." Drew gave Nicole full marks for the way she isolated DeLon as the wealthiest man at the table, a position every one of the others coveted. Vernon Singh knew what he was doing, sending his daughter in his place.

"My father remembers, as I'm certain many of you do as well, the hard times stable owners had after the Feeding Frenzy days of the Clan invasion. No one had it easy. The MechWarriors made the difference, giving people champions to rally behind. But champions need their enemies, or they become faceless beings again."

DeLon shook his head, though lightly. "I still do not like it."

"We could vote on it. Whether or not to intercede." Gaalf again. Drew tired of his interference. Gaalf didn't want the vote any more than he did, though he tried to make it seem so. But suggesting a vote and actually calling for it were two different things. Again, the Montenegran was letting someone else do all the work to defuse the situation.

Still, the sides were forming. Drew counted DeLon, Gaalf, and Tran Ky Bo against him. Nicole Singh made an unexpected but welcome ally. It would look good for a Davion and a Steiner-affiliated stable to stand together, while Tran Ky Bo split the Davion ranks. No one could claim that national rivalries had influenced the voting for the worst. Only for the side of better business.

"It seems," he said, "that Lion City and Blackstar stables agree to disagree. And yes, we *could* vote, though I should tell you it won't do much good. The vote binds us, not necessarily our fighters. And Michael Searcy is making a press appearance even now." He smiled in feigned good humor. "If he and Vandergriff meet tomorrow, it should be a fight to remember."

Tran Ky Bo had leaned in when Drew said that such a vote would not apply to the MechWarriors. He scoffed in open amazement. "You can't control your own fighter?"

Drew's smile turned nasty. "Coming from a man whose contender started a fight under Boreal Reach, I find that an inappropriate question."

"It was self-defense," Tran Ky Bo retorted, though his voice fell a few degrees in strength.

"So say you. Regardless, that was the heat of the moment. Michael is entertaining the press because it's good business. And you all know it." He speared Tran with an appraising look, knowing that everyone in the room was aware of the Edward-Payne grudge match Tran had rescheduled for the following night. "Tell me honestly that you haven't profited more in your Davion-Steiner rivalry fights."

Tran Ky Bo remained mute, but Drew noticed Jerry Stroud watching carefully, critically. Drew may have been facing down his rival for power in the Black Hills, but it was really to Stroud that he was appealing. Stroud, who now held the swing vote in the dispute. Without the open rivalries, Stroud could not make an issue of coming after Blackstar Stables, and Drew Hasek-Davion, in particular. He could challenge, yes, but without expecting the usual boost in publicity. And that hurt the bottom line, made a feud far less profitable. Jerry Stroud was strong, but did not have the deep resources available to Drew Hasek-Davion.

Drew knew that Stroud might also vote against him just for the sake of being contrary. So instead he turned his attention to Thomas DeLon, who was conducting his own silent poll of the table. Nicole Singh obviously stood with Drew, just as Tran Ky Bo offered Thomas his silent nod of support. Gaalf remained noncommittal, though if forced he would certainly vote with DeLon. That left Stroud, and even now the Lyran shifted in his seat to face Thomas more directly. He would obviously not side with DeLon Stables should Thomas call the vote.

Knowing better than to push a losing position, Thomas DeLon folded his hand and stood up. "I have made my concerns known. That is all I wanted. Kobe is not yet afflicted by this insanity you play at, so I will not try to force my views upon you. Let us get on with the Grand Tournament. When a Champion has been selected, or *confirmed*, perhaps we shall visit this subject again."

There it was. Drew also stood up across the table from Thomas. They both knew the fight was merely delayed, not settled. "Shall we adjourn?" he asked. Thomas nodded to second the motion.

Everyone else voted with their feet.

Garrett sat waiting in Drew's own sedan, affecting an air of disdain for the world around him, but Drew knew it was all an act. He was careful to keep his amusement in check, knowing the renegade Smoke Jaguar might too easily take offense. He also knew that the only time Garrett wanted to enter Kobe was for the purpose of stomping snakes in Ishiyama.

The Combine-affiliated sector always set the Clanner on edge. The Star League had driven the Smoke Jaguars from the Inner Sphere in shame, and then followed them back to their homeworld to smash them into extinction. Garrett felt a killing hatred for the Star League and anyone or anything connected to it, but even he realized it was futile to set himself against the whole of the Inner Sphere. Because his Clan had occupied the Draconis Combine and the Combine military had been instrumental in defeating the Jaguars, Garrett focused his rage against anything remotely hinting of House Kurita.

That had proven most rewarding, financially. For a while.

"You are amused. Everything went as you planned, quiaff?" he asked Drew.

Drew would have to be more careful if Garrett could read him so easily. He had survived the rout of his Clan, then made his way to the Game World with a Clan OmniMech. In private he sneered at Solaris VII, but the arenas were his only outlet for wreaking vengeance on those who had annihilated his Clan. His meteoric rise in the standings had been incredible. His quick fall slightly less impressive in Drew's eyes.

"Yes, Garrett. They have decided not to decide anything. Though I'm sure Thomas DeLon thought he had me for a moment. He'll wait now and hope to use Theodore Gross' fifth Championship as leverage against me." Drew laughed inwardly as Garrett physically recoiled with each contraction, the corner of his eye twitching. Clan warriors had a total aversion to such "lazy" forms of speech. "There's a chance it'll happen, but I'm betting heavily it won't." Twitch-twitch-blink-twitch.

The driver pulled the sedan out of the Paradise's protected parking onto Pillar of Gold Street, from there turning onto the avenue dedicated to Theodore Kurita. Drew settled back for the ride. Garrett sat ramrod straight, disdaining the luxury of the car's plush interior. "You should have let me kill Gross. Then the problem would not exist."

So that was the reason behind this requested meeting. Drew sighed, though the argument didn't surprise him. "You didn't get close enough to threaten his position. Once you lost to Srin Odessa, it was all over." Drew didn't add that it was Kasigi Mihabu, the most junior Kurita warrior, who had bumped Garrett from the Top Twenty altogether.

"So long as I live, it will never be over. There are more Clansmen here now, fighting up through the lesser arenas. When we are ready, you will bring us together under one crest. *Our* crest. I have your word."

As easily rescinded as given, Drew thought, but he let the Clanner believe what he wished. Garrett had fought well at first, furious and full of fire. All that changed once word came back that the Smoke Jaguars were dead and their military eradicated. His earlier fire had simply vanished. He still fought well, making few mistakes technically, but the drive was gone. It was as if the cloak of invincibility that had shielding him for so long had been torn away. The first time Drew heard Garrett referred to as the *Smoked* Jaguar, he knew it was time to concentrate fully on Michael Searcy. Garrett had even failed to win a spot in this year's Grand Tournament.

"We shall have to see, Garrett. Let me get through this tournament, and then . . . maybe."

Garrett wasn't giving up so easily. "You will let me fight Searcy for the top position in Blackstar Stables?"

"No." There was no profit in it. Drew knew he must always give the public what they wanted, or at least what they could be persuaded to want. And either way, Clan Smoke Jaguar was old news.

"Michael will be Champion, and there is more to that position than winning fights in the arenas." He looked at Garrett for a moment. "You could learn much from young Searcy."

Garrett glowered fiercely. To imply that a Clan true-born could learn warfare from an Inner Sphere freebirth was an insult. Like every Clan warrior, Garrett was the result of genetic engineering. "Combat is the ultimate teacher," he said, voice almost a growl.

"There I might be able to do something," Drew said. It was time to turn Garrett back toward his enemy. "Our recent schedule changes have opened up a slot on Day Five. A match in Ishiyama and against a junior DeLon 'Warrior." He saw the hungry gleam in Garrett's eyes. "If I slate you for that match, can I count on a solid victory over our enemies?"

"Aff!" Garrett said.

"Can you kill him?"

The Clanner's eyes narrowed into unreadable slits. "What do you put against his life?"

Though taken aback for a brief moment, Drew silently commended Garrett. Before, he would have accepted that order as a gain in itself. Now he was ready to set a price on such actions. Perhaps the Jaguar renegade was not finished in the games after all. He studied Garrett's face carefully. "You fighting Michael Searcy. The idea is . . . interesting."

The predatory grin Garrett gave him was all Drew needed to see that the man was hooked. It always paid to know what a person most wanted. Of course, what Drew Hasek-Davion most wanted right now was a diversion to occupy Thomas DeLon while Drew turned the rest of Blackstar Stables against the Skye Tigers. Jerry Stroud's time was coming, and Drew didn't intend to wait for the fight to come to him. He would go on the offensive today, with a series of grudge matches and clandestine operations. And so what if Garrett was now setting his sights on Searcy? Michael could look after himself, and it wasn't as if Drew had *promised* to arrange the match in an arena.

Besides, there was the very real possibility that Michael might someday outlive his usefulness. Careful planning always demanded that contingency plans be set in place.

And Drew Hasek-Davion was a very careful man.

6

On top of the world, and deservedly so.

Exactly how Michael Searcy felt standing before the holocams of the three news crews, holding his press conference atop the Viewpoint. The highest promontory in the Black Hills sector, it towered over the city and was enclosed by a concrete guard rail on all sides. A brisk wind whipped across it, ruffling his short blond curls with cool fingers, but otherwise the weather cooperated beautifully. The rains had lifted their gray veil, allowing for a magnificent view and a wonderful backdrop.

Michael felt himself master of all he surveyed. Soon to be Champion. Or so Drew Hasek-Davion kept promising. Those promises were barely worth the air behind them, though, when it came to the bottom line. Drew could not gift him the Championship. *That* Michael would have to win on his own, which sat perfectly fine with the Davion favorite.

"So you aren't worried about tonight's match against Kelley Metz. Think it's a foregone conclusion and already looking forward to tomorrow, Day Five."

Michael smiled for the cameras and the small audience that had gathered to watch the free show. He knew how to play to the media. "Was that a question, Adam, or are you working on your mind reading?" His touch of humor won a laugh from the crowd and even some spontaneous applause. Adam Kristof chuckled dryly and bowed his head, acknowledging the point.

"For the record, then. No, I am not concerned about Kelley Metz. I respect her skill, but she's already coming in under three handicaps. She was hurt in last night's match against Karufel. Doctors are calling it a cerebral contusion. She bruised her brain when her 'Mech toppled during the fight. She can compete, but she'll be fighting some light nausea and dizziness as well as me. Second, her *Emperor* gives up ten tons to my *Pillager*. And then there's the fact that we're in Boreal Reach, my home ground. Despite the tonnage difference, I've won enough points to choose the simulated terrain. We'll be fighting in Hell's Canyon among the lava flows, which won't help her heat curve."

Federated Suns Broadcasting edged in with the next question. "A *Pillager*? A Davion fighter in a St. Ives assault 'Mech?"

The other reporters shook their heads wearily. Fed-Suns Broadcasting was not known for stellar field journalism. Michael treated the question as serious, though. No sense making an enemy—even an incompetent one— in the Black Hills. "The *Pillager* design was made possible with information recovered by NAIS on New Avalon. HildCo fielded the trials and first few production runs, but GM on Kathil has been turning out limited numbers since 3060. I had one brought in for the second half of the tournament." He tried for a crooked smile. "Time for the big boys to come out and play."

"So you expect an easy match." Adam Kristof again, trying to pin Michael down on his personal opinion of Metz as a contender.

"Metz isn't about to go down easy. But I'd rather see her bow out than risk combat. I've no reason to want to see her get hurt."

"There's more than MechWarriors getting hurt this tournament, though," put in Veronica Sherman of the

Solaran Broadcasting Corporation. The Lyran-based SBC had sent out their ace video journalist to try and set him up. Michael saw her delivery coming from kilometers away. *Now* the game would turn more interesting. "It took the Silesian police force until nine this morning to declare the riots under control. Those weren't the fights that started in the heat of the games around Boreal Reach or the Coliseum, but Black Hills residents prowling Silesia intent on destruction and mayhem. Sixteen deaths reported as of an hour ago. Comments?"

Adam Kristof tried to head off the trouble. "You can't put all that on the Black Hills, Ronnie. You know full well that your police arrested three Silesia citizens in connection with some of that trouble."

Sherman ignored him. "Comments, Mr. Searcy?"

"If you're looking for my personal take on the matter, Ms. Sherman, just ask. I don't have details of what goes on in Silesia. Neither do you, from the sound of it." Michael threw Adam a conspiratorial wink. "But let me say that I *do* take the damage done to Boreal Reach very personally. Not just the collateral damage caused by the impromptu 'Mech battle in the bays, either. But every broken bench and smashed window and all the graffiti that has appeared in the last twelve hours. I admit that when I heard about *that,* I felt like walking my *Dragon Fire* into Silesia and kicking down some doors. Whoever was responsible ought to get a taste of their own medicine."

"Is that how you justify Craig Orme?" she asked, trying to edge in with a low blow. "His death in exchange for Stephen Neils?"

Except Michael had purposely left the opening for her. He frowned darkly, no need to feign his anger. "Neils's death is just as much a tragedy as Orme's, though the SBC has gone to great lengths to imply otherwise. A finding of 'no fault' has been handed down from the officials, but your *impartial* journalism seems to ignore that."

Michael waited for Sherman to just begin speaking, then cut her off. "If Solaran Broadcasting wants to boost its ratings in the Alliance, that's no concern of mine. But

I will not allow you to do it at the expense of the Federated Suns. You've even played up Victor Vandergriff, of all people, as a local hero defending Alliance honor, since he's Silesia's last hope for a Champion this year. But that's not choice, that's a lack of options. I actually wish Vandergriff luck tonight, because if he wins, then *I* get to meet him tomorrow in the Coliseum, where I'll show everyone what he really is."

Icy stare. "And what is that, Mr. Searcy?"

His challenge had been accepted. Michael grinned cruelly. "A Lyran pretender to a Federated Suns crown."

That drew a round of hearty applause from the Davionists present. Adam Kristof waved down a heated rebuttal from his Lyran counterpart, then waited for the applause to subside before leaning in with the logical follow-up. "By your statement, should we infer that you also disagree with Archon Katrina Steiner-Davion's attempt to steal her brother's throne?"

"Attempt? Adam, what papers are *you* reading? It's stolen." Michael crossed his arms over his chest, twisting just enough that the Blackstar Stables crest on the sleeve of his jacket would be highly visible. Time to feed out the material handed him by Drew Hasek-Davion. The material he agreed with, at any rate. "But to be fair, it's not her brother's throne. Not exactly. That throne belongs to the people of the Federated Suns. Not to any one man, and certainly not to *her*."

"Is that why you've never dedicated a fight to Prince Victor?" FedSuns Broadcasting again, voice eager and eyes glowing with delight. "Because you don't recognize him as the legitimate ruler?" The reporter even earned a jealous look from Adam Kristof for that question. No reason that an inexperienced reporter can't get lucky, though.

Careful now. On the Game World and throughout most of the Inner Sphere, being a die-hard Federation citizen and a staunch Davionist were thought of as one and the same. "I think *Precentor Martial* Victor Steiner-Davion was once our legitimate ruler. And maybe he will be again someday. But he has, in fact, refused to press his claim. And his isn't the only family we can look to in times of crisis. We've got the Haseks and Hasek-

Davions. The Sandoval family on Robinson. The Duvalls, whose ancient family helped found the Federated Suns. I'm proud to dedicate fights to them."

As if on cue, the clouds broke in several places, and some thin shafts of sunlight fell onto Solaris City. One just happened to shoot down on the Viewpoint, like a sudden spotlight. Michael paused to lift his face to the warm rays, then looked back into the cameras. "I'm a loyal *son* of the Federation. I'll defend that honor against any enemy, foreign or domestic. Just as I'll defend my personal honor and that of my stable.

"And if Victor Vandergriff gets in my way, it will be his turn to look to his life."

Ranking right up with "appearance is so easily accepted as reality" was another of Drew Hasek-Davion's cautions: "Know when to walk away a winner." Michael had accomplished all that he wanted to in the interview. He'd given the media their show, had made all the statements he'd planned, and so thanked the cameras for their time and made a rapid exit.

And not a moment too soon. The brief sun break over Viewpoint vanished almost immediately, and within five minutes not a ray of golden light still shone over Solaris City. SBC had already packed up and driven off, with the various Federated Suns services not far behind. The first peal of thunder rolled through the sky, and a light squall spattered Viewpoint with fat drops of rain.

You could quickly sort out the tourists from the Solaran natives by who bothered with umbrellas or ran for their vehicles and who simply stared up into the sky to welcome those first few drops. Michael laughed and walked to the concrete railing, pleased with himself as he surveyed the whole city from here. Across the river, Ishiyama rose dark and brooding over the sluggish Solaris River, and in Montenegro the Factory was nearly hidden back among other abandoned industrial sites. Then his gaze traveled to the long, gray pillbox of Boreal Reach and over to Cathay, where the Jungle loomed like a huge temple devoted to the gods of war. And further east the Steiner Coliseum.

All his domains.

That was what the Grand Tournament was all about, wasn't it? Mastering Solaris City and proving that no one could hope to stand against you. That no one else *could*. Seven fights in seven days to make Champion. Victories in all five arenas. All manner of 'Mechs and MechWarriors out there as opponents. House-affiliated stables, the independent cooperatives, and the rogues. One way or another they all took their shot at you this week. The Champion would have to survive them all. And that's what he was— what he would be. Sole survivor. Champion.

He would beat Kelley Metz because no Liao—especially a brain-addled one—ever had a prayer against House Davion. Tomorrow he'd take down Victor Vandergriff, showing the Lyrans once again that the Federated Suns knew no equal in thirty-first-century warfare, reminding them that it was the Federation armies who'd defended them when the Clans came. As for Theodore Gross, wasn't the heir of House Kurita alive and free right now because of help from Victor Davion? And in the finals, maybe it would be Jasmine Kalasa, the Diamond Shark trueborn now fighting for Lion City Stables, that he'd have to beat. Wouldn't that be fitting, the final match fought between Inner Sphere and Clan?

Standing atop Viewpoint it all seemed so clear. Part of the natural order. He would beat them all because he was the Federated Suns favorite. Davionist and Black Hills and Blackstar Stables all rolled into one package of natural talent and skill. So what if he'd been railroaded out of the AFFC? There he'd been subordinate to the weaknesses of his superiors. His rise to the highest levels of the Game World vindicated his worth—the trials and *trial* of New Canton notwithstanding. And if Drew Hasek-Davion had helped him create his Solaris persona, it was only possible because the foundation was already there. If it all rested on him, then it all had to be a part of him. He *was* Stormin' Michael Searcy. Had always been, in fact. He couldn't lose.

There could be no other way.

Even if he'd tried, Michael couldn't have picked a worse terrain for Kelley Metz. A short five minutes into the battle, he knew he had it won.

Boreal Reach comprised roughly half a square kilometer and boasted technological sophistication matched only by the Steiner arena's detonator grid. A system of holographic projectors, solid terrain modules, and full climate control could simulate almost any imaginable terrain and conditions. Hell's Canyon, with its rough, broken ground framing islands of impassable terrain such as lava flows and deep fissures, was a recent favorite among the stadium-goers. It was easy to end up cornered in a bad location unless the MechWarrior had the skill to maneuver in the ever-changing maze of small eruptions and shifting flows. For most 'Mechs that meant jumping.

Kelley Metz couldn't jump.

Her *Emperor* was equipped for it, certainly. Pitban LFT-50 plasma jets had been built into its legs and back, enough to cover a solid ninety meters of ground. But Michael had made some inquiries that afternoon about cerebral contusions. All the experts he contacted agreed that unstable motion and jarring impacts would aggravate the condition. Well, riding ninety tons of upright metal through the air wasn't necessarily smooth sailing, and landing a jump-capable assault 'Mech often kicked a 'Warrior's spine up into her skull. It seemed that Metz was out of luck.

Michael used his own jump jets whenever possible, goading Metz by taking positions she couldn't reach. When finally she was forced to jump because Michael's *Pillager* had pinned her against an expanding lava flow, the landing was more like a crash. Her *Emperor* fell, sprawling very unmajestically onto its left side where it lay helpless while Michael hammered with the gauss rifles built into each arm of his new *Pillager*.

Then he noticed that the *Emperor* wasn't even trying to right itself. Keeping his targeting reticle over the 'Mech's broad-shouldered form, Michael moved in closer. He dialed for their shared frequency, dropping his jaw to engage the contacts for transmission. "Kelley? Are you okay?"

"No, Michael. I don't think so. I've fallen, and I can't get up."

"You have to flash a surrender to the judges. I can't break off unless you do."

"If I could find the switch, don't you think I would have by now? I think I'm going to be sick."

A new voice broke in. It was one of the arena officials monitoring the channel in case their chatter would make for good dubbing over the video later. "Ms. Metz, this is arena control. Do you surrender and do you require medical attention?"

"Yes. And, I think, yes."

Then it was over. Michael stayed on site until the paramedics arrived to remove Kelley, then took his *Pillager* on a victory tour around the stadium. Blackstar Stables and the Boreal Reach managers had arranged a little publicity stunt. Every four hundred meters the holographic projectors materialized an enemy 'Mech in front of him. First a *Striker,* which disintegrated under a single hit from his large laser. Following in quick succession were a *Devastator,* a *Zeus,* a *Banshee,* and a *Berserker*—all of which went the way of the first. A new *Hauptmann* guarded the door to the 'Mech bays. With one shot it crumpled to its knees, where it remained as the *Pillager* stalked past in disdain. Each was a 'Mech design common to the Lyran Alliance. Each was painted in the well-known color known as Steiner blue.

The message was clear, especially for Michael Searcy. He would let nothing stand in his way. Vandergriff would beat Albert Mayetska this evening, and tomorrow afternoon he and Michael would go 'Mech to 'Mech in the Steiner arena. And there Michael would destroy Victor Vandergriff.

There could be no other way.

=== 7 ===

Thor's Shieldhall, Silesia
Solaris City, Solaris VII
Freedom Theater, Lyran Alliance
14 August 3062

Michael hadn't planned this event.

"FedRat bastard threatening me!" Victor Vandergriff's bellow overrode all other conversation. "Come on, Searcy!"

Vandergriff was just about to pass through the main door of Thor's Shieldhall when he turned and caught sight of Michael using the VIP path roped out along the entrance. He actually shoved Trevor Lynch, his own stable master, aside as he fought his way back, hands outstretched to wrap around Michael's neck. A righteous anger raged up in Michael. Stormin' Michael Searcy was not about to pass up a challenge.

Except that Larry Acuff stepped in first. A Cenotaph gladiator and Grand Tournament contender himself, Acuff blocked Vandergriff's path and shoved him back into the arms of Roger, the Shieldhall doorman. Trevor Lynch moved to help restrain his fighter while Acuff spun around to catch Michael around the chest in a bear hug, pinning one of Michael's arms to his side.

Karl Edward, who was part of Michael's group, leapt

forward. But instead of helping his friend against Acuff, he grabbed hold of Michael's free arm to help restrain him.

Michael struggled to get free. "Let me go, damn you!"

Karl shook his head and held on tighter. "Not here, Michael." Karl glanced back, possibly concerned for the third member of their group. But Garrett simply stood by, sipping the Vita-Orange sports drink he'd carried from the car. The Clanner's pale eyes missed nothing, but he made no move to assist or hinder.

Also of little help was the line of arena fans queued up to gain entrance to Thor's Shieldhall, the most famous—some would say infamous—bar in Silesia or, in fact, the whole of Solaris City. Its ultra-exclusive Valhalla Club attracted the top MechWarriors of the Game World, and the Shieldhall filled nightly with those hoping to catch a glimpse of an arena star. Now here as a new entertainment that many would have paid good money to see, a fistfight among two of the top tournament contenders. Some shouted encouragement to one or the other, or even both, in hopes of keeping it going. A few punches were thrown as Silesian and Black Hills residents decided to settle their differences themselves, adding to the chaos and merely fueling Michael's desire to reach Vandergriff.

Lynch and others had managed to wrestle Vandergriff through the door and into the neon-lit bar beyond, the Lyran still cursing Michael with a spacer's fluency. Michael made another effort to break free of his restrains, but Vandergriff was already gone.

Acuff appropriated a drink carried by his date—from an earlier party apparently—and splashed the last of it into Michael's face. The alcohol-tinged fruit drink burned in Michael's eyes, and he breathed a slug of it down his throat. That took the last of the fight out of him as he lapsed into a choking fit.

Cameras were flashing, and security for the Shieldhall moved out to cordon off the fistfights and protect the small group of MechWarriors from getting further involved in the growing fracas. Acuff and Karl pinned Michael against a nearby wall. Though Michael was no longer struggling, he noted that Acuff turned his body away in case the young fighter decided to use his feet. Smart man.

Acuff also moved to block the cameras trying to immortalize the fight. "Michael, cool your jets. Calm down!" He leaned in close, holding Michael's eyes with a calm determination. "We don't bring our fights to Valhalla, right? I said, right?"

With his challenger gone, Michael slowly got himself under control. It wasn't easy. He was angry at Acuff's interference. The man was an enemy, a future opponent.

"Right," Michael said finally. He shrugged Acuff away, pulled rudely away from Karl, and rubbed a hand over his face to wipe away the excess cocktail. Not quite the way he'd imagined making his entrance into Valhalla tonight. The story wouldn't play badly to the press, but it wouldn't do much for his prestige among other 'Warriors. Well, that he could make back in the arena.

Larry Acuff rejoined his own party, returning the empty glass to his date. "We'll refill that inside, Meta," he said. "After you."

Looking completely unruffled, Roger was already back at the door, holding it open for Acuff's party and then Michael's. "A pleasure to see you again, Mr. Searcy," the doorman said, only a hint of displeasure in his voice. Michael smiled back thinly. It was the closest Roger would get to an apology, but he owned the doorman something.

"Enjoy your stay in the Hall of the Dead," Roger added as the group went past him.

"Hall of the Dead?" Garrett asked as the three of them moved through a darkened stretch of the bar toward a curtained door set off to one side. The Smoke Jaguar trueborn sneered in contempt at a couple drugging themselves into bliss at one table. The touch of flame to an opium pipe added its flowery perfume to the already smoke-filled atmosphere. "That was a joke, quiaff?"

"It can be," Michael said. "It all depends on your point of view." Karl held the curtain back, allowing Michael and Garrett to pass through first. They ascended a ramp that doubled back over the main door to the Shieldhall. There a new door of dark glass waited, with a security agent to one side in a booth protected by bulletproof glass.

Michael still hadn't figured out why the Clanner had asked to come along tonight. The way Garrett kept studying him, asking questions, it was obvious there was something he wanted. It left Michael wondering if this was another of Hasek-Davion's games.

Still, there was no harm in talking. "Valhalla is the legendary place from Scandinavian mythos to which kings and outstanding warriors were escorted after death. Their reward."

"So it is a place of honor, then," Garrett said.

Michael shrugged and repeated, "Depends on your point of view. If you're in Valhalla, you died. So it's also a place of the vanquished."

Garrett was still trying to work his way through the contradiction as the door of reflective glass finally slid open. "Is nothing ever simple on this world?" he asked, though it was more like he was talking to himself.

Michael answered him anyway, raising his voice to be heard over the roar of conversations that spilled out of the cavernous room beyond. "Not usually," he said. "Only in the arenas."

Valhalla.

No matter how often he'd been here with Michael, the place always left Karl Edward slightly in awe. The long, wide hall made him think of older, more heroic, times. Rougher times, too, the days when warriors created and toppled kingdoms.

Central pillars constructed from genuine and rare woods still showed the axe marks that had felled the trees and knocked off their branches. Animal hides from a dozen or more different worlds were stretched over any open wall space. A large holographic bonfire crackled at the center of the hall, and holographic torches threw flickering light into the furthest recesses of the room. Huge tables and matching benches marched down the length of the hall, breaking only at the bonfire. Each had been handcrafted from rough, thick planks.

At the far end of the hall another table and an assortment of high-backed chairs sat on a dais. The one in the middle, at the hall's place of honor, belonged in a throne room and was currently empty. Theodore Gross sat at the right hand of the throne, his rightful place as defender of the Championship. Thomas DeLon was also seated among Gross' party, which presided over the Hall of the Slain. Other warriors crowded the open floor space, mingling with comrades or coming and going from the many alcoves that lined both sides of the hall. Heraldic banners and shields identified the owners of the alcoves.

This place honored the MechWarriors of Solaris above all else, the gladiators who fought each other in the arenas. Outside the walls of Valhalla, money and titles and national loyalties meant nearly everything. Here none of that mattered, or at least mattered far less. This was a place for the best of the Game World to meet on equal footing. It was reserved for the elite—the top fifteen percent of all MechWarriors on Solaris VII—and their guests. Karl would have been refused entry into Valhalla if not in the company of Michael or another of the chosen few. Such selectivity only reinforced the hard path ahead of him—the numbers Karl faced if he was ever reach the upper echelon. If the warriors from all the various stables and cooperatives and independents were brought together, they would add up to over ten regiments of BattleMechs—more than a thousand warriors and their machines.

Roger alone managed whatever complex formula decided who was allowed in at any given moment, which gave him a very tangible power. Karl had been sure to tip Roger generously once the near-fight broke up at the door, guarding his friend's back at a time when Michael wasn't even aware of his own discourtesy. The doorman also assigned the alcoves, reserving them for retired Champions and other impressive warriors or those few nobles and merchants powerful enough to warrant access to Valhalla and wealthy enough to pay for it. Still, these latter were not allowed to overshadow the warriors, and were arrogated to the foot of the table or those alcoves furthest from the dais.

"Full house for certain," Michael said, nodding toward the packed tables and crowded floor.

Karl brought up the rear as Michael led the way, trading cautious greetings and occasionally a word or two with his peers. Garrett was careful to keep abreast of the Federated Suns favorite rather than accept an inferior trailing position, but Karl didn't mind hanging back. It gave him the chance to observe the scene, to sample the mood of the room.

Tensions were high, which was to be expected. The quarterfinals began tomorrow, with only eight contenders left. Valhalla was usually a place where fighters could relax and temporarily drop their rivalries. Not this night. It was almost as if the squabble between Michael and Victor Vandergriff had infected the atmosphere. Bad blood seemed to be tainting everyone.

The Combine warriors and their guests played at being masters of the Hall, with Gross in the place of honor, joined by three others still in the tournament. Stables associated with House Marik tried for a superior detachment, as if the rivalries meant nothing to them, but no one bought that. And even they slipped on occasion, bristling anytime one of them came near a Capellan. Kelley Metz simply snubbed Michael, one of the better reactions he got from the Liao-affiliated warriors. But if they were cold to the Davionist faction, the static buzzing between the various Cathay stables was decidedly lethal, and Karl was glad it wasn't directed their way.

As for the Federated Suns and the Lyran Alliance, the rival sides had practically divided the room between them, treating any other faction with pure disdain while reserving a real hatred for their one-time allies. And if Karl was too far down the ladder to draw much of the Lyrans' hostility, Michael was not. His friend's face darkened with every malevolent glance, the undercurrent of hostility that permeated Valhalla a very palpable presence. Several other Federated Suns fighters gravitated toward Michael, like clouds circling the deceptively calm eye of a storm.

"Stormin' Michael Searcy," a nearby voice commented dryly, as if reading Karl's mind.

Then someone reached out a hand and took him by

the elbow, pulling Karl to one side and away from his friend.

In Valhalla, all warriors are equal. Some are just *more* equal than others.

The old saying haunted Victor Vandergriff, who moved through the Hall of the Dead feeling like a true ghost among the living. He nursed a stiff drink along with his anger and the sting of humiliation. He was a quarterfinalist in the Grand Tournament, a serious contender for the Championship for the first time ever, yet few Silesian 'Warriors acknowledged him and fewer still seemed proud of his accomplishment. They could throw his name in the face of their Federated Sun rivals, but beyond antagonizing the FedRats, his compatriots treated him as someone to be *tolerated*, not respected. And that bled over into the judgment of other factions present in the hall, most of whom considered him an oddity.

His past trailed him like a dark and heavy cloud, despite his recent successes. When the others looked at him, they saw the epitome of a long but relatively undistinguished career. A MechWarrior could be many things on the Game Word, but *undistinguished* was not one of them. Victor was a Top Twenty warrior cast out of his old stable as a poor bet and now the struggling star of the desperate Lynch Stables. That shame still weighed on him, stooping his shoulders and slowing his step. What would it take to cast off that cloak of humiliation? The Lyran media had been painting him in an idealistic light since the death of Stephen Neils, and the people cheered for him once again, but Victor knew how fleeting their favor could be.

Someone stepped into his path, but Victor brushed past, lost in thought.

"Trees that brace the sky so tall do not see dark clouds at all."

He recognized that voice. The line of verse was as out of place in Valhalla as the person who spoke it, and the voice belonged to someone who had not deigned to speak with Victor in several years. He turned back toward the man who'd spoken.

"Your vision seems a bit clouded, Victor," said Jerry Stroud, nodding a greeting to his former gladiator. "You should be celebrating. You've fought well this week." The owner of Skye Tigers wore his hair cut military-style, an odd contrast to his expensive suit. A gold and silver tie clip showing the traditional Steiner crest of a gauntlet against a square field winked back the hall's flickering holographic torchlight.

Victor nodded slowly, not sure what Stroud was up to. "Quarterfinals. Best I've ever done." And then, he couldn't help himself. "Sorry none of your fighters made it this far," he added. His caustic tone belied his words.

Stroud came back with a careful smile. "Not this year, no. But they've done well enough. They usually do."

That was true. Stroud had traded away his two best warriors in '57 when he took control of the Skye Tigers, wanting to disassociate himself from its previous owner-ship. Then he built a 'Mech stable of strong comers and now possessed an excellent feeder system with contend-ers in every arena class. None of his fighters had yet broken the Top Twenty, but his stable was one of the strongest in the city. Victor would never admit it openly, but he'd have liked to be part of that new beginning. It was hard to envy and hate this man at the same time, but then nothing ever came easy for Victor.

"I haven't seen Erin Hoffman yet," Victor said coolly, naming Stroud's highest-ranked warrior. "Is she here?"

Stroud's smile faded to a grim line. "Actually, she's in the Riverside Hospital. She barely survived an attack tonight at Skye Tiger Estates. I lost a shipment of 'Mech actuators and armor as well. Hijacked."

Victor raised his eyebrows. "Too bad. I wonder who dislikes you so much?" Besides Victor, that was.

Nodding toward the other side of the hall, Stroud said easily, "Perhaps the master of the man who has threat-ened to kill you?"

Victor followed the gesture, though he knew who Stroud was talking about. Michael Searcy, of course, and Blackstar Stables. Victor hadn't been able to help watch-ing Searcy out the corner of his eye the whole time he'd been in the hall. He'd seen how Searcy attracted a reti-nue of warriors, while Victor's only company was a man he would call an enemy any other time. Would, in fact, call an enemy right now except that they were united in their hatred of the Federated Suns and of Blackstar Stables, in particular. In the entire room, had anyone else shown Victor any measure of civility? At least Stroud had implied that they were, in a way, equals.

Catching Searcy's eye for a moment. Victor gave him a mocking bow. In their mutual enmity, the two warriors were equal as well.

While Michael moved on ahead through the crowd, Karl lagged behind. For the moment, Michael seemed to have forgotten him completely.

Tran Ky Bo, owner of Starlight Stables and Karl's patron, still held onto Karl's arm, forcing him to keep a more sedate pace. "Off on another rampage," Tran Ky Bo said, voice neutral. Then added, "Stormin' Michael Searcy."

"That's not who he really is," Karl said, instantly ready to defend Michael. But even he was starting to wonder. That cocky warrior might not be who Michael *was,* but in the last two years his friend had certainly grown into the role. Especially in the last few weeks.

Tran Ky Bo smiled slightly. His Asian features seemed ageless, but just then he looked even older than his considerable years. "He's your friend. I know that," Tran said. "He is also a young Federated Suns firebrand with a burn against anything Lyran."

He studied Karl's face. "But you are not, though it would be easy to emulate your friend, who has had more success on the Game World. I'm wondering why that is."

Karl shrugged. "Does it matter?"

"Perhaps I'm simply concerned that you will not play to the fans as most of the fighters do, in which case I should think about trading you to Thomas DeLon." He gave a short laugh at Karl's obvious shock. "Actually, you've spoken out for Prince Victor—and against Katrina Steiner-Davion—enough that I know you don't mind using the warrior's platform to voice politics. But you don't seem to let it get personal."

Karl gave a slight shrug. "Maybe it's because I was born and raised here on Solaris VII. I grew up watching the rivalries and feuds, which cured me of ever wanting to get mixed up in them. I transferred my citizenship to the Federated Suns because I grew up admiring Prince Victor, and I think Katrina was wrong to seize the throne. That makes Lyran Alliance warriors my *opponents* in the arena, but the Lyran people are not my enemy because of it."

"Well spoken, but not convincing. You don't believe others can share such a viewpoint?"

"On Solaris VII, you can change citizenship like some people change auto clubs. At most, you move across the city to a new sector. What other Inner Sphere world allows such freedom? But you may have to be born to it to appreciate it. Most warriors show up here with a strong prejudice toward their own nationality."

He looked around the room. Another Starlight warrior shouldered roughly past Isaak Kremms, the Steiner fighter who had gained a bye in the tournament due to Sarah Wilder's disqualification. At another nearby table three stabled MechWarriors were harassing Gerald Knight, a warrior with the independent Renegades cooperative who had finally been knocked out of the tournament only tonight. Yes, there was a lot of bad blood this evening. And not just between the Federated Suns and Lyran Alliance. Karl mentioned all this to Tran Ky Bo, as well as his thoughts that Michael's near-fight outside Valhalla had seemed to heighten the existing tensions. If that was possible.

Tran Ky Bo nodded. "Remember, nothing is impossible on Solaris ViI."

"You just have to find a new bookie who will cover the odds," Karl said, finishing the old joke. Only it didn't seem so funny anymore. If someone was to give him odds against Valhalla making it through the night without a brawl, he might have covered it himself.

And won, when not ten seconds later two MechWarriors dove for each other over one of the tables, scattering glasses and a few meals over their former owners. Curses flew as well as fists, but Trevor Lynch and a few others quickly moved in to separate them.

It was Michael Searcy and Victor Vandergriff.

Again.

"Those two are going to kill each other," Karl said, partly in resignation over his friend's behavior and partly in a dark jest. Right now, too many people in the room would have been on the same side as Karl on that wager.

But who in the room would have dared cover it?

Karl Edward sighed. On the game world there were battles, and then there were simply *struggles*.

See, see
Oh playmates
Come out and
play with
me. . . .

8

The Coliseum, Silesia
Solaris City, Solaris VII
Freedom Theater, Lyran Alliance
15 August 3062

A line of security guards decked out in riot gear held
the mob back from the Coliseum. Most of them wore
the black and gold uniforms of Hollis Security, Silesia's
largest private security firm, contracted for the duration
of the Grand Tournament. Visored helmets and thick
plastic shields protected them from the occasional bottle
or chunk of paving material thrown in their direction.
No guide chains tonight. No polite signs to mark a
boundary. The mere implied threat of hands resting on
the grip of holstered weapons was enough to hold the
riotous crowd at bay.

Still, to Megan Church that security line seemed dan-
gerously thin next to the thousands of fans already
massed outside the Coliseum. These were ticket-holders
for the evening set, ignoring the intermittent rains and
waiting for the afternoon matches to conclude so they
could flood the arena stands and take the places of those
watching the current fight. Many had brought radios,
cranking the volume up so everyone could enjoy the
soundcasts of the Grand Tournament bout already in
progress.

It was the Searcy and Vandergriff match, possibly the hottest ticket set for Day Five and, from the sound of it, being viciously fought. People crowded nearer those with radios, and it was within these islands of spirited fans that the fights first began. Julian Nero's commentary fanned their passions until tempers flared and arguments quickly turned to insults and jostling. Just as quickly, these became shoving matches, with drinks thrown and radios smashed. Then followed a few wild punches, until full-blown brawls broke out in several places among the crowd. And they were spreading.

The fights had started without Megan's help, but she worked to keep them going and would certainly claim credit when it came time to collect her paycheck. A girl had to make a living, after all.

Megan Church knew how to handle such a crowd. There was no need to dive into the middle and get involved in the thick of the fighting. Those fools were already hooked on the adrenaline rush of violence and their own rage. Instead, she worked at stirring up people on the perimeter, goading them with the aim of getting more people into the conflict.

After nearly tripping over a trampled umbrella, she picked it up and stripped the last of the cloth and wire supports away. She wielded the handle and rod like an *épée*, dealing stinging slaps against the sides of people's heads and then fading back as those individuals rounded on the closest enemy. Only one man was a bit faster than she'd given him credit for. He was big and overweight, with the sun-and-sword crest of the Federated Suns painted on his face. Just another couch-warrior out for a little excitement and hoping to get a two-second shot on the main screen during a slow combat sequence. Megan dealt him a slash against his right ear, perhaps harder than she originally intended, drawing blood and knocking him off balance.

He recovered quickly, catching sight of her and barreling through a pair of fellow Davionists to give chase. Megan dodged around another arm of the growing riot, but was knocked aside when someone threw a man into her. She tripped over a manhole cover that had gotten pulled out of its seating. She went tumbling over the wet pavement, scraping skin from her hands, until fetching up against the body of a former—now unconscious—rioter. A large hand fastened onto the front of her leather jacket, hauling her to unsteady feet. A painted face glared down at her. One meaty paw slapped out, aiming to backhand her across the face.

"Steiner bitch!" he growled.

Megan was not about to get into a contest of strength with the big man. She hunched one shoulder, partially deflecting the blow, and then rolled with the slap to absorb most of its remaining force. The side of her face burned with the slap, and one eye teared up. Megan sagged back, spitting out the salty taste of blood from biting her tongue, cowering away as much as his grip on her jacket allowed. She tugged with little strength against her jacket front as if trying to free herself, then looked off to one side and screamed, "David, do something!"

Megan's assailant made the mistake of looking over toward her fictitious boyfriend or husband or whatever, while she twisted from his grasp and lashed out with a sidekick to his knee. She could break four boards with that kick, against which the poor engineering of the human knee stood little chance. She felt his leg give under the blow, twisting in the wrong direction, then stepped in with a palm-heel strike that certainly broke a rib.

Megan Church also knew how to handle herself. Solaris taught you that at a very young age.

The man stumbled forward, then collapsed alongside the unconscious form Megan had bumped into earlier, moaning through pain-clenched teeth. It reminded her of her own roll across the ground and that misplaced manhole cover that led her to—

The open manhole. It yawned a few steps to her left, a spot of darkness against the light gray pavement. One man was just crawling free, then turned to help a second up the ladder that extended down into the darkness. Megan knew of the extensive tunnel works beneath Solaris City, tunnels big enough to let BattleMechs travel from one side of the city to the other without ever seeing daylight. There was no way of knowing whether this hole led down into those tunnels or to a simple utility shaft, though from hand-held flashlights the men carried, she was willing to bet on the latter. One also carried a tool pack slung over a shoulder and had wrapped several loops of det-cord around his wrist.

One of the men noticed Megan's interest and took a step in her direction. His friend, more interested in his watch than any potential witnesses, grabbed at his companion's shoulder and pulled him back away from the open manhole. There was no mistaking their look of concern as both men then worked to put distance between themselves and the manhole.

Megan turned at a right angle to their retreat and sprinted away, directly into the heart of the brawl but with no time to be picky. She counted each pounding step, marking time. Surely they would give themselves room for an escape. At fifteen she caught a hurried blow against her shoulder, the jacket's padding absorbing most of the wild punch. At thirty a bottle smashed into the pavement nearby with a resounding crack that tricked her into slowing, thinking the danger was past.

She was still glancing around at forty, when the first explosion belched flame in an inverted cone not twenty meters in front of her.

A good thing she had slowed, actually. Her dash for safety had taken her out of danger from the first manhole but placed her closer to a second. The cover had been replaced on this one and went flipping into the air like some kind of giant coin tossed to settle a wager. People yelled in pain, panic, or anger, depending on their distance from the explosion. Another fiery eruption flared up beyond this one. The ground shook only lightly as the underground detonations spread their force over a wide expanse of thick pavement.

Megan had relocated to the damp ground as a cautionary measure. Now, with the danger apparently past, she got back on her feet. She scoped the area, looking for the quickest path out of harm's way. The fracas had staggered back down to shoving matches and a few wild punches around the areas where the explosions had occurred. Most of the brawlers were trying to figure out what had happened, while only the truly dedicated used the distraction to score a few more blows. Maybe the fighting would re-ignite. Maybe it would gutter out. Didn't matter to her. She'd done everything she'd been paid to do.

Megan would leave the rest of the night's work to the professionals. Whatever else was going on, she knew it meant . . .

Serious trouble. Four separate utility shafts had been demolished by planted charges, three on the coliseum's east side and one on the west. The ground and broken pavement caved in above one site, leaving a crater four meters across by fifteen in length. Over two dozen manhole covers blew out of their seating under the force of the blasts, causing several broken arms, concussions, dislocated shoulders, and a fractured clavicle. One also smashed square into the head of a Montenegro resident who'd pulled a hold-out laser on a Cathay rival, killing him on the spot. Fortunately for the mob—at least for the short term—most of the force was contained in the tunnels where the explosions ripped apart conduits and shattered piping.

Fiberoptic cables supporting the stadium's public pay-phones were severed, more inconvenient than danger-ous. Also hit were security lines, and the damaged network fed several false alarms to nearby fire stations and police precincts. Fire trucks, paramedics, and cruis-ers were dispatched to the scene, pulling important sec-tor security assets out of place. The Silesian Police Department even deployed a light 'Mech equipped for riot duty, just in case.

But the real problem was that the Coliseum's four primary power feeds had been severed, causing a sudden and massive undervoltage condition on the local main bus. In the sub-levels of the Coliseum, sensing devices registered the problem and a backup fusion reactor sparked to life, quickly powering up in an effort to help handle the load. Crucial seconds were lost as non-critical systems tripped off-line on the undervoltage condition. By order of priority, power-sensing breakers on all important equipment and systems automatically switched over to the auxiliary bus while waiting for the main bus to re-gain power.

Except that the auxiliary bus wasn't meant to handle such a demand. Designers had never planned for a complete loss of the independent main feeds, not with the fourth conduit for auxiliary power routed in on the far side of the Coliseum. As the breakers switched over, a building overcurrent condition now threatened to trip out the aux bus. More loads were automatically dumped according to designated priority, and all safety-affiliated systems were routed back onto the main bus and local power.

This included the detonator grid—the technology that provided the destructive forces released in the arena. The fusion reactor could not possibly keep the system at full strength, though a margin of safety had been built in that allowed it to function at reduced-effect capacity while human controllers responded to the problem with appropriate actions. The current match would be called, and unless repairs could be made immediately, the Coliseum might not be able to host any more Grand Tournament fights. Which had likely been the saboteurs' plan.

They would eventually get their wish.

In the arena's electrical control room, also in the sub-levels of the Coliseum, journeyman electrician Keith Mick responded quickly to the problem of a complete loss of main power. He saw the fusion reactor come up and accept the high demand of the detonator grid. Even at reduced capacity, the grid threatened to overload it. He picked up a phone to call in to Coliseum Control. The arena was unsafe.

The line, however, was dead. Somewhere, sometime, someone had decided that internal stadium communications between the sub-levels and upper control rooms were less important than the ability to retain full recording and broadcasting capability. Keith wasted all of two seconds stabbing at the On button, and another few in realizing that the breaker was not immediately accessible. Then he was out the door at a full run, abandoning his station as he made for the elevator—no, the stairs!— and hopefully the Coliseum control room before disaster occurred. No, too late for that. This was already . . .

"An exciting match, game fans. The southern barricade is rising, catching them on opposite sides just when it looked like they might come to physical blows. Stormin' Michael Searcy isn't about to wait. He's heading for the eastern edge of the barrier. The fighting is brutal in there. Vandergriff's customized *Banshee* might be an older design, but it's standing up to Searcy and his *Pillager* remarkably well. If you're not here for the Coliseum's afternoon set, I'm telling you, you ought to be."

Julian Nero sat in the soundcast booth, just off the Coliseum's main control room. He was taking his turn on the live feed going out over radio, teasing the fans who'd decided not to purchase tickets for the Coliseum's live show. He hated the soundcasts, but his contract obligated that he do them once a week. More often than not he was competing with live video footage, the arena junkies who had bets on matches at Boreal Reach or the Factory and had brought in small receivers so they could keep tabs on the outcomes. He had to be part commentator and part salesman, trying to hook them into the Coliseum fights the next time around. And besides, just how many ways were there to say that a PPC hit melted armor off a BattleMech's chest?

Well, twenty-three so far. That included the new one he'd thought of tonight when describing Vandergriff's opening shot as "an azure knife *brutally rending* Searcy's armor from shoulder to hip." He had them all on a list, taped onto the glass wall that protected him from the noisy arena-controllers in the main room. Likewise, cheat sheets for lasers, autocannon, and missiles. With those lists, he could, theoretically, keep going for hours. That plus on-screen histories of both fighters and separate screens to dig up info on their 'Mechs, giving him access to plenty of background material. And he had one of the best views in the stadium, with the controllers feeding him holovid segments from three different camera angles.

Julian Nero was still the *man in the know*.

Time to get back to work. "If you're just tuning in, we have a sensational match underway in this first of Day Five's tournament bouts. These two fighters are out for blood this afternoon as Victor Vandergriff defends the honor of the Lyran Alliance and Archon Princess

Katrina Steiner-Davion against Davionist—I'm sorry, make that *Federated Sun loyalist*—Michael Searcy."

Not too much sarcasm, Julian reminded himself. He shouldn't appear biased. "It's been billed the 'Battle of the Bruisers' ever since word got out that the two warriors came to blows in Valhalla last evening, and they're doing everything they can to live up to it. Michael Searcy is spending gauss slugs like they were Solaris scrip, but Vandergriff has surprised the Federated Suns favorite at least once by showing off the jump jets custom-installed on the *Banshee* by the great Lazlo Falcher. And if you want my opinion, I'd say it's . . ."

Only a matter of time now. And Michael Searcy knew it. Vandergriff could hide for only so long.

He worked the *Pillager*'s controls, stomping the one-hundred-ton 'Mech to the end of the chevron-shaped southern barricade. Sweat streamed down his face from the hard-fought battle, despite the *Pillager*'s reputation as one of the coolest-running designs and the top-line coolant suit Hasek-Davion had invested in for Michael. The exertion came more from fighting the terrain than Vandergriff, though.

The Coliseum was in "chaos mode"—MechWarrior slang for the way the pop-up barricades and pylons would randomly rise ten to twenty meters high or plunge back into the floor, making an ever-shifting maze in which the two 'Mechs hunted each other. The stadium managers were also trying to spike interest with strange effects again, strobing the lights to break up fluid movement and make the 'Mechs look as if they were being shifted about the arena by some invisible hand.

FLASH—Michael's *Pillager* slammed a gauss slug into the *Banshee*'s side. FLASH—Victor relocated thirty meters to the right, one of his PPCs slashing a deep furrow up the *Pillager*'s left leg.

Michael stood at the eastern end of the barricade. This was where Vandergriff would expect him to come around. Certainly the Lyran wasn't about to risk his neck in a frontal assault. Vandergriff would run away and hide. It was what Lyrans did best, running away and then striking out from ambush.

Just like Michael's old C.O. had run away, leaving him alone in the path of that Liao advance. Arranging a flanking maneuver, the officer had claimed. Steiner blue—what a laugh. Their color was yellow.

But such generalities aside, there was also the matter that the *Banshee*'s heat curve was far less than optimum. Every few moments Vandergriff *had* to break off and cool down or risk becoming incapacitated by the heat buildup. He would run, Michael was certain, and wait for the *Pillager* to round the barricade.

It wasn't going to happen *quite* the way Vandergriff wanted it. And that would make all the difference.

Cutting in his jump jets, Michael decided to "skywalk" the Coliseum. The high-ceilinged arena allowed for it, and with his range he could just clear the barricades. The customized *Banshee* had demonstrated a similar capability early on in the battle, catching Michael off-guard once, but he doubted Vandergriff had the spine to use it again.

FLASH—the *Pillager* rose on a hellish cloud of vented plasma, pulled from the fusion reactor and routed out special ducts built into the back of the assault 'Mech. FLASH—it came down right on top of the barricade, fifteen meters above where it had started. Its weapons pointed straight down into the arena, ready to pound twin gauss slugs into the head of the *Banshee*.

Only Vandergriff wasn't there.

The warnings wailed at him too late. Showing more backbone than Michael had given Vandergriff credit for, his enemy had walked his *Banshee* further down the wall and now rose up on his own jump jets to perch atop the same barricade. Blue-white lightning from twin particle projection cannons stabbed out as Michael hunched the *Pillager* down to decrease its targeting profile. One stream of energies flailed into the ferroglass protection of nearby private boxes, those spectators getting a closer look at the action then they'd bargained for. Fiery-white sparks and arcs of electrical energy jumped off the detonator grid—an effect Michael had never seen before and mentally catalogued automatically for later review. The other PPC carved deeply into the *Pillager*'s left arm, deeply scarring the star slab armor.

His ambush sprung, Vandergriff ran his ninety-five-ton *Banshee* along the top of the thick barricade toward the *Pillager,* pinning it against the end of the barrier, which dropped off on three sides. He obviously planned to rush Michael's 'Mech, shoving it off the wall before pouring more firepower into it from above.

"Treacherous, money-grubbing Lyran!" Caught on the left flank and in no good position, Michael abandoned his own chance to fire and instead cut in his jump jets again. The *Pillager* rose off the barricade five meters, then ten—a good twenty-five meters off the floor of the arena and coming even with the levels of main seating. He planned to sail up and over the closing *Banshee,* then come down in its rear quarter, carving into the weaker armor that protected Vandergriff's back. That was the plan. It should have been a simple maneuver for a MechWarrior of Michael's caliber.

It should have been a simple maneuver.

It should have been.

Vandergriff's paired medium lasers sliced more armor from the *Pillager*'s left side and hip, followed by hammering blows from the *Banshee*'s shoulder-mounted short-range missile system and the autocannon that replaced the *Banshee*'s usual gauss rifle. The *Pillager* trembled under the fire, one missile drilling into the side of its head and throwing Michael against the limit of his safety harness. His head slammed back against the padded headrest of his seat, but was further protected by the lightweight impact helmet he wore in place of the usual bulky neurohelmet.

Then the *Pillager* suddenly lurched heavily to one side, its left-leg jump jet suddenly shutting down without warning. Michael hesitated on the controls, still shaken from the rough treatment and unsure what was happening. Telltale lights flashed a blockage of the venting port on his left leg.

In his mind's eye, he saw the emerald laserfire he'd weathered melting enough of the star-slab composite to splash molten armor into the vent, though that knowledge came late as he struggled to bring the *Pillager* back under control. If he couldn't land correctly, the fight might be over—No! He wouldn't give up the Championship so easily. Not now and certainly not to Victor Vandergriff! But the strobing lights made the visual cues he so desperately needed impossible to find, and he overcompensated with his right and centerline jets.

FLASH—the *Pillager* drifted into a tight leftward spin, out of control. Its head rocked back as it sailed out from over the barricade, still rising on its remaining plasma-vent lifters.

FLASH—one hundred tons of armor, weapons, and control systems hurtled back against the ferroglass shield and detonator grid protecting the main stadium seating. Protecting thousands of cheering, bloodthirsty fans. A cascade of bright, white-hot sparks lit up an entire quadrant of the arena as the underpowered grid overloaded trying to push back such a large mass. In its reduced capacity, there was simply no chance.

FLASH—the *Pillager* smashed through, detonator grid, ferroglass shield and all, to plunge into the Coliseum's packed stadium seating.

9

The Coliseum, Silesia
Solaris City, Solaris VII
Freedom Theater, Lyra Alliance
15 August 3062

"It's bedlam in there. The lights are still flashing, freezing the action into a series of rapidly changing still shots and making it hard to ascertain the full extent of the damage. But Michael Searcy is definitely into the stands. Fight fans, he is through the detonator grid."

Julian Nero kept his voice just at the edge of control, his delivery professional but letting his excitement bleed through to charge his listeners with a sense of frantic energy. For Julian, what began as an irksome duty had become a once-in-a-career opportunity. That he was on soundcast at the very moment when the Coliseum's safety features were breached could be thought of no other way, and he wasted no time pitying the video commentators. It would be Julian's voice first carrying a report of the tragedy to Solaris City, the Game World in general, and perhaps the whole of the Inner Sphere. The great Nero. The man in the know.

The man who had been dealt one incredibly large stroke of luck.

"I think I see Searcy standing back up." He saw a

dark outline, framed by the continuing shower of sparks and electrical discharges of the ruined detonator grid. "Yes, the *Pillager* is back on its feet and hovering at the breach in the ferroglass shield. The arena controllers seem to be having trouble bringing up the Coliseum's main lights. I can see them in the control room arguing with someone from the maintenance crew."

A trail of bright fire clawed up through the darkened arena in between light strobes, careening off the left arm of the *Pillager,* throwing flinty sparks and shards of armor over the assault-class 'Mech's left shoulder. Julian bent over the monitor as if pressing his nose to the screen might improve his sight. Was that—could that have been . . . ? Was that the *Banshee*'s autocannon fire ricocheting off the arm of the *Pillager* to range deeper into the packed stands?

The question was only half-formed in Julian's mind when the monitor suddenly brightened with a cascade of brilliant azure striking out from the top of the barricade and whipping manmade lightning up through the breach.

"By the Archon! Victor Vandergriff is continuing to fire! The detonator grid is down, and that PPC—two, *two* PPCs—spent their hellish destruction into the lower level seating. I don't know if Searcy's *Pillager* back-stopped the damage or if it bled directly into the crowd there. These strobes make it difficult to tell. But *there's* the *Pillager*. It's still on its feet, framed by the wide hole smashed into the ferroglass shield. If you could only *see* this. Is Searcy attacking? I can make out . . ."

Twin, muted flashes of blue light. Victor saw them. It was the discharge of electricity from heavy capacitors dumped into the acceleration coils of two gauss rifles, one in each arm of the *Pillager*. The flash of energy would create a strong magnetic field in each weapon, latching onto the nickel-ferrous slug with an invisible but unbreakable grip and rapidly accelerating it along the length of the barrel.

The silvery was not visible in that instant of travel, not with the chaotic lighting of the arena, but Victor Vandergriff knew the telltale flash of the coils and tensed for the blow. One of the slugs tore into his *Banshee* just right of the centerline, screening off the angular torso and smashing to impotent shards his protective armor. A fault indicator for one of his heat sinks spiked the cautionary amber straight to red as the crushed armor caved in over a faulty support and ruptured cooling equipment.

Victor was sweating freely in the sauna of his cockpit, the pair of extended-range PPCs driving his heat up quickly. Coupled with his earlier jump they had worked to drive his fusion reactor output into the yellow band. The reactor's waste heat bled into his 'Mech and up into the cockpit. If not for the coolant lines threaded through his vest, he might have passed out from the roasting temperatures. But he couldn't pass out—wouldn't allow himself.

Not while Michael Searcy was still trying to kill him.

From the start of the fight, there was little doubt in Victor's mind on that score. Searcy had all but threatened it on the news vids, hadn't he? And then the despised FedRat had chosen one of the deadliest *headhunter* 'Mechs out there—the *Pillager,* with its twin gauss rifles. The same weapon Stephen Neils had used against him, also trying to kill him.

It wasn't enough anymore that Victor be defeated—sent back to the ranks of the has-beens and wannabe-warriors where he had labored mostly unnoticed ever since the trade to Lynch Stables these last six years. They wanted him dead for daring to hold his head up proudly again. They all wanted him dead, the 'Warriors and stable owners and fans, rooting against him in the games and waiting for him to take the final fall while making jokes at his expense. A member of the Top Twenty, ridiculed! "Placeholder" was another of his nicknames. It bit at him every time he heard the news channels list the top nineteen MechWarriors on Solaris VII, as if he didn't deserve mention.

Victor himself might have wished for his death. Wouldn't it be better to die in the games, which were all he lived for anymore, before suffering an ignoble defeat? But now he decided he wasn't going out so easily. A champion—a *Champion*—never gave up the fight.

Victor would take his enemy with him. He would give them all something to remember him by, and that vow colored tonight's battle as he fought with a savage ferocity he hadn't felt in a long time.

Victor had seen Searcy's second sky-walking maneuver, the *Pillager* rising above the barricade on which they stood. Anticipated it, and turned his short-range weaponry on the 'Mech while preparing for the tight turn when Searcy came down at his back. Then the *Pillager* had veered hard for the stands, smashing into the protective shields. Did it force its way through? The strobing lights made everything seem so disconnected. So out of focus, though he relied on thermal imaging over truesight.

How many seconds had he lost between flashes? One? Two? He triggered his light gauss rifle by reflex, then stabbed out with his paired PPCs. But Searcy was already in the stands, and Victor's attack looked as if it had stabbed deeper, past the outline of the *Pillager*. His hands loosened on the control sticks for a second, trying to make some sense of the disaster.

And that second of inattentiveness almost cost him his life. The gauss slug that punched down at his head just barely missed, ringing off the *Banshee*'s right side and throwing a hard tremor into its step. Walking a tightrope, even a thirty-meter-wide tightrope, was no place to be lapsing. The fight was still on. Searcy was still after him.

There were Lyrans up there—Silesians—but Davionists from the Black Hills as well. And residents of Cathay, Montenegro, Kobe, and the outlying districts. No one could tell who had claimed what section, and to Victor it really didn't matter. Something inside him simply turned off—the remorse for the tragedy and any pity for the vultures in the stands who had tormented him all these years with their fickleness and sneers. The ones who had abandoned him. The ones he supposedly fought for. No, Victor Vandergriff fought for himself. First and foremost. He walked forward under the guns of Searcy, ready for a gauss slug to punch through his cockpit canopy at any moment and end his existence. But it didn't happen. The fates were not finished with Victor Vandergriff, and he meant to push their generosity to the fullest measure.

He cut in his own jump jets, ready again to meet Michael Searcy in a head-on challenge and settle their fight once and for all. The *Banshee* rose on fiery jets, angling for the same hole the *Pillager* had already made.

"Stop me if you can!" he called out into the tight confines of the cockpit, enjoying the sound of his own voice—defiant to the end.

Searcy gave way, as Victor had known he would. The *Banshee* settled into the destruction, the sloped levels of seating now crushed beneath the feet of an assault-weight BattleMech. Shadows scurried around him, vague forms in the uncertain lighting, scrambling over the ferrocrete slabwork like cockroaches heading for their cracks in the walls. One particularly large crack was just about BattleMech-sized, a place where the *Pillager* had fallen through the sloped floor and created a tunnel leading out to the huge system of walkways and ramps that circled the entire Coliseum floor by floor. A huge shape moved within it, backlit by the red emergency lighting of the hallways beyond.

Drifting his targeting reticle into that gap, Victor smiled when the cross hairs burned the dark gold of target lock. He snapped off a single PPC blast, the swirling blue-white energies streaming out to slam into the *Pillager*'s back. Damn that bizarre lighting! If Victor had known he had Michael by the rear quarter, this fight might be finished right now.

The scarlet lance of a large laser speared back as the *Pillager* turned to face him, hitting the *Banshee* in its broad chest. Armor melted and runneled to the floor below, but the assault 'Mech hardly missed it. The gauss slug that tore into his right leg was another matter, scraping the limb nearly clean of any protection. The *Banshee* stumbled under the onslaught, threatened to totter back through the hole in the ferroglass shield. Victor bent forward, his own sense of balance fed through the neurocircuitry to the *Banshee*'s massive gyro. He held his feet, if barely.

The *Pillager* was gone, having gained the outer ramps. Probably waiting now in a Davion-style ambush, Victor decided. FedRats were rather unsporting that way. He smiled grimly and walked around the lower level, each step crushing more of the arena seating. Three sections, he decided. Then he would smash a new exit some way down from Searcy's. Victor Vandergriff was not about to be predictable, and he wasn't about to give up. Not now.

The hunt had only begun.

10

The Coliseum, Silesia
Solaris City, Solaris VII
Freedom Theater, Lyran Alliance
15 August 3062

The siren wailed like a banshee through the 'Mech storage and repair bays in the Coliseum's lower level. On the wall a red light began to spin in warning. But a warning of what? Karl Edward had been resting against the foot of his *Cestus,* in partial repose and partial contemplation of his upcoming fight. He quickly scaled the gantry ladder up to his cockpit, thinking that whatever the reason for the alarm signal, he'd be better off facing it strapped in, powered up, and ready to move.

The other thought that crossed his mind was whether his grudge match against Tom Payne of Overlord Stables would be postponed, again. Their fight was scheduled between the two Grand Tournament tickets on tonight's lineup, but if something was wrong, his would be one of the first bumped from the program. The Grand Tournament took precedence, and rightly so. After all, it wasn't *that* big a grudge, was it?

Reaching the gantry platform, Karl peeled off his jacket and threw it aside. He already wore his cooling suit, the newer life-support technology available to a few of the more prominent stables and replacing the old ballistic cloth vest. Though he still relied on the tried-and-true neurohelmet, it would be a simple matter to hook into the 'Mech's life support and control systems and bring his *Cestus*'s reactor up to power. Halfway through the hatch, though, he glanced again at the flashing red warning. Damn if that didn't sound like an attack alarm. Here? On Solaris VII? Karl pushed down an instant of dread, then ducked inside and began to bring his sixty-five-ton avatar to life.

He wasn't alone. All around the big bay other warriors also scrambled for their rides. Karl could imagine the same scene throughout the Coliseum warrens, the adjacent tunnels and bays that were part of the vast underground tunnel system beneath Solaris City. Tom Payne, just across the way, was already powering up his Steiner-variant *Hunchback*. In the next rack over Estelle Goulet, another of Tran Ky Bo's Starlight "starbrites," walked her *Penetrator* onto the main bay floor. Most of the others weren't far behind. Karl plugged into his communications system. Already the commline was alive with chatter as everyone requested information or made wild speculations.

"Fusion reactor online," the soft voice of the computer informed him. "Initiate security procedures."

Because BattleMechs represented a huge investment, sometimes in the tens of millions of C-Bills, tight security measures prevented just anybody from walking off with one. In the several hundred years of Succession Wars and numerous minor skirmishes, very little was as valuable as control of a 'Mech.

"Karl Edward," Karl said, activating the voiceprint match. "Starlight Stables."

"Pattern match obtained. Cross-check requested."

The technology to fake a voiceprint did exist, though to do it correctly usually required a decent amount of expertise. So a second level of security was installed: a code phrase known only to the 'Mech's primary operator. Without it, the 'Mech would shut right back down. Karl's dated back to his childhood and the name his little brother had bestowed on him. "I am the High Tyrant of

Munchkins," he said, doubting anyone could ever delve far enough into his past to unravel that one.

"Security procedures confirmed. Welcome, Karl Edward. Remember, little brother is watching."

Karl stepped his *Cestus* onto the main floor and came face to face with an *Emperor* painted Steiner-blue and bearing the crest of Silesia Coliseum Security. His commline crackled to life on the emergency frequency, overriding all others. "There has been a breach of Coliseum safety," the voice said. "All MechWarriors will stand down immediately."

Used to obeying the regulations and restrictions that governed the games, especially with regard to arena safety, Karl reached for the bank of toggles that would begin shutdown procedures. But a niggling doubt stayed his hand over the switches. Nothing he could put a finger on, just a vague uneasiness that something didn't make sense.

A feeling others apparently shared. Estelle Goulet's voice came in over a private frequency reserved for Starlight Stables. "Karl, you got any clue what's going on here?"

None. Especially when Tom Payne and two other Lyran fighters continued to walk their BattleMechs out of the bay. The *Emperor* made no move to stop them— even moved aside to allow more room for a squat, wide-shouldered *Bushwacker* to pass.

Karl dialed for the emergency channel the *Emperor* had used. "I thought *all* MechWarriors were to stand down," he complained.

"The Silesian 'Mechs have been authorized to assist in containment. *You* will shut down at once!"

"He's full of it, people. This is Aubry Larsen of Blackstar Stables. I was listening in on Michael's fight, and they went through the wall. Nero's saying they're still fighting it out in the parking area now, though Vandergriff is beginning to fall back toward the river. Pick it up on civilian freqs—channel setting seven, should be. These guys have been called out to put the fighters down. Want to bet who they'll be shooting at?"

No takers here. One *Emperor* was left to contain the rest of them while three other Lyrans went hunting Michael Searcy. Karl slowly drew his hand back from the toggles, aborting the shutdown sequence. Tran Ky Bo might disapprove. There was no love lost between him and Michael. But that was a *MechWarrior* out there, dammit—the best the Federated Suns had to offer on Solaris VII. And he was Karl's friend.

"I doubt Silesians will be trying too hard to bring Michael back in one piece," he told the *Emperor* pilot, wishing he was dealing with another arena fighter rather than a die-hard Lyran Alliance soldier. "We'll go out and bring him in. Stand aside."

A *Tempest* painted the purple and white of Fitzhugh, one of the Montenegro stables, stepped forward. He was followed by a stable-mate piloting an *Anvil*. "No, we'll go. We've no personal stake in this. Let cooler heads prevail here."

Several 'Mechs throttled into slow walks, including Aubry Larsen's *Dragon Fire* and Estelle's *Penetrator*. The *Emperor* pilot was one step away form losing control of the situation, and obviously knew it. He had a few options on how to handle it. He chose poorly. A large laser flared from the *Emperor*'s right arm, followed by a second from the left. Rather than flash warning shots or tag the forward-most 'Mech, which was the Fitzhugh *Tempest,* he chose to reach back into the stable for Estelle Goulet's *Penetrator*. The emerald beams slashed away armor from her 'Mech's left shoulder and then stabbed deeply into the side of the head.

"I said stand down!" he commanded.

The *Penetrator* staggered forward, reeling from the hard-hitting blow against its most vulnerable point. Karl froze for a crucial second, his own anger warring with his shock at seeing the Lyran direct such heavy fire against a non-hostile opponent. But only when the *Emperor* pressed forward did he realize the threat posed to his stable-mate. He throttled forward, trying to insert himself between Estelle and the Lyran, but before Karl could intervene, the *Emperor* triggered its LB-X eighty-millimeter autocannon. Cluster rounds spat out in a high-velocity stream, fragmenting into a wide spread of lethal destruction. The deadly shower sanded away at the *Penetrator* while Karl stood there in impotent rage.

In the tight confines of the bay, that was overwhelming firepower. Several of the submunitions pierced the thin armor left protecting the *Penetrator*'s cockpit, and the 'Mech crumpled like a puppet with its strings cut, landing heavily on its left side.

Karl punched in the private Starlight Stables frequency. "Estelle? Estelle!" No answer. He could see the jagged holes cut into the right panes of the ferroglass canopy. Karl wanted to believe she was all right, that the damage might simply have severed her communications ability, but from the way her 'Mech had collapsed, the only real explanation was complete failure of the gyroscopic stabilizer system. The housing protecting the gyro itself was intact, hadn't been touched in the brief assault, which meant the system had been destroyed from the other end—the neurological signal taken from the brain and fed down into the stabilizer on a feedback loop.

The signal that relied on a living MechWarrior.

Seized by a white-hot fury, Karl turned his *Cestus* on the *Emperor* while toggling his targeting system alive and dropping cross hairs over the Lyran's outline. "Nail that murdering son of an *Archon*!"

So close, he couldn't possibly miss. Tightening up on his main triggers, Karl fired ruby lances from both his large lasers. The concentrated energy runneled molten armor from the *Emperor*'s center and left chest. Then the *Cestus*'s gauss rifle punched a silvery slug in right behind the second laser, pounding the last of its armor into impotent shards that now littered the ground.

The *Emperor* rocked back under the onslaught, but would have walked through it to hammer at the *Cestus* next if not for Aubry Larsen's *Dragon Fire*. Another large laser scarred the *Emperor*'s left leg, while her gauss rifle slammed a second of the devastating rail-accelerated slugs into the Lyran's left side. The impact pierced to the internal structure, smashing titanium supports and crushing the physical shielding that helped contain the fusion reactor burning away at the heart of the 'Mech. It released in a furious blossom of uncontrolled energies, bleeding reddish-gold fire out of hip and shoulder joints before bursting through to consume the *Emperor* in one final explosion.

Burning metal and myomer flew out in a fiery hail, a few large pieces slamming into Karl's *Cestus*. He rode out the shock wave, holding his 'Mech under control.

"Into the tunnels and then up to the surface," he said. Sparing Estelle's fallen *Penetrator* one last glance, he walked his machine toward the 'Mech bay exit. His friend was up there, alone and hunted. "If it gets in your way, and it's Lyran, burn it down. It's that easy."

And just then, it really seemed so.

On the closed-circuit trivid, four 'Mechs painted the black and copper of Blackstar Stables pressed through a screaming blizzard against a like number of Skye Tigers. Gem-colored laserfire washed the driving snow and sleet into neon sparks. The thunderous tumult of autocannon and missiles shook a distant glacier, causing it to calve some small icebergs into an ice-rimmed pool. Where one of the war machines stepped, snow banks melted from the residual heat bleeding off armored feet and legs. For a holographic environment, Boreal Reach showed a strict attention to detail that left many professionals stunned and drove the videophile crowds to near frenzy.

Drew Hasek-Davion sipped at a bourbon neat, hardly tasting the expensive, smoky liquor as he concentrated on the fight. The sounds of battle, reproduced by a top-line sound system, echoed in the booth he shared only with a bodyguard. He had opted to forgo attending the Coliseum match between Searcy and Vandergriff. Instead he'd taken his private box at the Black Hills arena where four of Blackstar's lower-echelon fighters were competing in a rare lance-on-lance event against the Skye Tigers. Though a bit strange, his presence here demonstrated his support for the up-and-comers, as well as a strong measure of confidence in his premier fighter. He glanced at his watch, his lips pressing together in a thin, humorless smile.

And if everything had gone according to well-laid plans, the Searcy-Vandergriff match would have to be re-fought anyway. Drew eagerly anticipated the windfall of a rematch—moved from the ruined Coliseum over to the Boreal Reach arena!—on the next morning. A Grand Tournament first.

For most, the team match in the simulated blizzard was only a lead-in for a Grand Tournament bout. For Drew it would be the night's main event. While everyone focused on the Grand Tournament, he would preside over the beginning of the end for Jerry Stroud and his upstart stable. Tonight Stroud would lose one of his better warriors, as well as one of his better BattleMechs, in a tragic accident. A damn shame, really—about the 'Mech, that was.

Reaching down to his belt, he tapped one finger against the side of his wireless pager, which had been redesigned with a new feature for this occasion. At the press of a button, it would send a signal through a number of relays until reaching the arena. Torrence Klein of the Skye Tigers would fight in his new *Barghest,* one of the rare quadruped 'Mechs and a very efficient killer. Unfortunately, he had trusted the 'Mech to a tech with dubious loyalties to the Alliance and a gambling habit to support. A useful man to have in his pocket, Drew had found. All he had to do now was wait for a solid body-hit against the *Barghest.*

All according to plan.

He toasted Klein with the last of his bourbon, draining the highball with one indulgent slug. Wouldn't be long now. The Lyrans were falling back in obvious distress, while Blackstar's MechWarriors continued their lethal barrage. Although Drew saw no reason for such an early rout, he didn't mind it one bit. Then Klein's *Barghest* suddenly turned its broad-shouldered back on its foes, unleashing the fury of its heavy weapons against the arena's camouflaged southern door. The holographic cliff face crumbled as the projection lost its backing. The *Barghest* leapt forward, disappearing into the opened cavern that led back down into the underground bays. Two more Lyrans followed, also escaping the arena. The fourth, a hatchet-wielding *Nightsky,* sprawled awkwardly to the floor as a final salvo from the Blackstar lance shredded its rear armor and carved out its gyro.

It happened so fast Drew forgot all about the control unit he wore at his belt. He stared dumbly at the screen, at his lance, which had paused in apparent confusion. "After them!" he shouted at the trivid, willing his men forward. Two of them did move toward the shattered door, slowly at first but picking up speed once they committed.

Now he stabbed at the pager, sending out the killing signal. The indicator light remained dark. No return signal. The *Barghest* was already too far away from a relay, protected by the thick ferrocrete walls of Boreal Reach. Drew had never imagined anything like this, that Torrence Klein would make such a dramatic exit. What was going on? Drew had turned off the commentator feed, preferring to watch and enjoy the destruction as if the skirmish were a real battle. Now he grabbed up the controls from a nearby table and selected the appropriate audio channel, catching the handicapper Mason Wells in the middle of an excited ramble.

". . . to Silesia where the riots have spread over several blocks as the Coliseum and 'Mech yards continue to deploy BattleMechs intent on bringing down Michael Searcy and any other Black Hills 'Warriors on hand. We've even received reports that Montenegro 'Mechs have been fired upon and returned that fire, though at this time it isn't clear whether the Eagles are working for or against the already-overmatched fighters of the Federated Suns.

"We've finally gotten a video feed of the Boreal Reach 'Mech bays, where the initial fighting broke out between Lion City and Gemini Stables following soundcasts of the events in Silesia." The video cut to static for a brief second, then over to one of the large underground bays where a half-dozen BattleMechs exchanged fire at point-blank range.

"It's developed into a free-for-all down there. We know that Sheridan Lang is dead—you can see the remains of his *Ti Ts'ang* in the lower left corner. The Cathay champion was set for his Grand Tournament match against Lion City's Jasmine Kalasa tonight and went hunting Kalasa when the fighting broke out. She ripped him apart and then headed into the tunnels. Not too surprising, that outcome, considering she was favored five to three in the latest—"

Drew switched off the trivid. Mason Wells had reminded him of the soundcasts. That would let him stay abreast of events without chaining himself to this booth and this building, which would soon be the center of more intense rioting as the arena fans spread into the streets. Better to be mobile. He had interests to protect and plans to see through. Drew was always one with an eye out for opportunity.

This day certainly had possibilities.

The Solaris City underworld was a very real thing, but not in the sense of old action-adventure holovids where the criminal element lurked in the shadows of alleys, run-down warehouses, and secret hideaways. In Solaris, the crime lords inhabited high-rise boardrooms, while the underworld belonged to the BattleMechs. A vast network of tunnels, underground repair bays, and storage facilities ran under the city, allowing 'Mechs to move around without disrupting traffic in the streets. Each arena was tied into this network, as were the spaceport and the main 'Mech yards for each sector. The tunnels connecting these hubs were fifteen meters high to accommodate even the tallest BattleMech and sixty meters wide at the narrowest point.

Still, natural bottlenecks did occur. Only four tunnels crossed under the Solaris River, for one. Another was the difficult, deep stretch under the Cathay lowlands, where water seepage was a problem throughout Solaris VII's wet months—which were most of the year. And then there was the hilly terrain of the Davion sector of the Black Hills, which compounded one problem area with another.

Aligning the tunnels of the Black Hills with those of the Cathay lowlands had been extremely difficult, so that only three main passages existed to pass from one sector to the other. Two of them had required the construction of ramps that allowed above-ground travel for a few blocks. These rose up in the middle of the Black Hills' extensive slums where no one minded inconveniencing the residents. It was toward one of these ramps that Torrence Klein in his *Barghest,* his stable-mate in a *Scarabus,* and a Cathay MechWarrior they'd picked up in the tunnels under Boreal Reach were headed. The *Bar-*

ghest and *Scarabus* led, with Kym San Lee's *Cataphract* close behind.

Klein had given up on the main tunnel right away, as it ran directly under the Federated Suns Police Department. He was sure the FSPD would have the area locked down with BattleMechs and static turret defenses. He and Kym had decided they would go up the ramp at Radler and Frances Avenue, then through the Danning Street greenbelt, which would let them out at the Cathay border. Once there, Kym guaranteed them access back into the tunnel system. That would let Klein and his stable-mate continue on to Silesia, where the fighting raged out of control.

Not that the fighting in Boreal Reach was any less vicious, but Silesia was home. And at the eastern edge of the sector was Skye Tiger Mall, the complex that housed their stable's training facilities and main 'Mech bays. Klein couldn't stand to think about the Davionists striking there, leaving him a fighter without a stable. The Capellan 'Warrior's reasons for fighting his way free and heading for Cathay were less clear to him, though apparently Liao stables were also brawling beneath, within, and around the Jungle arena. Kym wanted a piece of that action, whichever side he supported. Klein shrugged. This was an alliance of pure convenience that would dissolve as soon as each got what he wanted from the bargain.

At the ramp, the Davions upped the stakes.

A pair of new *Enforcer III*s held the lower edge of the ramp, proudly wearing the sword and shield insignia of the FSPD. They didn't wait for hails, but opened fire as soon as the Lyran 'Mechs rounded the corner leading to their position. Gem-colored beams lit the tunnel, concentrating on the *Scarabus* and followed quickly by the hammer of autocannon fire. The light 'Mech shuddered under the savage assault, shedding armor in molten-orange splashes and a rain of glittering fragments that became a rainbow of colors in the backwash of laserfire. The *Scarabus* held to its feet, accelerating at a run to force a breach through the pair of *Enforcer*s and gain the relative safety above.

But before Klein's stable-mate could bring any

weapon into effective range, the FedRats fired again with lasers and autocannon. One stream of high-velocity metal slugs walked a line from the *Scarabus*'s crotch out to its hip, chewing past earlier laser damage and blasting through part of the titanium skeleton beneath. The leg separated, leaving behind a short stub of framework, and the light 'Mech toppled into a disastrous skid that threw up sparks and fragments of armor.

Even the greenest garrison warrior couldn't miss while shooting down a narrow tunnel filled with one hundred-seventy tons of war machine. The *Scarabus* pilot, limited to short-range weaponry, had no chance. Klein decided it was time to show the Davionists what made Solaris arena fighters among the best in the Inner Sphere. Closing at eighty-five kilometers per hour, he drifted his *Barghest* to the left to clear Kym's line of fire while dropping his targeting reticle over the *Enforcer* on the right.

The cross hairs burned the deep gold of a hard lock, and he cut loose with both large lasers as well as a rapid-fire burst from his twelve-centimeter autocannon. The laser turrets on the *Barghest*'s left shoulder tracked in against the *Enforcer*'s right torso, burning away the Star-Guard armor composite. The depleted-uranium slugs from his heavy-bore autocannon bit in at centerline and drifted right, raining a shower of shards and splinters onto the tunnel floor until the *Enforcer* had lost protection across its entire chest.

The Black Hills security 'Mech teetered back, unbalanced and on the edge of falling, when Kym San Lee's *Cataphract* hammered in with its light- and medium-weight autocannon. Exploiting the *Enforcer*'s ruined armor, the forty-millimeter slugs and eighty-mill fragmenting rounds he fired tore at the 'Mech with the savage force of a jungle cat eviscerating its prey. The cluster-round shrapnel carved away at internal supports, engine shielding, and the ammunition bin for the *Enforcer*'s autocannon. The ammo went off in a series of hard-hitting detonations, ripping apart the *Enforcer* and freeing the fusion reactor. Golden flame lanced out, scarring the second FedRat 'Mech as the first ended its usefulness in an explosion that filled the tunnel with fire and flying parts and equipment.

The *Barghest* leapt through the wall of flame, as fierce and undaunted as the mythological creature for which it was named. Klein did not waste time with the second *Enforcer* picking itself up off the ramp, but made for the surface instead. Kym, with a deeper grudge to assuage, paused his *Cataphract* long enough to hammer away with all weapons at point-blank range.

Klein broke free of the underground tunnel system while Kym stayed there, blasting away, so he wasn't certain what was happening down there.

And never would be certain, as his own fusion reactor detonated not two seconds later.

A thrown rock skittered off the bullet-proof glass of Drew Hasek-Davion's hovercraft sedan. His driver threw a sharp "S" into the vehicle's glide path, spoiling the aim of the vandals—probably would-be carjackers—then turned down Danning Street.

Leaning forward in the car's plush seat, ignoring the city-wide riot, Drew gazed through gray-tinted windows at the shattered and smoking remains of the *Barghest*. He clipped the modified pager back onto his belt, then tensed as a damaged *Cataphract* limped up the ramp and plunged into the nearby greenbelt. His hovercar was not armored against a BattleMech, but the surviving Cathay MechWarrior was more interested in making it to his home sector than taking unsporting shots at civilian vehicles.

Drew would never have been out among this insanity on the streets, except that he wanted to personally guarantee that Klein never left the Black Hills alive. Too much effort and money had gone into this operation, the first nail in the Skye Tigers' coffin. Sometimes the gains outweighed a little personal risk. Drew could see no other way of attempting to head off the *Barghest* but to get within range for the small transmitter to detonate the petroglycerin charge planted during the 'Mech's last maintenance cycle.

A lucky guess, really, tracking Torrence Klein to the Frances Avenue ramp. It also brought Drew toward a most dangerous area where the vast slums of the Black Hills had erupted into street fighting, widespread looting, and vigilante justice. The riots were spreading fast. The same ferocious mania that had seized the warriors under the Coliseum and Boreal Reach had now spread to the population of Solaris City. Drew knew that could make for opportunities, although ones better exploited from a safer location. He punched the intercom that connected him to the driver's compartment up front. Still looking ahead, he could see the street choked off with swarming rioters.

"Back to Green Mansion," he ordered his man. "And you slow for nothing less than twenty-five tons."

11

Under Ishiyama, Garrett was seated at the controls of his battered *Mad Dog*, awaiting his match of the day. He was proud of his ride, a Clan-design OmniMech that the brainless vidcasters insisted on calling by its Inner Sphere name of *Vulture*. He didn't know which made him angrier, that they ignored the *Mad Dog*'s true Clan name or that they dishonored the 'Mech and its 'Warrior with their ignorant stupidity.

The *Mad Dog* was no scavenger, but a rabid fighter—a 'Mech designed to go head-to-head against mightier opponents and still give a good accounting of itself. It was barely recognizable after a year and a half of battles and inept repairs by Blackstar technicians, but it was still *Clan*.

It was still his.

Because he'd decided to wait without distraction in his cockpit, he was late in realizing what was happening out on the streets. When the big underground bay suddenly exploded with activity and sporadic weapons fire, his reflexes took over. He quickly powered up while patching in to the commline to find out what was going on.

The news was sketchy, but one thing was clear. Fighting had broken wide open in the streets of Solaris City. Some stables were taking advantage of the chaos to settle old grudges. Others were apparently using it to start new ones. From what he heard, there wasn't a single faction in the city that hadn't taken hostile fire from somewhere, and many 'Warriors had simply "gone rogue." Across the river, the fighting between the Black Hills and Silesia was reported as exceptionally brutal.

And now here in Kobe as well. Two 'Mech battles already raged across the bay, filling the air with a storm of destructive energy. He waited, as if invisible, his 'Mech still racked in its berth awaiting the signal to move up into the arena. His would have been a "filler" match, one of several preceding tonight's Grand Tournament bout in which Theodore Gross of the hated Draconis Combine was slated to defend his title against another fighter from Garrett's own stable. Now one of those men suddenly burst into the bay on foot, heedless of the 'Mech fire going on all around him.

Theodore Gross!

Gross practically ran under Garrett's cross hairs, dodging the feet of other 'Mechs on the move as he made a beeline for his own Omni. With the *Mad Dog* powered and its weapons hot, Garrett almost burned him down right then and there.

Yet he held back, watching as Gross scooted between the legs of a lumbering *Sirocco* quad-Mech from Bromley Stables to reach the gantry alongside his *Warhawk*—misnamed a *Masakari* by the Combine—and one in beautiful condition. If it wasn't travesty enough that an Inner Sphere barbarian fought in a Clan Omni, the 'Mech had been a *gift* to Gross from the ruler of the Draconis Combine. Not only had they stolen this beautiful piece of work from the Smoke Jaguars, but then they shamelessly put it into service among their own. By comparison, Garrett's *Mad Dog* was a battle-ruined shell of its former glory. Gross didn't deserve that 'Mech. Hardly anyone on the Game World did, except perhaps Garrett himself.

Still watching, he couldn't deny that what Gross was doing took courage, but it wasn't enough to change Garrett's mind. The man was scrambling up the gantry ladder now, still under Garrett's cross hairs. Without remorse, he triggered the forty-millimeter autocannon mounted on the *Mad Dog*'s right arm. It chattered out a quick burst, sending a hail of lethal metal across the mounting gantry and into the Solaris Champion. What chance did flesh and bone have against a weapon intended to use against other BattleMechs? Blood erupted in a geyser of crimson, staining the gantry and spraying red mist in the air. The body, torn and battered beyond recognition, tumbled awkwardly to the floor, where it piled up like a rag doll.

"Same chance you gave my Clan," Garrett said out loud.

Methodically and without haste, he unbuckled his safety restraints and opened a small compartment under the control panel. He selected two printed circuit boards, one controlling basic 'Mech security and the other fine-tuned to interface his brain waves with the neurocircuitry link to the gyro. Inner Sphere 'Mechs were rigged to prevent theft by others. Among the Clans, theft was inconceivable; besides, 'Mechs were often assigned to different warriors when necessary. Unless the Combine engineers had radically reworked the *Warhawk*'s computer system—which Gross always boasted was in pristine condition—the extra layers of security typical of Inner Sphere BattleMechs would be missing. If so, it was a simple matter of replacing circuit boards and the *Warhawk* would be Garrett's. Deservedly so.

He released a retractable ladder from his cockpit hatch and climbed down to the bay floor. He walked calmly toward the *Warhawk,* looking neither right nor left, not once worrying about a stray laser beam or bullet. He knew nothing could touch him or stop him from taking command of the 'Mech. His Clan was dead and Garrett should have died long ago.

Perhaps at the controls of the *Warhawk,* both could be reborn.

Michael Searcy limped his *Pillager* west along Narvik Street, which led through Silesia's fashionable Riverside district. A few high-rise hotels and the occasional cluster of condominiums broke up the grounds of rambling estates and luxurious single-dwelling homes. The crowds had not yet converged in force on the area, but as more of Silesia's poorer residents figured out what was happening, the looters wouldn't be far behind.

He tapped open the commline. "Give me a read, Karl."

A burst of static announced the incoming transmission, whispering a soft crackle in Michael's ear. "Northbound on Liszt. Aubry and I left Thor's Shieldhall behind us a minute or so back. Coming up on the Grateful Burger." A pause, likely for a sensor check. "Two heavy Romans and a MadCap bruiser still chasing us, spoiling for a fight." Michael recognized the slang for two Lyrans and a Capellan warrior. "You're out there somewhere, aren't you?"

"I'm here," Michael said. He checked their positions on an auxiliary screen showing a detailed map of Solaris City, currently scrolled to the Lyran sector of Silesia.

"I'm calling the ambush at Hewitt and Ninety-first Street. You come straight up Liszt to Barer, then break over to Ninetieth and try to pull them onto a parallel track. Don't lose our friends."

Michael switched channels, checking in with the others relying on him to coordinate their actions, then switched back over to the frequency he and Karl Edward had claimed for their own.

For the last hour, Michael and Karl had worked on joining up with little success. In fact, Michael was currently coordinating about four different running battles through the streets of Silesia, but none of the Federated Suns friendlies had yet been able to link up. There were too many enemy units in the streets, herding the Davionists first one way, then another. So, besides fighting sporadic encounters on his own, he had to keep track of the others as they played a deadly game of hide-and-seek among the rioter-filled streets.

Caught up in their own concerns, no one on the ground seemed to care much about the lethal firepower being exchanged between the 'Mechs towering over their heads. They either had their own Lyran-FedSuns scores to settle or were simply the have-nots looking for the haves. One enterprising tong or street gang had painted a large bull's eye on the side of a bank, hoping a passing MechWarrior would oblige. Michael hadn't, but returning that way five minutes later, he noticed that someone else had. The looters were now swarming over the spot like ants at a picnic.

Not that he worried overmuch about the people scurrying about below. They were only the dregs of a money-loving but morally bankrupt realm, or so he kept telling himself. Yet, he couldn't help the slight twinge over his escape through the stands at the Coliseum. Was it his fault that the detonator grid and shielding hadn't held? Or that Vandergriff had kept firing on him, forcing him to choose between fighting a live duel amid the spectators or burrowing back into the Coliseum to escape outside? Certainly he couldn't surrender! No one could have expected that. If anyone should have surrendered, it was Vandergriff. Anyway, the Lyrans had only their faulty engineering to blame for putting him in that kind of position in the first place.

That was only one of the ways this spoiled fight in Silesia reminded Michael of the debacle on New Canton. Once again he'd been abandoned by his commander— this time Drew Hasek-Davion, who hadn't even been present at the match. Nor had Drew responded to any attempts at communication, even though Green Mansion had a high-powered comm system connecting with the Blackstar training facility to the north. Then he'd been set upon by a large force with nothing in the way of support. It was almost as if the erratic lighting of the Coliseum was still affecting his vision. First, he would see the streets of Solaris City. Then, in a blink of an eye, he was back on New Canton, caught in a stretch of steep-faced canyons as the Capellan forces stormed his unit's position.

Vandergriff had pressed hard, just as that Capellan 'Mech had done, forcing Michael's 'Mech into a shutdown from overheating. He hadn't a moment's respite. Vandergriff had pursued him through the Coliseum, where they'd traded ineffective fire among the arches and short passages of the stadium. From there, they'd continued on into the parking area, then into the Silesian streets beyond.

Only this time Michael rode his heat curve more carefully, wiser now about where it paid to take a risk and slowly gaining the upper hand. His *Pillager*'s gauss rifles reached out at range to smash open the *Banshee*'s chest and expose its fragile innards. Vandergriff had been wading through acres of cars in the parking lot, kicking them aside in his haste to close with Michael. Suddenly it was his turn to back away, worrying that another high-velocity round might cripple his 'Mech.

Michael had pushed Vandergriff toward the river for several blocks before losing him among cramped apartment buildings. An *UrbanMech* rigged for riot control—its lasers replaced by water cannon—had intervened briefly, its single autocannon chipping away at the *Pillager*'s armor. Michael fired a well-aimed gauss round that took the other 'Mech's leg clean off, the titanium femur snapping just above the knee joint.

With one enemy driven off and another beaten, nothing remained to remind him of New Canton. He was no longer a lowly member of the Kestrel Grenadiers but one of the best MechWarriors on Solaris. When the other Davionist 'Mechs finally escaped the Coliseum, it was only natural that they looked to him for leadership. Karl had led them up from the tunnels, but the trouble he had holding everyone together proved that they needed someone stronger.

Slowing his *Pillager* for a corner, Michael moved onto Ninety-second, heading south for Hewitt. A burnt-out upper leg actuator made the turns difficult, though a light touch on the controls coupled with his own sense of balance fed down into the gyroscopic stabilizer corrected that problem. Speed, though, was uncertain. Never a fast 'Mech, the *Pillager* was now limited to forty-some kph—slower if Michael wanted to avoid a debilitating skid on the slick pavement. He pushed it for top speed, working more to correct the hitch thrown into the *Pillager*'s step as he raced to set himself up for the ambush.

Karl had warned of two heavy Romans. That meant two MechWarriors from the Coliseum, piloting heavy-class BattleMechs. Also a MadCap bruiser. If Michael was reading Karl's half-slang half-code correctly, it was a warning that a Capellan assault 'Mech pilot had thrown in with the Lyrans for reasons of his or her own. That made for even odds, maybe weighted a bit toward the Lyrans.

Michael Searcy would even things up.

The *Pillager* gained the intersection at Ninety-second and Hewitt just as Karl's *Cestus* turned onto the same avenue two streets to his right. Aubry Larsen's *Dragon Fire* followed him through the turn, then both 'Mechs raced away at a right angle to their original course. Michael nodded his satisfaction, throttling down and dropping his cross hairs over the back of his fleeing allies. Good enough.

"Michael, be warned. One of the Romans might have split wide through an alleyway."

Warning lights flashed for attention, and Michael's sensors wailed. A short hundred meters further down Ninety-second, a *Falconer* stepped out from between two store fronts, flanking him. At the same instant a Capellan-marked *Emperor* moved up Ninety-first to place itself between the *Pillager* and the retreating pair, already committed to going after Karl. The *Emperor* spitted its broad back on Michael's cross hairs.

"Anything else you forgot to tell me?" Michael shouted in frustration, tensing for the hit while squeezing into his own salvo.

The Capellan had chosen sides poorly. Michael's large laser stabbed a scarlet lance into the rear right flank of the *Emperor,* slashing deeply before his twin gauss slugs slammed in behind it. One silvery blur careened off the hip, raining armor fragments onto the rain-slick street. The other followed the scar already melted into the back, smashing aside several support struts as it burrowed into the medium pulse laser and a heat sink. The attack might have been enough on its own to take out the ninety-ton assault 'Mech, but Michael wasn't finished. He punched three of his four medium lasers into the *Emperor,* two of them grouped together into one large cascade of energy that completely gutted the right side of the Capellan BattleMech.

By some miracle the savage assault missed the ammunition bin stored in the *Emperor*'s right side, and the

'Warrior managed to engage the dampening fields before the reactor blew out of the weakened physical shielding. But as an instrument of warfare, the machine was finished. It continued to turn in a lazy pirouette, then tumbled onto its right side. Its arm, caught against the ground, smashed through the ruined torso—driving into the gyro housing and adding insult to the grievous injury.

Michael had no time to gloat over his victory or worry about his heat spiking into the red bands except to slap at the shutdown override. The *Falconer* was already on the offensive, firing with its PPC and lasers. The PPC carved into the freshest armor Michael owned, on the *Pillager*'s right arm, and burned through an upper arm actuator. Two of the lasers worried at his gimped left leg, weakening supports and completely destroying the clogged jump jet that had originally landed him in the Coliseum stands. The only saving grace was that in its rush to engage, the *Falconer* missed with its own gauss rifle. One of the nickel-ferrous slugs skipped off the pavement and further down the street, where it became the problem of looters and rioters. And welcome to it, in Michael's opinion.

Michael lumbered a half-dozen steps before turning the *Pillager* around out of sight of the *Falconer* and throttling back into a rearward walk. "Guard my back," he ordered Karl, counting on his friend to field the second Lyran wherever it had gotten off to. "Where's he at—where's the third 'Mech?"

Waste heat bled through the cockpit, and the *Pillager*'s reactor spiked with the power draw his lasers had demanded. Sweat beaded and ran down Michael's face, burning his eyes, though his coolant suit quickly brought his core temperature back toward normal. He blinked away the tears of sweat, concentrating on drifting his cross hairs back into the intersection he'd just vacated. He waited for the *Falconer* to round the corner. The Lyran second-guessed him, taking to the air on his jump jets to cut the corner and come in over and behind Michael's hundred-ton titan.

The gauss slug flew true this time, cracking the back of the *Pillager* dead center and weakening the skeletal structure, though failing to do much more. The PPC flayed more armor from Michael's left arm, while the lasers again flashed out in a spread of damage that fanned across his back. The *Pillager* shook violently under the assault, but Michael kept the machine upright with a quick repositioning of its feet. He twisted about to bring at least his right arm into play against the *Falconer*. Fortunately for him, his back armor was mostly unscathed and had absorbed the lethal damage fairly well. Michael had to admit it was a gutsy move, though, the kind that won games in the arena.

Except that this was no game, and Michael no average 'Mech jock to be dismissed so easily.

His throat parched and constricted by the scalding air, Michael reached out with his right arm to point the laser barrel straight into the cockpit of the enemy. Scarlet energy lased out, splashing its destructive power over the ferroglass canopy and back off the cockpit's right side. It wasn't enough to penetrate the armor protection, but the head-shot had surely shaken up the warrior inside and left him fighting the dizzying effects of flash-blinding for a few seconds.

It gave Karl Edward and Aubry Larsen their chance. The two had turned back, and now gained the same advantage against the *Falconer* that it had held against Michael's *Pillager*. Short-range and by the back. Aubry was faster on the trigger, her *Dragon Fire*'s large laser spearing the *Falconer* dead center, while the LB-X autocannon showered it with fragmenting cluster rounds, sanding away more critical armor. Everything else missed.

Karl, more cautious but twice as effective, lanced out with two more lasers, which tunneled through the *Falconer*'s back to carve away the gyro housing. A gauss slug hammered in immediately and finished the job, crushing the delicate equipment and punching out through a flaw in the *Falconer*'s front armor. The slug, its momentum mostly spent, bounced off Michael's *Pillager*. Michael stared down at the misshapen slug, battered and carved from its trip through the innards of the *Falconer*. Then a shadow fell across the ruined ammunition as the *Falconer* collapsed right over it.

Michael stepped forward, bringing his whole hundred

tons down on the Lyran's arm, crushing it beneath gargantuan metal-shod feet. Another step ruined one leg, and the other followed a few seconds later. Certain that the enemy 'Mech wouldn't get up anytime soon, or even be considered salvageable, Michael limped off to rendezvous with his two comrades.

"Not a bad piece of work. Score one *Emperor* on my record. Karl, good shooting—nice assist. We'll make a contender out of you yet."

"The third 'Mech bugged out when the *Emperor* went down," Karl transmitted, ignoring the remark. His voice was flat, hinting at displeasure.

Did Karl expect solo credit on the *Falconer*? Michael frowned. Well, that wasn't going to happen. The *Falconer* had been so focused on Michael's *Pillager* that it had ignored the others to its own detriment. And Aubry had gotten a piece of it before Karl touched it. So had Michael, in fact. No clean kill there. Michael would have to arrange a talk with Karl later, if there was time.

"Now what, Michael?" Aubry asked, automatically deferring to the senior Blackstar fighter.

He took a slow turn with his *Pillager,* trading his attention between the view out the canopy and his sensors. He picked up neither enemy contact nor friendlies. Just rioters and the occasional vehicle speeding down streets trying to bulldoze its way to its destination. Back toward the Coliseum, pillars of greasy smoke roiled into the gray sky.

Somewhere out there Victor Vandergriff had found a place to hide, to escape his fall and prevent Michael from claiming the victory he was due. Michael wanted to search him out, finish the battle Vandergriff had forced outside the arena, but now was not the time. Not in a wounded 'Mech and while being hunted by Silesia security and any warrior belonging to a Steiner-affiliated stable. Not to mention the other factions with a grudge against Blackstar or Michael personally.

"Now we hold the door open and try to route the others in this direction," he said finally. "Narvik Avenue can take us all into Cathay, and the three of us alone should be able to spearhead a drive along the riverfront if the MadCaps try to give us any trouble. Then it's an easy run back to Boreal Reach, where we can make repairs. Maybe get some ideas of where things stand in the city. Who we can count on, and who's against us."

"Can't say I'm sorry to be leaving," Aubry said, "though I wouldn't mind kicking in the side of a few more banks. Doing my part to accelerate the Lyran trickle-down theory of economics."

Karl cut in over the end of her signal. "Maybe we should be trying to figure out how to stop this before things get too far out of hand."

"Too late for that, Karl." Michael was already planning his next moves to bring in another set of Federated Sun MechWarriors. He'd save who he could, and then they'd all pick up as much salvageable parts as they could carry and head for the Black Hills. He glanced around once more, searching for a target. For Victor Vandergriff.

"No, this fight isn't over. Not by a long shot."

The clock crawled slowly past midnight, and Julian Nero rubbed at his eyes. Stepping before the cameras, he had a bad taste in his mouth from the sweetened coffee he'd been relying on for energy. His live soundcast had eventually turned into a video-feed commentary as arena camera crews managed to get footage of the riots and 'Mech battles taking place in Silesia. It wasn't their specialty, nor was the back room of the mostly deserted Coliseum the perfect stage for his ongoing reports. However, changing location and fighting to depose the normal studio anchormen would take time. Julian wasn't about to give up the narrow advantage he held in being first on the scene. The man in the know. The infallible Nero didn't plan to fiddle while Solaris City burned down around him. He was going on his sixth straight hour with no relief—he'd refused it—and no pre-canned commercials. That had to be a first in the industry.

Someone off to the side said, "You're live in three, two . . ."

A finger stabbed out on the invisible count of one. A red light glowed to life on one camera. Julian looked over at it as if he'd just been consulting with someone off stage, getting the latest news for the viewing audience. Those who were still watching, that is, not out in the streets helping to create the news itself.

"Word of the catastrophe that began here in the Coliseum tonight spread through Solaris City like sparks in a forest fire," he said in one long breath. "Jumping from one danger spot to another and lighting new blazes, which then spread until the conflagration burned firmly out of control. Not one sector had been spared, though Montenegro may suffer somewhat less because its large industrial parks were practically tailored to 'Mechs fighting in the streets.

"The Kobe waterfront is devastated from Garrett's impressive run, which left behind a tangle of broken BattleMechs and one murdered body—that of Champion Theodore Gross. His calls for single combat have been met at least five times in the last several hours, and in the shadow of the Founder's Bridge he has defeated every one of them. He finally walked back over to the Davion side of the river not fifteen minutes ago, still crowing his derision for the once-proud Kobe warriors."

He paused for a few deep breaths to recharge his voice and let people work up a solid hatred for the Clan renegade. "Still, no sector, not even the Black Hills, has yet seen the devastation of Silesia. Madness rules in the streets as looting continues unabated and entire neighborhoods begin to organize into armed camps openly supporting either Victor Vandergriff or, surprisingly, Michael Searcy. What was once thought to be a silent minority has proven they have a voice and an impressive following. And riding the undercurrent of this unrest come the cries of support for either Archon Katrina or Prince Victor."

Julian Nero knew he had his audience, knew it in a way that told him to trust his instincts. He had them and could keep them coming back so long as he delivered on his promises. But to deliver, he first had to make those promises.

"And so we're left waiting. And wondering. Where is Victor Vandergriff? When will the Silesian Police Department restore order? Can they? Who will be next to follow Theodore Gross, Sheridan Lang, and Torrence Klein? Will they be avenged, or have they died in vain?

"More questions. And I'll be here to bring you the answers.

"This from Julian Nero. The man in the know."

12

Skye Tigers Estate, Silesia
Solaris City, Solaris VII
Freedom Theater, Lyran Alliance
16 August 3062

Victor Vandergriff watched as Jerry Stroud's technicians swarmed over his *Banshee* with welders, testing probes, and an assortment of other tools. Off to one side, he warmed himself in a patch of rare morning sunlight streaming through the open doors. He'd spent the night as a guest of Stroud, but hadn't slept much. All night there'd been the distant sounds of rioting and 'Mech battles, and then the clang of tools and shriek of welding that accompanied the repair work on his 'Mech.

Stroud's estate inside the city boasted a full maintenance and repair facility to serve the lance of BattleMechs normally posted there for protection. Victor had not given permission for work on his *Banshee,* but he certainly didn't object to his 'Mech being brought back up to strength.

In one hand he held a bowl of warm cereal he'd picked up off a bounteous table on his way out of the mansion. Even with a liberal dash of granular quillar, the fare tasted flat. Just like the sun's rays, which seemed to offer little warmth. Victor couldn't summon much appreciation for his near-royal treatment at the hands of his former employer. Nothing could really engage him this morning; the events of the previous evening hung over him like dark storm clouds of self-condemnation.

He'd lost.

That was the hard truth, pure and simple. This had been the big ticket—his last chance. All that had truly mattered was beating Michael Searcy, the Davion favorite. Even winning the Championship of the Grand Tournament wouldn't have mattered as much, at least not this year. Beating Searcy would have been enough to complete his resurrection. A contender serious enough to draw crowds and inspire large purses. The conqueror of the Federated Suns. Oh, how well that would've played in the pre-fight media circus.

And he'd let it slip through his fingers, forced to retreat when Searcy's damnable gauss rifles tore open his torso and exposed its vital equipment. Though the fight was technically a draw, Victor knew right then that Searcy owned him. Searcy knew it too, which was even worse.

He turned at the sound of footsteps and saw Jerry Shroud approaching. "Almost as good as new," Stroud said, gesturing to the *Banshee.*

"Almost," Victor said curtly. "But I don't get the meaning of that Skye Tigers crest on the right leg."

"Oh, that," Stroud said. "Seems only fair. We gave you sanctuary, put your 'Mech back together. I still have to keep my eye on the benefits of sponsorship. I've lost millions in the past forty-eight hours. Not counting four BattleMechs. I can't afford to be philanthropic."

Victor half-turned to study the other man. Stroud was dressed casually, but affected a clean-shaven, paramilitary look. His speech was like the clipped sentences used in combat when seconds mattered, but his vocabulary spoke of a good education.

"You asking me to fight for you again, Jerry?"

Stroud seemed to be admiring his stable's crest painted on the leg of the *Banshee.* "Lynch Stables still owns the prominent position. And I did work this out with Trevor last night. He's hiding in Joppo, by the way, in case you want to speak with him." He nodded toward the Skye Tiger insignia, a tiger's head against a full, blue moon. "This will show some solidarity among the Lyran-affiliated stables. A pooling of resources. It's important. For Silesia."

Victor shook his head at the long explanation. "Are you asking me to fight for you again?"

Stroud blinked, glancing from the *Banshee* to Victor, obviously stalling. Then he nodded, once. "If that's what you want to hear me say, Victor. Yes, I want you to fight for Skye Tigers—for me—again. For the duration of this crisis."

Victor spooned up another bite of cereal, trying to conceal the instant of satisfaction those words gave him. "And how long is that? Riots don't last. The security forces will put them down soon enough."

Stroud shook his head. "The Silesian police force is stretched way too thin along our borders with Cathay and Montenegro. Most of Hollis Security as well. They're fighting a losing battle to prevent inter-sector clashes between civilians. That leaves very few to police Silesia itself, and entire neighborhoods are at war within the sector. Same with the Black Hills."

He pointed out two more battle-ravaged 'Mechs, racked in nearby stalls and waiting their turn with the technicians. "The MechWarriors, of course, are striking at each other wherever they can. The tunnels beneath the city are murder holes. Streets along the sector borders aren't much better—they've been hit the hardest by both the 'Mech battles and the rioting."

Frowning at the news, Victor studied the two Skye Tiger 'Mechs waiting for repair. He walked slowly over to the nearest one, trying to figure out what it was about it that bothered him. Then he had it. "This *Nightsky* took quite a bit of damage from behind." He shot a glance over at the second 'Mech, noting the run of melted armor now solidified into a permanent cascade. Until the techs took their grinders in there, at least. "So did that *Hollander*. Those are medium-class laser hits. Your people let FedRats in that close behind them?"

"That damage is from Lyran—ex-Lyran—BattleMechs." Stroud glared at the damaged machines, as if they were to blame for their condition. "A few of our own went over to the Davionists after being ordered to control a neighborhood openly declaring for Victor Davion. Doesn't matter to any of them that the prince shows no desire to retake his throne." He looked back at Victor. "My people were in the way when it happened."

The thought of Lyrans declaring for Davion turned Victor's stomach. "Setting 'Mechs against civvies is never a good idea," he said, stalling. "I'd say the riots should burn themselves out before too long. They always do."

Stroud shook his head. "This is no ordinary riot. I lost the eastern gatehouse last night. Obliterated. Similar attacks were launched against Skye Tiger Mall near the border. Infantry SRM packs, Victor. Since when do civilians find easy access to military-issue equipment?"

"Well, this *is* Solaris City."

Stroud didn't smile. "It's Hasek-Davion's doing. Has to be him. He won't be satisfied until he personally shovels the dirt over my grave."

Victor winced at the fresh reminder of last night's debacle. "You think Drew Hasek-Davion is feeding the riots?"

"I know he is. But my only witness is not what you would call credible, at least not in a court of law. I suspect Hasek-Davion is behind the sabotage of the Coliseum and my own losses as well. The man is powerful, especially so long as he controls Michael Searcy."

Victor nodded. Hasek-Davion's position rested heavily on Searcy's success or failure. No matter how strong a stable owner was, much depended on his premier fighter. If Victor hadn't been forced into a retreat last night, the troubles gripping Solaris City might already be a matter of history. But he hadn't. Now Jerry Stroud stood to lose even more as Blackstar increased the pressure under cover of the riots. Victor's only path to redemption still seemed bound to the rising star of Stormin' Michael Searcy.

"What about the Com Guards? Haven't they tried to maintain order?" he asked. ComStar maintained a full regiment on the Game World. They were posted well outside Solaris City, but could be brought in easily enough.

"They've been ordered to stand down, for now. Victor Davion is their new commander, don't forget. Would you want him claiming credit for putting down a civil war on a Lyran world?"

Victor should have thought of that himself. But if the Com Guards couldn't be allowed to interfere, that left five fairly evenly matched sectors struggling against one another, each with internal factions of stables and independent cooperatives looking after their own concerns. Solaris VII could draw together better than ten regiments of BattleMechs, but with no standing garrison force, the Lyrans couldn't hope to dominate.

"You paint a bleak picture," he said finally.

"That depends on what you're looking for, Victor. Drew Hasek-Davion has proven that any situation offers its opportunities, no matter how bad it looks on the surface. So has the Clanner, Garrett, who's taken his private war against the Combine into the streets.

"We can't just sit back and do nothing. That would make the Black Hills look stronger than Silesia. That's the reason I want you on my side. So the question becomes, what is it that you want?"

Turning back to his *Banshee,* Victor Vandergriff stared at the damage still to be repaired, damage inflicted by the one man who stood between him and redemption. A man who championed the cause of Jerry Stroud's enemy. What did he want?

Victor loaded his words with pure loathing. "Just give me Michael Searcy," he said.

In the tunnel system beneath Cathay's notorious Tenement Area slums, Michael Searcy struggled to maintain his balance as a torrent of water washed down the narrow tunnel and over the feet of his *Pillager.* The passage ran down a steep slope, diving into the deepest part of the Solaris City labyrinth—the tunnels running under the Cathay lowlands. Thousands of liters rushing by, riding a meter-high crest, impacted with enough force to throw him off-step. The gyro strained to recover, while Michael deftly worked the controls to remain standing. Water splashed off his legs high enough to hit his cockpit canopy. But it evaporated seconds later as the ruby energy of a medium pulse laser hammered a flurry of bolts into the side of the *Pillager*'s head.

The *Dragon Fire* that had fired on him ducked into a side passage to escape retaliation. Not so lucky was the *Penetrator* three hundred meters further down the narrow tunnel. Michael's large laser stabbed scarlet fire into its leg, then punched through the breach with a slug from one of his gauss rifles. The kinetic force imparted by the nickel-ferrous slug was enough to snap the titanium limb in mid-femur. From behind the *Pillager,* Karl Edward's *Cestus* shot a gauss slug just past Michael's shoulder to smash away a ton of armor off the hapless *Penetrator*'s right side.

Not necessary, Michael knew. He had already put it down.

Deprived of half its support, the *Penetrator* lost its fight with gravity. It collapsed against one wall, its other leg splayed out to partially block the tunnel like a makeshift dam. The mysterious flood of water broke wildly over the obstruction, knocking the 'Mech prone before making enough headway to continue. The canopy burst open under emergency-escape charges, and a MechWarrior quickly evacuated the flooding cockpit. He climbed out onto his 'Mech's chest, then apparently decided to risk the current rather than the good graces of his former-allies-turned-enemy. He jumped into the raging torrent and was quickly swept away.

"What's going on, Karl?" Michael asked. The water was getting deeper, now swirling around his *Pillager*'s knees.

Karl Edward was acting as comm officer for the two-man team, staying in touch with Boreal Reach, which Blackstar and most of the other Federated Suns stables were using as their command post. Even Starlight Stables, known for its long-standing feud with Blackstar, had contributed 'Warriors. Except for the three defectors Michael and Karl had been tracking through the tunnel system.

"It's the Solaris River," Karl said. "Apparently Tancred Stables and some Montenegro MechWarriors came to blows on the Cathay side of Steel Bridge. Someone blew the bridge, so the fight went underground as the

Montenegrans attempted to get home. No one is sure what happened next, but my guess is that someone lost containment in one of the under-river tunnels. The river is pouring into the tunnel system and running downhill, straight into Cathay."

"Well, Cathay always did need a good flushing out."

Michael walked his *Pillager* down to a nearby intersection, the same one that had sheltered the *Dragon Fire*. The turncoat 'Mech was nowhere on his sensors, having ducked out through the next cross-tunnel. South led deeper under Cathay. West would eventually lead to Silesia, no doubt the destination of the turncoats. East would take Michael and Karl home.

"Do we pursue?" Karl asked.

"They're your buddies. What do you think?" The three renegades were Starlight 'Warriors, and Michael saw no reason to make it easy on his friend. Everyone had to choose sides. Karl's stable-mates had chosen poorly.

"I think your *Pillager* has taken some good damage to the head and torso. If you've lost integrity and water floods in, you might lose your 'Mech down here." Karl's slight pause let Michael check the water levels for himself. "It's only going to get deeper the further we get under Cathay."

Karl was right about having to fight the water as well as the renegade Starlight 'Warriors if they took up the chase. Michael was glad that at least they'd gotten one of the fleeing 'Mechs. "All right. We wrestle the *Penetrator* back toward the Black Hills for salvage and forget the others for now. Maybe the MadCaps will get them if the flood doesn't." He couldn't resist gloating a little. "If someone doesn't get isolation doors down soon, Cathay might sink even further."

The two 'Mechs waded over to the *Penetrator*. Holding its seventy-five-ton bulk between them, they dragged it into the eastern passage, heading upslope and out of the water's immediate grasp.

"Too bad," Michael said, more to himself than anything else. Except that he'd left his throat microphone keyed open.

"Too bad about what?" Karl asked.

"That there's no media camera-system down here. Only security cams and our guncams. A running fight along narrow passages, ending with a flood and a pretty good finish taking the leg off the *Penetrator* would have made for some good video footage. Don't you think?"

Karl didn't answer for what seemed like a long time. "Yes, Michael. I suppose it would have sold quite a bit of Vita-Orange sports drink or the latest Sunspot concert holovid disk. Properly edited and cut with commercials, of course."

Well, of course. Karl made it sound like there was something wrong with it, but that was how Solaris VII worked, and no one could afford to forget it. Not if he wanted to stay on top of the Game World, which was exactly what Michael Searcy intended to do. The prize was within reach, and one way or another, he would have it. Arena fighting or battle in the streets, it was still faction against faction. Warrior against warrior.

Steiner versus Davion?

Michael thought back to the "MechTalk" interview opposite Jarman Bauer. He'd played the game but bent the rules where it suited him. He'd suckered Bauer into his trap and laid him out clean. The next day, Storming' Michael Searcy triumphed in Ishiyama over the "farmer." Presentation, and then demonstration. Appearance becoming reality. And really, that's all he was still doing. Wasn't it? He was the Federated Suns favorite, expected to defend the honor of his nation and Blackstar Stables.

Appearance and reality.

What really was the difference?

Green Mansion, Black Hills
Solaris City, Solaris VII
Freedom Theater, Lyran Alliance
16 August 3062

Security cameras set atop the high wall surrounding
Green Mansion panned back and forth, surveying the
streets for trouble. Remarkably, the roadways were
mostly clear. The neighborhood was too far away from
the city proper, and the mobs had not yet moved against
this high-end residential district of the Black Hills. For
those who wanted to try it, a *Blackjack* stationed at the
corner of St. Hellions Avenue and April Street would
discourage looting or other <u>mischief</u> while also watching
for hostile 'Mechs. The local tunnel system had been
blocked off by intentionally collapsing the arterioles,
making above-ground movement the only way to approach. The one security concern came from the nearby
border shared with Cathay, but the Free Cappella faction, always friendly to House Davion, still controlled
the far side of that border.

Which left Drew Hasek-Davion's personal estates in
the middle of one of the few relatively safe areas of
Solaris City.

Megan Church sidled along one of the five-meter-high

walls, listening for any hint of danger over the rasp of her leather jacket sliding along rough stonework. In her right hand she carried a one-meter-long shaft. A loop was attached to one end, and the head consisted of a hard ball covered by a special plastic wrap. Hugging the wall put her below the cameras' line of sight, though she could just see their lenses peeking over the rim, their asynchronous movement creating brief gaps in their coverage. It would be enough.

If the *Blackjack* pilot had noticed the instrument she carried, he'd have burned her down at once just to be safe. The device was a grapple rod, an infantry tool for scaling up the leg of a BattleMech to plant satchel charges in knee and hip joints. Except for this and a few other devices, MechWarriors were fully insulated from the threat of any mere foot soldier. Fortunately the *Blackjack* was facing the opposite direction, and Megan had no plans to get any closer than she stood just now. The grapple rod had many uses off a battlefield as well.

Watching the uneven camera motion, she peeled away the plastic coating from the head of the grapple rod, careful not to touch the special adherent that coated the hard ball. When both cameras crisscrossed their line of sight directly over her and panned away, she quickly stepped out, took aim over the wall, and thumbed the activation stud on the shaft. The ball shot away on a small compressed-air charge, flying ten meters before coming to the end of its wire tether. Wrapping over the wall, the ball fell against the other side, where its industrial-strength adherent glued it fast to the stonework. She pressed another button, and with a high-pitched whirring the motor built into the shaft began to reel in the wire.

Placing one foot in the stirrup, Megan rode the grapple rod up the side of the wall. Once she neared the top, it was a simple matter to stop winding in the tether, loop the cable around one of the iron spikes crowning the wall, and then drop down the other side. Hanging from the end of the grapple rod gave her a short two-meter drop to the lush grounds maintained below for Drew Hasek-Davion's personal enjoyment. She left the device there for his security guards to find later.

Megan would be leaving by the front gate.

A short run across well-manicured garden paths, fragrant with the scents of more flowers than she'd ever seen in one place, brought Megan to the base of a fountain. A concrete statue of a *Union* Class DropShip sat at the center of a dozen small water jets, whose broad base could have concealed two infantry squads. This was as far as she could approach by stealth. Although the walls possessed many security flaws, whoever had designed the mansion's defenses had been no slouch. From the best position it would still take a twenty-meter run to make any cover, and the cameras here were positioned to give no blind spots. Maybe if she waited near the drive, she might shadow a car in toward the garage. If she had that kind of time to spare today.

Megan stood and boldly headed for the front door. Reaching a corner wall of the manse, she ducked into the open garage. Hasek-Davion's chauffeur leaned against the side of an Avanti hovercar, nodding carefully as he watched her every move. She waved back a short salute, making for the door that led into the mansion proper. It opened even before she placed a hand on its latch. Garret stood there, gray eyes expressionless as he ushered her in and directed her to follow him.

So, another round conceded to Hasek-Davion.

"Ms. Church. A pleasure, as always, to see you." Drew Hasek-Davion waved with his pool cue as Megan was escorted into the billiards room. He leaned forward to line up his sight with the tip of the cue stick, and with a sharp crack sent a field of colored balls scattering over the felt. "I assume I have some camera motors in need of repair and that I will be billed for another grapple rod."

She struggled and looked around. Except for Garrett, she and the master of Blackstar Stables were the only ones present. Drew Hasek-Davion never met with her alone. The man trusted no one whose fate he didn't already rigidly control. Megan refused to give him that kind of hold over her. Bargaining with the devil of Green Mansion was dangerous enough without such complications.

The portly man set aside his cue for the walking stick he favored, idly tapping the lion's head into the palm of his hand as he spoke. "No trouble finding your way here, I hope. I was reluctant to call for you, with all the trouble on the streets."

"There's only trouble on the streets if you don't belong there to begin with." She hunched her shoulders, suddenly uncomfortable with the way Hasek-Davion stared at her with measured curiosity. "Cathay is a hell-hole mess," she said, shrugging off five terrifying minutes on her trip here in which she'd been caught between no less than five 'Mechs in a grand free-for-all. "But traveling through Silesia and the Black Hills is as easy as knowing when to cheer for Archon-Princess Katrina or Prince Victor."

Hasek-Davion scoffed. "And that's easy?"

"I could have drawn a map for you six months ago, letting you know where the pro-Victor element was keeping a low profile in Silesia."

"Then why didn't you?" Hasek-Davion snapped. "It might have proved useful."

Megan smiled. "My job was to keep them fighting. It was only important for *me* to know whose buttons could be pushed." She cocked her head appraisingly. "Besides, you didn't pay me enough for it."

"It seems I may be paying you enough for work you haven't performed, though."

Megan froze, a mask of indifference carefully drawn across her face. Slowly, allowing her mind to catch up, she asked, "I'm not certain what you mean. Sir."

Drew Hasek-Davion stood and walked around to the far side of his billiards table, where he leaned over the felt table top with his walking stick laid flat across it. "I mean that you have twice billed me for fights or events for which I know you are not responsible," he said, just barely containing his rage. "You had nothing to do with the rioters who attacked Skye Tiger Estate last night."

The distance Hasek-Davion had suddenly put between them meant that he acknowledged the possibility of violence coming from this interview. Megan did not dare turn to look for Garrett, but kept her yellow-green eyes focused on her employer while trying to divine exactly what Hasek-Davion might know. Was the attack against Jerry Stroud's estate coordinated by another in his employ? Had she been spotted on the estate grounds, away from the so-called rioters? Megan decided to play the middle, hoping his reaction would tell her which way to jump.

"I didn't lead them in against the estate, no. I assume you had someone else do that." She paused, watching, but Hasek-Davion was too experienced a player to give away anything so easy. She would, then, assume the worst. "However, I was already on the grounds and *did* facilitate the armed party that forayed out from the estate and ended up trading shots with your rioters. I believe four rioters were killed, which will escalate the tensions."

Drew's cold blue eyes tightened with suspicion. "Is that what you were doing inside? I wondered."

Megan thanked her natural paranoia of the night before, which had prompted her to infiltrate Skye Tiger Estate by going over the wall, much as she'd done today at Green Mansion. Likely, one of Hasek-Davion's other agents had spotted and recognized her. That told her several things right there. That he had other agents fomenting trouble in Silesia, that her face was known to them, and that Hasek-Davion was more dangerous than even *she* had guessed. Had she kept to her original plan of donning a Skye Tiger security guard uniform and slipping through one of the manned gates, Hasek-Davion's own paranoia might have demanded that he shoot her for the mere possibility of betrayal.

"I saw Victor Vandergriff's *Banshee* inside, being repaired." She hoped the information might turn the topic slightly, but his level gaze did not falter. Hasek-Davion played for higher stakes than worrying about Michael Searcy's current enemy. She shrugged, feigning resigned indifference. "I arranged for a few accidents that might be attributed to the rioters, especially after they blew the eastern gatehouse. It was also my idea, planted carefully, in the right ear, that a small force be sent out after them."

"Your report implied that you were in command of the entire situation." His voice was still hard, but his eyes no longer glittered with murderous rage.

"No one leads a mob," Megan said. "Not really. You

appear to lead it by figuring out where the people are going to go and then jumping out in front. That gives you some small measure of control." Time to get off the defensive. "*You* of all people should know that."

Drew Hasek-Davion blinked his surprise. "What do you mean?"

"Champion of the Federated Suns?" Megan asked, smiling. "Blackstar waving the Davion flag around? Six years ago you were denouncing the Federated Commonwealth and before that courting all opposition to the ruling Davion line. I'd say you've also made a habit lately of jumping out in front of the crowd to be seen as its leader."

One thin eyebrow crept up toward Hasek-Davion's hairline. "So we seem to have something in common." He nodded, conceding the point. "Most people can't—or at last do not care to—remember so far back. On the Game World, anything past last month's highlights on the Interstellar Sports Network is ancient history."

He walked slowly around one end of the billiards table. "I want to move you to the Black Hills. You might prove very useful in rallying Davionist support around Michael Searcy, and me. If we can bring our sector back under control, it would play well to the media."

Bringing the Black Hills under control would mean stamping out all Lyran pockets within the sector. "I would prefer to remain on assignment in Silesia," Megan hedged. "Over there the fighting is much bloodier, more chaotic, and I can work more effectively."

Smiling grimly, Hasek-Davion shook his head. "All right, stay in Silesia. But you shouldn't let it get personal."

"Let what get personal?"

"Fixating on one enemy—wanting to be in on the kill. It can lead to mistakes, especially since sometimes all you can do is *survive* your enemy." His eyes took on a hard gleam. "Knowing when that death is actually within reach, that is the hard part. That is when patience pays off."

Megan had a good idea who he thought was within his reach. "The voice of experience?" she asked.

Hasek-Davion looked at her strangely, as if suddenly

awakened from a vision only he could see. "You learned your lessons on the streets of Solaris City. I learned mine from the machinations of one Kai Allard-Liao. The man almost destroyed me, even though I was never his main enemy. Still, he showed me how far-reaching collateral damage could be and the power of a man firmly in control of the people of Solaris VII." His face darkened. "In fact, I probably wouldn't be where I am today without those lessons."

"You don't sound too grateful," Megan said cautiously, not wanting to draw his ire again.

He smiled, showing his teeth, and it looked more like the feral grin of an animal. "I never said I enjoyed the experience."

Megan returned his grim smile. "That just gives us one more thing in common then."

Seen almost in miniature on a holovid screen, the *Overlord* Class DropShip looked nowhere near as massive as one might expect. Its ovoid shape rested on a half-dozen blunt-footed landing pads that extended out from its base. Only one large ramp was still extended onto the spaceport tarmac, guarded by two sentries. And as they turned to walk up the ramp and into the DropShip, the final passengers to be loaded, someone might guess the vessel no larger than ten stories—twelve at best.

Until that person realized that those *passengers* were not people, but BattleMechs topping ten to twelve meters each. The tiny ants, now scurrying away to clear the area in their toy-sized vehicles—those were the people. The *Overlord* topped out at one hundred-thirty meters, about forty stories high. It was as if someone had plunked down a skyscraper in the middle of a desolate field of ferrocrete, but instead of steel and glass it was white-painted armor and weapon turrets looking out on the world of Solaris VII.

A world being bid farewell, as the first curls of fiery plasma scorched the field and roiled up from underneath the titanic ship. The force shook the ground. Even with the camera set back far enough to capture the entire ship in one shot, the image still trembled. Then slowly, majestically, the leviathan rose from the ground, picking up speed as the giant fusion drive lifted the DropShip out of gravity's embrace. The camera followed it until it became a false star in a pale gray sky and was finally lost to the near-eternal cloud cover that blanketed the continent of Equatus.

"That was the scene at Mantraa's Fulcrum Fields today, as the first three companies of ComStar's Eighth Army, Fifty-sixth Division, lifted off Solaris VII under orders from Archon Katrina Steiner-Davion. The Martial's Sword division, lately under the command of Precentor Celene Jussiaume, has been posted on the Game World for the past decade. The bulk of the division will continue to evacuate over the next twenty-four hours, leaving behind only a small logistics detachment responsible for arranging the relocation of personal effects of those family members not able to make such a rapid departure because of work contracts."

The scene cut to a live feed of Julian Nero. He was now the leading Silesian journalist covering the growing civil unrest and liked to think he'd brought his own personal flair to what was, in truth, a grim reality. Certainly he was in demand—the highest in his career. His commentaries led every news piece that left Solaris VII by HPG, bound for either the Lyran Alliance or the Federated Suns. Only Mason Wells, the popular Black Hills anchorman, came close to matching the Great Nero's current popularity. For the first twenty-four hours of the crisis Julian had even managed to avoid routines such as plugging sponsors, worrying about running long into the next feature, or toeing the line of state policy.

Though that was about to change. He felt the frown straining at the edge of his mouth, and instead gave the viewing audience a brilliant, false smile. Spreading his hands flat over the desk in front of him, drawing strength from a script he had played out hundreds, even thousands of times before, he launched into the prepared spiel.

"Never considered a garrison force, the Fifty-sixth Division has served more in the role of arbitrators for inter-sector disputes. However, this neutrality seemed to waver in the face of Victor Steiner-Davion's accepting the position of ComStar's Precentor Martial. There was even some vocal dissatisfaction when the unit was passed over as security during the seasonal tournaments this year. The chance of ComStar interfering in this time of turmoil and crisis, to further their own interests rather than that of the Lyran state, was too great. A wise precaution, it seems, especially when the major protests so far have come from stable owners in the Black Hills sector of Solaris City."

And at least this last part was completely true, so perhaps the Archon knew what she was doing after all. Though Julian was neglecting to mention that Overlord, the premiere Lyran stable, had also called for ComStar intervention and that notably absent on the Federated Suns side was Drew Hasek-Davion of Blackstar. Notably absent from *that* situation anyway. The letter Julian had received from Hasek-Davion felt as if it was burning a hole in his inside jacket pocket.

"Locally, Silesia is suffering more under the actions of Davionist vigilantes and others with a mind to exploit the situation for their own gain." Nero warmed up to his theme now that official business was out of the way and his teleprompter had moved on to the script he had prepared himself. "The Renegades, one of the stronger independent cooperatives that challenge the Game World's well-entrenched stables, have carved their own little territory out of Silesia's fashionable upper east side. They have reportedly struck a deal with the Black Lions in Montenegro that is basically a non-aggression pact, securing at least part of the Silesia-Montenegro border between them. And what began as looting in the Riverside district has turned into an armed occupation. Where the closet-Davionists have failed to take control, massive criminal elements from Cathay's Maze have poured across the border to claim their share of the spoils. Resistance is so heavy that the police have now declared it a total loss, concentrating their efforts elsewhere.

"Not everyone is giving up, however. Today Jerry Stroud of the Skye Tigers, apparently speaking for himself and Lynch Stables, promised to support a drive to put down the riots and retake control of the sector. Victor Vandergriff, also fighting under both crests, has made numerous sorties into the battle-scarred city, and so far claims two Renegade 'Mechs as well as a Starlight 'starbrite' who attempted to support the Riverside standoff. Against the Davionists, Vandergriff showed the same furious talent that has carried him so long in the Top Twenty. We'll have highlights of that battle, shot by one of our field cameramen, coming up next.''

Julian paused for a fraction of a second as the teleprompter reminded him to lead out with more description of Vandergriff's intensity in the fight. The footage was certainly worth the extra build-up. Still, at the back of his mind was the nagging feeling that Vandergriff was still not a good bet. Julian didn't need to tie his success to the fortunes of any one MechWarrior. What the people wanted—what he had to make them want—was simply more of Nero, no matter which fighter was currently at the forefront of the news. "And I'll be back at the top of the hour," he said, leading into his traditional sign-off, "with the latest coverage of events. A promise from Julian Nero. The man in the know."

"And you're clear," called someone from the wings as the screen was turned over to canned footage of the riots and on-site journalists commenting on the action. The studio was quickly abuzz with activity as aides and support personnel worked furiously to ready the set for the next live spot. No one hurried Julian Nero away from his desk, however.

No one dared.

Reclining back, stretching tired muscles, Julian worked a cramp out of his neck, then reached into an inside pocket of his jacket to draw out a folded missive. It had been delivered to him by private messenger five minutes before air time, delivered by a woman who had apparently evaded studio security with a quiet competence. He instinctively knew she would make a good feature, whatever her story. Listening to those instincts was how he had built his reputation for being infallible, that and a lot of hedged bets that let him claim success no matter what the outcome of any particular fight. But something in her eyes—yellow-green like a cat's—kept him from proposing such an interview. Instead he simply accepted the message, which he read three times after breaking the verigraphed seal. Once in haste and then twice more carefully. It was an invitation to attend a private meeting of ranking journalists from all across Solaris City.

An invitation and the offer of safe conduct to the estate of Drew Hasek-Davion.

He tapped the folded paper into one open palm, as if he could weigh its significance. What did Hasek-Davion have up his sleeve? Just when Julian thought he had pegged the stable owner into a particular group or on a given issue, the man shifted. He was a chameleon, always placing his own best interests first. But the message vaguely promised that the discussion would include ways to improve broadcast rights and place the vidcasters in a more prominent position. Isn't that what Julian was looking for?

The studio might balk, safe conduct notwithstanding, but in the end would go along with whatever he decided. It would have to be kept quiet, though. Julian had no doubt what Silesian officials would say, parroting the local Lyran Alliance governor who was Katrina's man through and through. No discussion. No room for negotiation, whatever the deal. The Archon's interests were unlikely to coincide with those of Drew Hasek-Davion.

But meeting with Hasek-Davion would land Julian a story if nothing else, and if that kept him on top of the world, then so be it. He would meet with the man, with them all. He would stay "in the know." Julian had his own interests to look after as well.

That was simply how the universe worked. Especially on Solaris VII.

14

Boreal Reach, Black Hills
Solaris City, Solaris VII
Freedom Theater, Lyran Alliance
17 August 3062

In the warrens under Boreal Reach arena, now sealed off from Solaris City's main tunnel system except for one well-guarded arterial, the MechWarriors and tech personnel supporting the Federated Suns moved with purpose about their established base. Damaged machines walked or dragged into the 'Mech bays were repaired as quickly as possible, made ready for the next day's fighting. 'Warriors grabbed food and rest as they could, some of them checking in with Michael Searcy for an update on events. The more practical-minded simply found a holovid station and tuned into any one of several news programs—the same channels and vidcasters that normally covered the arena games.

One such station was set to the Solaris Official Bookmaking Channel. Two exhausted pilots argued over the odds that had been assigned to the battle they'd fought earlier today. One of them had made a small fortune betting on the outcome of their raid against Silesia.

Not every area of the Game World suffered under the current chaos.

A host of armed guards—some members of the Federated Suns Police Department and others drafted into service from Boreal Reach security—kept careful watch over the access passages leading to the surface, wary of the rioters in the streets above. Several city blocks were no more than fire-gutted shells, and the violence continued. A new *Rakshasa* had already been lost when a crowd of Lyran fanatics stormed one of the BattleMech storage bays and lobbed grenades into the open cockpit, destroying the control equipment beyond repair.

Michael nodded curt greetings to a pair of guards as he passed their station, then bumped into Aubry Larsen at the door to the large room he'd commandeered as his office. Aubry was one of his aide-de-camps, mostly by virtue of having fought her way free of Silesia with him and Karl Edward. She handed him a stack of battle reports, which Michael dropped heavily on a table as he entered the office alone. His muscles protested the long days, having carried him through another six hours in his cockpit just this morning. A chair stood by invitingly, but he ignored it in favor of slow pacing along a giant high-resolution wall screen.

Originally a meeting room for technicians and engineers to discuss the performance of various BattleMech designs fighting in Boreal Reach, the large table now held a spread of reports on the fighting and the status of all units currently defending the Black Hills. The wall screen, usually devoted to showing a 'Mech's technical data, was currently loaded with a tactical map of Solaris City. Large red stars anchored each sector—marking important areas such as the spaceport in the International Zone, the various sector arenas, and other known BattleMech staging sites.

Arrows showed paths of advancement and retreat and told an interesting story of who was fighting whom. Cathay was a tangle of green arrows showing the various factions within the Confederation engaging in their own private wars. Tandrek and Zelazni Stables had practically beaten each other into bankruptcy with furious, no-holds-barred combat and would require years to recover their once-strong positions. Tentative stabs of green and purple over the Solaris River indicated the skirmishes

being fought between Cathay and the Free Worlds
League sector of Montenegro. Montenegro was also tangling with Kobe on the west and Silesia to the east.
Kobe's red arrows spread several strikes toward the
Black Hills, but many of them stopped on their side of
the Founder's Bridge. Michael knew that was due to the
tenacious efforts of Garrett and the other few Smoke
Jaguar renegades who had joined him in opposing the
Combine MechWarriors. Garrett was racking up an impressive set of kills, though he still remained back-page
news to most.

Regardless, Cathay's preoccupation and Garrett's line-
of-death defensive strategy left the bulk of the Black
Hills' combined military effort free to cope with the riots
and the Federated Suns' main opposition, namely Silesia.
Blue and gold arrows traded long-reaching strikes across
Cathay. On the sector's western border, shorter but
more numerous stabs lanced between Black Hills and
the International Zone, which was still controlled by the
Lyrans. But for how much longer? Michael studied the
map, doubting they would last another two days, not
with his latest plans being set into motion.

A voice at the door startled him, and he glanced over
to see Karl Edward standing there. "And Alexander
wept," Karl said, "noticing that out of the vast multitude
of worlds, he had yet to conquer one."

Michael frowned and turned back to the screen. "I'm
not Alexander the Great, and I'm not weeping," he said,
recognizing the lines from Plutarch, who was still taught
in the Federaled Suns academies. "But I will conquer
this world. It's the reason I came to Solaris VII."

He gestured to the map. For a moment, all the lines
and battlefield notations displayed for Michael reminded
him of the strategy board once laid out for New Canton.
There he had not been in on the planning, only expected
to follow. And look where it brought him. "I've never
had to plan a campaign before, and it certainly wasn't a
talent I thought would surface on the Game World. Not
quite how I expected it to happen, but it will serve."

Karl came up alongside him and also looked up at the
map of the city. "How wonderful. Have you decided
where they will erect the statue in your honor?"

"Atop Viewpoint," Michael said, giving no sign that he even noticed the sarcasm. Coming from his best friend, the implied criticism stabbed deep. "It's the highest point in the city. From there, everyone can see it." Michael rubbed one hand along the side of his face, the rasp of two-day stubble hard against his palm.

He turned back to Karl. "I missed you at the briefing this morning."

His friend's voice softened only slightly. "I was attending a quick memorial service for Aaron Harper."

The name tugged at Michael's memory, but he couldn't put a face to it. "Who?" he asked.

"He was the one killed by Victor Vandergriff in Silesia yesterday during the takeover of the Riverside District. I thought we agreed that it was too dangerous for one 'Warrior."

"You agreed and then turned down the assignment. I said I'd think about it." Or something along those lines. Had Michael actually agreed? So many decisions coming so fast. "I had to make the call," he tried to explain. "We have people on the ground there."

Now it was Karl's turn to ask, "Who, Michael? Who do we have on the ground there?"

"The people getting hurt. FedSun loyalists."

"No, who *exactly*? Who have you talked to and what are their plans to aid us?"

The questions stopped Michael for a few long seconds, mostly as he didn't have any answers. Silesia's Riverside District was now under the control of the Federated Suns. Wasn't that enough for Karl? He turned to face his friend, who stood with arms crossed defiantly and a look of frustration on his gaunt features. "What are you getting at, Karl?"

"I want to know if you made the call, or was it Hasek-Davion?" Karl asked quietly. "I didn't know we had infantry on the ground, anywhere. So why are we—why are *you*—supporting the rioters? We should be putting a stop to this madness, not making it worse."

What did Karl think Michael was trying to do? The crowds followed the MechWarriors, didn't they? The riots continued because there was no dominating faction. No Champion to set things right. Appearance was too often accepted as reality; Michael could not appear weak in the face of a Lyran advance. He had to meet it. Retaliate. Win! On the Game World, people only respected a winner. Stormin' Michael Searcy had to hold on to that respect if he was to do anything about the troubles.

He tried to explain that to Karl. "I'm not blind to the situation. I know people are getting hurt out there in the riots, but they won't follow if we don't lead. So we need to act, and I've got a plan." He turned back to the map, running a hand over the border between the Black Hills and the International Zone. "With ComStar ordered off planet by Katrina Steiner, she unknowingly left the spaceport undermanned. The Fifty-sixth may not have been an official garrison force, but the Lyrans relied on them nonetheless."

A shadow of doubt flickered in Karl's eyes. "What's so important about the spaceport?"

"The customs area," Michael said, stabbing a finger down on a cluster of buildings at the spaceport's northwest corner. "More specifically, the Solaris City 'Mech bays and warehouses, which are part of every sector's logistics chain. You bring a 'Mech or even any parts onto Solaris, and they go into this set of buildings until processed. The small Lyran contingent still guarding the spaceport is sitting on a treasure trove. If we can push them back, or simply aside, we can grab the supplies and use it to equip another two companies easy. Then we smash the Lyrans completely and hold the International Zone ourselves. It stops the two-front war we've been fighting and gives us access to a supply line." He glanced back at his friend. "What do you think?"

"Very high-profile," Karl said. "It will make for splashy headlines."

"Exactly." Michael beamed his satisfaction. "And I want you to lead the first strike."

"You what?"

Didn't Karl understand that Michael was trying to help him? They'd always watched each other's backs. Now it was Michael's turn to offer a hand up to his friend. "There's enough glory to go around, even if the riots do cast a shadow over everything. Look, I know Garrett's way isn't yours, but he's accomplished something for himself in his vendetta against Kobe. You could do the same. Build some prestige. Move to the forefront of the fight, with me."

"Another of your calls? Or did Hasek-Davion plan this move as well?"

"What does it matter who thought of it?" Michael asked, exasperated, though it was true the idea for this operation had originated with Hasek-Davion. Well, so what? The man had more years watching for opportunities such as this than did Michael. "It will take Mech-Warriors to make it happen. *We* make the difference."

"You really believe that? Michael, wake up! You're not 'Stormin' Michael Searcy.' That man doesn't exist except in the media. You're a MechWarrior, and you're being used. Hasek-Davion's plans benefit one man only, and that's himself. He's got his hooks buried into you so deep that when he twitches a finger your head jerks around like a puppet."

Michael shook his head. "You're wrong, Karl. This is an opportunity. And it's a necessary move."

"The last *necessary* move you made cost a friend of mine his life."

"Is that what this is about? That Aaron Harper was a fellow Starlight fighter?" Michael remembered Drew's warning—had it only been four days ago—that Karl was jealous of Michael's standing and might betray him. "Would it still be an issue if the dead man was a Blackstar or a White Hand gladiator?"

Karl Edward's face drained of color. "What's wrong with you? This isn't about stables or rivalries. People are dying out there! It's not a game anymore. It hasn't been a game since you and Vandergriff smashed through the Coliseum wall. Not when people's lives are at stake."

Michael couldn't believe Karl would turn on him like this. Was he hoping to use the downfall of Stormin' Michael Searcy to rise in the ranks himself? "You're jealous," he blurted without thinking.

Eyes wide with shock, Karl could only stammer out, "Excuse me?"

Righteous anger rose up in Michael. "Jealous, I said. Admit it. I've risen to the top of the Game World in only three years, and you can't stand that I've left you behind. But it's been no secret. You know what it takes to get ahead on Solaris VII, I've showed you. You've held yourself back. Even when I offer to share some of the glory, you throw it back in my face. So what is *your* problem, Karl? What stopped you from following a proven formula for success?"

When Karl spoke, his was voice deadly calm but laced with contempt. "Because if I had played the game your way, you wouldn't have a friend left on this world and you'd be even more the creature of Drew Hasek-Davion that you are now. A want-to-be Champion on a very short leash."

Venting his fury, Michael lashed out at the pile of reports sitting on the edge of the table, scattering them into the air. "To hell with you then! Go on, get out!"

Karl turned for the door, and Michael almost called him back—wanted to—certain the damage could be undone. His pride stopped him, however. Michael had expected Karl to back him, just as he always had. To discover instead that his friend had held a low opinion of him for some time, remaining close only out of some desperate loyalty, chipped away at his resolve and his confidence. It reminded him too much of earlier betrayals. Of the reasons why he had come to the Game World in the first place.

If not Champion, then what?

"Karl!" Michael's call stopped his friend just short of the door. The silence drew out for several long heartbeats. Finally, "Tell me something. Do you think I would have won?"

"Won?"

"The Grand Tournament. The Championship. If things had proceeded normally, do you think I would have won?"

Karl looked at him sadly. "I don't know, Michael. You're good, no one can deny that. But Champion?" He paused, shrugged. "Most of the Champions I've ever seen didn't need someone else to tell them so.

"Goodbye, Michael."

Tran Ky Bo had been right, Karl decided, the taste of failure bitter at the back of his throat. The master of

Starlight Stables had predicted that Michael wouldn't listen to him. Argued against even attempting to influence the Black Hills' self-anointed champion, worried that *Stormin'* Michael Searcy might turn against his former friend. But Karl thought he owed it to Michael to try.

He'd failed, and now his decision weighed heavily. It would put him on a path leading away from his friend, who wouldn't listen, wouldn't see that he was being used. Or if he did see, he wouldn't admit to it. Just as Michael did not hear the finality in Karl's goodbye.

Someone else had, though. Garrett waited just outside the door to Michael's lair, pretending to relax against a corridor wall, though Karl doubted the Clanner had relaxed once from his militant vigil ever since arriving on the Game World. Or since losing his Clan. Garrett looked upon everyone as an enemy. Even those few Smoke Jaguar renegades who'd also come to Solaris VII were potential rivals. Karl pitied the man his lack of peace, but that didn't mean he felt sympathy.

"Going somewhere?" Garrett asked.

"Valhalla. Thought maybe I'd toughen up our competition for network time." Karl stopped as Garrett stepped into his path. "Why? You want to come along?"

Some of the Solaris elite had been at the exclusive club when the fighting broke out. Hollis Security and a few Silesian PD 'Mechs quickly cordoned off Thor's Shieldhall, allowing Lyran warriors out to join Silesia's defense but leaving the others under a kind of house arrest. Over the last several days there'd been talk among the Black Hills defenders of going to "Free Valhalla." Talk was all it was, though. Most of the gladiators didn't miss the competition, seeking their own fifteen minutes. Any effort to free the 'Warriors trapped in Valhalla would have to come through an independent effort.

It was a lie that Karl would make that effort with the meager resources available to him, but he hoped it sounded credible. Especially in light of his actual plans to quit Solaris City, answering Tran Ky Bo's summons to rendezvous with a number of disillusioned MechWarriors at Starlight Sables' remote training grounds. Karl felt like he'd do anything that would get him back to his *Cestus*.

"You aren't heading into Silesia," Garrett sneered. "We know you've been talking to Tran Ky Bo."

We. Karl knew that meant Hasek-Davion. It was amazing how the man kept himself hedged against any flanking maneuvers. He looked past Garrett, at the intersection that would take him toward his 'Mech and away from the nightmare that had descended on Solaris City.

"Out of my way, Garret," he said, his voice deadly cold.

Garrett bristled. "Try another direction."

Karl started to turn away, as if avoiding a confrontation, then spun back around for a hooking punch that Garrett was too slow to ward off. The right hook smashed into his jaw, sending him sprawling.

Karl looked down at him, fists still clenched, but Garrett didn't move. That surprised him, but he quickly stepped over the Clanner's unconscious form. In his anger and desperation, Karl must have mustered a blow hard enough to catch even Garrett unprepared. He'd downed his enemy, but no video cameras, no witnesses were present to trumpet his victory.

And that suited Karl Edward just fine.

15

Green Mansion, Black Hills
Solaris City, Solaris VII
Freedom Theater, Lyran Alliance
17 August 3062

The media room in Green Mansion made a big impression on the quartet of video journalists Drew Hasek-Davion had gathered together. They sat in overstuffed leather chairs pulled up to a table in the beautiful grain of New Syrtis golden oak. Cocktails of their choice rested on linen napkins, but mostly went ignored as they swiveled about to follow the panorama of news reports displayed on four large wall screens. The scenes were constantly shifting between the numerous feeds pulled in from all across Solaris City, and a state-of-the-art sound system delivered the voices of the commentators.

The commentaries had been expertly edited to make a huge audio collage of the troubles on Solaris VII. Not more than a few seconds ever followed the cut to the next report. Though it would have been a dizzying assault on the senses for most people, these were media pros, used to such rapid-fire deliveries and crisp summations. They followed along, caught up in the spell of the moment.

In an adjoining room, peering in through a hidden

camera, Drew Hasek-Davion smiled whenever he noticed someone straighten perceptibly as they recognized a fragment from one of their own reports.

He had left them alone to view their own handiwork—mostly footage of the violence that still ruled the streets of Silesia and the Black Hills. They listened to reports on the fires that broke out in Kobe the night before, reducing a large section of its slums to ash and charred brick and even now barely under control where it had spread into neighboring areas. An illegal tap into the closed-circuit feed of Cathay's Jungle arena provided some close-up shots of the ongoing 'Mech battle between warring Liao stables, then cut back to a failed push by Federated Suns police to retake one of its own security compounds captured by Lyran sympathizers. They also saw clips from the Tong war for control of the Black Hills riverfront and of Skye Tiger 'Mechs defending Jerry Stroud's estate from a raid by a lance of Blackstar 'Warriors.

Many of the clips showed today's heavy assault against the spaceport. No control facilities had been touched, only the auxiliary buildings. The spaceport proper was the only area that all sectors recognized as neutral and no 'Mechs had threatened it. The fighting had edged closer, however, as Black Hills forces sought to flank the small Lyran contingent guarding the port warehouses. In the background, DropShips continued to arrive with their manifest of tourists and future gladiators.

One screen froze on a shot of a Monopole Lines DropShip touching down on the tarmac, about a full kilometer back from one exchange of firepower. Soon a second screen paused on the same scene. Then the third. Carrying his usual bourbon neat, Drew timed his entrance to coincide with the fourth wall screen turning to the same static image.

"Interesting, don't you think?" he said, obviously startling his four visitors from their contemplation. "For all the danger of the riots, of BattleMechs fighting in the streets and not the arenas, we continue to be flooded by aficionados—the gamblers and spectators and simple tourists. Very few have altered their travel plans or are remaining in safety at the recharge station facilities. The current unrest seems only to have heightened the appeal of the Game World. Yes, an interesting situation." He paused. "Which *you* all help to promote."

Veronica Sherman of the Solaran Broadcasting Corporation glared at him. She was antagonistic to Drew as she'd been to Michael at the Viewpoint press conference. "We *report* the news. We do not create it. That is easily left to deviants such as *your* Michael Searcy."

"Or Victor Vandergriff," Adam Kristof reminded her. "Also Srin Odessa and Jasmine Kalasa and any other MechWarrior who has taken to the streets." He glanced at Mason Wells, the popular Federated Suns journalist, apparently looking for support.

But it was Julian Nero who spoke up next, which pleased Drew. "The MechWarriors may take center stage," he said, "as always, but the riots are fed and maintained by the ordinary citizens of Solaris City." He shrugged uncomfortably. "We bear some responsibility for that, being the self-declared opiate of the masses. But I'd say it's safe to assume that no one in this room is about to cut them off 'cold turkey,' as it were. That would be professional suicide." The others nodded agreement.

So did Drew. "You mistake my intentions, Mr. Nero. I've no desire to limit your journalistic freedom. Only to regulate it . . . *slightly.*"

He sipped at his drink, appreciating its heady taste and enjoying the looks ranging from consternation to sheer rage on the faces of his guests. Each one acting predictably—so far.

Drew meant to have the cooperation of these four people. He needed it. Solaris VII was a media-driven world. Normally the stable owners wielded the controlling influence, deciding who would fight where and which media would be allowed to cover it. With most stables currently lacking any real authority over their fighters—except for *his* stable, of course—the media now held the upper hand. As usual, Drew was ready to take his place at the forefront of the crowd, to be seen as its leader. To *be* its leader.

Before any of the four could take issue with him, he went on. "The betting, both legal and illicit, is as heavy as ever. The odds are fluctuating like nothing ever seen now that the controlled environment of the arenas isn't functioning, and the money is pouring in. Even Solaris scrip is seeing the strongest upsurge in some time, with everyone wagering their House-bills on the violence."

He set his drink down on a low table. "Be that as it may, we've all been hurt in the second-most profitable venture of the Solaris VII, which is the commercialization of the games." The vidcasters were only cogs in the wheel. Their livelihoods depended on the profitability of their networks. "You've been enjoying some extra freedoms lately, but the truth is it's hurting your studios and owners. I don't have to tell you that no one is immune to the imperative of the bottom line."

Mason Wells leaned forward in his seat, hands folded elegantly on the table. "What are you suggesting, Mr. Hasek-Davion?" His voice gave away nothing.

Drew smiled and spread his hands expansively. "Merely that you provide more of your old showmanship-style reporting and help me in coordinating sponsorship efforts. I've made arrangements for several high-stakes deals that will benefit your studios, and you specifically. The sponsors cannot possibly show favoritism to the MechWarriors or to any of the various factions. It would limit their cross-market appeal. However, they *can* sponsor independent reporting of the events here on Solaris. Bluntly put, the media is currently more marketable than endorsing the fights."

"Then allow me to be blunt as well," Julian Nero said. "Why do we need you?"

Drew held his temper in check, knowing it would give him no advantage at the moment. Nero's question was a fair one. "You may have the talent, Mr. Nero, but you haven't the contacts the stable owners have developed over the years. And you've no time to acquire them. You could leave it to your studios, but they've no reason to cut you in. I would arrange the sponsorships directly, which can then be negotiated with the studios at more favorable terms than you normally receive."

"This is an outrage!" Veronica Sherman slammed one hand flat down against the table. "I see no reason that the Lyran news agencies should bow to your management."

Drew turned to look at her calmly. "I don't see why not," he said, a wintry edge to his voice. "They've always been responsive to the influence of the Solaris Stable Owner's Association. Within two days, other stable owners will recognize the value of this opportunity, and the SSOA will formally take over as your representative."

Mason Wells smiled cynically. "You expect to remain head manager of the project, of course."

"Of course." Drew shrugged. "Someone must be in charge and held accountable." He didn't say that he intended to reap the benefits of being in control, while holding the journalists themselves ultimately responsible.

Adam Kristof glanced around at the others, then back at Drew. "You don't mean for this to end with the four of us, then, do you?"

"Not in the least. Once other media representatives and studios see the deals being struck, they'll come aboard as well. But that shouldn't matter to the four of you. As the first, you will automatically receive the best deals. It will also let you remain at the forefront of this crisis. More air time. Wider distribution of your commentaries into syndicated broadcasts. Greater recognition and prestige."

These four people had been in the game long enough to know the score. Hadn't they watched the same scenario play out with the MechWarriors who dominated the arenas? The 'Warrior became hot property, leading to bigger purses and a demand for more fights.

"You did mention returning a touch of showmanship to our reports," Mason Wells said.

Nodding, Drew warmed to his secondary motive for bringing the media under his control. "Love them or hate them, the MechWarriors are the property we sell. Even at their worst, the riots can't compete with video footage of BattleMechs blasting away at each other. There is no denying that the strong central personalities of the Game World have been sacrificed for a more generalized view of the fighting. I want to see that competitive flavor brought back to your reporting."

"With an emphasis on Michael Searcy's exploits, no doubt."

Veronica Sherman was determined to force Drew's hand. All in good time, though. If she could not be brought on board, he would simply redouble his efforts to snare Julian Nero. "Michael Searcy is a man in search of his own destiny. In fact, I'd go so far as to say that he has very few ties left to Blackstar Stables. He is a 'Federated Son' warrior. You should treat him as such in your reports."

Even Veronica Sherman couldn't help showing an interest in that surprising bit of news. Was Blackstar Stables officially relinquishing all ties to its favored 'Warrior?

Drew's words certainly suggested that, even though it wasn't true. It was all part of his insurance plan. Eventually, the price for the riots would have to be paid. Drew had every intention of coming down on the winning side, which meant he had to be ready to sever all relations with Searcy should the young hot-blood fail to carry the fighting for the Black Hills. Drew wasn't about to leave his future in the hands of any one person.

"If we play up the divisive factions any more than we do now," Nero said, "we open ourselves to charges of feeding the violence."

"Or, of trying to put the focus back on the various fighters," Drew returned calmly. "Lure the people back to their screens and leave the fighting to the professionals." It was the justification that would cover everyone's actions if played correctly to the viewing public. And weren't these the people responsible for the presentation? "As for the MechWarriors, you will be instrumental in declaring the champions and the vanquished. Tried in the media. Judged by the public."

"It could work that way," Nero said cautiously. "Though I think that each sector—each nation—will prefer to choose their own champions. And enemies."

"Which means we eventually reclaim the same system Solaris VII has been operating under for the past several years," Drew said. "Either way, it makes for one hell of a story."

In the SSOA meeting of four days prior, Drew Hasek-

Davion had carried the day through a well-played game against Thomas DeLon. Manipulating his peers, dominating them where necessary, he had steered the outcome of the meeting to within a hair's breadth of the victory Jerry Stroud then handed him. He still savored the memory of that maneuver, with all its tension and the delicate care he'd needed to take with each step.

Compared to that meeting, this one was child's play. He'd owned Adam Kristof and Mason Wells from the start. The lure of direct sponsorship was too enticing. Also, the journalists recognized the power Drew could bring against them in the Black Hills and were wary of him. Julian Nero was nobody's fool, though, and could retreat back into Silesia where Drew's reach was not so long. Or so he might think. Still, Drew read it in his eyes that the Lyran 'caster was nearly solid. The benefits far outweighed the dangers of dealing with Hasek-Davion. That left . . .

Veronica Sherman shook her head emphatically. "I'll have nothing to do with any scheme proposed by a Fed-Rat. By the time I've had my say, I doubt many others will either."

"Damn it, Veronica," Kristof chided. "If it had been one of your Lyran merchant-masters who had come up with this, you would be first on line with holocam already running."

"Well, it wasn't. And that makes all the difference to me."

Watching her with his own mask set carefully into place, Drew simply removed the wireless from his belt and asked, "Is that your final answer?"

"Close enough," she said. "In fact, I think Adam's right. I see no reason why the same plan can't be put into effect by going through a Silesian stable master. Jerry Stroud can be counted on, I'm sure."

Veronica had gone one step too far, her fate sealed by her refusal. Not that Drew would think to harm her directly. Nothing could turn the media against him any faster than to threaten their persons. But he had many other ways to accomplish the same end, ones not so easily traced back to his hand.

He speed-dialed one of his agents at Boreal Reach on

his wireless, then spoke into it. "I'm concerned about some reports I'm getting," he said, gaze centered unwaveringly on Veronica Sherman. "I want the SBC protected. Yes, the Solaran Broadcasting Corporation. We have forces in the International Zone? Good, make certain they respond. And I'll put up a fund of one hundred thousand C-bills for any warrior who can hold out against the expected Lyran attack." He snapped the wireless closed.

Veronica Sherman's face paled. The others shifted uncomfortably, realizing the implied threat to all media concerns. "You can't do that," she demanded. "Everyone needs the SBC facilities to put on their programs."

"No," Drew disagreed. "The SBC only makes it easier. It wouldn't be impossible to get along without it, though most studios would certainly be harder pressed to rely more on their own talent and facilities. Which is why I want it protected." Of course, by sending Black Hills troops to defend the site, it would become an instant target for the Lyran forces. "Not one Federated Sun warrior will fire on the buildings intentionally." And so it would appear that Drew Hasek-Davion had worked to defend Solaris City's central broadcasting facilities.

And appearances were, indeed, everything.

"They won't have to. The Lyran forces will destroy it."

"I do hope you are wrong. But if the worst should happen, I'd say you would be out of a job, Ms. Sherman." Time to clinch the deal. "What do you think, Mr. Nero? Would your studio be likely to offer Mrs. Sherman a place to voice her opinions?"

Julian Nero's struggle played out quickly. Drew could practically read the other man's mind, knowing the options left to him. Should he show solidarity with the Lyran-affiliated media and risk a similar ploy to drive his own studio out of business, or should he work within the parameters just outlined in this room? Drew counted on Nero being a newsman before he was a patriot.

The man did not disappoint.

"Very unlikely, sir," he said, throwing a quick glance at his former associate.

Sherman seemed to have collapsed inwardly, her leg-

endary stamina deserting her with the implications of
Hasek-Davion's actions. If the others had similar reser-
vations, they were careful to keep them hidden. Power
had just been transferred this afternoon, shifting from
the media concerns back to the stable owners. Perhaps
any true independence had never been the media's to
begin with. Until now, power had been spread among
the stable owners; it had never rested in the hands of
single master.

All in an afternoon's work for Drew Hasek-Davion.
He was now the most powerful force on Solaris VII, and
he meant to hold on to that newfound strength with
every means at his disposal. Searcy would either carry
the fight and be dependent on Drew's media influence
to vindicate him, or he would fail. In which case Drew
was now in position to denounce Searcy and still come
out the winner. Garrett remained a secondary insurance
plan against Searcy, just as Searcy remained one against
the Clan renegade. And always there were Jerry Stroud
and Skye Tigers Stable to contend with. Drew's nemesis
could not help but fall now. Stroud had no real hope.

Not so long as Drew Hasek-Davion remained in control of the Game World. And, so far, there was no one
in place to stop him.

16

The palatial estates of the Triad on Tharkad demonstrated a regal splendor of immaculately kept grounds, grand arches and cathedral ceilings, rich tapestries and richly carpeted halls. As the seat of power for the Lyran Alliance, it demanded nothing less.

Nondi Steiner's office in the Triad's executive wing, however, showed more Spartan tastes. As General of the Armies, she thought it more seemly. The tiled floor had been polished to a mirror shine, and the room's only furnishings were her desk and chair and two seats for visitors. The expansive desktop of pale blue marble streaked with gray was kept fastidiously clear. A small holovid monitor sat on its left side. A large nameplate was place prominently on the front edge, as if anyone entering the office would not know who presided there. On the desk's right-hand corner was a miniature flag in a pedestal. It showed the symbol of the Lyran Alliance, a blue gauntlet set against a field of white.

Only two pictures had been hung on the walls. One was a shot of her first BattleMech, an old ZEU-6S *Zeus,* with Nondi as a young lieutenant standing atop one metal-shod foot. The other was a glamour painting of Katrina Steiner, Nondi's young niece and the Archon of the Lyran Alliance. Though Katrina was a Steiner-*Davion* by name and ruler of the Federated Suns as well, to Nondi's way of thinking Katrina would always be a Steiner first and proud champion of the Lyran state.

As evidenced by the holographic message ComStar had recently delivered by priority routing.

Katrina's face filled the three-dimensional viewer, the close-up so lifelike that Nondi could pick out the actual brush strokes of the light touch of blue shadow applied to Katrina's eyelids. Her long, gold-blond hair hung in a thick braid over her right shoulder. Ice blue eyes, hard and penetrating, stared out from the screen. It was almost as if Katrina was in the room, though the message had originated half a day prior and hundreds of light years away.

"I have already ordered the Com Guard Fifty-sixth Division off Solaris, preventing my brother from using them to win a public relations coup by quelling the riots. It would be just his way, using an ostentatious display of force to command the situation. All under the pretense of *keeping the peace*"—Katrina's tight-lipped frown deepened—"though seen and trumpeted by his supporters as a successful challenge to my rule."

That could not be allowed to happen—not on a Lyran world! Nondi had little use for Victor Davion, to the point that she refused him the honor of his mother's maiden name.

Katrina's message continued. "I had hoped that our forces on planet and the Silesia stables could restore order on their own, but many of my missives to the stable owners have gone undelivered or perhaps even ignored." Katrina's eyes tightened at the idea of being slighted.

But worse, Nondi knew, was the fact that Katrina had no direct control over the situation. She was currently on New Avalon occupying the throne she had assumed during Victor's long absence from the Inner Sphere, unable to return to the Lyran Alliance.

"The riots have turned into a bloody conflict, covered

by some of the most prominent journalists of the entire Inner Sphere, and the unrest is spreading to other worlds via these reports and news footage. I will *not* have this in my realm! Circumstances force me to remain here on New Avalon, ready to deal with any move on my brother's part to reclaim the throne, so I expect you to safeguard my people of the Alliance. Put an end to the riots, dear Aunt, and make an example of those responsible. By whatever means necessary."

The image winked out in an eyeblink, at first leaving a fathomless darkness on the holovid monitor that was quickly replaced by the Lyran Alliance crest. Nondi leaned forward eagerly, pulling a glass touch pad from its slot just under the marble desktop. The facsimile of a keyboard had been etched into the glass. As she stabbed at the keys, the Lyran crest dissolved, and her monitor came to life with new data.

Displayed before her was the table of organization and equipment of the Lyran Alliance Armed Forces. The simplest move was to send forces from the Freedom Theater roster. But whom to send? This mission couldn't be trusted to a unit of less than certain loyalty to Katrina. The threat was too great. Solaris VII had always been a problem waiting to happen. That the disaster should come now, when public sentiment was building for Katrina's dethroned brother, was timing of the worst possible order. Small hints of unrest had even surfaced here on Tharkad—Tharkad, for the love of the Archon!—with the underground tabloid *The Federated Son* stirring the normally calm waters.

Scanning the data before her, Nondi searched out the Seventeenth Arcturan Guards, the only unit based near Solaris that Nondi emphatically trusted. The unit, however, was currently on Wyatt and a few lights years too distant to make a timely arrival. Katrina wanted—needed—the riots stopped before the flames of unrest burst into the uncontrollable fire of civil war.

Nondi silently cursed her own lack of foresight. Why hadn't she garrisoned Solaris VII with Lyran troops?

Falling back to her second tier of choices, she came upon a stroke of good fortune. The Thirty-second Lyran Guards were currently garrisoned on New Kyoto, with one battalion just returning from training exercises on Hyde in the Cavannaugh Theater. Her sources labeled the Thirty-second as neutral in any possible power struggle between Victor and Katrina, but under the command of Leutenant-General Gustav Van Buren, Nondi would worry less. Gustav was old-school Lyran and could be counted upon for sterling advice. And his troops were green. Hardly the kind to upset the chain of command by going rogue, and perhaps idealistic enough to turn the situation around on Solaris VII.

What truly tipped the scales was the fact that they were due to arrive back in the New Kyoto system in six hours. That placed them already at a jump point, saving the six days of travel time it would normally take to get there from a planet's surface. Nondi would order the unit to commandeer a ready JumpShip, to which they would transfer their DropShip and travel to Solaris near instantaneously. Because the Solaris system was so well traveled, there would be any number of known intermediary jump points at which to arrive, further saving travel time.

"Thirty-six hours," she said aloud, figuring up the total travel time. "I can have them on the ground in thirty-six hours." Her voice echoed off the barren walls of the office, a reminder of the solitude that came with high command. But it was all for the good of the Lyran people. Her people, and Katrina's.

One battalion might not be enough to put down the fighting, not when any given stable could call upon almost as many 'Mechs. Nondi would back them up with the Seventeenth Arcturan shortly after the Thirty-second's arrival. In the meantime, Leutnant-General Van Buren could do what Nondi needed done, the thing about which Katrina was most adamant. Make an example of those responsible.

"A fire needs heat, fuel, and oxygen," Nondi said to herself. "Remove one component, and the others are harmless. That is what I will do. Send Gustav and the Thirty-second to smother the fuel source.

"To crush the forces hiding in the Black Hills."

Ashes Ashes
All fall down . . .

17

Star League Park, International Zone
Solaris City, Solaris VII
Freedom Theater, Lyran Alliance
19 August 3062

The Star League Park, a wide expanse of grounds in the International Zone, had once been a rare island of calm and beauty in an otherwise gray and oppressive cityscape. Filled with trees and flowering plants that thrived in terminally wet environments, the place was a riot of color year round, making the gardens one of the few Solaris tourist attractions not centered around the arenas. An extensive network of roofed walkways allowed access to all areas of the park in any weather, while covered cook-out grills and picnic tables were set up for those who wanted to spend the whole day in peaceful respose. No betting terminals here. No monuments to past Champions or favorite BattleMech designs. Just a place to restore body and soul.

But not anymore.

Michael Searcy walked his *Pillager* through the destruction left by the battle that had occurred here earlier that day. He passed shattered walkways, fire-gutted alcoves, and trees toppled or uprooted. He saw crushed flower beds, lawns torn up by the lumbering tread of

BattleMechs, and armor fragments glittering silver among the wet greenery. He came upon amputated 'Mech limbs and an odd assortment of blasted-off equipment, which marked the path of the running battle. Every so often he even encountered the corpse of a fallen BattleMech, the once-powerful machine now a monument to the violence that had claimed Solaris City. At least until the salvage crews arrived.

The battle had begun just south of the river in the Black Hills district, the Thirty-second Guard engaging a joint force of Starlight and Overlord Stables—Federated Suns and Lyran!—working together. The hard fighting had leveled two city blocks and killed both the Thirty-second Guard commander and his *Atlas*. With the loss of their commanding officer, the Lyrans had retreated south to the International Zone, a path that took them directly into the Star League Park. From the evidence, Michael counted no less than three rear-guard actions, all failed.

Why Overlord Stables had sided against the regular Alliance troops, Michael still didn't know. Had the Overlord 'Warriors defected? Had Karl returned with this force? With the discovery of each new 'Mech corpse, Michael dreaded the possibility that it might be Karl's *Cestus*.

Along with the story of this battle, Michael now understood why the Guard force that had attacked the Black Hills earlier today was smaller than predicted. No one doubted that the unit would be spoiling for Davion blood or that they didn't know that the Black Hills base was in Boreal Reach arena. From the moment news came of their landing, Michael had been expecting an attack by the full battalion.

Instead of coming at him directly, however, two Guard lances and armor support had first paraded through the Black Hills, laying waste to streets and property with no regard for the occupants. Or even whether the neighborhood might be a supporter of Katrina Steiner. Julian Nero had characterized the unit as a neutral force here to enforce martial law, but they weren't acting like it. Michael and his people had beat them back.

He tread far more carefully now, wary of the people

who still huddled under the roofed walks or wandered the grounds in shock at what they'd witnessed. A few, however, were snapping pictures, while others shot footage with holocams. News crews were also on the scene, probably arriving on the heels of the paramedics. The reporters had people climbing up onto fallen Battle-Mechs to pose while giving interviews, though Michael wondered what more there was to say amid the devastation.

He noticed the accusatory glares some of the civilians threw him. They seemed to know who he was, which was no surprise. Who wouldn't recognize Stormin' Michael Searcy after the way the media had hyped his involvement in the struggle? The hostile stares made him feel ashamed even though none of this was his fault.

Isn't it? Karl's voice whispered at the back of Michael's mind.

The swath of destruction continued to the southern edge of the park, where it broke through another thick stand of trees and continued into the International Zone's administrative district just beyond. Most of the ferrocrete buildings were still standing, though none had escaped unscathed. The Council Hall, however, was a pile of rubble, collapsed into a mess of brick and plaster. One fluted marble column still stood a lonely sentry, holding up a small piece of what had once been a marvelous marble and granite overhang. Michael waded into the ruin, then stopped short at the sight of the General Court building, half of which was piled in the street like some improbable snowdrift.

Half buried in the rubble, lying on its back, was Karl's *Cestus*.

An emptiness welled up in the pit of Michael's stomach. Though the comet-and-stars insignia of Starlight Stables was partially hidden by debris, the Mech's blue and silver color scheme was Starlight all the way. And on the lower right leg, half-covered by the spill of bricks, was the crest of Solaris VII—a torch held aloft in a 'Mech's hand. Karl, one of the few Solaran natives who'd worked his way up in the games, was the only Starlight 'Warrior who displayed that crest.

The upper half of the *Cestus* also protruded from the

spill, mangled almost beyond recognition. Armor had been breached in several places, and a mess of half-scorched myomer musculature hung from its right side. The right shoulder was similarly ruined, with a half-melted actuator visible through a large rent. The 'Mech's rounded cockpit crest had caved in over several places, and the ferroglass canopy itself had been punctured. From the looks of it, by light autocannon fire.

Approaching slowly, he thought about his last meeting with Karl, and how he hadn't even returned his friend's goodbye! He hadn't dreamed that it might be a final farewell, but what did that matter now? Standing over the *Cestus,* Michael got a look into the 'Mech's cockpit. Empty! A small hope blossomed that maybe Karl had gotten out alive, perhaps recovered by his own forces or taken prisoner.

Because he'd been expecting the whole battalion to attack, Michael had been forced to pull in his sentry 'Mechs to be ready for the assault. If not for that, he might have been alerted to Karl's return and been on hand to guard his friend's back. Whose call had that been, his or Drew Hasek-Davion's? Was Michael really calling the shots or was Karl right in saying he was little more than a puppet on a string?

Misting rain dropped a soft gray shroud over Solaris City, and tiny rivulets beaded down his cockpit canopy. Standing in the ruins, shaken by the sight of his one true friend's ruined 'Mech, Michael knew that Karl had been right about one thing for sure. This wasn't a game. Not anymore.

This was about as real as it could get.

The overhead florescents were dark. The only lighting in Michael's office came from the wall screen that switched between different channels at irregular intervals. He sat slumped in a chair, one hand rubbing at the side of his face and the other cradling a remote with his thumb poised over the channel-changer. A feather-touch blackened the screen, throwing the room into complete darkness for a split second before the next station came up.

In a way, it reminded him of his fight against Victor

Vandergriff in the Coliseum, but now it was bright snatches of holovid reports that periodically lit up the shadows. DARK. Then—Tanya Oshia of the Kobe Information Network rained down scathing indictments against Garrett for his headhunter tactics. The body count of Kobe MechWarriors fallen to the Smoke Jaguar renegade had mounted to eleven. "The intentional destruction of the Dragon Arch, the gateway to Kobe, is just one more casualty in the Clan warrior's pogrom against anything Combine-related, and—"

DARK. Then—". . . about what the point spread suggested would happen." The bookmaking channel. Clips of battle footage bought, borrowed or lifted from the regular news channels played out in silence as the hidden announcer continued to cover the betting. A scrolling tape at the bottom of the screen showed the payoffs on today's favorite wagers. "Tomorrow's favorites so far cover a new drive from Montenegro across the Solaris River and deep into Cathay, with four-to-one guaranteeing they reach the Jungle. Eight gets you three if a Kobe MechWarrior manages to put down Garrett, the *Smoking* Jaguar. Eight returning five if they kill him. Any Silesia-Black Hills match-up pays even money for now. If you plan to wager on a better tomorrow, the odds might give you an incredible return when considering that today we—"

Another feather-touch to the channel tab, and DARK. Then—". . . found Stormin' Michael Searcy at the site of this afternoon's defeat of the Thirty-second Lyran Guard." Mason Wells, the old handicapper himself, was framed against a shot of Michael's *Pillager* moving through the Star League Park. "The Lyran assault caused an estimated fourteen million D-Bills in damage to the Black Hills. The cost in lives lost is still being tallied. Searcy's *Pillager,* the same 'Mech used in the interrupted Coliseum match against Victor Vandergriff, shows remarkably little damage after such a brutal engagement, which only testifies—"

That Michael hadn't been there for the fighting! He stabbed at the feather-touch contact again, switching stations.

The next two channels, Solaris Broadcasting Corporation affiliates, were off the air. A test pattern ran in their place.

"There is no such thing as bad publicity," a voice said from somewhere behind Michael, startling him. "At least, not on Solaris VII."

Glancing back over his shoulder, Michael saw Drew Hasek-Davion silhouetted in the open office door. "I wasn't even there for the fight," he said, voice low. "Yet every station has segued from that fight to me, as if trying to tie me to it."

Drew moved further into the room. Against the flickering shades of gray as the picture changed on the wall screen, he looked washed out in his light-colored suit. "You are a leader, Michael. I've told you that from the beginning."

"You told me a lot of things," Michael said, leaving the rest of his thought hanging unspoken in the air: *Not all of them true.*

"I told you that Karl Edward was jealous and would betray you when the time was right. He knew two days ago that Starlight Stables was bringing the bulk of its warriors over from their west coast facility. He knew it when you and he argued here in this room, but he never told you."

Michael couldn't help glancing about suspiciously. Was the office bugged? Or had Garrett been outside the entire time, then gone to report back to his master? "I wouldn't listen," he said, defending Karl.

"You believe he would have told you that a combined force from Starlight and Overlord Stables meant to take control of the Black Hills? To take control away from you, dear boy?"

Away from *us*, Michael knew he meant to say. It would ruin the plans of one Drew Hasek-Davion. He brushed the contacts again.

DARK. Then—Julian Nero, full front to the camera and a picture playing behind him of a 'Mech battle. ". . . and two abridged companies of the Thirty-second Lyran Guards—two lances left to each—fought their way through the Black Hills' southern reach. Here you can see Aubry Larsen's *Penetrator* leading a company formed from Blackstar Stables and Federation Police

'Mechs in a flanking attempt to catch the Guard before they could reach the relative safety of Cathay."

An attempt Michael knew had failed, though the hard fighting cost four BattleMechs and one life from each side. And by all reports Michael had read, the Thirty-second lost another 'Mech and its pilot once they got inside Cathay.

Nero frowned as the battle footage froze to catch Aubry's *Penetrator* giving the coup de grâce on a fallen Lyran *Scarabus.* "Two Lyran MechWarriors died in that attempt to bring relief forces over to Silesia. Our field journalist met with Victor Vandergriff at Skye Tiger Mall, who had this to say."

The video cut to Skye Tiger Mall, panning over an assortment of partially salvaged BattleMechs. They had been arranged so that crests from Starlight, Blackstar, and even one from Gemini Stables could be seen. Black Hills stables, every one.

"We've held our own," Vandergriff's deep voice came from off-camera. "And with elements of the Thirty-second to aid us, we can hope to restore order and take the fight back to the Black Hills where it belongs."

Not where it *started,* Michael noted, but where it *belongs.* The camera opened up to show Victor's freshly armored *Banshee* standing over the salvage field of wrecked machines, his 'Mech showing the crests of Lynch Stables and the Skye Tigers and now also a small emblem of Eichenberry Stables as well. The shot blurred and swung right for a close-up of Victor Vandergriff. He wore a light blue—a *Steiner* blue—cooling uniform similar to Michael's own. Gone was the combat cooling vest, though Michael noticed that he cradled his bulky neurohelmet in the crook of one arm. The suit did not have a neurosensor cowl, then. Still the old stuff for poor Victor, though by the looks of it he was coming up in the world.

"I plan to make the Davionists in the Black Hills pay for those two lives and for all the others this conflict has cost us. Michael Searcy will answer for his actions, that I promise."

Julian Nero reclaimed the screen, looking pleased with himself. "Now a word from our sponsor, Earcandy

Music and Entertainment, bringing you the unbiased reports of the Solaris conflict."

The mute feature silenced the high-pressure sales pitch while Michael shook his head at the news. Of course, no one mentioned the swath of destruction the Thirty-second had cut through civilian neighborhoods of the Black Hills in their efforts to cross the city. And nothing about the Lyran-affiliated Overlord Stables becoming part of the opposition to the Thirty-second. Or about any fighting but that between Silesia and the Black Hills. Always, came back to Steiner versus Davion. Victor versus Michael.

"Lies," Michael said softly, answering all at once Vandergriff's bluff, Nero's dedication to unbiased reporting, and Hasek-Davion's earlier accusation that Karl had meant to betray him. "All lies."

Drew Hasek-Davion did not sound pleased with the assertion, catching the implied insult. "Really? Then why hasn't your *friend*"—his sneer turned the word itself into an accusation—"Karl Edward contacted you? As of this afternoon, the battered Starlight-Overlord force controlled the Solaris 'Mech bays at the spaceport. And the warehouses. That's been *your* goal over the last several days, hasn't it?"

Michael straightened up angrily. "You mean *your* goal. You are very well informed, Drew. So you tell me, how did the Thirty-second know to skirt my defenses and hit the incoming Starlight-Overlord force? Karl apparently wasn't the only person who knew they were inbound."

Drew had been caught off guard, but he seemed to coil back into himself, a serpent readying to strike. "Going against that battalion would have accomplished nothing we couldn't gain by diverting its attention elsewhere. And as inexperienced as they are, you still might have been killed. I can't have you dying in a meaningless battle. No, Michael, that wouldn't play well at all."

"I'm a MechWarrior," Michael said hotly. "That's the risk I take every time I fight for you." He took a breath trying to calm himself down. "Or at least it was. I'm through with this conflict."

Drew barked one quick laugh, brutal and mirthless.

"You don't understand—never truly have. You don't have to do anything." He shrugged. "Maybe I'll have another warrior parade around in your *Pillager,* just to keep up appearances. But do you honestly think you can just walk away? Disappear? I've made you the Federated Suns favorite. A Davionist hero, though not necessarily a Davion supporter. You're an icon, Michael. The people will not forget." He jabbed his walking stick in the direction of the wall screen. "*They* won't let the people forget.

"Not," he said with quiet menace, "unless they have something better to push in front of the masses."

Drew's eyes narrowed slightly. "You are no simple MechWarrior. Those 'Warriors are out in the streets, walking patrols or fighting our enemies. You are hiding in a dark room, my boy. What was the charge against you on New Canton? Pusillanimous conduct? If you thought your commander betrayed you with his testimony, what do you think the press would do if such a story broke here and now?"

Michael felt as though the world was slipping away under his feet. Since coming to Solaris he had done everything possible to bury his past, but apparently not enough. If the vidcasters ever got hold of *that* story, any appearance of impropriety would quickly substitute for reality. It would be all over at that point. Michael would never be the Champion. Not even a contender after that. But . . .

"That would be cutting your own throat as well."

The innocent expression appeared out of place on Drew's face. "How often have you heard my name mentioned in vids over the last few days?"

Not very, Michael thought. And now he saw Drew's hand in the way the press had become preoccupied with Stormin' Michael Searcy. It was a way for him to distance himself. Not enough to rob Hasek-Davion or Blackstar of a share in any victory, but carefully applied insurance against tragedy. Michael took Drew's meaning all too well this time. In the blink of an eye, his stable master could sever all his ties with Michael and leave him to sink on his own.

Smiling, Drew reached down to pat Michael on the

shoulder. "Don't worry, Michael. All a MechWarrior can do out there is win, lose, or die. Remember when you asked me if I wanted a pet 'Warrior? Well, now you know I don't. What I want is a Champion!"

Again he pointed at the wall screen with his walking stick. "The Champion will be named by the media, and it will be you. No one will be able to challenge that, so long as we—you and I—work together.

"And when you kill Victor Vandergriff, who will be left to challenge?"

18

Skye Tiger Mall, Silesia
Solaris City, Solaris VII
Freedom Theater, Lyran Alliance
21 August 3062

Try as he might, Victor Vandergriff couldn't deny it. The *Banshee* looked a thing of beauty, especially compared to its ignoble origins. Gone was the Frankenstein quality of the mix-and-match weapons systems, where weapon casings and armor did not exactly blend together. Gone were the hastily installed armor panels to patch holes where weapons had been yanked out to save weight for the Luxor jump jets. Gone was the coat of dark paint slapped over the 'Mech to make it presentable enough to go before the cameras.

The Skye Tiger techs had worked on his 'Mech to make it deserving of the Lyran favorite. The ill-fitting paneling had been cut away and molded armor fitted into its place, streamlining the *Banshee's* blocky torso. They'd adjusted the LBX-class autocannon so that it no longer looked like it had been grafted on as an afterthought. They'd moved one of the PPCs into the left arm, giving the *Banshee* an extended left-side range of motion with its weapons. And then they'd painted the whole machine metallic blue with gold highlights. The

ferroglass canopy was backlit with a subdued blue lighting, as were the inside of both PPC barrels. The missile
ports of the SRM four-pack riding the right shoulder,
however, shone with a harsh red illumination. It would
be worthless once battle began and missile exhaust covered the ports in soot, but until then it gave the *Banshee*
a lethal appearance.

From the ground Victor studied the 'Mech with a critical eye. Jerry Stroud waited nearby with Maria Utley,
the Skye Tigers' chief tech who'd overseen the work on
the *Banshee.* A small part of Victor still detested the
BattleMech for its antique design. Although customized
and beautified, the machine was still not the same
cutting-edge caliber generally assigned to top contenders. But it was his, and one of the best machines he'd
ever owned in his long if undistinguished career.

"It's perfect," he said to Maria. "Don't change a
thing."

She nodded and smiled. That was what she wanted to
hear, not for the praise but because she could now turn
to other work still waiting to be done. After a quick
handshake, she went off quickly to supervise another
project.

"You'll like this even more," Stroud said, coming up
alongside Victor. "Today, Victor. You'll fight him
today." There was no need to identify the "him."

"Searcy?" The name came out a curse. "He's coming
to Silesia?"

Four frustrating days Victor had waited for the
chance, damning the necessity that kept him chained to
the Lyran sector while Michael Searcy concentrated on
the International Zone. He'd watched the trivid and
studied the newsfaxes as his enemy continued to dominate the reports and claim the headlines. The media dar-
ling, still. Even in Silesia it was Searcy's actions that
were the top news, leaving Victor the role of struggling
opponent in his own brief interviews.

"You'll go to him," Stroud went on. "Now that the
Thirty-second Lyran Guard is here, we can hold our own
if Cathay or Montenegro pushes at us. There are reports
that Overlord Stables may be cooperating with Starlight,
but I'm not sure that's been well-received by the Black

Hills types. The hard-line FedRats don't trust Overlord and are holding their western border against their approach."

"That's where Searcy will be," Victor said, "facing off with the International Zone. Even if I have no problem crossing Cathay, I'll have to fight to get through the Black Hills. That's hostile territory all the way." Not that Victor was unwilling to make it happen. Already he was planning the mission into enemy territory. "If we can use the flooded tunnels beneath Cathay—"

"No need," Stroud interrupted. "Searcy will be at the southern edge of the Black Hills, easily accessible. You can skirt south of Cathay, through the Brahma Slums. Then you'll find him on the grounds of the Running Fox Country Club."

Victor was stunned. "You arranged this?"

"Not exactly. Searcy will be heading out to Green Mansion today to guard Hasek-Davion's estate, and the news crews will shoot some footage of him in the *Pillager*. You'll enter the Davion sector by the way of the country club, which is only minutes from Green Mansion. Searcy will be the closest 'Mech. He'll have to respond, with news crews in tow." Stroud nodded in satisfaction. "My people intercepted a wireless call from Hasek-Davion to his estate. Because of the location of the call, it bounced off a hilltop repeater controlled by Alliance patriots."

"Convenient."

"Not convenient. Planned. Hasek-Davion knew I'd intercept that call. That's why he made it where he did. He wants you two in a rematch. It's as simple as that."

"And Trevor approves." It was not meant to be a question. Trevor Lynch, safe outside the city, was doing little more than echo Jerry Stroud and other Lyran stable leaders who were holding the line in Silesia.

"Actually, he doesn't," Stroud admitted. "Lynch heard through the Lyran Guard that more troops are on the way. Direct orders from Nondi Steiner herself. He suggested we button up tight and wait for the military, let them shut down any resistance to the Alliance government and take control of Silesia."

No! That wasn't the way this would end. Victor had

come too far, through five days of the Grand Tournament and now six more of open warfare in the streets of Solaris City, to sit back while some wet-behind-the-ears army unit claimed headlines that were rightfully his. Or to let some officer use martial law to take control of the Game World—to make himself *Champion*. Victor would let nothing keep him away from Searcy.

"You said Trevor *suggested* we wait."

"That's right, should. We agreed to let you decide." Stroud's grin was humorless, almost predatory. "You got us where we are today, after all."

"We go after Searcy," Victor said.

"That's what I thought you'd say. I'll give you a lance of Sky Tigers as an escort to the Black Hills. They can field any friends Searcy may have in tow." Stroud stared at Victor levelly. "Then it's up to you."

Victor nodded. No arena walls to hem the battle in or judges to save his enemy. Today he and Stormin' Michael Searcy would meet again.

And this time Stormin' Michael Searcy would die.

With determined stride, Megan Church headed straight for the main entrance of Jerry Stroud's mansion. She'd tailed him here from Skye Tiger Mall, which his stable was using as a base of operations separate from the one in the Coliseum. It had been slow getting here because of the need to avoid areas of the Lyran sector still deemed unsafe. She also had to go easy with the tail, not race ahead in anticipation. Cautious, she had to be cautious. Even when time didn't allow for it.

Especially then.

She'd parked her stolen truck a block over on Inverness Avenue and changed into the black and gold paramilitary uniform of Hollis Security. Like most Silesian stables and other large businesses, Stroud had hired a few detachments of Hollis guards to supplement his own security at the Mall and to act as couriers running face-to-face errands across the sector. An observer might assume that the metal briefcase handcuffed to her wrist contained important documents—reports on the stable's military readiness or on the latest assault by the Black Hills.

In truth, however, it contained the tools and explosives for the afternoon's work.

Megan didn't like it. Not one bit. For one thing, it was all happening on too short notice. In the early hours of the morning she'd been called to an emergency meeting in a deserted office building near Boreal Reach. To get there from the relative safety of Silesia, she'd had to cross Cathay and then make her way through the Black Hills, no routine commute. When she arrived, it was just the two of them, Megan and the demon of the Black Hills. No guards or surveillance—none that she could detect anyway. Some things were better kept between the two of them, he'd said. The set-up was almost too good to be true. If only she'd had some advance notice . . .

But she hadn't. And no time to improvise either. Her orders were simple. "The situation has changed in the last forty-eight hours, with the arrival of the Lyran Guard battalion on Solaris," he told her. "There's also some doubt about Michael Searcy's willingness to cooperate. The plans have to go forward more quickly than anticipated." Then came that smug smile that spoke of confidence in Megan's abilities but also the knowledge that she was forced to obey him. "I want you to take a more direct hand in events."

Damn him! It wasn't that she minded getting dirty on an assignment, not since she was sixteen and working as a courier between the Triads. Money helped wash the filth off afterward, she'd discovered. But this was a bit extreme. Any other time and she would have refused, but the pressures mounting on her left her no choice.

Her nerves stretched taut, she approached the guard and flashed the Hollis Security identification. "I'm expected," she said tersely, and was waved through a side gate that the guard buzzed open. If someone were watching, that would have seemed way too easy, she thought. She should have been questioned, at least briefly. And shouldn't the guard have called up to the mansion and sent Megan there with an escort?

She could have come over the wall, but that would have meant a night-time penetration, and Hasek-Davion had been firm that it had to be today. This very afternoon. And she had to be off the grounds by sixteen-hundred hours. She had only forty minutes till then, having lost time in the trip from Skye Tiger Mall to Stroud's estate. A daytime intrusion risked giving her away, and the rushed nature of the job risked a mistake that could cost a life, her own included. But if she was under observation, not to follow through meant also risking the fragile relationship she'd built with Hasek-Davion. Which she'd finally gotten so close to where she wanted it.

He had even promised to get her off Solaris after this. "The world won't be safe for me," she told him, hoping to beg off the job. "Even for someone who knows when to cheer for Katrina or Prince Victor. Jerry Stroud is too important, too well-connected."

"He's also vulnerable, my dear. Now more than ever." Hasek-Davion would brook no argument. "You said it could be done."

"It can be. But then what do I do? Solaris VII is all I've ever known."

If one thing was certain about Drew Hasek-Davion, it was that he took care of his own—and the further you slipped under his control, the more valuable a possession you became. "I promise you that will not be a problem. When we're done here, I can find work for you on New Syrtis, Robinson, even New Avalon."

Megan recognized all three as March capitals, especially the last, which was the seat of power for the entire Federated Suns. She couldn't help but wonder if it was a coincidence that the one he'd named first was the capital of the Capellan March, long-time political bastion of the Haseks?

"I'd rather stay in Lyran space."

"I told you before, my dear. Don't let it get personal." She wouldn't.

Stroud's Deuceman Blitz-Zweisitzer, a big car with a powerful engine more suited to a race track than city streets, was parked in a carport to the rear of the mansion. No fancy chauffeured hovercar for Jerry Stroud. He wanted control of his own fate, even when driving.

Megan was just glad the vehicle's engine was internal combustion; messing with a fusion engine was a lot more dicey. She snapped off the handcuffs with a fast-release catch and opened the briefcase. This part of the operation was actually the easiest, provided no one walked in on her.

She slid under the rear end of the car, and in a matter of seconds planted a small brick of petraglycerine into a space between the lightly armored fuel tank and the driver's-side frame. Then she pushed a detonator into the soft material, careful that the wire ends were still wrapped in their protective caps.

This wasn't some holovid-adventure method of wiring an explosive to the ignition system—start the car and *boom*. That would have required her to get under the hood or inside the car. Even a simple space sensor would be hard to defeat once her body mass broke the plane of the hood or got past the car doors.

She used a small but powerful drill with a carbide tip to make a small hole in the left-side exhaust pipe. Then she glued a sensor about the size of a big bottle cap over the hole with Bond-it (a thousand and one uses). A few more adjustments and everything was ready. A single spark would trip a contact when the pressure in the exhaust system indicated a running engine. The contact would fire one heavy spark, and that would be enough. Megan carefully stripped the wire ends of their caps and attached them to the sensor's small terminals. Her work done, she slid out from under the rear of the car, got to her feet and dusted off her uniform.

Before she left, Megan stooped back down to check her handiwork, which looked like a small, irregular bump on the exhaust. The bomb's trigger would be easy enough to find if someone knew where to look. Otherwise, only a careful sweep of the car would give it away. That would take time.

If Hasek-Davion's deadline was any indication, time was the one thing Jerry Stroud would not have.

A sense of dread shadowed Megan as she walked around to the front of the mansion, leaving the live bomb behind her. It was all part of the job, she kept telling herself. Another day at the office. Yeah, sure.

Just like she'd told herself that Hasek-Davion and Stroud played their games of dominance far over her head. It didn't matter who came out on top, so long as she could keep making a living with a mostly clear conscience. Heading back to the street, briefcase swinging lightly at her side, Megan knew she'd crossed the line, that she'd sold another piece of herself here at Jerry Stroud's mansion.

And that another debt would be called due. Soon.

"Got a *Rakshasa* to the west and a *Dragon Fire* to the east. They're tearing me apart here!"

"Someone back up Blue Five before . . ." Silence. "Blake's blood! Never mind. Pull in. Close that hole."

Victor Vandergriff stared out his canopy at the lush grounds of the Black Hills' Running Fox Country Club, clenching his teeth so hard his jaws hurt. The voices on the commline were coming from the battle being fought back in Silesia. The signals were faint, interspersed with static from bouncing up into the Black Hills, but it sounded like the Thirty-second Guard was being hammered by a strike staged from the Black Hills that aimed to roll right over Skye Tiger Estate. The Guard was trying to evacuate Jerry Stroud, though in the confusion no one knew if he was already hell-bent for the more secure Skye Tiger Mall or was still trapped inside his walled estate.

"Watch it, sir!" Some overlapping chatter bled together into a cacophony of noise and a few recognized words, then, "The lieutenant's out. Clean ejection."

"Tiger One to Vandergriff." Tiger One was the lead element of the lance that had escorted Victor to the southern edge of the Black Hills. "They're getting slaughtered. Do we return?"

"We do not," Victor said with authority.

This was more important.

Leaving his escort behind and well out of sight, Victor had gone alone into the country club. He would share this moment with no one. Cutting his *Banshee* across five fairways of the eighteen-hole golf course, he now stood on the first green within sight of the opulent clubhouse. News teams began arriving almost at once, setting up in the shadow of the clubhouse.

He saw no sign of Michael Searcy, but here he would wait. If anyone was going to save the Thirty-second, it would have to be reinforcements out of the Coliseum or maybe Skye Tiger Mall. Even if Victor and his escort left the Black Hills at a full run, they could never hope to get back to Silesia in time to turn the tide of battle. For now, he listened and waited.

Nervous sweat trickled off his brow. Soon heat build-up in the *Banshee*'s cockpit would have him sweating rivers, but he was counting on his new cooling suit to do its job. This was it—the fight he'd been denied six days prior. The one that would settle the question of Champion or vanquished. Vandergriff or Searcy. Steiner or Davion. Victor already knew the answer, but he still had to prove it to the rest of Solaris—and by remote video feed to the rest of the Inner Sphere. Through his canopy he could see camera crews setting up on the far side of the first tee. Searcy could not be far behind.

"Blue Seven. I've jumped into the estate courtyard. It's a mess—the Sworders have been here already. We've got a downed *Enfield* with Skye Tiger colors. I can see what looks like it used to be a garage with the burning remains of one . . . two cars. People are running from the mansion toward the back of the estate, waving at me and pointing back at the house. What the—they're diving out of windows now, even from the second floor."

Victor reached for his communications panel, ready to switch his transmitter over from the private channel he shared with his escort to that of the Lyran Guard frequency. He knew what was about to happen in that fight, even if the green 'Warrior did not. But before he could warn Blue Seven, Victor's own sensors suddenly warned him of a threat approaching on the left flank.

It was a BattleMech, and he was sure it couldn't be anyone but Searcy at the controls. He had no solid reading on it yet, but by turning the *Banshee*'s head, he could see something large pushing its way through a thick stand of trees in the bend of the fourth fairway. One tall pine fell over, crashing down as other boles stripped away its branches with rifle-shot cracks. In the gap Victor saw a flash of gray armor. It still wasn't enough for his computer to identify, but to his practiced eye it looked like a small 'Mech, one smaller than a *Pillager*.

He wrote that off to a trick of the terrain, the tall pines dwarfing Searcy's big 'Mech.

"By the Archon!" It was the voice of Blue Seven again, but Victor had no time to warn him of the 'Mech coming at him *through* the mansion. The one the running and pointing people had also tried to warn him about.

"A Blackstar *Pillager* just gutted the mansion." The Lyran Guard 'Warrior's voice bordered on panic. "Taking damage. I'm trying—ejecting!"

Victor had been turning his *Banshee* to face the approaching 'Mech, about to switch off the chatter from the battle in Silesia. He nearly wrenched his neck muscles twisting about to look at the comm panel. A *Pillager*? Blackstar owned only one of those.

It belonged to the stable's premier 'Warrior.

"Searcy!" he shouted, alone in his cockpit. "Impossible! You can't be in Silesia. You're out here!" How else could Victor explain that 'Mech hiding just within the dense stand of trees. Refusing to believe the report, he throttled into a walk, moving against the gunshy enemy.

Shy no longer. A forty-ton *Watchman,* one of the lightest of medium-class BattleMechs, it took to the air on its jump jets, rocketing up and right to keep its distance from Victor's *Banshee.* At the apex of its jump, its large laser tore a molten scar across the *Banshee's* chest. Though not more than a scratch, the hit stung Victor's pride.

Now he understood. This was all a set-up. Searcy hadn't been sent to guard Hasek-Davion's estate today! Stroud had intercepted the wireless call, but not because he wanted to arrange a rematch between the Davion favorite and Victor. If anything, it was a way to pull Victor out of Silesia so that Searcy could attack Stroud's estate. A way to humiliate Victor by sending an inferior 'Mech to play games with him while his enemy remained solidly out of reach.

Rage warred with chagrin. Did they expect him to chase the faster *Watchman* around the golf course, looking every bit the frustrated Lyran? Or did they hope he'd ignore the FedRat 'Mech and make for Silesia?

Either way it was a losing proposition, with the local media on hand to record him waiting here like a stooge while Searcy grabbed more headlines.

Not that Victor could let the *Watchman* off without at least an attempt at returning fire. Dropping his targeting reticle over the stand of trees where he'd seen the Fed-Rat land, Victor tightened up on his two main triggers. Azure whips of manmade lightning streaked out from the *Banshee* toward the wood. One energy discharge buried itself in the underbrush, setting it on fire. The other might have scored, but the *Watchman*'s 'Warrior obviously had no intention of committing suicide by tangling with an assault machine like the *Banshee*. The other 'Mech faded back through the woods, coming out the other side in a run that quickly separated the two BattleMechs.

His fury far from spent, Victor slid his cross hairs down into the trees and among the denser brush. Two more PPC discharges flared, bursting boles and scarring the ground as it touched off scattered fires. He walked down the length of the first fairway, the *Banshee*'s enormous metal feet ripping up the manicured lawns as its energy weapons ate again and again into the surrounding stands of trees. Sweat beaded and ran freely down his face, soaking into his cooling suit as the temperature in the cockpit spiked upward. Victor slapped at the shutdown override every few seconds to keep the fusion reactor online and pouring more energy through his PPCs at the terrain around him. Soon a dozen fires raged over the Running Fox course, darkening the skies as they consumed a healthy part of the grounds.

By the time Victor reached the clubhouse, the video crews were scrambling for the parking lot, though several cameramen were still shooting as they ran. Victor didn't care. He ignored them just as he ignored his *Banshee*'s protesting systems. He simply hit the override again and hoped the crews had a good camera angle as he slowly blasted the clubhouse to a pile of smoking debris. From there he could work over any remaining vehicles in the parking lot. And then it was on to Green

Mansion before a Federated Suns patrol offered any serious threat.

He'd give that treacherous Davion-dog something to come home to.

19

The activity level under Boreal Reach had stepped up several notches toward frantic since the previous evening's raid against Silesia. The large bays smelled of acrid hot metalwork and the sweat of technicians working around the clock to keep machines fit for combat. Any MechWarriors present were either sleeping, eating, or suiting up for a new excursion. Not an hour went by that BattleMechs weren't on the move, their footfalls shaking the walls as they patrolled the tunnels or engaged the enemy in battle on to the streets above.

They didn't have far to go this morning. A few patrols guarded the western border, the Black Hills combined militia still uncertain of the Starlight-Overlord force that held the spaceport and remained under communications blackout. Most 'Mechs were shifted to the nearby eastern edge of the sector, where Silesia pressed hard in a series of attacks being led by Victor Vandergriff. The fighting there was savage. Reinforced by the Thirty-second Lyran Guard, the Silesians were demonstrating a fanatical drive after learning of the destruction of Skye

Tiger Estate and that Jerry Stroud was missing, pre-
sumed dead. Cathay was no longer much of an obstacle
between the two sectors. The Capellans were busy with
their own internal fighting and ignored the Lyran and
Federated Sun forces passing through so long as their
battles occurred outside Cathay's borders.

So far the flood of forces was fairly one-sided, and the
slums hugging the northeast border of the Black Hills
looked like the ruins of an old battle-torn city. Silesian
'Warriors had crossed in staggered waves during the
night, fighting to clear a free-fire zone from the Solaris
River down to the Danning Street greenbelt—a swath
of destruction half a kilometer deep and over two kilometers in length. The rubble and ruins now choked the
largest arena ever seen in Solaris VII, one under the
watchful (remote) cameras of ever major media concern
on the Game World. The battles raged violently for a
time, no-holds-barred brawling that wasted machines
and MechWarriors, until both sides were forced to retreat for repairs and whatever further reinforcements
might be scraped together.

Michael had spent a difficult night, experiencing the
helplessness of being dispossessed for the first time in
three years. Drew had made good on that much of his
threat; he'd given Michael's *Pillager* to Aubry Larsen
for its appearance the evening prior against Skye Tigers
Estate. Michael had already resolved to take action, no
matter what it cost to him, but was forced to wait anxiously for technicians to repair his 'Mech. From all reports, the fighting was sporadic but savage.

The feeling of helplessness made him begin to wonder
exactly when he'd begun to buy in to the illusion spun
by Drew Hasek-Davion. When had he begun to believe
that he and the media creation of *Stormin'* Michael
Searcy were one and the same? When had he begun to
believe that he was in control of his life and could seize
an imagined destiny from the cockpit of his 'Mech? Michael had wanted so desperately to reclaim his honor
after New Canton that he'd persuaded himself that all
he needed do was prove his talent. Illusions of victory
enticed him forward, but it was all a mirage of his own
creation.

Karl's departure and Drew Hasek-Davion's blatant manipulations had shattered those illusions. Now Michael's eyes were wide open, perhaps for the first time since setting foot on the Game World. Now he'd changed course, deciding that from now on he would turn his talent to ending the terrible violence that gripped Solaris City instead of his own best interests. It had nothing to do with fighting in the games, nothing to do with achieving his own ends. He just wanted to help put a stop to the madness.

The underground hangar Michael had entered held four BattleMechs racked in separate maintenance bays. One was being rendered down for parts, and technicians were swarming over two others in anticipation of the next battle. Only Michael's *Pillager* stood ready for combat, eleven meters of lethal design freshly armored and ready to walk. Even under the stress of the last twelve hours, someone had found time to touch up the paint and add a few Federated Suns crest. The sword-in-sunburst design covered the entire torso, the blade extending up to the 'Mech's head and reaching its point in the titan's armored brow. Nice work for a machine that was supposed to remain out of combat except for a few special appearances.

Too bad Michael intended to ruin that paint job today.

Wearing coveralls like those of the techs and astechs working in the bay, he went unnoticed until he stepped onto the gantry lift that would take him up to the cockpit. He was six meters above the floor when someone called out to him. It was an engineer looking up with a quizzical expression.

"Take about four minutes, sir," Michael yelled back as if answering a question. The man was still watching when Michael slipped through the hatch and dogged it shut behind him.

He moved quickly, knowing he was on a timer. No telling if Drew Hasek-Davion had someone watching the *Pillager* or looking for Michael. Regardless, the news would eventually break. Michael stripped down to the cooling suit he'd worn under the coveralls. Pulling up the cowl on his suit, he settled the neuroreceptors firmly against his forehead, temples, and at the base of his skull. Then he climbed into the command couch, strapped into the five-point safety harness, and plugged his coolant and command lines into the appropriate sockets built into his combat suit. The last thing was to strap on the light-impact helmet for protection.

The power-up sequence proceeded with the speed of familiarity. Michael shivered when the coolant instantly began to lower his body temperature, though he would be glad of that soon enough. As the Vlar fusion power plant thrummed to life in the *Pillager*'s chest, he sped through the checks of weapons and subsystems. Finally, he initialized the computer to accept piloting commands and to process the signals the neuroreceptors would feed into the gyroscopic stabilizer.

He had personally reinstalled his old security system during the night, careful to stay out of sight of anyone who might report back to Hasek-Davion. So when he identified himself as "Michael Searcy," the computer accepted his voice print.

"Initiate cross check," it prompted for the secret code phrase known only to him.

The security code caught in his throat, the words reminding him of too many past events all at once. The media circus of a trial that had followed New Canton. His 'Mech Talk interview opposite Jarman Bauer and the later press conference on Viewpoint. His last conversation with Drew Hasek-Davion.

"It's not whether you win or lose, it's who reports the game," he said softly, hating the truth in those words. Because no matter that his motives might be selfless this time, his plans still necessitated use of the media. On Solaris VII, one always had to count them into the order of battle.

Except there was never any telling on which side the media would enter.

"Again. We have unconfirmed reports that Michael Searcy has terminated his contract with Blackstar Stables, citing irreconcilable differences with management. Discreet sources claim that Searcy has taken to the streets of Solaris City in his *Pillager*. Stable owner Drew

Hasek-Davion has been unavailable for comment. At this time we can only wonder—"

In the offices he had commandeered near Boreal Reach, Drew snapped off the holovid, erasing Adam Kristof's visage from the screen and terminating the infuriating report. What game did Searcy think he was playing? It was one hell of a way for his star MechWarrior to give his notice. And now he was capitalizing on the supposed strained relations Drew had already hinted at in the media. Hints Drew had set in place in case he found it expedient to sever ties with Michael—not the other way around!

Michael counted on his celebrity status giving him free rein in the Black Hills, protecting him from any attempt to use the combined militia against the wayward 'Warrior until further plans could be made public. And there would be more news in the making, of that Drew had no doubt.

Drew only briefly debated calling in to Boreal Reach before deciding not to waste the effort. There was no reason to doubt the rest of Kristof's report. Michael was already gone, taking the *Pillager* as he set about his own plans. He had probably called in the news of his leave-taking, preempting any attempt by Drew to turn the defection to his own advantage. Now Drew had to play catch-up. It was not a position he relished, and he vowed to make Michael pay for it with interest.

"I should have had him killed yesterday," he complained aloud, snatching up his wireless and speed-dialing the communications room of Green Mansion. Killed him and dumped the body among the ruins of Skye Tigers Estate. A hero's death would read better than a defection any day.

When his communications controller answered, Drew ordered that his call be patched through the equipment. The station could reach anywhere in Solaris City and, in fact, over most of the continent of Grayland. Searcy couldn't hide. All he could do was refuse to answer. Drew delivered the frequency he knew Michael Searcy and Karl Edward used to reserve for their private use. It might be enough to catch Michael's attention and perhaps give Drew a chance to further poison the friendship between him and Karl. Always thinking two steps ahead, that was the way Drew did things.

"Michael, where do you think you're going, dear boy?"

The light hiss of static filled his ear for a moment, then he heard Michael say, "Didn't waste any time, did you? The story broke, what, two minutes ago?"

Drew's voice turned hard. "I asked you a question."

"What am I doing? I'm going to put an end to this madness. One way or another."

An end to the fighting was the one thing Drew did *not* want. Too many opportunities remained to be exploited for the situation to come to a premature end. He needed confirmation that Stroud was dead and that the Skye Tigers were also only a memory. Then *he* would bring things back under control, as spokesman for the SSOA, of course, but the savior of Solaris nonetheless. He would never allow Michael Searcy to interfere with those plans.

Time, then, to start working on appearances.

"You're going into Silesia. Michael, I told you to stay out of there. You've already brought enough down on us in the last week, haven't you?"

"Not bad," Michael congratulated him. "I'm sure you're recording the conversation, and it will play well for the media and to the authorities when they finally retake control of Solaris VII. Providing I never get the chance to tell my side, that is."

"No one will believe it, not with your past. Think before you do this, Michael. About what you risk." Drew could do plenty of damage to Michael if he tried to stand in Drew's way.

"There's nothing you can do to me that I haven't survived before. And if I win, it won't matter near as much. Appearances will out. You taught me that."

"It will matter," Drew snarled. "I'll make certain it matters. You won't enjoy any victory for long."

"Long enough. And if it means that every day for the rest of your life you'll have to remember that I beat you, that will be victory enough. One you can't spin for the media."

Drew stabbed a thick finger at the Disconnect button,

breaking the connection. He was almost on the verge of losing his temper, but he wouldn't allow it. Getting angry would serve no one but Michael. Cold calculation, that was Drew's strength. If Michael wanted to play at the bigger games, then Drew would teach him a few final lessons on who truly ruled the Game World. A single MechWarrior couldn't hope to compete, not in Drew's arena. And as he began reviewing his various insurance plans, his spirits buoyed again. The worst that could happen was a break-even proposition.

Especially when he could call in a player in Michael's own league. Warrior to warrior, then. Drew would find a way to reclaim some of the prestige the wayward gladiator had carried off with him.

On its backward-canted legs, the *Maelstrom* stalked forward with a hunching step like some giant bird of prey. There any resemblance to a creature of nature stopped. The right-arm PPC spat a lethal stream of energies that missed wide, blasting a large piece of ferrocrete railing from the Founder's Bridge. A large laser on the 'Mech's lower left arm lanced out with scarlet destruction to dig up the ground where Garrett's *Warhawk* had stood not a second before.

Running his OmniMech at sixty-five kilometers per hour, Garrett raced forward in an oblique attack to close with the thick-bodied *Maelstrom*. He speared the 'Mech with cross hairs far more accurate than any he'd seen for some time, and the twin PPC system mounted on his left arm flayed two azure whips into the *Maelstrom*. One finished off the armor protecting an arm, and the other cored into the internal supports of the right side.

Though almost even up on armor, the *Maelstrom* was seriously outgunned by the Clan-designed *Warhawk*. Its only advantage was a superior movement curve. But the Kobe MechWarrior at its controls misjudged the approach, throttling into a backward walk too late to prevent Garrett from bringing his large pulse lasers into range. Sapphire needles darted out in a flurry of bright energy, the first pulses eating into the armor over the *Maelstrom*'s chest and allowing the small cloud of misted metal to dissipate before the next darts chewed deeper.

The BattleMech shuddered violently, a sure telltale of gyro damage, but the pilot kept it on its feet.

Late, the *Maelstrom* staggered back into the cover of a ruined building once belonging to a Virtual World franchise. The gutted shell provided cover for the 'Mech, and Garrett immediately backed off. Already fighting a power spike in his fusion reactor that shot his cockpit temperatures up several blistering degrees, he returned to the end of the Founder's Bridge rather than charge into a possible trap. It wouldn't be the first attempt by Combine-affiliated stables, for all their talk of higher moral standards, to lure him into an ambush sprung by hidden 'Mechs.

Of course, the next one to succeed would be the first.

The Ghost Jaguar. That's what they were calling him lately. An avenging spirit for his Clan. Unstoppable. Some of this world's play-warriors had complained that he might have a sensor-jamming device. No truth to that, though his survival quotient might suggest it. Since fighting his way free of Ishiyama the afternoon of Day Five, Garrett had never returned from a foray into Kobe with critical damage worse than a wounded actuator. Well, once. That afternoon when Karl Edward caught him off guard, knocking Garrett unconscious for the first time in his life. He'd had a rough time of it on his next duel in which an *Avatar* opened him up from shoulder to hip, burning away engine shielding and nearly crippling his gyro. If the DeLon Stables 'Warrior hadn't been over-eager in pressing the advantage . . .

A burst of static echoed inside his neurohelmet. Then, he heard, "Garrett, this is Hasek-Davion. You are to return to the Black Hills at once."

The master calls, so he was to obey like a trained surtax? The *Maelstrom* hadn't reappeared, which surely meant Garrett had given a more crippling blow than he'd taken. The Jaguar did not abandon its kill. "Neg. I am not finished here."

"You will be, Garrett, if Michael Searcy has his way."

Searcy? What did the Blackstar champion have to do with his personal war? Keeping on eye on the hunkered-down *Maelstrom,* Garrett pulled back another fifty meters to the partial shelter of a smashed security post. "Explain."

"He defected, Garrett. He abandoned Blackstar. My guess is that he will try to join Karl Edward and the Starlight forces that are holding at the spaceport. Your *Mas*—your *Warhawk* is faster. You can intercept him." A pause. "You once asked for my permission to challenge Michael. Well, now you have more than that. I give you my full support. You will have everything you desire for your resurrected Clan here on Solaris VII."

The scent of blood from the wounded *Maelstrom* almost made Garrett refuse. A warrior fought for himself first; the last few days had reinforced that as he reveled in bringing down one Kobe MechWarrior after another. But now that Searcy's inviolate protection had been removed, Garrett could bring him down and perhaps Karl Edward as well. The opportunity was too great to be refused.

The smoke jaguar *might* abandon a kill for worthier prey.

One step backward. Then another. With each meter, his hunger for the *Maelstrom* receded. There would always be Combine warriors to hunt. But imagine the glory of bringing down a Game World icon, of taking his place as the premier Blackstar fighter. What wouldn't be within his reach then? In his mind Garrett saw a stable composed of his former brethren, all prepared to beat the Inner Sphere at its own game. Nothing could be more glorious.

Already, Garrett was adding both Michael Searcy and Karl Edward to his list of kills. The media had gotten that much right at least; he was unstoppable.

Garrett would simply be proving it again.

"What do you mean, you don't know where Vandergriff is? We're supposed to have a field man on him twenty-four seven. Find him! And double-check for sightings of a *Pillager*."

Julian Nero punched the Disconnect and threw the wireless at his assistant, then rocked back in his well-padded black cloth chair. Around him the studio's secondary news station bustled with activity, while he ruled

Silesia's news empire from his own little domain. Several news anchors threw him questioning looks; one shot him a hard glance, jealousy mixing with curiosity. Julian stared them down. They all wanted to know what he had working. Wanted to ask him for some extra material they could weave into their own reports and commentaries. During his thirty-minute respite, however, no one dared interrupt him, and he could try to reach his decision.

Was today *the* day?

Events were coming to a head. The landing of the Thirty-second Lyran Guard and subsequent arrival of a joint force from Starlight and Overlord promised that. There was the free-fire zone Vandergriff had cleared along the eastern border of the Black Hills and also Michael Searcy's *possible* defection. And this rumor—still unsubstantiated—that Garrett had walked away from a battle in Kobe, recalled to the Black Hills. It wasn't hard to read the signs of an impending and explosive confrontation, but it would require more to attempt any kind of solid interpretation. Julian Nero, Mr. Infallible, the man in the know, had to make the call based on second-hand information and one hurried conversation with Drew Hasek-Davion.

"Crucify him." That had been Hasek-Davion's suggestion—demand, actually. "The rogue Davionist, out for his own ends. Hype it until every Silesian MechWarrior is looking for a piece of Searcy. Then we give him Vandegriff." By all indications, everything was going according to plan.

Except that it made no sense, from a purely public relations viewpoint, that Hasek-Davion was the instigator of the rupture. It would deprive Blackstar of its share of any glory won by the Federated Suns favorite. This move only made sense if Hasek-Davion expected Searcy to lose. Or was actively working against him.

The only conclusion Julian could draw from the tangle of half-truths and hidden agendas was that Hasek-Davion's little empire was caving in. Somehow Drew had lost control over Searcy and now wanted Julian to stoke the fires that burned between Silesia and the Black Hills. And if Hasek-Davion wanted to keep the fights going, then Searcy must be working to stop him. The two were in a race to see who could complete his objective first, stable owner or arena 'Warrior.

Julian Nero snapped his fingers at his assistant, holding his hand out for the wireless. One thing he had learned early on. You generalized on the stable.

You bet on the 'Warrior.

20

The *Cestus* had kicked its way through the rubble-strewn streets, pausing near the ruins of what had once been the city's main monorail station. The bullet-shaped train slept on the elevated rails, no longer running but miraculously untouched by the violence that had destroyed the station. He continued along Hotel Row, where several of the city's luxury-class hostelries were still filled to capacity as the greatest show in the Inner Sphere continued.

Upon leaving the safety of the spaceport area in his salvaged *Cestus,* Karl Edward had no idea what kind of opposition he'd find when he reached the border between the International Zone and the Black Hills. If someone had offered him a bet, he'd never have wagered on running straight into Garrett in his OmniMech.

But there he was, the *Masakari* standing dead center in the street, blocking Karl's path, framed by the elevated rail system to one side and the Imperial Hotel on the other. Spectators filled the hotel windows, people intelligent enough to keep off the streets yet believing that the double-paned glass windows offered some kind of protection. It didn't matter that collateral damage from a weapons exchange could ravage the hotel front in seconds; they'd come for the show and seemed determined to get one.

"I didn't expect to find *you* here, Garrett. I thought you'd be in Kobe."

"I was. About to claim a victory, too. As always." Silence for a moment, then, "The *untouchable*. That is what Kobe warriors are calling me."

Karl smiled grimly. Explaining what that word really meant to Combine culture wouldn't be politic at the moment. He sidestepped his *Cestus,* thinking to lead Garrett away from the hotel. The eighty-five-ton *Masakari* swung at the waist to track him, raising its left arm menacingly. The apertures of its twin PPCs were threat enough to keep Karl from taking another step.

"So why are you here?" he asked. Karl needed to know who he could still trust, if anyone.

"I am here to claim what is rightfully mine. It seems I have beaten Searcy in getting here, but that is acceptable. You and I have our own score to settle."

Karl tasted the nervous sweat that beaded on his upper lip. He wasn't afraid, but duly concerned. The *Masakari* was designed to be a killer. Against the *Cestus,* its energy-weapon configuration would quickly destroy his armor protection. The only thing Karl had going for him was that Garrett had apparently come here straight from another battle, and some minimal damage showed across the *Masakari*'s chest and arms. If Karl acted quickly, he might be able to exploit that damage.

He was troubled, though, by the implication that Michael was also on his way and that Garrett was expecting him. Were the two working together, Clanner and Champion? Was Michael hunting the task force put together by Starlight and Overlord, thinking it threatened his position as leader of the Black Hills force? Karl had wanted to tell his friend about those plans, to enlist his help, but Michael had been in no mood to hear him. He'd become the creature of Drew Hasek-Davion.

"And that's why you're here, Garrett? To settle up with me?"

"You think too highly of yourself, like most Inner Sphere barbarians. My purpose here is higher than that, and a great reward awaits me." There was a touch of amusement in Garrett's voice. "An offer I could not decline. Is not that how you play-warriors phrase it?"

"Close enough," Karl said, stalling. He paired his arm lasers into medium and large combinations, tying them into the primary triggers for each control stick and leaving his gauss rifle on the right-hand thumb button. He selected his targeting system to passive mode, relying on his own skills rather than computer-aided sensors. It was less accurate, but would give Garrett no warning. "You've become a true mercenary, then, haven't you? Where paymaster counts for more than person?"

Karl was baiting Garrett, and it looked like the Clanner had taken it. He moved his 'Mech forward threateningly. "We are not under Boreal Reach now. Out here, you are no match for me."

Tightening down on his primary triggers, Karl carefully dropped his targeting reticle over the *Masakari*'s outline. Without active sensors, the cross hairs did not change to a golden hue to indicate target acquisition. So near point-blank range and two non-moving BattleMechs, Karl hardly needed a computer to assist him. But with the hotel so close, he couldn't afford to miss, and every second of easing into the shot increased the chance for clean hits. "This was Michael's biggest mistake," he warned. "Don't do it, Garrett."

The *Masakari*'s left arm reached out, leveling its paired PPCs at the *Cestus*. Cautionary alarms rang a warning that another 'Mech had sensor lock. But Garrett held off. Perhaps it was because Karl had invoked the name of Michael Searcy, the man who was the bane of Garrett's existence within Blackstar Stables. Or maybe Garrett believed he actually was "untouchable."

"Do what?" Garrett asked.

"Start believing your own press," Karl said, carefully squeezing his triggers.

Both of his 'Mech's arms extended toward the *Masakari*, spearing out intense, gem-colored light. Molten scars opened up on the Omni's right arm, slashing across the chest and then down toward the left hip. Armor sloughed away, opening up the breach in the 'Mech's right side that Karl's gauss slug slammed through a split second later with devastating force. The hit rocked the *Masakari* back on its feet but failed to unseat it.

"You are very *touchable*," Karl said grimly, throttling into a backward walk and waiting for his weapons to cycle. He braced himself for the blistering counterfire.

The assault spun the *Warhawk*'s gyro off-balance, even with the compensating signal fed to it by Garrett's neurohelmet. The 'Mech swayed back precariously, fighting the pull of gravity, while inside the cockpit Garrett wrestled the controls to keep the eighty-five-ton machine upright. He spread the 'Mech's legs into a wider stance and thrust its arms forward in counterbalance. Ducking the *Masakari* hard at the waist, he hoped to rob the shove of its momentum. All of these were automatic responses to the hard-hitting assault, trained into his reflexes like instincts. And they accomplished their aim. Slowly, the *Warhawk* came under control, rocking forward to regain a fighting stance.

Garrett was not about to succumb to the filthy surat's opening salvo.

The damage, though, had been done. Insistent lights flashed red and amber cautions at him while alarms rang for attention, warning of damaged or upset systems. That one salvo had left him with only fifteen percent armor mass, the rest of it now a mess of molten splatters smoking on the ground. A heat sink mounted in his right torso had ruptured, which would also cost him in heat dissipation.

So he would sweat a bit more. Garrett pulled his cross hairs across the holographic head's up display his *Warhawk*'s computer painted over his main canopy. The reticle would blink out for a long second before reappearing, jumping across the HUD to finally settle over the retreating *Cestus*. Jerking back on the trigger, he unleashed twin cascades of azure destruction from his paired PPCs. The energy arced out, flailing at the wide-shouldered BattleMech.

And missed.

The energy discharge spent itself impotently against a

pile of bricks and plaster, geysering scorched rubble into the air. Except for a few shards of ferrocrete that rang off the *Cestus*'s head, the salvo accomplished little.

Garrett stared in disbelief, the shock wasting several precious seconds. Another glance over his system monitors confirmed what the flashing cross hairs had hinted. The gauss slug had smashed deeper into his side than he'd thought, crushing his targeting computer. An irreplaceable piece of Clan engineering, lost in the opening seconds. Garrett had been caught unprepared.

Now he had to make up for it. He killed his targeting computer, falling back on straight sensor feed and his own skill in acquiring target lock. This time he saw the reticle burn gold before easing into a shot, lancing out with his PPCs and the sapphire darts of his large pulse lasers.

Karl fired at exactly the same moment, a second salvo almost as effective as the first, minus one of his large lasers. The *Warhawk* shook under the onslaught, giving up more of its armor as destruction walked across the chest and also cut deep into the left leg this time. The cockpit heat spiked hard and brutal as the *Cestus*'s laserfire cut away a good portion of the physical shielding around the *Warhawk*'s fusion engine. Coupled with the heat spike created by demand of Garrett's energy weapons, his cockpit temperature shot straight through the yellow band and well into the red.

Garrett gasped for breath, the scorching air burning in his lungs as he overrode the automatic shutdown safeguard. The Clan-designed *Warhawk,* usually so responsive to his touch, performed sluggishly now, the heat interfering with its internal systems. Why had he wasted time talking and grandstanding for the spectators cowering in the nearby hotel and the cameramen he'd noticed set up in the shadow of the elevated monorail tracks? Sweat streaked his face and burned at the corners of his eyes, blurring his vision. He blinked them clear and looked out his canopy onto a restorative sight.

The *Cestus* was leaning drunkenly against a wall, having nearly fallen, one arm neatly amputated just below the shoulder.

Garret's second set of PPCs had not failed him this

time, their lethal discharge combining to melt away armor and sever the titanium bones underneath. In a single salvo, he'd robbed the *Cestus* of half its laser power. It reminded Garrett once again of how lethal was the machine he piloted. This was no ordinary 'Mech. It was Clan. It was *his*.

Still, the wire-frame schematic displayed on an auxiliary monitor might have been enough to unnerve many another MechWarrior, those without the experience of a hundred arena duels or the genetic superiority of being trueborn among the Clans. His armor was ravaged and breached over his right side, while the heat flooding his Omni was creating massive system failures. Worst of all, the fusion engine was borderline critical.

None of that mattered. Garrett would never give up; he was made of sterner stuff. He was a Clan and always would be. Swallowing some moisture back into his parched throat, he trailed his reticle back toward the *Cestus* even as the other machine straightened up to resume the battle.

The *Warhawk* responded too slowly, the efficiency of its myomer musculature devastated by the internal temperatures, allowing the *Cestus* to throttle up and move out from under the cross hairs. Garrett stabbed at his triggers, his twin PPCs pouring out streams of hellish fire in hopes of another solid hit. That's all it was: hope. The coruscating energy lanced over the *Cestus*'s right shoulder, burning harmlessly into the air over several buildings before finally dissipating. The single gauss slug Karl returned smashed more armor from the *Warhawk*'s left side, opening up a breach there as well.

Karl Edward cut inside Garrett's firing arc then, racing his machine forward in a curling pattern that boiled the fight down to a race. He would surely go for one of the *Warhawk*'s critically wounded flanks, betting against the heat-addled turning speed of the OmniMech. Garrett wrenched on his controls, fighting to wrestle more performance out of his 'Mech than it had ever been designed to give under such circumstances. Pushing the machine into an awkward turn, he twisted the torso to its limits and then reached to the side with the 'Mech's right arm.

It gave him just enough range of motion to thrust

forward the two pulse lasers directly into the chest of his opponent. Sapphire darts hammered into the *Cestus*'s chest, chewing into the Durallex armor. A gray mist of flashed metal covered his torso, the cloud spitting out small molten gobbets in sizzling arcs. Enough to wound the other machine gravely, though not enough to stop it. Karl Edward had built up too much momentum in his charging attack. Too late, Garrett realized that the other MechWarrior meant to smash into him.

He shoved the throttle forward so violently that it broke one of its mechanical stops, wrenching the stick. The *Warhawk* managed one half-step—not nearly far enough—before the *Cestus* slammed into its weakened right side.

The impact rattled Garrett hard against his restraining harness, digging deep bruises into his chest and shoulders. The grinding sound of crushed armor roared in his ears. The *Warhawk*'s right hip took a glancing blow from the *Cestus*'s knee, and the Omni's arm, already bent awkwardly back, wrenched at the shoulder joint. Then the smaller 'Mech's shoulder dug into the ruined right torso, smashing the bulky flank shielding the *Warhawk*'s fusion engine back into the main body, where it impacted against the gyroscopic stabilizer and reactor.

There was no saving the *Warhawk* as it stumbled back, caught in gravity's embrace. Even if it could have held to its feet, the fusion reactor had taken too much damage and nothing could bring it back under control. Already its dampening system was failing, golden fire leaking out the caved right side and bursting through both hip joints. What little armor was left protecting the chest melted, sagged, and fell inward. Black smoke belched from the seams surrounding the head.

Garrett smelled the scent of molten metal in the split second before the loosed inferno ate its way up through the floor of his cockpit. Then he felt the searing heat as it consumed metal and flesh and filled the space around him with a glorious blaze. But buried down deep, in a place his screams of pain could not reach, was one final spark of pride, of satisfaction. His Clan was dead. He had died with it, in fact, though he'd refused to acknowledge it. And now there would finally be a peace of sorts.

Peace that he would not outlive *this* disgrace.

"I always knew you had it in you."

Michael walked his *Pillager* forward, careful of the still-smoking ruin that had been Garrett's *Masakari*—a machine the Clanner had insisted on calling a *Warhawk*. The explosion of the fusion engine hadn't left much recognizable, just blackened and twisted metal. A few larger pieces were scattered about the street, having blown clear of the inferno. Among them one arm had gone smashing through the wall of the Imperial Hotel, bringing the fight closer to some spectators than they would have liked. Most of the hotel's windows had shattered under the explosive force. The people moved about over there as if in a daze, slow and aimless, but at least they were alive. Most of them.

No answer from Karl. The *Cestus* lay on its side, unmoving. Unable to hold to its feet after the impact of its charging attack and the violent destruction of the *Masakari*, it had fallen into the ruins of the monorail station. Michael was worried. Caught against the force of such an explosion, slammed down against an unyielding street with only one 'Mech arm to break the fall, Karl might be hurt. Hurt bad.

Michael crouched the *Pillager* down beside the fallen *Cestus* to get a better look. A prickling sensation crawled over his scalp, the same touch of dread he'd felt walking through the devastation of the Star League Park.

In the other cockpit, something moved.

"Had what in me?" Karl finally asked.

Michael smiled in relief. His friend was alive. "The showmanship," he said. "That last attack was a true showstopper. Grandstanding for the audience."

Silence for a long moment, as if Karl wasn't certain whether this was some new game. Finally, he said simply, "It hurt."

"I'll bet it did. No one said fame was easy, pal."

"That's not why I did it." The *Cestus* stirred, rolling over onto its front and working its one arm beneath it.

Michael straightened up his *Pillager* and waited for the *Cestus* to rise on its own. "That's not why I did it, either, not at first anyway. But fame follows victory on

Solaris VII as sure as newsmen can smell a story." He turned the *Pillager*'s head just far enough to indicate a direction. "Over there, in the shadow of the elevated rail. I counted at least three different crews. Like it or not, my friend, they'll already have you cast as the Jaguar-slayer. You'll be very popular in Kobe, I'd think." Michael knew he was playing hard on the "pals" and "friends," and wondered briefly who he was trying to convince, Karl or himself. Maybe both, he finally decided.

Karl wasn't giving him much to work with. "Why are you here, Michael?"

"I came looking for you, Karl. You, Starlight, Overlord. Though I didn't think to find you so easily. Or so *involved*."

"I was waiting for you when Garrett decided to settle an old score." A pause. "It's settled."

"How did you know I was coming?"

"A little bird whispered it in my ear."

Michael frowned, not catching the reference. "A little bird?"

"Okay. Would you believe a fat vulture squawked on the wrong channel?"

So Karl *had* heard the earlier conversation between Michael and Hasek-Davion. And he'd come out alone to gauge Michael's attitude. All right, then. "I need your help," he said.

"*Stormin'* Michael Searcy never needed anyone," Karl retorted.

"Yes, he did," Michael answered wearily. "He needed the media. The media and Drew Hasek-Davion made his reputation. But it was a reputation built on hype and happenstance, though for a while he even believed it himself." For a long while—too long, in fact. "That's over."

When Karl spoke again, his tone had softened somewhat. Not that all was forgiven, but Michael could at least hear some definite hope in there. "So who are you now?" Karl asked.

That was the question Michael kept coming back to. *If not Champion, then what?* "I don't know yet. But whoever Michael Searcy is now, he belongs out here trying to set things right—if that can be done." He ran his gaze over the ruins around them, and he knew that further east, between the Black Hills and Silesia, the battleground looked even worse. "What have you got left here?"

"The battle with the Lyran Guard hurt us, but between Starlight and Overlord Stables and a few odd hangers-on we've attracted, we can field two disjointed battalions. That's enough to hold the International Zone, or at least the spaceport, to keep either sector from acquiring the stockpiles stored there." Karl paused, then admitted, "But it can't stop the fighting. The Black Hills alone can field a regiment or more, and that belongs to Drew Hasek-Davion, your defection notwithstanding. Silesia is even stronger with the Thirty-second's arrival. Neither side is about to back us for a peaceful solution."

Michael frowned, considering, then nodded to himself. "One side might," he said haltingly, "if it's done correctly. What's missing is someone on point, to clear a
• path."

"Always out in front, eh?"

Michael heard the edge in his friend's voice, but wasn't sure if it was sarcasm or dry humor.

"One more time, Karl." He could hear the weariness in his own voice. "Stormin' Michael Searcy still has one final appearance to make."

21

Hazelwood Heights, Black Hills
Solaris City, Solaris VII
Freedom Theater, Lyran Alliance
22 August 3062

Michael Searcy watched as a lance of four 'Mechs shook out into a ragged line halfway down the slope, claiming a small park along Regency Street. The Black Hills' main police station crowned the hill, a monolithic structure overlooking Hazelwood Heights and, much further down, the residential slums settled into the lowlands that eventually gave way to Cathay. Though it had the capacity for a thousand policemen, the station never garrisoned more than a light BattleMech lance here for riot duty. Times had changed, though, with the FSPD upgrade in recent months.

These were no light 'Mechs. A new *Enforcer III* and a *JagerMech III* stood slightly forward of a pair of *Centurion*s, the lance of a height with the stands of birch trees from which the area took its name. The armor on all four was a bit worse for wear, Michael noted. But all proudly displayed the insignia of the Federated Suns Police Force—the sword-and-sunburst set over a golden shield.

He halted his *Pillager* a quarter-kilometer away, his

cockpit seat giving him a good view over the rooftops. His computer identified the lance as a security patrol, tagging their icons on the heads-up display in neutral blue. That was all well and good for the computer, but Michael wouldn't be satisfied unless he was sure these 'Mechs weren't under the direct control of Hasek-Davion. Until then they were hostiles.

Michael was bound for Boreal Reach, there to face the self-proclaimed Black Hills Militia, and then on to Silesia. Already he'd met three pickets on his way through the Davion sector, but here, in the shadow of the main precinct, the stakes were higher. He could have swung wide of the area, but that would have meant conceding authority to Drew Hasek-Davion. Stormin' Michael Searcy never shied from a challenge, but in this game, if he resorted to firing a single shot he would have already lost.

Selecting the Black Hills' frequency, always monitored by police forces, he dropped his jaw long enough to engage his transmitter. "State your business."

"It's the other way around, Searcy," came the immediate response. The *JagerMech* shifted slightly on its feet to indicate who led the police lance. "This is Lieutenant Rand of the FSPD. That's my line, and I want to know what you think you're doing here."

"I'm passing through. You can move aside or be moved."

A nervous laugh. "You and what army?"

Michael knew that Rand didn't want this fight any more than he did. The police lance had the numbers, so far, but Michael commanded a far superior machine and owned three years in the arenas. It helped balance the odds. "Karl, show them," Michael said.

On his HUD, icons painted the gold of allies moved out of the sensor shadows cast by some of the taller buildings. From behind Mirabilis House, one of the landmark mansions that existed side by side with the eyesore slums, Karl Edward appeared at the head of a double lance of Starlight MechWarriors. Then a company from Overlord emerged from around the Davion Arms Condominiums to the direct south. Further back, another combined-stables company came from between some of the larger buildings that flanked the Black Hills' mercantile district. In that last group were the three police pickets Michael had already recruited to his side while traveling here from the International sector. Two of them displayed the same sun-sword-and-shield crest as these new officers.

Karl remained on point in his *Cestus* as the battalion moved up, his 'Mech damaged from the fight with Garrett but still ready for more. "Did we interrupt something?" Karl asked over the open frequency. His threatening tone was a scripted part of Michael's bluff. Then, over the closed channel, he added, "I hope you know what you're doing, Searcy."

Michael hoped so too. As the battalion positioned itself in a wide arc three hundred meters back of his *Pillager,* he said, "That answer your question, Lieutenant?"

Rand's next transmission was more subdued. "I count at least fifteen Lyrans in that force."

"And you'll notice that I've trusted them at my back. No one's shot at me yet."

A lengthy pause followed, which Michael figured was either a conference between Rand and his lancemates or with someone higher up the chain of authority. It wasn't too hard to guess who that later might be. Michael had his own ace to play, but he hoped to save it for later in the game. He took several more menacing steps forward, halting the *Pillager* again only when his sensors warned of multiple target locks.

"Fire or stand aside, Lieutenant Rand. I don't have time for discussion."

"Yes sir. I mean, no, of course not. But—we were advised that you had abandoned us for the Lyrans." The words came out in a rush. "For *her.*"

So, Hasek-Davion's propaganda machine was already hard at work accusing Michael of defecting to Katrina. A smart move, but this time Drew was also going to have to fight the persona of Stormin' Michael Searcy— a persona he'd helped create. The lieutenant obviously didn't want to believe Michael was a traitor. Appearance *and* reality—this time Michael had both on his side.

"If you truly believe I could turn *merchant,*" he said, using the common slang for a Lyran citizen, "that I would turn my back on the Federated Suns, then you should fire." He throttled into a slow walk, letting the *Pillager*'s arms swinging normally for balance rather than held in position for an attack. He wasn't about to fire on these men.

The *Pillager* ate up the distance in six-meter strides. Michael's sensors continued to complain of target locks, and he tensed for an assault. Nervous sweat trickled down the sides of his face. His first half-dozen steps past the four police 'Warriors seemed to stretch on forever— enough time for them to hit him from behind at point- blank range. That would ravage both Michael *and* the *Pillager* beyond any hope of salvage or survival.

And then one after another, the cautionary alarms of multiple target locks faded away.

Karl's voice was a brief whisper in his ear. "Well played, Michael."

The police *JagerMech* fell in behind the *Pillager,* quickly followed by its three companions as the lance now accompanied Michael's forces down from the hills and into the tenement area. It was a victory, but Michael knew his troubles weren't over. They were only beginning.

It seemed he had come full circle. The Davion favor- ite and one of the most celebrated gladiators on Solaris VII, at this moment he was as nervous as the first day he'd walked a battered *Blackjack* into one of the Game World's minor arenas. Heart pounding, throat dry, fear warring with adrenaline.

He even had an audience again as he walked his 'Mech through the tenements. They were refugees, displaced by the savage Lyran assault against the Black Hills. Their tenements were threatened or already destroyed as the free-fire zone expanded on the eastern border that sepa- rated the Davion sector from Cathay. Hundreds of peo- ple trailed along the walks as Michael and his men moved deeper into the sector. Many simply stood and watched, awed by the leviathan machines that a week before had commanded the arenas and now ruled the streets of the Game World. A few threw rocks or bottles plucked from the garbage littering the streets, but the protestors were quickly put down by the greater numbers who cheered and waved, recognizing what was certainly the most celebrated 'Mech in the Black Hills. Along every street some few dozen would jog along for a few seconds, thinking to match the pace set by the *Pillager*. The 'Mech was slow compared to some others, but no one on foot could hope to match its thirty-two-kilometer per hour speed.

Most gave up, but others continued to trail along in the *Pillager*'s wake. Michael continued up Danning Street, then turned onto Marx Way eight short blocks from the Davion arena. The battalion remained a respectful distance behind him, at times disappearing completely in the shadow of larger buildings. Only the security lance remained at tight quarters, having become his official escort through the streets and right up to the titanic gray ferrocrete bunker that was Boreal Reach.

Two companies of Black Hills Combined Militia guarded the approach, formed up into a five-tier, triangular phalanx. Aubry Larsen's *Dragon Fire* stood out in front like an arrowhead aimed straight at Michael.

After scanning an array of channels, the *Pillager*'s communications equipment centered in on Larsen's voice transmitting over the Blackstar Stables general frequency. "I'd have bet real money against you coming back, Michael. Hasek-Davion was sure you would, though." Her transmission wasn't coming in on the coded channel, which meant she wanted her words intercepted by the media. "And he's always right, isn't he?"

Michael grinned without humor, readying himself to play the game. "It *appears* so," he said. The security lance fanned out to either side of him, while Karl led the battalion up to within a half-kilometer. "Though I've heard several interesting rumors concerning my current relations with Blackstar Stables."

"You defected, Michael. Abandoned us for Starlight and Overlord—Overlord!—right when we needed you most."

"It had to be done to bring in Starlight and Overlord," he admitted calmly. "It was the only way we'd ever end the fighting."

She laughed scornfully. "At the expense of Blackstar and the Davion sector?"

Michael was jubilant. Aubry had just given him the opening he needed to play his ace in the hole.

Right on cue came the voice of Adam Kristof over the commline. "Most people would say that ending the violence would be worth any price. Especially those who've been put out of their homes. Or are you saying, Ms. Larsen, that Drew Hasek-Davion doesn't want the fighting stopped?"

The accusation left her speechless for a long five seconds, then, "Who is this?" she demanded.

Kristof identified himself, and Michael smiled at how well the pieces were falling into place. Adam Kristof had been in charge of one of the news teams reporting on Karl's fight against Garrett. Michael had brought him along, leaving the *Sun Times* van well protected back among the Starlight contingent, and by Karl in particular. He'd wanted to be prepared for any chance to ram his own media support down Hasek-Davion's throat.

With any luck, now Drew would choke on it.

Michael keyed his transmitter, keeping up the pressure. "So what do you intend to do now, Aubry?"

"Nothing," she said calmly.

Nothing? Michael had expected the full-out assault Hasek-Davion threatened him with several days before, including the revelation of Michael's own dubious history and blame for causing the riots.

"So long as you don't try to force your way into Boreal Reach," she went on, voice calm and even, "I've been instructed to let you proceed toward Silesia. Whatever your reasons."

"The reason is to end the fighting," Karl said quickly. "Any way we can."

"So you say. And by your bringing along a small Lyran contingent, the Silesians might believe it as well."

Listening to her, Michael began to wonder if this might be another trap Drew had set in his path.

Kristof tried again. "Shouldn't Hasek-Davion also be concerned about trying to end the violence?"

"Of course he should. And he does!" She paused. "But not when other matters are more pressing. Such as the rumor of the Lyran Alliance landing another battalion at the spaceport this afternoon. No green unit this time, though. The Seventeenth Arcturan. We have more immediate interests than trying to force a resolution with Silesia. Or should Drew Hasek-Davion not concern himself with the defense of Federated Suns' citizens?" Her voice ran to smooth poison as she threw Kristof's own words back at him.

A chill ran up Michael's spine. How had he missed such a rumor, when he'd been leading the Black Hills militia only a few days before and had still been in the intelligence loop just last night? Hasek-Davion couldn't have isolated him from this information. From what he knew, that battalion of the Thirty-second Lyran Guard had already been in transit and conveniently routed to Solaris VII. Could another unit have been brought in so quickly?

"That's news to me," Kristof said to him privately, "but it's possible. Depends on how desperate they were to move in military troops and whether they had a ready JumpShip and didn't mind risking another jump into the system's gravity."

A couple of strong *if*s that depended on how desperate Katrina Steiner was to put down a challenge to her power. Especially if her dethroned brother could benefit from her defeat.

"A full battalion, even an assault company with armor support, might be enough to retake the warehouses," Karl said, obviously worried for the small force left behind to guard the site. "Especially if they drop with aerospace assets this time. We left only a skeleton force to garrison the spaceport."

And Michael had stripped the sector's western border of its picket patrols, adding them to his force. If new forces did arrive and targeted the Black Hills with the same ferocity as the first wave, they would lack sufficient defense. He could send those pickets back again, perhaps split off another few lances . . .

There it was, the hand of Drew Hasek-Davion hiding in plain sight while manipulating various pieces on the game board. Michael cursed him silently. Even without moving directly against Michael, Drew had still managed to diminish him in the eyes of others. Especially if the report was true and Michael could be blamed for weakening the Black Hills' defense. He couldn't afford not to accept the report as true and split off forces to prepare. *That* would put his remaining force at greater risk in Silesia, where the Blackstar master would no doubt have more surprises waiting.

The reach of Hasek-Davion was long indeed.

Michael quickly released all members of the security force as well as two lances from the battalions mixed-unit company. It added up to a strengthened company, which he placed under the command of Lieutenant Rand.

"Why under *him*?" Aubry asked, no doubt feeling snubbed in her new position as leader of the Combined Militia.

"Because the Federated Suns Police are empowered *to protect and serve.* Not to *attack and provoke.*" That left no doubt about his position to anyone listening in on his transmission, which he was sure was being recorded by several news teams. Aubry Larsen wisely remained silent, but Michael thought she should have quit when she was ahead. He ordered the withdrawal of his remaining units.

Karl tried to offer some small comfort as the main force moved away from Boreal Reach and headed into the free-fire zone, toward Cathay and Silesia beyond. "You did it," he said. "And all without firing a single shot. Hasek-Davion tried to cut our legs out from under us, and we beat him. *You* beat him."

With the force he planned to take into Silesia reduced to less than he'd begun with in the International Zone, Michael didn't quite agree. "This time we managed a draw. Nothing more. For every move we make, he's already been there and prepared for it. Isolating himself from the risk. Maintaining deniability."

Michael slammed one hand down open-palmed against the arm of his *Pillager*'s command couch. "Drew Hasek-Davion is just too powerful. I wanted to bring him down," he said, "but I'm beginning to wonder if anyone on this world is strong enough to do that.

"Maybe winning a draw is the best any of us can hope for."

Drew Hasek-Davion reclined on the leather chaise he'd ordered moved into the media room at Green Mansion and watched the news. He found little pleasure in his many diversions, even in his quest for power, but he still experienced anger. Savored it, in fact, with the appreciation of a connoisseur.

He would never let it show. Only his walking stick, held in a knuckle-white grip and slapping the side of the chaise with increasing violence, expressed his agitation as he listened to Adam Kristof finish his on-site report. The reporter allowed a few precious seconds of silence to trail out as Michael Searcy's two companies passed from sight between buildings.

Brandishing his walking stick as a sword, Drew slashed the air in front of the holovid screen as if he might reach out and strike down Michael himself. With his other hand, he used a small remote to cut to a Silesian news channel. He muted the audio on a pitch for SeraVideo Entertainments' latest home holovid system while he pondered Searcy's latest move.

"Well played, dear boy," Drew murmured. He had to admire Michael's gambits despite how frustrated and angry he was. Well played, yes, but unfortunately—for Michael—there was no way for the 'Warrior to hurt him. Drew had seen to that early on, always guarding himself. Too many tools had turned in the hands of Drew Hasek-Davion over the years for him not to have developed a strong sense of precaution. Too many plans had withered before they could bear fruit.

Adopting the Davion name had been one of them. He'd used it to build a small base of power in the Federated Suns' Capellan March, but that had fallen through when young Morgan Hasek-Davion had returned his hereditary line to the original *Hasek* name. Then he'd attempted to capitalize on the anti-Federated Commonwealth movement, but had been kept in check by other Solaris stable masters. Poor planning, that one. It had actually hurt rather than helped his interests in the Capellan March. His ambitions were next thwarted by Kai

Allard-Liao. And then the failure of Garrett to amount to anything on the Game World. Now Searcy . . .

Michael Searcy—what a Champion he'd have made for the Federated Suns, and for Drew. So much time invested, so much effort. And Drew had come so close. Next time, he'd be better prepared. The good thing about mistakes was that he could learn from them. Besides, he'd won most of what he'd set out to accomplish.

Stroud had to be dead. Megan Church reported no sign that he'd escaped the raid on his estate. And by her reports, the Skye Tigers were seriously hurt. Not yet past the point of recovery, but close. With the fall of Stroud's stable and the boost given Blackstar this last week, no stable—no *two* stables—would be able to bring Drew down. DeLon and Tran Ky Bo might try, but they lacked the strength to do so. The other stable owners could be played off against one another easily enough. Drew had won. Not a total victory, but enough to satisfy him. For now.

Only Michael's efforts against him kept the victory from being complete. What the boy did not realize was that his actions no longer made any difference. Drew was ready for what was next. He knew it was time for the civil unrest to end, and he'd be ready to shift blame away from Blackstar or its master in any number of directions.

He could also play the approaching showdown in Silesia to his own advantage, whatever the outcome. Victor Vandergriff was too far gone down the path of rivalry with Michael for him to be satisfied with anything less than a fight to the death. The very same rivalry Drew had helped to foster. Now, that fight would be something to see, and hopefully Julian Nero or another media hound would catch in on holovid.

Those two 'Mech companies under Michael couldn't hope to prevail over the force Vandergriff would throw at them. If—*when*—Searcy fell to Vandergriff, the bad blood between the Steiner and Davion supporters would only intensify. Drew might even be able to milk another week of violence out of it before stepping in to end it himself.

If Michael won . . . Well, Megan Church *had* evidenced interest in other work. There were always ways of dealing with a 'Warrior.

One way or another.

22

DBC Studios, Silesia
Solaris City, Solaris VII
Freedom Theater, Lyran Alliance
22 August 3062

A map of Solaris City filled the wallscreen behind Julian Nero, the appropriate sector flashing as he mentioned it in his vidcast. Lines of movement were sketched in where studio resources tracked the 'Mech battles still raging across four of the city's sectors. Heavy in-fighting continued among factions in both Cathay and Montenegro, though several assaults had speared across the river in both directions even today. Only Kobe wasn't caught up in the troubles, though they had problems of their own.

"Kobe officials claim they've finally gotten all the fires that ravaged much of the tenement area called the Poisoned Hills for its sanitation difficulties under control. Use of BattleMech forces, recently freed from the fighting, to create fire-breaks are credited with turning that battle. Meanwhile looting continues to plague the Lotus District as the disadvantaged turn on their more affluent neighbors. Sector Manager Osha Minawa promises strong measures to end the looting and to ensure public safety."

His prepared delivery scrolled over the 'prompter, but Julian mostly ignored it. The Great Nero did not need the device. What he did need was to generate a few seconds of drama as the map enlarged to show an image of the southeastern cityscape. Arrows indicated where the Davionists had recently thrust back into the Lyran sector after being pummeled initially.

"No official word yet regarding Michael Searcy's push toward Silesia at the head of a large force," he said. "Intercepted transmissions indicate that the Federated Suns favorite is planning to end the fighting 'any way he can.'"

That quote was courtesy of Karl Edward, but there was damn little else. Julian was furious that his people hadn't scraped up more for him to work with thus far, but he'd be taking matters into his own hands soon enough. "Victor Vandergriff has put out a call to the defenders of Silesia, rallying them at Skye Tiger Mall. After which he intends to confront what he calls 'this latest challenge to Lyran dignity.'"

Julian hated doing it, but he knew the subtle twist of his tone made Vandergriff's vow sound more petulant than bold. It probably wasn't fair, but at least he wasn't kowtowing to Hasek-Davion any longer. Whatever he did or said now was his own decision. His instincts were telling him to give a boost to Michael Searcy. Those instincts had gotten him this far and he had learned to trust them.

"And as the two titans close—with the fate of peace for Solaris City riding in the balance—you can be certain I'll be there to keep you informed. The promise of Julian Nero, the man in the know."

Julian didn't wait for his *clear* from the studio crew. The instant the red light winked out over the camera, he was on his feet and shouting for his assistant. "Where's that VTOL I asked for?"

"Sitting on the roof, Mr. Nero. Your video crew is already there."

Julian nodded brusquely and headed for the elevators, suppressing a laugh at the shocked expressions on the faces of his fellow vidcasters. Julian Nero, abandoning his throne? How many would scramble for his hourly spot, never realizing that by then he would be commanding from the field and the studio would be robbed of the limelight? Big events were afoot, and he wouldn't rely on second-hand information any longer. Today would be *the day.* He would make it so. Julian had been fortunate once, the big story breaking on his watch. It had dropped right into his lap, virtually prepackaged and ready to bring him instant acclaim. This time, however, he didn't intend to wait for the story to come to him.

He would seek it out himself and make it his. Next to that . . .

Nothing else mattered. Searcy would die beneath the *Banshee*'s guns. Vanquished in combat, just as Katrina Steiner had mastered her brother in politics. It would vindicate Victor Vandergriff's worth as a 'Warrior after all these years and restore his place among the finest.

There could be no other way.

Or so thought Victor as he raced across the 'Mech bay at Skye Tiger Estate, then scaled the ladder to his cockpit and quickly fastened himself into the command seat. What did it matter that Adam Kristof was championing Searcy as the answer to Solaris City's troubles or that the damnable Julian Nero was making it sound as if Victor were all talk and no action. Had they forgotten his raid into the Black Hills? The very same strike that brought the war home to the Davionists as his forces carved deeply into their sector?

No, they hadn't forgotten. The media had decided to simply ignore his victories—always that. After a week of building him up as the Lyran champion, possibly for lack of a better candidate, they'd now decided to cut him down. Maybe that was because Jerry Stroud was still missing, leaving no one to crank up the Lyran propaganda machine. Regardless, it would cost Victor the grudging respect he'd won among the Lyran fans and MechWarriors. It wouldn't be the first time he'd been betrayed by the media, then abandoned by public and peers. By the Archon, though, it would be the last!

He tightened down his restraining harness, then pulled the bulky neurohelmet over his head, setting it on the padded shoulders of his cooling suit. If only he'd been allowed to finish out the Grand Tournament, how different everything would be now. His career resurrected and the media fawning over him as they did their golden boy. Searcy had only three years on Solaris, yet everyone thought he could do no wrong. But what was that against Victor's fifteen years? Michael Searcy didn't have a chance now that Victor had regained the confidence and pride of the old days.

"Today we finish this, Searcy." His voice echoed loud in the helmet's tight confines.

The computer winked its startup sequence across the *Banshee*'s control board. Lights flashed on, then burned steady as systems were cross-checked and found in good operation. He felt more than heard the heavy thrum of the assault 'Mech's fusion engine powering up. The sensation vibrated up from the cockpit floor, into his feet and up through his legs. Then the chill touch of his cooling suit gripped him. He felt plugged in. Alive.

"Please identify," the computer prompted, its synthesized voice cutting into his helmet's built-in comm system.

"Victor Vandergriff." Victor had removed any reference to a stable the day Jerry Stroud released him from the Skye Tigers, trading him to Trevor Lynch.

"Voicepoint confirmed. Please initiate security check."

Victor's breath caught in his throat, something of his security phrase key worrying the back of his mind. He shook away the discomfort. "*Battuero ergo sum*; I fight, therefore I am."

His personal lance waited for him outside in the courtyard, already powered and holding a perimeter about the grounds. Though Searcy's raid of the day before had all but destroyed Stroud's estate, the main 'Mech bay still stood. And it was stocked with some of the best equipment money could buy. Victor had moved his headquarters here from Skye Tiger Mall for its access to central Silesia. The Mall, situated on the eastern edge of the city, was too far away for rapid deployment. It was from here he'd organized the strikes into the Black Hills and would now venture forth to meet Searcy's counter assault.

A full company of medium and heavy-class BattleMechs stood a silent vigil on Inverness Avenue, just outside the estate's toppled walls. MechWarriors from the various Steiner-affiliated stables had banded together. Some came from Lion City and others from independent cooperatives now contracted to Lynch Stables. Leading his lance through the broken walls, Victor took the head of a column formation and paraded his force along the short stretch to the Coliseum. An additional two companies surrounded the Steiner arena, the few remaining members of the Thirty-second Lyran Guard mixed in with stabled 'Warriors. They pulled in on his arrival, forming up across the vast parking grounds. Only a few vehicles remained, ones crushed or abandoned that first night when the Grand Tournament had spilled into the streets outside the Coliseum.

Victor dropped his jaw to engage his neurohelmet transmitter. "Who's got them? Where are they?"

A Lion City *Penetrator* stepped forward. "It'll be easy enough to follow from here." A metal-clad arm pointed west. "Just watch their escorts."

Victor saw copters, four of them, swarming over the border between Silesia and Cathay. They might have been closer, but he wasn't used to judging distances against the sky. Those would be the news teams, out to cover the battle wherever it took place, tracking in above the force advancing from the Black Hills. Like carrion birds circling their prey, Victor thought.

One of the aircraft was larger than the others; an armored VTOL, military-issue. At least one of the newscasters had some common sense about flying into a potential combat zone. Victor centered on it as his telltale. At roughly a half-klick he pulled everyone back into the Coliseum's shadow or sent them to the flanks along the cross avenues. They formed three sides of a large box, leaving room for maneuvering in the open parking area, an island of gray ferrocrete that he alone commanded. That was how he wanted to be seen. Recorded. Remembered.

The Davionists came down Luisen, the triple-wide street that fed several arterials into the Coliseum's main parking area. They came two abreast, one long double-column. The ground shook under the footfalls of fifteen-hundred tons of war machines on the move. At the front, Searcy's *Pillager* marched alongside a damaged *Cestus*. The large sword-and-sunburst crest covering the *Pillager*'s chest looked freshly painted.

Victor drifted his targeting reticle over that insignia, the gold-burning cross hairs properly overlaid against the sunburst. He knew that at least half his assembled force had the *Pillager* covered, and the alarms ringing in Searcy's ears must be near deafening. The *Pillager* ignored the Lyrans, however, and continued on at the head of the line across the Coliseum's front drive. The assault machine and its crippled companion finally came to a halt in front of Victor's *Banshee,* but the *Pillager*'s arms were not in firing position. The rest of the Davion force continued to move on by until they were spread out along the length of Luisen. The Black Hills' short battalion capped the open square framed by Victor's forces, now encompassing the entire parking grounds.

Why hadn't anyone fired?

For that matter, why hadn't *he*?

Victor suddenly realized that he, too, had been caught up in the drama of watching the media's favorite march in like royalty while Victor's own force seemed to wait like subjects to receive them. That made him angrier than ever. Here they should be equals. MechWarrior champions. Blackstar and Lynch. Black Hills and Silesia.

Davion and Steiner.

Victor selected an open frequency, wanting the moment immortalized. He took a deep breath and pitched his tone hard and cold. "Ready to finish what we started?"

"You sound so proud of yourself, Victor. Do you honestly approve of what's happened to the city?"

Victor glanced skyward at the hovering eyes of their audience. Searcy was playing with words, angling for the sympathy of the viewing public. He was a master at such games.

Searcy was still talking, not even waiting for Victor to answer his question. "We didn't start this, Victor. It was started for us." Searcy sounded weary. "We only helped escalate the situation out of control."

Victor struck back with the first thing that came to

mind. "Ducking your responsibilities, just like you ducked out of our fight at the Running Fox? Like you abandoned Blackstar? FedRats are so good at running away and then pointing a finger, casting blame onto others."

"Oh, the blame is mine as much as it is yours, Victor. And it also belongs to the stable owners, the fight promoters, and the bookies. And to the politicians and the media. To everyone who helped prime that explosion. If you and I hadn't lit the fuse, it would have been someone else. The whole thing was a powder keg just waiting to go off."

What was Searcy saying now? That he wanted to put the lid back on? No, that couldn't be. Michael Searcy had to want this fight as much as he did. Unless he thought he didn't need it—not like Victor did. Why wouldn't he try to seize the crown, though? Unless . . .

Searcy was afraid! Now Victor smiled. There could be no other answer. Victor had the advantage of three to two in numbers, not to mention the possibility that Overlord Stables might revert to the Lyran side when the shooting began. And maybe Searcy thought he couldn't win a straight-up fight against Victor. Maybe he believed he'd have lost their Grand Tournament match if it had proceeded along normal lines. Belief was a powerful tool. Now that Victor had it back within his grasp, he intended to wield it powerfully.

"This isn't 'MechTalk,' Searcy. You can't argue your way out of this." Victor tightened on his triggers, riding the edge of their pull. "No friendly reporter can spin this for you. You've paraded into Silesia with a Davion-backed force, a fact that's being caught on multiple camera angles as we speak. Do you expect anyone to believe that line you fed the media earlier, about stopping the fight? 'Anyway you can,' is it? Well, there's one way, and we both know what that is."

"I will not be the first one to fire, Victor."

There was a simple solution to *that.* Victor triggered his weapons, and twin scars of lethal energy raced across the short distance between the two 'Mechs, the PPC discharge gouging deeply into the *Pillager*'s body. A stream of autocannon slugs ripped in behind them, smashing more of Searcy's protection into useless fragments. As the *Pillager* stumbled under the assault, bleeding molten armor onto the gray ferrocrete, Victor Vandergriff throttled his *Banshee* forward.

"That," he said, "should no longer prove to be a problem."

23

The VTOL's rotors thumped heavily overhead. Its quick passage over the Steiner Arena's parking area rushed air past the craft's open side door with a sharp whistling sound, tugging at the clothing of those belted into its seats. The wind's touch was chill and clammy against Julian Nero's exposed skin and carried the smell of smoke and ash, a scent that had hung over the whole city this last week. His face tingled with the cold, but his ears were warm, protected by a pair of headphones that let him listen in on any 'Warrior chatter passing over unprotected frequencies.

Over the competing noise and muffling effect of the headphones, Julian picked out the crackling scream of the *Banshee*'s twin PPC blasts. Or at least he thought he did. Either way, the directional microphones employed by his video crew would grab the sound well enough for his audience.

"A devastating assault by Victor Vandergriff, who is obviously refusing any attempt at reconciliation," Julian said into his mike. "Michael Searcy gets credit for trying, but it's cost him plenty. The *Pillager*'s armor is literally melting off onto the ground."

The customized *Banshee* moved forward in an oblique line of attack, its torso-mounted autocannon spewing a burst of cluster rounds. "And now Vandergriff is following up with the LB–X autocannon he swapped in for the *Banshee*'s standard gauss rifle. Most of the shrapnel seems to have missed the stumbling *Pillager*, instead hitting Boi Yardii's Italian restaurant behind Searcy and across Luisen Street."

Julian spot-checked the cloud of debris raining down along the side of the building, but it looked like the damage hadn't penetrated into the dining area, so he didn't mention it further. He had enough to do craning his neck to keep the battling machines in view as the VTOL rolled off its original line. He elbowed the pilot and made a circling motion in the air. Covering the microphone wire that extended down from his headset to keep his voice from going out over the air, he nodded back toward his right. "You bank around tight and keep those 'Mechs in our camera range." His voice brooked no refusal. The pilot was a studio employee, and Nero had spoken.

"Searcy is holding to his feet, though it looked like touch and go there for a few seconds. The *Pillager* is no easy mark to cave in so early into a battle and Michael Searcy no rookie 'Warrior. We're looking for a hard-hitting return, and there! Laserfire from the *Pillager* spitting into the gap between Searcy and Vandergriff. But no gauss rifles! Michael Searcy is holding back on his most devastating weapons."

And Julian couldn't figure out why. Vandergriff was already recovering from Searcy's blistering laser attack, tracking the *Banshee* back to its right in order to keep it under his guns. Without the gauss rifles, the match was far more even than Julian would have liked. The *infallible Nero* had softened his approach to Michael Searcy—damn that unreliable Davionist—wanting to keep his options open should the fight go in Searcy's favor. He had to be ready to come down on the side of a peace initiative, strange as it was coming from a Solaris gladiator. Maybe things weren't what they seemed and

Searcy hadn't come here prepared to back up his peace resolve with combat.

Whatever Searcy's game, Julian had to figure it out quickly. Because without some sign . . .

It all came down to instinct.

Alarms already triggered by the multiple targeting locks could not warn Michael of the impending attack. And most of the *Banshee*'s primary weapons had already been trained on the *Pillager,* with no telltale shifting of an arm to betray the assault. Nor had Vandergriff spoken at the moment of attack, giving away his intent.

Yet Michael had sensed it coming. Maybe he realized that his words about not firing first could be misconstrued as a challenge. A dare, even. Maybe it was that sixth sense most arena warriors experienced from time to time. Whatever it was, something had warned him. Not in time to escape the ambush or even to fire a preemptive strike, but enough to prepare for the onslaught. His quick reactions saved the *Pillager* from toppling under the hard-hitting blows, the fractional turn lessening his targeting profile. Because of it Vandergriff's follow-up autocannon fire only skipped a few cluster fragments off the *Pillager*'s armor, and the bulk of the attack hit the buildings behind him.

Bracing back on the 'Mech's left leg, Michael recovered full control, selecting and firing weapons more by reflex than thought. The temperature in his cockpit soared momentarily as the energy draw of so many lasers spiked the power output of his fusion engine. Fresh sweat broke out on his brow. But it wasn't until his sensors reported the damage effects, or lack of them, on the wire-frame schematic display that he truly recognized his mistake in not using the paired gauss rifles. He still wasn't sure why he hadn't.

The *Banshee* came in right-oblique, crossing his line of sight and then Karl's. Vandergriff was probably intending to take out the already-damaged *Cestus,* claim a kill, and reduce his understrength enemy by one sixty-five-ton machine. Michael recognized the intent, saw his window of opportunity in that fraction of a second, and activated the *Pillager*'s HildCo jump jets. A one-hundred-ton assault 'Mech rocketing thirty meters into the air on vented plasma would draw anyone's attention, especially a nearby enemy. It might choose to land near you. Worse, it might choose to land *on* you—a maneuver MechWarriors called "death from above"—a hundred tons of BattleMech dropping directly onto the head of another.

Michael landed the *Pillager* hard in Vandergriff's right rear quarter, knees bending to absorb the shock. The *Banshee* twisted about violently trying to bring its weapons back to bear. But with Michael so far past the limit of its turret-style waist, only the short-range missile pack on the *Banshee*'s right arm would extend back far enough. The exchange was fairly one-sided, with three missiles arcing out from the *Banshee*'s SRM launcher answered by another blistering laser blast from the *Pillager*. The energy barrage splashed away more armor from the *Banshee*'s right side. In return, Michael took two missiles against the chest and the third against the *Pillager*'s armored brow. The impact threw Michael violently forward against his restraining harness and then back against his seat. He tasted blood from a bitten tongue and felt a tearing pain in his neck muscles.

His vision swam, but not so much that he failed to see Karl's *Cestus* stepping forward with its one remaining arm thrusting out toward Vandergriff's *Banshee*.

"Karl, hold!"

Again, Michael reacted from sheer instinct. The split-second decision was like so many made in the heat of battle, where time was often measured in fractions of a second.

Turned from its original purpose, Vandergriff now came after Michael with a dedication worthy of an arena champion. The two assault machines circled out into the parking area, gaining some distance from each other as their weapons continued to probe for critical weaknesses. Vandergriff had to worry over heat-buildup in the *Banshee* more than did Michael in the cool-running *Pillager*. He could tell by the way the other 'Warrior routinely switched out one of his PPCs for the autocannon or a pair of medium lasers in an effort to control his heat curve. Michael kept to lasers only, straining even the *Pillager*'s known ability to dissipate heat as he worked to push Vandergriff back toward the Coliseum and away from any MechWarrior affiliated with the Federated Suns.

As Michael and Vandergriff traded weapons fire over the open territory, relying on the heavy armor reserves of their assault 'Mechs, Michael gained a few precious seconds to make some sense of how he'd gotten himself into this. By coming to Silesia he'd hoped—expected, even—that Victor Vandergriff might join him in a call for peace on Solaris VII. Being confronted by the ugly truths of the last week had been enough to break through Michael's own delusions. The truth had let him see that the real enemy was Drew Hasek-Davion. The Lyran MechWarriors were fellow competitors, not mortal foes. Solaris VII was not New Canton, and Michael was not—should not be—at war.

Michael had been shamed into seeing that his obsession with proving himself had turned him into the kind of person he'd loathed before coming to Solaris. Someone who thought only of himself. Someone like his Lyran commander on New Canton, who'd ended Michael's military career with a lie to save his own hide. Or maybe not a lie. Just a slanted way of viewing the situation. Appearance was, indeed, a powerful argument.

But where Michael had only three years on Solaris, Victor Vandergriff had lived with the ups and downs of the Game World for much longer. It would be that much harder for him to throw off his illusions. And who, in the last week, had made any attempt to break through the fantasies ingrained into every MechWarrior on the planet? Michael, the man Victor believed to be his worst enemy—the Davion favorite come to destroy what little respect he'd managed to win in this last week.

Michael saw how easily he might have ended up the same way. He'd been on that path, no doubt about it. And except for the overreaching ambition of Hasek-Davion and the friendship of Karl Edward, he might still be lost along that road.

A PPC from the *Banshee* struck him square in the chest, finding a flaw in his armor and stabbing into the internal works of the *Pillager*. It melted the barrel of his one medium laser, ruining the weapon that could still perform as additional centerline armor that prevented the PPC from gouging deeper into his gyro or engine shielding. As if summoned by the threatening blow and Michael's thoughts of him seconds before, his friend's voice whispered through on a quick burst of static. "Michael, what's the problem? Finish Vandergriff before he wears you down. Is there something wrong with your gauss rifles?" Without waiting for an answer, he offered, "Let me help!"

"No. Stay out of this, Karl."

Karl's transmission had drawn Michael's attention to the fact that no one—not Federated Sun or Lyran—had fired a shot while he and Vandergriff continued to hammer away at each other under the watchful eyes recording the fight from helicopters and VTOL above. It was as if the two sides, drawn up for battle, were now content to allow their leaders to settle the question. Davion and Steiner stood their places in a giant square, their followers framing the Coliseum's parking grounds and forming a giant arena for the two gladiators. Even when a stray laser struck one of the spectator 'Warriors, no one retaliated.

But then a laser couldn't decapitate a 'Mech with one shot. Couldn't crush a cockpit inward so fast that the 'Warrior inside had no chance to escape with his life. And now Michael realized why he'd refrained from using his gauss rifles until now. Those were *headhunter* weapons, among the most dangerous ever mounted on a BattleMech. With the gauss rifles in play, Michael could end this fight with Vandergriff prematurely, and permanently. That would send the assembled Lyran battalion into a murderous rage, and no telling what kind of spin it would receive from the several news teams hovering over the parking grounds. Enough to spark another murderous assault against the Black Hills? Even a win that left Vandergriff alive was no guarantee against military reprisal. Not when it would take just one Lyran MechWarrior, feeling he had nothing left to lose and hoping to stave off the possibility of total defeat, to incite a full-scale battle.

But if Michael couldn't afford to win, he certainly

couldn't afford to lose either. Leaving Vandergriff victorious and at the head of a large Lyran force wasn't much of an option. So Michael had fought a delaying battle until now, leaving his primary weapons powered down and stalling for time. As another cerulean lash flayed away protection from over his left arm, he knew he couldn't go on stalling much longer. Not as the *Banshee* and *Pillager* slowly worked through each other's armor. The fight would be measured in minutes.

If that. A medium laser hit the side of the *Pillager*'s head, costing Michael more armor and shaking him again like a leaf caught in a tempest. Time was running out. Michael selected his gauss rifles, tying them into one of his main triggers. He would have to wait for just the right moment to try and disable Vandergriff. He had to keep their battle private. It was the only way to keep the arrayed forces sidelined and prevent the fight from escalating into all-out fighting again.

Then the idea hit him. What if the conflict could be settled between two 'Warriors, as in the arenas? After all, everyone knew . . .

It was how things were done on the Game World.

Julian Nero recognized Searcy's problem after he backed off Karl Edwards. Searcy was trying to prevent a blood bath while eliminating the one factor—Vandergriff—that stood in the way of a cease-fire. To do that the fight had to remain between the two of them. Searcy could not accept help.

Of course, Victor Vandergriff might command it from his force, but Julian doubted that would happen while Vandergriff was so intent on defeating his enemy. Julian shook his head in wonderment. There Vandergriff was, with enough backup to destroy the Black Hills expedition to the last man and possibly claim the mantle of Solaris *Champion* by right of conquest, and instead he played the game being called by his opponent.

Julian had always known Vandergriff to be a poor bet.

"It's a brutal slugfest taking place in the shadow of the Coliseum," he reported, watching as the two assault machines continued to spar almost exclusively with energy weapons. "Though Michael Searcy has apparently foresworn his gauss rifles, weapons that would shift the odds radically in his favor, he has still managed to force Vandergriff back until the *Banshee* looks like it's standing in line waiting for admission into the Steiner Arena. Back where the two of them started their rivalry on Day Five of the Grand Tournament. A match never finished, until today."

It wasn't much, but the continued soft-sell of Searcy's part in this battle was the best Julian Nero could do. The best he *would* do, at any rate. He would stick his own reputation out only so far, and that he did so at all for a gladiator of the Federated Suns surprised even him. Especially after his own part in Hasek-Davion's plans, which had contributed to fueling the violence.

He knew it had to end, even though the war had thrust him into greater prominence than ever. Hasek-Davion himself had reminded Julian of how much the media had done to whip the situation into a civil war. The fighting of the last week had become a media sensation, an event that had sold many cars and boxes of soap and entertainment discs.

Now it was time to sell the audience on a return to sanity.

"Not one other 'Warrior has so much as fired a shot or moved to interfere in this most spectacular of duels." Refocus, he told himself. Maybe reinforce their neutrality if any of the military down below were tuned in to his reports. "This is no invasion. What we have here is the most intense grudge match the Game World has ever seen. A war, yes, but personal, and private.

"No call to arms in the service of Archon Katrina Steiner *or* Victor Davion, but a duel between two champions, contenders for the *Game World* throne."

And if he could sell *that* to his audience, the *Great Nero* would have accomplished something important. And he would still be the man in the know. Mister Infallible. Because to him . . .

Everything was now very clear. The stakes riding on this battle. What it would take to win them.

Victor Vandergriff had listened as Julian Nero turned against him. His communication scanner pulled in the vidcaster's reports among the few warnings and cheers his battalion offered. He heard the subtle digs aimed his way, no doubt influencing his Lyran listeners against Victor. The implication was that the only reason for so close a match was that Michael Searcy must be holding back. That Searcy had still managed to push Victor back, despite a hold on the *Pillager*'s main weapons.

Push him back! Victor had spat dryly at that idea. Nero might be good at secondhand observations, but knew nothing about being a warrior. Victor had traded ground for maneuverability, making himself a harder target in case the treacherous Davionist decided to bring his *mankillers* into play. He'd used the *Banshee*'s mobility to counter the *Pillager*'s heavier armor load and superior weapons, his one advantage—and damn Julian Nero if he couldn't see that. In the long minutes so far, Victor estimated he'd hit with at least twenty percent greater accuracy than Searcy. On a few salvos, Searcy failed to reach him at all! And according to the wire-frame schematics his battle computer painted of both 'Mechs, Victor was within a ton of eliminating the *Pillager*'s advantage in armor. Not that his *Banshee* looked any better, but at least it put him within striking distance of victory.

Of *vindication.*

With that thought, Victor brought both of the *Banshee*'s arms up to level his secondary weapons at Searcy. His heat scale edged deep into the yellow, making his cockpit a sauna. The heat also threatened to rob him of the 'Mech's precious mobility as its myomer musculature turned sluggish in the high temperatures that plagued the *Banshee* design. He selected for the autocannon as well, spending more of his limited cluster ammunition; only four salvos left there.

Searcy caught the movement and, judging correctly that Victor would rely on his smaller weaponry, jumped back ninety meters to create targeting difficulties. A successful gamble, though it threw off his own aim. Victor's missiles arced wide of target, and both left arm-mounted lasers burned impotently into the parking ground's ferrocrete surface, bubbling the paving material. The fragmenting rounds of his autocannon threw a wide enough spread to reach the *Pillager,* however, sanding away more of its thinning armor protection.

Only one medium laser struck the *Banshee* in return as Victor sidestepped out of Searcy's direct line of fire, retreating further toward the Coliseum and turning the BattleMech's still decently armored left side into the blow. He caught the intense, scarlet light against his arm, shielding his savaged torso. He throttled into a backward walk, ready to trade his longer-reaching weapons against the *Pillager*'s lasers, retreating between two giant Romanesque pillars that framed the arena's northern entrance.

Mobility, the first precept of professionally waged warfare.

But if Nero couldn't quite recognize the tactics—the *artistry!*—he at least put his finger on the prize. He'd called it the throne of Solaris. And that was so much more than the high seat in Valhalla. It meant respect. Acclaim. It would be the crowning event of his professional career. Exoneration, ten years of fighting—the last six years of sneers and condescension from fans and fellow warriors alike. That elusive prize.

To be *Champion.*

Spitting the advancing *Pillager* on his cross hairs, Victor released another energy barrage of PPC and laser fire. He caught Searcy at the point of a right turn, hoping to carve through the critically weak armor remaining on the 'Mech's left side. Except the FedRat had held a trick or two in reserve. He threw his *Pillager*'s one-hundred-ton weight into a harder pivot that turned its back to the *Banshee*'s weapons.

And old but tried and true maneuver. Though a 'Mech's rear armor as the weakest, in an assault 'Mech it was still enough to turn one hard-hitting barrage. The azure PPC discharges burned twin molten furrows starting just inside the left shoulder and then down to its center waist. Large red-orange gobbets spat from the wounds, like blood spurting from an open vein, but nothing more critical than armor composite melted under the cascade of burning energies. Certainly not enough damage to truly wound the assault 'Mech and buying the insufferable *Sworder* time to close again.

Victor railed at the cruel turn, knowing what his attack might have accomplished against the already ravaged armor along the *Pillager*'s front. The shot had spiked his heat scale into the red from the energy demand to his fusion engine. A wave of heat washed through the cockpit, shortening his breath in the stifling air and flash-drying sweat into a salty residue that burned on his lips and in the corners of his eyes.

The *Pillager* completed a full turn, arms thrusting forward in a widespread reach. Victor had no more room to maneuver behind him. Unless he wanted to smash his way through the Coliseum's glass and steel entryway, his choice was between jump jets or taking the assault. As the *Pillager* had just done, Victor pirouetted into his own turn that would bring his *Banshee*'s unblemished rear armor into line with Searcy's lasers. The *Banshee* was better armored across the back than the *Pillager*. It would be the first time Victor enjoyed an obvious edge in protection, and he was already planning his next salvo when silvery blurs streaked out from the *Pillager*'s torso-mounted gauss rifles to smash with crippling force into the back of the *Banshee*.

One of the nickel-ferrous slugs, launched at incredible velocity, impacted directly centerline, smashing aside nearly every ounce of armor but failing to penetrate to the vulnerable skeleton beneath. The second slug hit the *Banshee* against the right hip, cracking the armor case protecting its side and pushing support struts through the bulky shielding of the 'Mech's extralight fusion engine. Following up the devastation, the *Pillager*'s lasers stabbed at the *Banshee*'s back as well. The larger laser missed wide, spending itself against the arena, but both medium-class weapons bit into the ruined rear armor, probing for critical equipment.

Treacher! Davion dog! Victor had caught the telltale flash of the gauss coils on a rear-facing auxiliary monitor, knew even as the brutal shove from behind pushed his command couch hard against his spine that he had played right in Searcy's hands. He fought his controls, fighting a losing battle to hold ninety-five tons of upright metal against the pull of gravity. The *Banshee* toppled forward, its head and shoulders smashing through the entryway that—until last week—had allowed thousands of fans to pass through routinely for the nightly Silesian duels.

Victor caught his fall by quickly thrusting out his arms, but the move cost him nearly a ton of armor scraped off his arms and a ruined hand actuator as the *Banshee*'s right hand overextended and partially crushed the 'Mech's wrist. Then the shielding breach made itself known as cockpit temperatures again spiked, making his vision swim and stabbing fiery pokers into his lungs with each gasping breath. He sagged down against his restraining harness, shaking his head clear of the fall and heat stroke, then quickly levered himself back to unsteady legs. Julian Nero was shouting excitedly in his ear. Victor cut him off with a quick stab at his communications panel.

As the *Banshee*'s internal temperatures hit critical levels, the *Pillager* closed with weapons cycling for its next salvo. Victor did the only thing he could. He retreated into the grand halls that surrounded the Coliseum arena. Every step brought him new pangs of loss that once again he was running from Michael Searcy. He had to or be destroyed. But he wouldn't run far or for long. It was only a change of venue. He was not about to concede *this* match.

Victor wouldn't back down this time. He would not lose—he *could* not lose! He tightened his grip on the *Banshee*'s control sticks until his muscles ached and his fingers were numb with exertion.

This was all that he had left.

24

The Coliseum, Silesia
Solaris City, Solaris VII
Freedom Theater, Lyran Alliance
22 August 3062

Julian Nero winced, expecting a mid-air collision as the VTOL pilot crowded another copter away from the Coliseum rooftop landing pad. He nearly snapped out a rebuke, then thought better of it and sat back with eyes closed for the rest of the descent. The pilot was an employee of Donegal Broadcasting and a professional doing his job, just as Julian was doing his.

Protecting the studio's interests.

Julian was out of the VTOL and heading for the rooftop access door the moment the skids touched the circular pad. He used his master key card while the video crew hurriedly unloaded their gear. The heavy thump of the rotors whipped a storm of sound and dust over the roof, and then the large machine lifted skyward and set up station to protect the Julian Nero exclusive. None of the other lighter-weight news copters would risk playing a deadly game of brinksmanship with the pilot of an armored, military-grade VTOL. *He* was almost guaranteed to survive a crash.

Their footsteps echoed hollowly in the stairwell as Julian

led the way down several flights to the arena's control rooms. Red emergency lighting brightened the way, offering some relief from the cold, dead feel of the deserted space. The silence was eerie. No dull buzz of a thousand conversations, muted by the near-soundproofed window. No trembling of the floor from BattleMechs on the move. No sounds of combat, and that Julian found strangest of all.

He went over to the main window looking down on the arena, a spot he'd often occupied in his years of covering the Silesian duels. His people worked to bring the banks of monitors to life while Julian stood gazing down through the black ferroglass at the ghostly arena illuminated only by the red-lit emergency signs.

One of those signs moved!

There, at the west end of the arena, directly opposite the BattleMech entrance. The blue glow outlining the *Banshee*'s cockpit had been subdued by the harsh red backlighting of the missile launcher. But now Julian had it fixed in his mind. He could just pick out the box-shaped "cheeks" of the *Banshee*'s head down in that darkness and the soft blue spotlights that illuminated the ends of its PPC barrels.

It was Victor Vandergriff, back in the arena where it had all begun, waiting for his opponent.

"We have limited access to lights and sound, Mr. Nero," said one of the crew. "I'm sorry, but we're stuck with our own cameras."

Why be sorry? Julian had covered the opening battle of this last week on mere soundcast. If they didn't have full video capabilities right now, he would just make do. "Get a spot onto that *Banshee*." His orders were delivered softly, almost reverently. He nodded out into the darkness. "Stand by with another on the 'Mech entrance. And be ready! It's . . ."

"Not much longer now." Michael whispered the words to himself repeatedly, a calming mantra, having just found the hole Vandergriff had smashed through to the arena's access tunnel.

To his left the titanic archway sloped down into the holding center and repair bays, where it would link up with the city's underground tunnel system. To his right was the path into the arena proper. A good ambush stratagem on Vandergriff's part would have been to retreat back down into the tunnels just out of sensor detection to surprise Michael from behind as he made for the formal combat area. Had it been any other opponent on any day before this, Michael might have been concerned about that choice. Not now. Not after their duel began on the parking grounds. He was sure Victor waited for him in the arena.

It was where their fight belonged, whether or not Vandergriff realized it for himself.

Walking the *Pillager* into the tunnel, Michael was momentarily blinded when a bright light flashed out over the arena and settled over Vandergriff's 'Mech. It made the *Banshee* an easy target for visual tracking, illuminated in every bit of detail. Some cosmetic work had been done to the other 'Mech, but it hadn't lost its ungainly lines. Its torso resting on turret-style waist, the square-cast legs and the awkward barrels that protruded like an afterthought. How different from his *Pillager*'s design perfection, its molded armor and weapons. The *Banshee* didn't look much better on Michael's sensors. Its armor had huge rents for Michael to further exploit, and his thermal scan showed the right chest bleeding heat from the damaged reactor shielding.

Easing his fingers off the *Pillager*'s triggers, Michael opened the frequency he and Victor had shared during their tournament match. It was a channel designated for taunts and insults and for accepting capitulation, but now the only possible means of having a private conversation. The odds were long that Vandergriff would listen to him—assuming he'd even kept the channel stored into his communications system—but Michael had to try.

"It isn't too late, Victor," he said, halting the *Pillager* at the entryway into the arena. "We can both walk out of here under our own power."

Of course Vandergriff had kept the frequency set into his scanner. They'd never finished their duel. "An easy offer, *Davion,* when you send your media friends in first to catch my surrender on camera." There was no mistaking the hatred in his voice.

Media in one of the gallery control rooms? Michael could guess whom. That explained the spotlight on the *Banshee*. And on him as well, as a new spot stabbed down into the darkness to frame the entry and his *Pillager*. Two small islands of light, pinpointing the combatants in an ocean of black.

"Not a surrender. A draw. No one loses."

"I lose for not winning!" Vandergriff's voice was close to breaking. Not even the normal deadening of transmission could mute the fury and loathing and self-pity all boiling to the surface. "You've never understood what that's like. But you will!"

A mistake, transmitting right up to the point of his attack. This time Michael knew what was coming, that Vandergriff would stab down on his triggers with his last word. He maneuvered quickly away from the door and temporarily out of the spotlight. Twin streams of cascading energy washed by him, lancing back through the entry to be lost in the tunnel.

The *Banshee* moved forward, also abandoning the spotlight in favor of the darkness' meager protection. Enough, though, that Michael would not risk his gauss rifles. He was still under the same limitations as before. He couldn't afford to win, especially if it meant the price was Vandergriff's life. He couldn't afford to lose, either. The fact that cameras were recording this battle complicated any possible solution. Damn Nero anyway!

The scarlet lance from his single large laser stabbed back at the *Banshee,* accompanied by a trio of smaller emerald knives. They stabbed in against the BattleMech's left side, two of the medium lasers barely missing while the rest slagged away more armor from the arm and torso. Michael continued to circle right, distancing himself from the spotlight.

Blackness. The twin spots cut out at the same time, the darkness caving in over the two 'Warriors and forcing them to sensor targeting only. Michael accepted a partial targeting lock, then cut loose with another flurry of laserfire. It missed completely as the *Banshee* used jump jets to reverse its previous path but hold onto its full-front facing. Michael cut back inside, ready to turn the next salvo against his armor. He guessed that Vandergriff would continue to rely on his autocannon and lasers to relieve some of the heat created by PPC discharges combined with the reactor shielding damage.

He guessed wrong.

Vandergriff selected for his autocannon, yes. Also his lasers, missiles, *and* his PPC. The desperate all-out attack washed the darkened arena in a temporary iridescent light show that illuminated the space between the two battling machines. The flash of light revealed the *Pillager* being scoured by a PPC hit and the grinding sparks of fragmentation rounds against armor. The autocannon opened up the *Pillager*'s right side, slicing free the last of its armor protection. That left the interior vulnerable to the AC's cluster submunitions, which chipped and gouged at the 'Mech's skeletal structure, myomer, and the internal casing on one of the gauss rifles.

The only thing not pictured in that flash of energy was the single missile that also hammered in behind the savage assault, its detonation cracking the weapon casing and bursting through the highly charged gauss coils. The energy stored in those coils, enough to launch the heavy nickel-ferrous slugs with such devastating force, spent itself all at once in a secondary explosion that tore the weapon apart and destroyed a large piece of the *Pillager*'s reactor shielding. It also fed an immense feedback surge into the 'Mech's neurocircuitry system—the system that plugged a MechWarrior's sense of equilibrium into the massive gyroscopic stabilizer.

The feedback slammed into Michael's brain with stunning force. Shaken, disoriented, and now fighting to hold onto consciousness as well as fighting the pull of gravity, he again reacted from pure instinct. He turned the *Pillager* to take the fall face-forward, using his arms to cushion the impact and prevent further injury to himself. Still, the fall did throw him around, testing the strength of his safety harness and nearly knocking him unconscious.

In the dim light of the cockpit, Michael almost thought he'd blacked out when suddenly the full arena lights came up with glaring intensity.

"Not . . . yet . . ." His voice was shaky, but the sound

helped him focus. "Can't win . . ." His grip on the *Pillager*'s control sticks tightened. "Can't *lose*."

Pushing out with both of the *Pillager*'s arms, he raised its head enough to let him see across the arena's expanse, where the *Banshee* was lurching forward on unsteady legs. Wispy gray-black smoke trailed up from rents in its armor, from its joints, and from the ragged wound Michael's gauss slug had earlier torn into the *Pillager*'s side. A glance with thermal imaging showed the *Banshee* glowing brightly from heat buildup, a fiery red-orange blossom at its heart and spreading out to still-dangerous yellow in the head and limbs.

And as Michael watched, twin streaks of manmade lightning arced out from the *Banshee*'s PPCs—and heat be damned—to flail again at the downed *Pillager*. There was no more doubt that . . .

"Victor Vandergriff means this to be their final moment. Searcy is moving, but slow to recover from that crippling attack. One PPC misses high, but the other slashes and burns away more armor on the *Pillager*'s right leg. Nearly the last of it, by all appearances. The temperature inside the *Banshee*'s cockpit must be unbearable! I tell you, I can nearly feel the heat from here."

Though the balcony control room was still cold from disuse, Julian Nero had actually broken out into a hot sweat watching—and reporting—Michael's fall to the rest of the world. This wasn't the way he'd imagined the fight would go. Not even the way he wanted it to go, his Lyran prejudice notwithstanding. He'd made a decision to support Searcy's initiative to end to the violence, end the insanity plaguing Solaris City. And the Great Nero couldn't be wrong.

He was *the man in the know*!

"Another pair of PPC attacks. And both miss! The *Banshee*'s targeting system quite literally may have been burned out. Certainly those heat levels are affecting Vandergriff's equipment as well as his judgment. In fact, that last set seems to have gone a step too far. The *Banshee* is seizing up, barely able to move for the heatstroke." Julian willed Michael Searcy back to his feet as the *Pillager* finally began to rise, but slowly.

"Will Vandergriff back off? Will he risk his own destruction?" Another pair of cerulean streams streaked out with lethal intent. "He's attacking still! Believe it, Solaris. Victor Vandergriff is making his play for . . ."

All or nothing.

No mistake. Neither eagerness nor impatience. Desperation drove Victor Vandergriff forward against the limitations of his 'Mech, forcing yet one more step out of the heat-addled machine. He slapped repeatedly at the shutdown override even as each new attack drove his heat scale further into the red. The scorched air constricted and scratched at his throat and felt as if it were blistering his lungs.

The all-out strike was a desperate maneuver, classic Vandergriff. Right then, in the darkness and with the *Pillager* opting for a non-evasive pattern, Victor had known that Searcy would be open to a surprise assault. Fortune had been on his side, but only so far. He'd been able to deal the *Pillager* solid hits, critically damaging the 'Mech and toppling the mighty Davion favorite. That must have been humbling, but it wasn't lethal. Wasn't enough to win the fight.

Then the commline crackled and he heard Searcy murmur, "Can't win. Can't lose."

Victor doubted the other man realized he'd actually transmitted those words. He could tell from Searcy's voice that he was shaken up from the gauss rifle's discharge and the fall. But he also heard his enemy's determination. Like himself, Michael Searcy would let nothing short of death stop him from rising again, no matter all that talk about ending the fighting. He provided the pronouns himself. Searcy saying that *he*—Victor—couldn't win. That *I*—Michael—can't lose.

His next salvo scored the *Pillager*'s right leg, a solid but non-crippling strike. And again, the *Banshee*'s heat levels spiked so high that the myomer musculature failed to respond. The 'Mech was barely able to stand and totally unable to take another step. The sweat poured from Victor's brow and dried to a salty crust before it could so much as drip onto his cooling suit. The suit that held his body temperature down to a livable state was being taxed to its maximum effort. The shutdown warning sounded, and again he slapped the override to silence the alarm and abort the safety precaution.

The *Pillager* had gotten one leg underneath itself to stand as Victor's next pair of energy cannon discharges blazed outward. One scarred the Coliseum wall far back of the assault 'Mech, but the second one seared into the *Pillager*'s left arm, cutting past the final shards of armor to sever titanium bone and laser barrels. Though the arm was still attached, it hung limply against the BattleMech's side, the lasers ruined and shoulder actuator slagged beyond use.

Searcy fired back with his remaining gauss rifle, which spat out a silvery blur. It came so close and so fast that it registered in Victor's mind only after the slug had slammed into his left arm, crushing the protective plates with a sickening squeal of tortured metal and bursting the innards from two arm actuators. Then the *Pillager*'s right-arm laser sliced into the *Banshee*'s left side to slice through armor and breach the autocannon casing beneath. The weapon flashed a red indicator light on Victor's panel display. Ruined.

Hauling around impotent ammo was never a good idea, especially in an overheating 'Mech, but Victor couldn't worry about dumping the autocannon ammo right now. Once more he had to override the automatic shutdown and try to force some life back into his controls to reset his intermittent cross hairs. And here came the *Pillager,* now on its feet and throttled into a slow walk directly for the *Banshee.*

Victor triggered off a hastily aimed pair of PPCs, but missed again. What followed was another routine of riding out Searcy's answering strike, then overriding the shutdown and stabbing out yet another barrage.

This time both weapons miraculously hit their target. Or perhaps not such a miracle, considering that the *Pillager* had walked directly into point-blank range. What armor was left to the 'Mech's centerline soaked up the energy discharges, and the little that bled inside found no critical components. Cursing, Victor pounded one fist into an auxiliary monitor, taking some satisfaction in the smashed display and even the sharp pain of a cut hand.

Then the *Pillager*'s answering laserfire hit the *Banshee*'s head, cutting across the brow and splashing scarlet fire across the ferroglass canopy.

Shaken against the limit of his harness, Victor nearly laughed aloud that Searcy's shot had found the only perfect armor he had left. A dangerous sense of glee, since so little remained of the armor protecting the MechWarrior himself. All or nothing, though. That had been his decision. To win, no matter the cost.

His skin burned anywhere the cooling suit did not cover, and his oxygen-starved lungs forced several painful gasps of the scalding air. Blinking away the ghostly afterimages left by his enemy's laserfire, Victor speared the *Pillager* on his flashing reticle even as he listened to the wail of the shutdown warning. One hand left the throttle to hit the override, the hand that had smashed the monitor screen, and it came back to the controls with bloody and heat-blistered knuckles.

His other hand squeezed into his next assault, loosing his final pair of PPC blasts.

The cascade of energy scourged the *Pillager*'s right side, burning through the arm and shoulder and carving deeply into the body of the assault machine, while alarms began to scream inside the *Banshee*'s cockpit. Shutdown warnings. Equipment malfunction. Cooling system failure. Intense heat radiated throughout the core of the *Banshee,* scorching myomer and bursting heat sinks taxed beyond their capacity. It was a cascading effect that drove the heat beyond the limit of the computer's scale to measure. Beyond all design limits.

Beyond correction.

The remains of his autocannon ammunition cooked off first, staccato detonations that shook the *Banshee* even as the blast gutted the 'Mech's left side and poured further destruction into the centerline equipment. Then his SRM missile ammo erupted, a few in sympathetic detonation with the autocannon munitions but quickly turning into a devastating inferno on its own as the warheads combined into a consuming force. Neurosystem feedback from the near-simultaneous ammo detonations flooded Victor's mind, searing pain deep into his brain and lighting up his spine with electricity. Still, he remained mercilessly aware of the destruction he'd visited on himself even as the *Banshee* tore itself apart. Explosions ripped limbs away and collapsed the magnetic containment that normally held the fusion reactor in check. Golden fire spread through the ruins of the BattleMech. It ate quickly through the weak areas between engine and cockpit, turning the MechWarrior's small command center into a ready-made crematorium.

But even when the pain from the fire forced one final scream from him, Victor saw through the *Banshee*'s shattered canopy the *Pillager* falling as well. And nothing else mattered if Victor could pull his enemy down with him into death. Clenching his 'Mech's unresponsive triggers, he fought for consciousness, wrestling against the pain and refusing to submit.

These were the final seconds of Victor Vandergriff.

It was all he had left.

All-ee All-ee
All in free . . .

Solaris Spaceport, International Zone
Solaris City, Solaris VII
Freedom Theater, Lyran Alliance
25 August 3062

"I still say you should paste Hasek-Davion to a wall," Karl said. He gave Michael a grim smile. "Preferably with a gauss rifle."

Michael glanced quickly around the spaceport waiting area, checking to be sure no one could overhear—even by accident—their conversation. For the first time in his yeas on Solaris he wanted no audience. That was proving much easier than he'd have thought, especially in *this* crowd.

The third-class level of Solaris Spaceport teamed with travelers, the human flood heavier than ever. Most of them were newly arrived on DropShips, here to experience for themselves the dark adventure promised in the holovids, touring agencies, and especially the recent newscasts. Some looked annoyed at having to deal with the minor irritations of long-distance travel. On the faces of others, though, Michael saw a star-struck expression he understood so well. Eyes bright, these visitors cast around for the nearest betting terminal or hoping to spot a famous gladiator. Repeatedly their gazes swept up and then right past Michael without ever recognizing him.

But then who would, with his blond hair buzzed close and the stubble of a beard darkening his features? It was the best he could do on short notice, but the disguise seemed to be working just fine. He also wore yellow-tinted glasses, the ones known as "shooter's glasses" in law enforcement and military circles. And the capper: the former Federated Suns favorite was traveling in the simple uniform of the Solaris Constabulary—a *Lyran* police force. Just one more beat cop, heading out for a vacation *away* from the most popular tourist trap in the Inner Sphere. The disguise had been Karl's idea, and the black humor was not lost on Michael.

This was how Michael Searcy would depart Solaris VII, the Game World. Three years older and just maybe a bit wiser. But once again *dispossessed.*

"Drew Hasek-Davion knows how to quit when he's ahead," Michael said. The other few passengers also awaiting the outbound call seemed singularly uninterested in him or Karl. They looked gloomy and self-absorbed. Perhaps they hadn't found what they'd come to Solaris for. Or had they found a bit too much of it?

"He's had years to learn how to manipulate the whole Solaris propaganda machine." Michael gave a small sigh, his voice running almost bitter. "I can do the song and dance, but he's still a master choreographer."

Karl nodded reluctant agreement. "Having Aubry Larsen broker a cease-fire with the arriving elements of the Seventeenth Arcturan covered his six. And I suppose the Archon's *reluctant* appreciation of his assistance means that she won't take punitive action against him either." He shook his head sadly. "Yeah, he burst your heat sinks all right."

Michael shuddered. The old MechWarrior expression was too close to Victor Vandergriff's final moments. Surrendering the *Pillager* to gravity, he'd seen the golden fire consuming the cockpit of the *Banshee.* Couldn't win. Couldn't lose.

"But the cease-fire is only a temporary solution," Michael said, "and we all know it. Relations between the sectors are still strained, especially between the Davion and Steiner loyalists. If I were to show up now, alive and well after Julian Nero played up mine and Victor's mutual annihilation, it could easily set off a violent Lyran backlash and a new surge of pro-FedSun sentiment. So we leave it at a draw."

He smiled at his friend's sudden display of curiosity. Karl had been unable to resist asking about the battle's final seconds. Had the *Pillager* been mortally wounded by Victor's last salvo or had Michael's fall crushed the 'Mech's gyro. Had Stormin' Michael Searcy thrown away the victory to salvage a draw?

All Michael would say was that *Stormin'* Michael Searcy would never have done such a thing. It wasn't important for anyone else to know what happened in those moments.

"Better I remain dead to them. I'll travel under this identity long enough to get resettled someplace where Michael Searcy can start again."

"And you trust 'the man in the know' to keep that secret?"

Michael shrugged. "Do I have much choice? Besides, Nero is a Silesian. He has no burning desire to help create a Black Hills hero."

"Maybe," Karl admitted. "But it still isn't right that Hasek-Davion just walks away unscathed."

"Is that you speaking or Tran Ky Bo?"

A slight frown darkened Karl's features. "I speak for myself, Michael. I always have."

Michael winced and was sorry. "I know, Karl," he said gently. It was *he* who had so often spoken with another's voice. He who'd acted as a puppet for Hasek-Davion while believing he pursued his own ends in the character of Stormin' Michael Searcy. And appearance had *almost* become a reality for him, in both cases.

Deciding that train of thought had nowhere good to go, he decided to redirect the conversation. "Is Tran Ky Bo still holding against Drew's call for a new Grand Tournament?"

Karl brightened visibly. "He and Thom DeLon were losing ground with the other stable owners until some of the Game World's top fighters got behind them. Those from the Top Twenty who are still *officially* alive, that is. Larry Acuff, Kelly Metz. And Srin Odessa made it through, though Odessa's going to need a prosthetic leg. It's shaping up into the Top Twelve for now, and most of those refused to participate." He tried not to look too proud of his fellow gladiators, then sobered. "I think Acuff said it best. 'This time we all lose.'"

"This time we all lose," Michael repeated, knowing it was true.

The overhead speaker called his flight for boarding, and he stood abruptly, pulling Karl along in his wake as he moved toward the gate.

"Don't worry about Hasek-Davion," he said. "Too many people out there have his number now, and they'll watch him closely. Sooner or later he'll slip, and the fall will be a long one. That's the problem when you build an empire on appearances. You start believing in your own illusions, and sooner or later you overreach yourself grasping for one." Thinking about it, he walked on for few steps. "And there's no greater illusion than victory without a price to pay."

Stopping near the gate, Karl stretched out his hand. "You'll keep in touch?"

Michael gave Karl's hand a warm clasp that he held for a moment longer than normal. "I will, my friend. And I'll be watching, too. I expect great things from you, and someone's got to keep the others honest." He smiled ruefully. "Trust me, they need it."

Karl glanced toward the gate, where the first passengers were making their way out to the boarding gantry, then back to Michael. "What will you do?"

"Best I can, Karl. Always the best I can."

One final pump and then Michael broke their handclasp. He turned toward the gate and continued on alone, without looking back. He'd come to Solaris intending to prove himself by winning the highest honor the world had to offer. In some ways he'd lived the hero's life in the arenas, but that had also meant living according to what others thought of him. He hadn't won the Championship, but he'd learned some hard lessons, ones that only the arenas of the Game World could have taught him. The knowledge was hard-won, but it was a prize no one could ever take away from him.

If not Champion, then what? Karl had asked him. If not Stormin' Michael Searcy, then just *who* was he?

Michael now had his whole life to find the answers.

Epilogue

Green Mansion, Black Hills
Solaris City, Solaris VII
Freedom Theater, Lyran Alliance
31 August 3062

A *Dragon Fire* stood guard at the gate, protecting Green Mansion even though the riots and looting were now a week past. The 'Mech stepped aside, and the gate rolled open with mechanical smoothness to permit the luxury sedan to enter the grounds. The *Dragon Fire*'s pilot watched the sedan on his head's up display rather than visually tracking through the cockpit canopy. Doing that deprived him of detail better seen by naked eye.

That was how he missed the figure hunched low at the tail of the hovercar, coasting along on roller blades. She was being towed by the sedan, as she had been for the last block.

It was the simplest of plans. Megan Church was allowing Drew Hasek-Davion himself to escort her onto the grounds of his estate. As the Avanti settled down onto its skirting, she used it to shield herself from security cameras, then dodged to the side behind a small mechanic's station. She rubbed grit from her eyes, residue of the dirt and small gravel kicked up by the hovercraft's fans. It was a small price for her first successful penetration of Green Mansion since entering the employ of Hasek-Davion.

She stashed her small backpack in the garage, waiting for the master of the house to enter into his empty mansion.

Drew realized Megan's presence into his second break, which missed and sent the ball off bouncing off the side rail before glancing into the racked set. He sensed more than saw her. First it was a slight motion at the periphery of his vision, the awareness of someone leaning against the supporting pillar of the open entryway. That was strange because only his driver and the guard on post in the security room were on the grounds today. Then he heard a rasp of leather against the pillar's textured finish, and the ghostly image resolved into Megan Church.

He frowned at the table, then at Megan. He'd been expecting her, which was the reason the estate was almost empty, but he should at least have gotten a warning. The security agent would be reprimanded severely for this lapse. "Very good, Ms. Church, though it's no longer necessary to play these little games. My"—he paused—"*employees* are allowed to use the front door."

Megan shrugged. "I prefer discretion whenever possible. Makes for fewer mistakes in the long run." She smiled slightly. "And you never know what kind of opportunities might avail themselves of a discreet entrance."

Drew ignored whatever that was supposed to mean and tossed his cue stick onto the table. "Shall we?" He motioned toward an arch leading to the drawing room, then grabbed up his walking stick propped against the wall and followed Megan into the next room. He laid the walking stick across the corner of his desk, the silver lion's head close to his reach, and pulled out a small stack of papers from one of the drawers. "Passport. Identification. DropShip passes. Everything you need to get you to New Syrtis. I have quite a bit of work for you there, capitalizing on the growing unrest George Hasek is attempting to control."

The provocateur shook her head in a curt negative.

"We've gone over this already. I would prefer to remain in the Alliance. In fact, I intend to stay on Solaris VII."

"I've told you before, the faces—the nationality—shouldn't matter. You've played your part well on Solaris. Now it's time for a larger role." His disapproval of Megan's obstinacy told in his lecturing tone. "Never allow business to turn personal."

"But my work is *very* personal, by nature, Mr. Hasek-Davion. And while there is some draw to the prospect of stirring things up on New Syrtis, Solaris—the Alliance—is my home."

Difficult woman! After everything Drew had done for her, all he was offering, and still she found a way to complicate matters. Here on Solaris VII he would have to walk carefully for a time, but if she could be half as effective in the Capellan March as she had been in escalating the violence on the Game World . . . "People are looking for you, Megan. They don't have your name—not yet." The threat was rather blatant, but judged necessary. He would have her on New Syrtis. "Friends and associates of the late Mr. Stroud."

She waved off the concern. "They have already found me. In fact, they found me first. About a year ago."

"A year? But you've only worked for me . . ."

The threat in her admission became clear with the chill that settled into Drew's spine, shivering his large frame. Her calm refusals. Megan's arrival by stealth. For the first time he felt acutely the loss of Garrett, who had always chaperoned his assignments with Megan Church, and the absence of his mansion security staff. Only one man in the security control room and Aubry Larsen on post in the street. If he could somehow signal for help—

The chime on his wireless broke Drew's train of thought, the large man's strained nerves causing him to startle.

"Answer it," Megan said.

Mechanically, he lifted the tiny device from the clip on his belt and brought it up to his ear, never taking his eyes away from the dangerous woman. He summoned enough strength of voice to bluster, "This is Drew Hasek-Davion."

"You *were* Drew Hasek-Davion," a cold voice answered. Stroud! Alive, and turning his own weapon back at him. "Equal footing, Drew. Time to settle accounts." The click of a disconnect and the line went dead.

Nothing in his life brought the anhedonic stable owner actual pleasure, but Drew felt terror acutely enough. It froze his muscles, and set his thoughts stuttering through a list of past failures leading up to this grand climax. He had never understood before the concept of one's entire world falling apart. Jerry Stroud's voice, however, back from the assumed grave and delivering his final promise to see an end to the master of Blackstar Stables, shattered every victory he'd thought to have won these last few weeks. And worse. The other stable owners would bleed him dry, leaving Blackstar a ruined husk of its former power, if they left it intact at all.

And only if he managed to avoid the trap set for him here, in his own home. Stroud had called this the final game, and Drew's own life hung in the balance, with no champion to defend it.

"I can pay you much more than Stroud." He tasted the metallic dryness of fear choking his breath. Hoped to buy his way out; the easy solution. Everyone had a price, after all.

But it wasn't always hard currency. Megan shook her head. "It's not about the money, Mr. Hasek-Davion. It's *personal*." She paused, as if uncertain what to say next. Then, "Something you never understood. I followed your orders because it meant hurting FedRats. Never a Lyran, not directly. It was never an act, inciting riots by pretending to be a Steiner loyalist. It was real, every ounce." She offered him a pitying smile. "You saw what you wanted to believe."

Her words freed Drew from the near paralysis that had gripped him. Her taunt was that Drew had critically misjudged the difference between appearance and reality. And more than once. He'd lost Nero and Searcy and Garrett, and every other plan had gone astray throughout his life. Only this time the consequences were high. Too high. The strength of fear flooded him, and he grabbed up the walking stick never far from his side. A quick pull, and the hidden cane-sword slid free of its wooden sheath. He brandished it at Megan, cutting the

air between them as he backed for the door of the drawing room. The silver head felt slick against his sweaty
palm, but he gripped it with life-crushing force.

"Insurance!" he barked at her. "I am never without
a way to protect myself. *That* is something very few people take into account, my dear. And as I said before,
people don't know your name yet, but they *will,* Ms.
Church. They will."

Drew fled the room, backing down the short hallway
until he'd rounded a corner, then he ran for the nearby
security room. The door stood open, a clear violation of
his orders. He paused in the doorway, chest heaving with
the sudden and unusual exertion. Empty! Powered
down, the darkened monitors stared at him with blank,
unseeing eyes. Megan had been here first!

Panting, wiping at the terrified sweat dripping down
his face, he took shallow breaths trying to ease the painful binding of his heaving chest. In his mind, he heard
Megan's footsteps behind him, echoing through the mansion like the thundering footfalls of a BattleMech. They
pursued him, hounded him down the long hall leading
toward the mansion's western entrance. Escape was the
only thought in his mind when he burst into the garage
and ran for the Avanti hover sedan. More footfalls
echoed in his ears. Louder. Were the Skye Tigers closing
on his estate? What had happened to Aubry Larsen in
the *Dragon Fire*? He glanced around wildly.

No chauffeur. No sign of anyone. Except somewhere
back in the mansion Megan Church still prowled. She
was coming for him. They would all be coming for him.

Drew wrenched open the door on the driver's side and
saw the keycard still inserted in the dash. With one final
fearful glance toward the empty doorway, he climbed into
the sedan. Pain lanced through his breast, a death's grip
on his pounding heart. Even then, Drew would not give
in, would never make it so easy for his enemies.

He stabbed at the starter controls, defiant to his
final second.

How easy.

Megan stood a safe distance outside the mansion, near
the edge of a hedge maze where she stopped at the

moment of the explosion. She heard the roaring cacophony as fire gutted the garage, debris and smoke belching through the shattered door, setting Green Mansion ablaze. It was Drew Hasek-Davion's funeral pyre. The demon of the Black Hills. In her eyes, no one more deserving.

The driver and security agent lay on the ground just behind the manse. They were safe enough there and would soon be found. If it wasn't the emergency services arrived in answer to the explosion, then it would be Hasek-Davion's private guard or any of the neighborhood's idle curious—those always looking for a new show.

The *Dragon Fire* was first on the scene, of course, and Megan faded back into the grounds before the 'Mech could spot her. She moved quickly to the back wall and climbed over into the street, confident she hadn't been seen. She dusted off her jacket and strolled back around toward the front of the estate. Only the guilty fled. She joined the throng of spectators already blocking the gate, reviewing her handiwork.

Of course Hasek-Davion had run for the sedan. The man was a coward—one of the first things she'd seen in him those several months ago. He cowered behind his net of security, striking out at anything that seemed a threat. He was also soft, sending messengers where secrecy did not demand his own presence and living vicariously through his stable of pet 'Warriors. When threatened, he would only run so far as necessary.

And the choice of a car bomb had, in fact, been his own. Jerry Stroud had predicted it the night the match between Searcy and Vandergriff spilled out into the street. In his plan to assassinate Stroud, the master of Blackstar had named his own death. She remembered well her talk with Stroud.

"Hasek will come for me, Megan," he'd said. "And I'm sure he'll use you to do it. If he makes that mistake and orders my death, you will begin immediate plans to bring him down the same way. On equal footing. Just as he wanted."

Megan shuffled aside with the rest of the curious crowd as the first police cruiser wailed by. Yes, she had sold another piece of herself to Jerry Stroud for this act, but then everyone was responsible to a higher authority somewhere. At least this was in the service of her own people. Solaris-born, she was Silesian.

A Lyran.

If her hands got a little dirty, that was the job and she collected a good wage for her efforts.

And that, she silently told Drew Hasek-Davion, was life on Solaris VII.

Illusions of Victory is Loren Coleman's fifth BattleTech® novel in the series published by Roc Books. He is also author of *Into the Maelstrom,* the first in FASA's Vor™ novel series. In addition, he has written game fiction and source material for such companies as FASA, TSR, and Wizards of the Coast.

Loren currently resides in Washington State with his wife, Heather Joy, two sons, Talon LaRon and Conner Rhys Monroe, and a new daughter, Alexia Joy. He works in the company of three Siamese cats, who collaborate in his writing by offering the frequent paw and occasional body check against his keyboard.

Preview more BattleTech® action in
Blaine Lee Pardoe's

Measure of a Hero,

coming from Roc in July 2000 . . .

Prologue

Archer Christifori was uncomfortable, but moving only made things worse. With three broken ribs and numerous sprains, just about any position was painful. They'd given him painkillers, but the drugs left him trapped somewhere between agony and consciousness.

He stared up at the ceiling fan that spun overhead, wondering just how long he would be stuck in this field hospital. He hoped it wouldn't be more than a few more days. He yanked at the sheets with his right arm—the uninjured one—for what seemed like the hundredth damn frustrating time, attempting to find a position that was bearable.

It had been one hell of a week. Months of tedious space travel from the Inner Sphere to Clan space, shattered in sudden, quick terror. Task Force Bulldog had arrived in the Huntress system only days before, and not a moment too soon. Operation Serpent, the other arm of the campaign to end the Clan invasion, had been ground down to only a handful of operational units. So far from home, the Serpents lacked the men and materiel to complete the destruction of the Smoke Jaguars.

Archer's unit, the Tenth Lyran Guards, were part of Bulldog when it came to Huntress. He remembered the approach of his DropShip through the planet's stormy skies. He and the rest of his unit were mounted up in their 'Mech cockpits, awaiting the signal for the drop doors to open. Their orders were to cover the retreat of the Northwind Highlanders, who had been fighting the Jaguars in the thick, stinking mud of the Dhuan Swamp.

As he drifted in and out of consciousness, he heard footsteps in the hall. It wasn't the soft padding sound of nurses' shoes, but the familiar jingle of spurs, the unmistakable trademark of officers of the Armed Forces of the Federated Commonwealth. He lifted his head to see who was approaching, and several blurred figures entered his field of vision.

"Major Christifori," he heard one of them say. Archer blinked to focus his eyes.

"Sir," he managed to respond, bringing his good right arm up for a salute even though he was flat on his back. He immediately recognized Prince Victor Davion, his commander and the overall commander of Task Force Bulldog, but not the other officers with him.

"I've read the after-action reports submitted by Colonel MacLeod on your relief and rescue mission, Major," the Prince said with a slight smile. "That was one hell of a stunt you pulled."

Archer shook his head slightly. "Not really, sir. Just following orders."

The Prince cocked his head slightly. "I don't recall giving the order to drop right into the middle of the Smoke Jaguar advance, Major."

Archer closed his eyes slightly. Memory flooded back through the haze of his drugged brain.

The DropShip quaked. "Captain Strong, bring us in right between the Northwind Highlanders and the Jaguar," Archer ordered.

"Roger that, Major," came Strong's reply in Archer's headset. "You are one minute to drop and counting. LZ is hot."

He switched to the Command Company's frequency. "There's not a lot of time, so listen up. Our

_mission is to relieve the Highlanders. These people
have paid for this operation with their blood, and
we're here to make sure they live to celebrate the
victory. I want a wide dispersal directly between the
Jags and the Highlanders. Form a battle line with
Command Lance on the left flank, Striker in the
center, Stalker on the right._

_"Your orders are simple. No Jaguars are to
punch through to the Highlanders."_

_"Sir," said Lieutenant Moss, "they outnumber
and outgun us. Second Company will be up in
twenty. Shouldn't we wait?"_

_"Those folks have already been through hell.
We're gonna finish what they started. Remember,
no Jags get through."_

Archer's eyes cracked open slowly. "Your orders were
to relieve the Northwind Highlanders, sir. If I had
waited, good warriors would have died. Too many had
already."

The Prince nodded. "I'm not criticizing what you did,
Major. I'm praising it. Not only did you assume a good
piece of ground, you also took the initiative without hesi-
tation. According to the reports filed by your command-
ers, you personally engaged a total of six Smoke Jaguar
'Mechs at once. That was a hell of a feat."

Archer drew a long deep breath, part of him still
caught in the memory.

_"I have multiple bogies closing fast, all weight
classes," said Lieutenant Friscoe over the commline.
His voice was tinged with fear._

The short-range sensors of Archer's Penetrator
_didn't paint a happy picture either. There were too
many Jaguar 'Mechs, and they were pursuing the
Highlanders like a pack of rabid dogs._

_"All right, people, this is where we pay back for the
Serpents. The Clanners have trashed their own engagement rules, so keep your heads on straight. Your
orders are to engage multiple targets—engage them
all. Fire at anything that even tries to break through
the line."_

The first oncoming 'Mech was a Jaguar Vulture, *its mottled gray camouflage already burned and gouged in several places. It crested the ridge off to his left, moving along the flank of his line. It didn't even try to engage him. It was pursuing the High-landers withdrawing through the surrounding marsh-land, and its bird-like gait made it seem to bob across his field of vision.*

Archer twisted his Penetrator's *torso and jabbed the joystick forward so that the targeting reticle drifted over the running* Vulture. *He locked a trio of his medium pulse lasers onto the same target interlock circuit and kept his 'Mech moving forward to keep the distance steady. He triggered the lasers, and the air filled with bright emerald bursts as the beams stitched into the side and rear of the Jaguar OmniMech. The beams found their mark, rocking the 'Mech and peppering armor plating. The Omni's running gait slowly ground to a halt as the Clanner turned to face his attack.*

Archer moved farther up the hillside as a Dasher *also attempted to burst past. Ignoring a* Vulture *also coming at him, he locked onto the light-brown* Dasher *and let go with his extended-range lasers. The temperature in his cockpit spiked, if only for a moment.*

"DropShip Hill, *this is Ironclad. What is your ETA?" he said, the sweat running into his eyes inside his neurohelmet.*

"Ironclad, this is the Hill. *We'll be on top of you in twelve."*

"Make it five . . ."

"The report overstates the engagement, sir," Archer said. "Second Company's DropShip was only a few minutes away. My right flank folded, but the center and left held. I just wanted to shoot at as many Jags as possible to get them tied up on me rather than the Highlanders."

"The rest of your company was eventually forced to pull back, but you held your ground."

Archer flushed red at the note of respect in the Prince's voice. "Sir, you've been in command of the

Tenth Guards for a long time. You know that combat situations tend to be fluid."

"But not like this, Major. When you were recovered, you'd already punched out. Your 'Mech had suffered almost eighty-nine-percent armor loss. Around you were six OmniMechs and three Elementals, and according to your *Penetrator*'s battlerom, you killed them all."

The Warhawk *stumbled as Archer's only remaining large laser sliced into its knee, popping the actuator in a muffled explosion of white and gray smoke. It plowed into the mud and sod of the hillside with such force that his own mangled 'Mech quaked under the impact. Archer hobbled past the fallen* Dasher *he'd downed a few minutes before and swept the field both visually and with his short-range sensors.*

A gray- and black-striped Galahad *was climbing up the ridge along the right flank of his position. It had been damaged long before the arrival of his unit. It was a survivor of the long fighting for Huntress and was battling for the survival of its Clan—its way of life. The* Galahad *aimed its gauss rifles up the long slope almost wearily. Archer understood the feeling. The last ten minutes of fighting had left his unit falling back and his 'Mech was more scrap metal than machine.*

He targeted his own four remaining medium pulse lasers and the one functional ER laser at the Galahad. *He somehow managed to fire first, releasing a wave of emerald bursts and bright scarlet beams on his foe. Two pulse lasers missed, sizzling into the muck and sod near the feet of the 'Mech. The large ER laser sliced into the* Galahad*'s head, right into the cockpit.*

It replied by firing a pair of gauss rifle slugs, silvery balls of metal accelerated via magnetic pulses to supersonic speeds. One missed totally, but the other dug into the tissue-thin armor of the Penetrator*'s right torso. The 'Mech sagged backward as warning lights flared, and a ripple of heat swept over Archer like a hot, wet blanket. Warning lights* *flickered on his damage display. His 'Mech was dying around him.*

He could barely keep the 'Mech upright as he maintained his target lock. He locked his medium pulse lasers on the Galahad *just as his 'Mech stepped on one of the Elementals he'd killed only a few minutes into the fight. Archer fired, and so did the Jaguar 'MechWarrior. He did not wait for the impact. He wrapped his hands around the ejection control and pulled the ring as hard as he could. There was a rush of cool air, the grinding of metal, and a flash of light that was all he remembered after that.*

"Yes, sir," Archer said simply. "I guess I did kill them all."

BATTLETECH®
Loren L. Coleman

❑**DOUBLE-BLIND** The Magistracy of Canopus has been the target of aggression by the Marian Hegemony, and in hiring Marcus and his gutsy band of can-do commandos, it hopes to retaliate. But the fact that the Canopians are armed with technology that is considered rare in the Periphery is the least of Marcus's problems. Marcus and his "Angels" will have to face the real force behind the hostilities—the religious cult known as Word of Blake. This fanatical group has a scheme deadly enough to trap even the amazing Avanti's Angels.... (0-451-45597-5—$5.99)

❑**BINDING FORCE** Aris Sung is a rising young star in House Hiritsu, noblest of the Warrior Houses that have sworn allegiance to the Capellan Confederation. The Sarna Supremacy, a newly formed power in the Chaos March, is giving the Confederation some trouble—and Aris and his Hiritsu comrades are chosen to give the Sarnans a harsh lesson in Capellan resolve. But there is far more to the mission than meets the eye—and unless Aris beats the odds in a race against time, all the ferro-fibrous armor in the galaxy won't be enough to save House Hiritsu from the high-explosive cross fire of intrigue and shifting loyalties.... (0-451-45604-1/$5 99)

Prices slightly higher in Canada

DEEP SPACE INTRIGUE AND ACTION FROM
BATTLETECH®

❑ **LETHAL HERITAGE by Michael A. Stackpole.** Who are the Clans? One Inner Sphere warrior, Phelan Kell of the mercenary group Kell Hounds, finds out the hard way—as their prisoner and protegé

(0-451-453832—$6 99)

❑ **BLOOD LEGACY by Michael A. Stackpole.** Jaime Wolf brought all the key leaders of the Inner Sphere together at his base on Outreach in an attempt to put to rest old blood feuds and power struggles. For only if all the Successor States unite their forces do they have any hope of defeating this invasion by warriors equipped with BattleMechs far superior to their own.

(0-451-453840—$6.99)

❑ **LOST DESTINY by Michael A. Stackpole.** As the Clans' BattleMech warriors continue their inward drive, with Terra itself as their true goal, can Comstar mobilize the Inner Sphere's last defenses—or will their own internal political warfare provide the final death blow to the empire they are sworn to protect?

(0-451-453859—$6 99)

Prices slightly higher in Canada

Payable in U S funds only No cash/COD accepted Postage & handling: U S /CAN $2 75 for one book, $1 00 for each additional, not to exceed $6 75; Int'l $5 00 for one book, $1 00 each additional We accept Visa, Amex, MC ($10 00 min.), checks ($15 00 fee for returned checks) and money orders Call 800-788-6262 or 201-933-9292, fax 201-896-8569; refer to ad #ROC3 (1/00)

Penguin Putnam Inc	Bill my: ❑ Visa ❑ MasterCard ❑ Amex _____ (expires)
P.O Box 12289, Dept. B	Card# _____
Newark, NJ 07101-5289	Signature _____

Please allow 4-6 weeks for delivery
Foreign and Canadian delivery 6-8 weeks

Bill to:
Name _____
Address _____ City _____
State/ZIP _____ Daytime Phone # _____
Ship to:
Name _____ Book Total $ _____
Address _____ Applicable Sales Tax $ _____
City _____ Postage & Handling $ _____
State/ZIP _____ Total Amount Due $ _____

This offer subject to change without notice.